CRYSTAL STAIRS

Blessings Jennifer,

May you find yourself within these pages!! You are such a dynamic jewel. KD Smith 2013

K.D. SMITH

CRYSTAL STAIRS

a novel

TATE PUBLISHING
AND ENTERPRISES, LLC

Crystal Stairs
Copyright © 2012 by K.D. Smith. All rights reserved.

No part of this publication may be reproduced, stored in a retrieval system or transmitted in any way by any means, electronic, mechanical, photocopy, recording or otherwise without the prior permission of the author except as provided by USA copyright law.

This novel is a work of fiction. Names, descriptions, entities, and incidents included in the story are products of the author's imagination. Any resemblance to actual persons, events, and entities is entirely coincidental.

The opinions expressed by the author are not necessarily those of Tate Publishing, LLC.

Published by Tate Publishing & Enterprises, LLC
127 E. Trade Center Terrace | Mustang, Oklahoma 73064 USA
1.888.361.9473 | www.tatepublishing.com

Tate Publishing is committed to excellence in the publishing industry. The company reflects the philosophy established by the founders, based on Psalm 68:11,
"The Lord gave the word and great was the company of those who published it."

Book design copyright © 2012 by Tate Publishing, LLC. All rights reserved.
Cover design by Leah LeFlore
Interior design by Lindsay Behrens

Published in the United States of America

ISBN: 978-1-62024-341-1
1. Fiction / African American / Contemporary Women
2. Fiction / Christian / General
12.05.02

DEDICATION

Writing was never one of my ambitions. The late Craig Mandeville commanded me to write and in submitting to his God-voice, I discovered we are not always conscious of our innate passions.

God gave me an invaluable gift the day I met the late Atisha McKanney. Life is truly limitless and endless when we are able to live beyond the now and adverse circumstances.

Our Father knew precisely who I needed as parents. Thanks to my greastest supporter, Janet E. David, for always being there with love and strong guidance. Mom, you've been the priceless example of fortitude, faithfulness and godliness. You are an amazing woman.

There are great men who are committed to living a life of love. To my daddy, H. Theo Smith, thank you for having the courage to embrace God's creation all over the world, as if the farthest corner of the earth contains precious Jewels whom the Father desires. I have inherited your DNA. You are the first man of influence in my life and I love you for being a fine example. To my best friend for every moment of my life, Wendell Smith, thank you for being you (brother). To Patrick Purcell, you have shown me the greater capacity of how much God really does love us because He gives us the absolute best to bring out the best.

If God gave me a kit and said, "Make the perfect friends," I would have fashioned the same "girlfriends", sisters and brothers who God created. Words cannot express how much I need and love you!

To you, yes you, as you keep on living, you may have to climb some *Crystal Stairs*. I hope you succeed and cherish the best possible life.

ALIYAH
Ghettrocities Personified

Sunlight attempted once again to barge its way through the crack in the palatial window dressings in my master bedroom. What used to be a welcome indication that a new day has arrived has long been a reminder that I had to wake up and face reality. Sleep had not been a haven for recouping and resting for, I can't even remember, how long. Sleep was only a temporary delay and hiding place from dealing with the mess of the life I've known since I was a little girl. I must admit, I've seen mostly good days, but the few bad days I survived were devastating enough to affect the quintessential core of my being. If I could hibernate like the northern black bear for seven months straight, God knows, I just might.

Yet, as I hit the snooze button on the alarm for the fifth time, these words of power flowed through my inner man over and over again as part of the morning ritual. *This is the day that the Lord has made. I shall rejoice and be glad in it. This is the day that the Lord has made. I shall rejoice and be glad in it.*

Sunlight won the battle again. And if natural light wasn't enough to pull me out of bed, a phone call from Aliyah always did the job.

"Morning Aliyah," I uttered with a groggy morning voice.

"Jewel, I'm sorry to bother you, but I need you to help me out," Aliyah pleaded.

Well, knowing Aliyah, there was a thirty-three and one-third chance of guessing what her urgent need was this time. Homegirl only calls when she needs me. And I am perfectly cool with this arrangement. Although it has never been codified in words, we both know that I am the one out of our cliché who best deals with her temperament. Danne, Noey, Laurel and Chante can only take Aliyah with a grain of salt or over some good pasta dinner at our favorite Italian spot, Café Bacci. So I dared to act as if there was the possibility that her need didn't revolve around the sickness, her dishonorable husband, or a new stunt from one of her two BeBe's kids.

"What's going on?" I asked. There is nothing like someone else's drama to pull me out of my own.

With a panicked tone, Aliyah responded, "BJ wrote me this nasty letter. I just can't take this stress right now."

BJ, Elder Barron Jason Jones, is Aliyah's no-good husband who needs to be shot one bullet at a time, toe by toe, limb by limb, until he cries mercy. Oops. This is not really what he needs, but I can't help but wonder what it would be like to see him jacked up for just a few minutes.

I responded with a halfway concerned tone, "Aliyah, what did he say?"

Aliyah had to be embarrassed by now with this foolishness. "He told me that he knows I'm sick and what I am going through, but so is he. I need to make sure that when I can't get to the store and get him his stuff I need to let Rashaun have my card and send him his package."

Suddenly, I was on the bridge again: the mental bridge that spans from the place in your mind that wants to go all the way there to the place where after crossing the bridge, the tongue is bridled and good thoughts breed words of life. Meanwhile, my eyes were rolling to the back of my head while listening to this madness again. I cannot believe that a Black man could be so inconsiderate and trifling. BJ knows his wife just got out of the hospital, and he dares to suggest that she give her bankcard to her son, who everybody knows is two steps from a halfway house. BJ doesn't want to miss his Haribo Gummi Candy, Nestle hot chocolate with marshmallows, soups, cereal bars, and all the crap he puts on a list that he wants his wife, who is unemployed, lives on her hook-and-crook income, and who has AIDS, to continually send and supply. This is exponential gall to the 1,372nd power.

Listening with disbelief-not that BJ could threaten Aliyah from a jail cell with his powerful weapon of no communication, but that she would put up with his broken-down self-I suppressed the urge to break and remained silent. Remember, I was on the bridge.

Aliyah asked, "Are you there?"

"Yes, I'm listening."

Aliyah needed someone who was concerned enough to act like she cared, so I had to listen to her and let her vent. My best friends support me when I know they want to bust me in the head, too.

"I keep telling him he can't manage the house while he's locked up. He don't know what I deal with from day to day with these kids. I wish they could go with his family. I can't take it anymore. I know you probably busy, but I need you to go pick up my medication from the pharmacy for me, and get BJ's stuff and mail it for me. He said he ain't gonna send another letter till he gets a package." BJ was up to his same old control from the jail cell routine again.

"Aliyah, I know you don't think I have anything better to do than wait to run errands for you, but—" and then I made it over to the other side of the bridge.

Even though Aliyah and I are stratospheres apart in thinking and demeanor, she stretches to do me when she knows I need her. And out of the entire syndicate, she is the one who fights for me in a second. When Aliyah is good, I hardly hear from her. She does her own thing and is on the street from sun up until sun down doing something, mostly some church functions. So when she is unable to get around, I feel compelled. Although I can't stand her husband, she loves him enough to let withholding of communication wreck her nerves.

As usual, I gave in. "Okay, I'll be over in a bit. What does he want?"

"Well, you know get the hot chocolate and make sure it's with the marshmallows. Please don't forget I don't want to hear his mouth," she uttered as she scrambled off the entire monthly "stuff for husband in jail" list.

I can't stand these Negroes sometimes. You would think I have nothing better to do than to pick up stuff for an ungrateful nut job in jail. During these frequent ghettotastrophies, which usually occur with Aliyah or some one of her people, I often wonder, albeit an unhealthy thought, why I haven't been able to discover the value in the no-conscience low down criminal.

Like a good soldier, I continued to focus on making sure I didn't miss one detail in transposing the shopping list, because Aliyah's husband makes Hannibal Lecter look like a patron saint.

The good old Elder Barron knew he had AIDS and chased Aliyah down. She shook him off at first, but he was persistent. Homegirl thought he was a good man because he was always at church, always served in the ministry and appeared to have himself together. Since Aliyah came off the streets, her initial outlook was that most of the people she encountered in the church were honest. Most of them were good people. Elder BJ seemed to fit the pattern. So she thought.

BJ knew Aliyah was from the streets and knew she used to give up the bootay for some crack back in the day. And, Aliyah has back and plenty of it in all the right places. Since the day Aliyah got saved, she was radical for Christ. She was once a thug on the streets, and had that same personality and influence in the church when her life was transformed. Although missy had seen many days with pimps on the street, she didn't know pimpology had its kingpins right in the pulpit. She knew slick greasy cats on the corner and in the alleys but didn't think there were pimps who fished for silly women as prey right in the house of God.

Elder Barron drove a white Mercedes that was always so clean you could eat off of the hood of the car. He was tall, medium brown complexioned, and worked out. His teeth were white and his skin was clear. God knows that man has some good skin. His fingernails were manicured with beautiful broad nail beds. Elder Barron has never been gaudy. He's a brother that's more the clean-cut type. His watch, shoes, belt and taste said brother has some mullah. Elder Barron supposedly had his own mortgage company and used to wine and dine the high-end ghetto princess quite often. He would get her some nice things, but she wouldn't take them. Aliyah knew game and wasn't trying to get caught out there. An Akris Punto, Alexander McQueen, or Carolina Herrera dress, maybe even a fierce pair of Guiseppe Zanoti sandals had become the "clean" addiction of choice for Aliyah. But girlfriend wasn't about to let the power of a pair of Christian Louboutin shoes cause a man to manipulate her to get a good high. No control through lavish gifts. She could work game and get whatever she wanted on her own.

What Aliyah didn't know was that BJ knew game too. And, he was better at it. The Elder had the patience to work his game and the strategy to win. The clean cut "mand" of God, the "good catch" waited over two years and never grew weary with "please," "yes mam" and "thank you." He opened endless doors and took Rashaun, Aliyah's oldest son, to Wrestlemania, football games and the ESPN cafe. BJ was determined to get Aliyah-not the woman who is a testimony to the power of God, but Aliyah the sex pro turned Jesus girl-to sex him.

It was only a matter of time before Aliyah broke down and thought it must be real love because no man pursues that hard—repeated phone calls every day, takes her everywhere she needs to go, loves her challenging son—that long. This man must have been the blessing God had for her after all of the nastiness and abuse she had known with men from her past. While over BJ's house one night, he asked her to check and see if this bump he felt on his back looked like something he should have to worry about. Aliyah said that was the moment she should have said, "I'm outta here." But once that chocolate Negro took his shirt off and she saw the cut of his chest and saw those broad shoulders, she knew she was no good. Eight years off of the street from an instantaneous deliverance from crack cocaine in a beauty parlor, and eight years of running for Jesus. Eight years of celibacy and I'll never give the devil another second of my life. In the heat of the moment, Aliyah fell with this man who, because of perversion and total degradation of women, desired a woman with her past. He sought after those hips that knew how to give him the sexual kill he fantasized about and desired. He probably never even saw the real Aliyah.

So BJ and Aliyah did the do and she turned him out. She figured, I know how to do what I do and make the do, do what it do. I know how to lock a man down. But once she slipped, she recognized that she played herself. Aliyah realized she should have never let the "put it on him" do happen because she was open again. So she continued to go for the gusto. Since she was out there, Aliyah just gave him what he craved and hit the bull's eye. BJ was hooked with his nose wide open. The elder asked her to marry him.

Rashaun thought Elder Barron was cool and he was one of pastor's right hand men, so he should have been all right. Aliyah, who spent a considerable amount of her life in the cold hard streets of Chicago, managed to get a "good" church elder before those of us who had been waiting for eons for a good husband. None of our cliché was feeling this engagement though. Although BJ appeared to be all that, we couldn't put our finger on the problem. The cumulative power of our female instinct wouldn't let us rest. The syndicate knew something just wasn't right. We had to take it to Aliyah at a Bacci's moment.

"Look, we are not trying to tell a sista what to do, but did you seek God about this?" Laurel asked.

"Just because he asked you to be his wife doesn't mean you have to find him to be worthy of being your husband and having your favor. You do have a choice to be found," I threw out there.

"We love you, and this isn't hating. Something just doesn't seem right, girl." Although Chante probably couldn't care less, she did have genuine concern for Aliyah. Every now and again, we were privileged to witness some compulsion within Chante to briefly take attention away from her lobster ravioli in Vodka sauce and act participatory. Chante inherited her callousness earnestly. She knew the horrors of corrupted living firsthand.

Chante's parents both died in a drunk-driving accident coming from one of their Black elite social galas, when she was a little girl. Her dad, an avid but respectable alcoholic and cocaine user, drove home with her mom, a beautiful arm-piece who loved her man and never refused to snort the white line. They both probably never knew what happened. The notable President of the Black National Urban Alliance and his wife of Yale intelligencia, were both so drunk that they entered into eternity and left Chante and her two sisters behind. So homegirl became a rebellious hoodrat, and shut down emotionally. As one of the newest members of the crew and a babe in Christ, Chante is learning how to feel again.

This is when Aliyah disclosed the sex thing. "Look y'all, we love each other and he's good to me. Beside we already having sex, and we know this is for real."

Oh my God. Aliyah, with all of her street smarts, was caught. All Aliyah ever knew was sex. She never had a clear picture of intimacy with a man, without it. Her uncle sexed her when she was a little girl, often, right in front of her father. Her dad and a bunch of his friends used to get high off of heroin with her as a piece of candy for the drug addicts. Her older male cousins used to feel her up, too. This is what prompted Aliyah to hit the streets at fourteen years of age.

During her sixteen-year tenure on the streets, Aliyah constantly tested for sexually transmitted diseases and never had HIV or AIDS. When AIDS awareness hit the south side of Chicago, the community advocates did round-ups to get street workers to test for HIV/AIDS. Although she didn't comprehend why at the time, Aliyah never ran from the testing. She always wanted to know, stigma or not. Even when she was "out there," she didn't want to harm anyone. She was a product of harm and didn't want anyone to be in jeopardy because of her. It was an absolute miracle. Even after eight years of a clean record since being treated for syphilis, chlamydia and genital warts a few times when on the street, her health was excellent. She had a case of herpes so mild and infrequent that doctors never even prescribed treatment for it.

"Aliyah, you are in too deep. You need to pull back and see this thing for what it is. I'm not saying this isn't right for you; I'm just saying you can't know because your foundation has been tampered through fornication." Danne always had a diplomatic way of getting the point across. She also held fast to the Word of God in all things. "You've got to repent and cut it out Woman of God. Then expect God to bless."

Noey is the "let me kill you kindly with a soft bullet" type. You'll die nonetheless. She told Aliyah, "At the very least, you need to make sure you have pre-marital counseling and address all of your issues because once you marry, baby, that's it. We don't do divorce, okay? We may have to do funerals, but once you say 'I do', that's it." Noey is always going to drop that marriage perspective because she is the only one out of our crew who is actually married. "You really don't know a [N-word] until you're married and live with him. Don't get me wrong, I love Jayden, but it is not easy. Sometimes I want to kill Jayden, and then there are times I want him to never let go."

Aliyah looked concerned but assured us she had her life under control. At least God did, so we didn't have to worry. It wasn't until the ride home that night that she asked me what two medications that are part of one of the latest AIDS cocktails are used to treat. I was immediately alarmed.

"How do you know about those medications?" I asked.

"Why do you always have to act like we're in court? Can't you just tell me?" Aliyah often misread my angles of questioning her as if I were being official. What she failed to understand is anyone who cared about her and saw the red flag would want to know the same thing.

"Okay, those are two drugs used to treat AIDS patients. Why do you ask?" I conceded the answer knowing that Aliyah would disclose the real juice after a while. As it turned out, none of us were really ready for the raw deal.

Aliyah's tone swiftly changed. Sounding like a girl who really knew the cold mean streets of Chicago, girlfriend came back at me, "Are you for real? Please tell me you are kidding?"

"Why would I joke about this? What the heck is going on Aliyah? Why would you ask me that all of a sudden?" Aliyah was taking too long to just let it all hang out.

Aliyah burst into tears. "Oh God. Jesus help me fo I kill that [N-word]."

"Calm down and tell me what is going on!" The wisdom of the matter was to pull over. This was clearly a moment that we both needed to stay calm and focused.

"Jewel, I saw a bunch of pills in BJ's medicine cabinet. I didn't think anything of them. But then I noticed lately that he carries some pills in a container with him when we're out late at night and I asked him why, and he told me it wasn't nothing to worry about. So, I went and copied down the names of the pills and thought I would ask you to figure out what's up with them." Tears were flooding Aliyah's face.

I couldn't help myself. The inquisition had to go on. "Did you see if the meds were prescribed to him? Was his name on the bottles?"

"Of course they were! I do have enough sense to make sure the stuff was his." Aliyah was irate, and rightly so. "Anyway, who else's pills would be in his medicine cabinet?"

The rational side of me kicked in. "Okay, let's not jump to conclusions. I know that if he has prescriptions for those meds, he has to have AIDS. But that doesn't mean you have to worry."

"What do you mean? I've been sleeping with him," Aliyah confessed.

I wanted to flip on homegirl. "Please don't tell me you put yourself out there like that with him? Are you crazy? Don't you know you can't trust your life and well-being to anyone else in this day and age?"

"Look Jewel, I can't go there this second. Please. Don't make me curse you out. I don't know. Oh my God. " Aliyah nearly screamed as she interrupted an ill-timed life lesson speech.

Optimism, the healthy alternative to suicide and murder, was the only way to go. "Look, come by my office tomorrow, and I'll make sure you get tested. Don't panic. You were on the street for years and you've been on top of your health, so maybe you didn't contract it, if he in fact does have something."

"I'm going to kill him. I swear fo God, I'm going to kill that [N-word]." Aliyah stated those words as if she meant every single one of them.

"No, you're not. First, we don't know anything for sure. Second, you may not be infected. Third, you are a grown woman. You, of all people, know the dangers of putting yourself out there. In this day and age, did you really think you could put your own well-being into someone else's hands? You can't use an excuse when it comes to your own life!" I stopped myself. The last thing Aliyah needed was a beating. If she did in fact get caught out there, she would live with the results of foolish judgment. Words would not change her reality so I continued, "You got caught and were weak, but let's cross that bridge when we come to it. Okay?"

Completely ignoring me, Aliyah continued, "I'm going to jack him up. You got your cell phone? I'm going to call his Black [a**] right now and—"

"And, he will know you violated his stuff and put his business out there. Calm down and wait until we know what's going on with you first. Please, I'm begging you." It seemed like a good time to try and change the subject. "And stop that foul language. You always want Rashaun to stop cussing but where do you think he gets it from?"

"Okay! But why would he do this to me? Why?" And these are the questions for which Aliyah would never get a reasonable answer.

One hour earlier, around the finest Italian food on this side of heaven, Barron was the man for real. He was God's blessing. After learning he takes AIDS medication, super-spiritual Aliyah decided he's a hot mess worth cussing like a sailor over.

Aliyah kept her word and didn't blast the slime ball until she had solid proof. Although I have looked into patients' eyes and told them they had HIV or AIDS about a thousand times, I couldn't figure out how to break the news to Aliyah. She was infected. We all presumed BJ gave it to her, because when she told him she just found out she had AIDS and asked if he knew anything about it, he told her it would be okay. She knew from his reaction that he already knew he had AIDS. Why else would he be so calm and encouraging as if she told him the circus was coming to town? Aliyah confronted BJ about the medications. The good elder told her that he had been living with the virus for quite some time. He opted not to tell her, because he knew she would not have chosen to be with him. And, he didn't want to "die alone." So the trusty church elder decided to willfully and knowingly pass the virus onto a woman whom he craved for her sexual prowess and expertise. A huck and buck shouting, dancing, "mand" of God, withheld deadly information from Aliyah so he wouldn't die alone.

Aliyah was crushed. She could not believe a human being could be so selfish and reckless with another's life. People on the streets didn't do each other like that. Those who you thought were your peeps would put you down. When people did the dirt like that, you knew they didn't have your back.

She also blamed herself amidst the irony. Sixteen years on the streets of Chicago and no terminal diseases. Two years with a church elder who hid a lethal sickness from her earned her the diagnosis. Aliyah was real with herself. She didn't try to take herself down Excuse Lane. The grace of God was still sufficient to cover her. But sin and living outside of the will of God earned Aliyah a bill that she could not afford to pay. Like many good people, she would learn to still live with God's grace and the consequences of sin.

Aliyah decided to go through with the wedding because she too didn't want to "die alone." Who else would want to marry her knowing that she had AIDS? She might as well marry him: the sex was fantabulous, he took care of her, and she was already caught. For someone whose daddy put her on a platter for his friends to play with, the situation wasn't ideal, but wasn't as big of a deal as the crew may have thought. At least he wasn't with anyone else, and the two of them had each other.

BJ gave Aliyah her dream wedding: a ghettolabra affair. A super duper long weave, airbrushed tips on fingernails and yes, fake toenails, adorned the beautiful bride dressed in a Paloma Blanca creation. We all stood with our girl as we danced all night at the Chateau Briand. Aliyah showed us how to really forgive. No one who didn't know the scoop, would have ever thought BJ wasn't the best thing next to homemade ice cream. Aliyah made a decision. She made the decision to love instead of being bitter. Another Black man made a sister's life change forever. While we were still rolling our eyes and checking our own pulses to make sure our blood pressure remained below stroke level, Aliyah was working hard to be a happy and loving bride.

Aliyah decided to forgive BJ and even gave him a baby. Although the crew thought Aliyah was insane to have another child, she insisted on living with AIDS, not depriving herself of the joys of life. She wanted another baby, and that was that. So we prepared ourselves for unofficial auntiehood once her new baby arrived. Tysheem was born infected, but took medications early enough to combat the disease. He's cute like his daddy. I prayed that God would truly heal Aliyah's hurt and heal our hearts too because the girls-the syndicate-seriously wanted to hurt that man for his craziness. This mess Aliyah has with BJ is something we had all seen at some point in time in our own lives. We were girls or women who, at one time or another, had been in a relationship where a man never ever viewed us as individuals. We were simply pieces that could fit into their lives, be it to fulfill a whim or a life-long selfish desire.

We all spent a lot of time in prayer for BJ. Many precious hours were spent re-directing thoughts of wanting to see him hung up on a coat hook because he was so selfish. Most of the ill will toward BJ was pent-up frustration formed from my own emotional identification about men who callously engage in one act that devastates the lives of women forever. In prayer, the Lord spoke to me and told me don't worry about BJ. BJ was His son, and He would chasten BJ. I told Aliyah to trust God concerning her marriage, because there would be some rocky roads ahead. God was going to deal with the good Elder BJ. A few weeks later, BJ was extradited to Kansas for some crime he committed as a teenager over twenty-five years earlier. Needless to say, there was a whole lot Aliyah never bothered to find out, or would ever know about her husband. They carted his derriere off to jail for twenty-five years to life.

While finishing up the last items of the tawdry grocery list and preparing to ship BJ his stuff-in-jail list, I told Aliyah, "Girl, if heaven is giving out rewards for those who do the right thing when others would use a machete, you are going to be the first in line."

Aliyah, being the true trooper, conjectured, "Don't even go there. I keep asking myself, Lord, how long am I going to have to forgive this man? He is really starting to wear me out."

"Well, forgiveness is not just for him, but more so for you. You have to keep your heart right so that you can live. It is easier to forgive than to carry on with this mess." Although I was on my own journey struggling to forgive, the need to let things go and turn over a new leaf in life still held true. "But, you really have to make some hard decisions for you and your boys now. This isn't just about the two of you. Rashaun and Tysheem are watching all of this madness and this does not need to be their normal. God has given you a way of escape, time and time again. You have to learn to recognize it and take it. Have you spoken to your pastor yet?"

"You know how hard it is to get an appointment with Bishop." One thing about Aliyah, she is going to have her bishop's back.

Aliyah used to be the chief administrator for Bishop Chauncey Deuce. Since she has had repeated bouts of illness, he had no choice but to replace her. To think, she now has to go through the mega church hierarchy to get an appointment to see her bishop.

While rolling my eyes and trying not to go back to the unproductive part of the bridge again, I objectively stated, "That's exactly why I go to Restoration Temple. My pastor may not be on every church channel five days a week, but at least we can get an initial meeting with him before we begin counseling with the pastoral counselors."

"Shut up, Jewel. Your daddy is the pastor and you can call him any time. And the sad thing is you don't. Anyway, this is not the time for all that, okay?" Aliyah could not comprehend why I never pull on my dad like hundreds of other people do all the time. Although I'm a faithful bench-warming member of the same church in which I grew up, I have seen and known too much to just override church corruption. But, Aliyah would be loyal to her spiritual father until the end. Who could blame her? Aliyah was in good company with thousands of believers who see their leaders as untouchable and faultless, even when proper church governing would have required that her Bishop spend some time in the Time Out Corner. "You have no idea who Bishop is to the world and everything he has to do. The mand of God can't possibly meet with everybody."

"You are not everybody, Aliyah. You dedicated your entire life to that dag on church since you've hit New York. You would think you should be able to at least get an appointment. Uhhhh, you've been in and out of the hospital fifty times. But you know what? That's neither here nor there. I am going to pray for you, but you really need to make some decisions." I had a policy with Aliyah. Say what needed to be said, regardless of the fact that when it comes to certain things, words go in one ear and out of the other.

Aliyah would defend her money-grubbing bishop while he robbed the bank and would drive the getaway car, if she had to. He could do no wrong in her eyes. And who could blame her? He is the only father she has ever known. When she came from Chicago, Apostle J. Merriweather sent her to Bishop Deuce. He made sure she had a place to live and food to eat. He fed her the Word of God to help her grow. She couldn't care less that the Board of Elders asked him to step down two years ago and charged him with absorbing over seventy percent of the church's income for personal expenses, down to his grandchildren's cell phone bills. It cost quite a bit to maintain two mansions, a yacht, a condo, and a home for each of his three children (one of whom isn't even a part of the ministry), the millions of dollars in jewels for his wife and daughters and all of the bling bling "harvest" of the Lord. The world was his audience for "seeds of faith" through an expansive television, Internet and radio schedule. Don't mention the fact that none of the full-time staff-persons received salaries commensurate with their experience and qualifications, while he and his wife commandeered million dollar salaries. The staff, servants of the Lord, should be grateful to labor in the Kingdom of God. This ideology only went as far as the hired help. Bishop Deuce and Evangelist Deuce's "anertings" warranted millions as the cash dropped in the buckets. Meanwhile, staff paychecks bounced from time to time, church accounts were backed up to the wazoo, and the church facilities were barely kept. But one thing was always for sure: those television bills would always be paid. The world needed to hear the gospel and Bishop needed to stay connected to the "seed faith" partners. Aliyah couldn't care less about the corruption. She gave every dime she had to make sure that the same anointing that destroyed the drug addiction bondage from operating in her life would be available to others.

Even though I couldn't stand her allegiance to the grimy church is a family business ministry, where the lineage and inheritance for the ministry could only be for someone with the Bishop's last name, where callings, skills and training are meaningless because lineage means more than stewardship and productivity, and the people honor the bishop more than they ever honor Christ, I could not discourage her from seeking God where she felt comfortable. With all of Bishop Deuce's arrogance and greed some people were legitimately learning the Word of God and Aliyah needed the Lord more than ever now.

Meanwhile, all I had to do was pull up the precise mailing information for BJ from my smart phone, because I had mailed so many packages to Aliyah's husband before. This routine was a bit annoying, but I was willing to do whatever I could to help bring Aliyah any bit of relief and happiness. I prayed the entire drive this day. Aliyah needed it, and so did I. My drama is just as telling.

BIDDIE'S OWN DRAMA
Blackout in the Lighthouse

This unplanned errand would give me time to think for the zillionth time what I'm going to say or feel like, when I see my son who I had not seen since my parents gave him up when I was twelve years old. The private investigator believed he finally found my baby. I know my son is a grown man now. Year after year, I could not help but wonder what he must have been doing at every stage of his life. In many respects, in my thoughts he is still the little baby boy I had only held in my arms a few times. My thoughts haven't been able to catch up to the reality of his existence and life.

What will I say to Brandon Chase? My son told the locator he has always hoped to one day meet his mother. I still hold back tears when I think about it, believing that I will say the right thing and that God will prepare his heart to receive me and mine to receive him. I have read a trillion stories online, seen many movies, and talked about it with the crew. A reunion of this sort could be catastrophic or incredulous. I hope for the latter. Lord, order my steps. I probably won't disclose too much too fast. God Himself only knows if I'll be able to keep my composure. After all, I was clinically depressed for at least one decade after I gave him up. Would he ever know the real story? Only time will tell. To think of it makes me shudder.

When I was twelve years old, one of the leading traveling prophets of the day came to hold a one-week revival at the church where my daddy pastored. Back then, the evangelists stayed in the pastor's home or parsonage. We didn't know what "first class flights and room service meals or else you can't afford the great and mighty servant with demands" was all about. We thought the gospel was about humility and the gifts of God realizing they were gifts given to men: The emphasis of the worth of the gifts are purposed and intended to bless the people, not to be unique vessels that have some sort of monopoly on God and His will for our lives, which are expected to be adorned, worshipped, and esteemed. The gifts came to be a blessing; the people to whom they came were those who needed to be set free, delivered, and empowered to do more with the life God had given them. Back in those days, the traveling evangelists were merited for their anointing, their preaching ability, and their ability to reach the people, not their ability to raise money for the church. The reward was in seeing people experience the love of God and look for heavenly crowns in glory for their work. If a minister or missionary saw great earthly wealth, that was a great thing, not an indication that God was prospering the ministry after raking in offerings for two hours.

The visiting prophet was traveling all over the country and had not been home to see his wife for quite some time. His meeting at our church "ran over." People were coming out and getting healed left and right. People were getting out of wheelchairs. One of the ladies in our church who had been born blind with her eyelids shut, who we ignorantly called Blind Esther, opened her eyes during one of the meetings. There was a light shining so brightly in the Lighthouse that anybody who needed direction could see. The light brought healing and showed us the liberty in which we have been made free. So, every night for over one month, great miracles were happening. And the prophet, by the unanticipated but abrupt end of the meeting, made his way to my bedroom that night. That was the night of the blackout in the Lighthouse.

I knew Prophet Swanson shouldn't have been in my room at all. By the time I was fully awake I realized what was happening. He put a pillow over my mouth and told me not to make a sound. I tried to scream but felt the weight of the bald-headed heavy man my father trusted on top of me. I knew enough about God to know that what he was doing was wrong. My body concurred with this conclusion while registering that every ounce of my flesh was throbbing in terror and pain. What I didn't know was that the first tear I shed that night would flow like an endless river that wouldn't stop for years. The physical pain from an unwanted intrusion into my inner parts was nothing compared to the years of agony I would know.

When the prophet finished appeasing his appetite with an underage and unwilling partner, he immediately apologized and told me he was so sorry before he left my room. Prophet Swanson asked me if I forgave him. I didn't want the pillow snuffed over my face again for a third intrusion so I told him I sure did. I lay awake all night, weeping, cramping, aching, and wondering. Do I pretend this never happened, or do I expose the man of God? To expose him would upset my parents. The next morning, I was so torn I could hardly move, so I had to tell Mama what happened. She immediately told my father.

I listened to my father "talk" to the man who I would years later understand raped me. There was no Starsky & Hutch beat down or Kojak investigation. In the same world where I got whipped for leaving a mess in the kitchen or for backtalk, the clergy sat in the same psychedelic kitchen with mustard walls and orange and garden green countertops to work things out. My father and other clergy agreed that the rapist prophet should leave immediately and talk with his overseer. There was no need for community action. They didn't have to hunt down the assailant. He was there, right in our home. There wasn't a need for police or a protest against a Black man. The devil had gotten the best of him. And between my father's greater allegiance to not wanting to see a "reproach against the move of God" and a so-called good family man who had gone wrong, fall, he was willing to let a church council govern the violent infraction against his daughter–a Black girl who would one day become a Black woman–in his own home. The devil used them to try to get the best of me. My father's failure to cover me made a horrible night the basis of torment for many years of my life.

I never ever heard of that prophet again. Maybe he really did get himself together. Maybe his overseer did take charge of that behavior. Maybe he truly repented and got delivered. Everything didn't end with a maybe, though. When the prophet left, we soon discovered the, back then, "inappropriate", but now "pedophile's", act left seed in me at twelve years of age. My menstrual cycle, which I had just gotten used to, stopped. I knew what I was dealing with, but could not believe it. I didn't believe the prophet of God gave me a baby. Maybe if I pretended it wasn't real, it would not be real.

The morning sickness in the morning, noonday and night was real. The vomit was real. Certain questions would never have a definitive answer. I was too young to know if the sickness was pregnancy-related or nerve-wrecking trauma. Yet, the heaviness was real. The uncertainty was real. The depression was real. All of sudden, through one act, thinking clearly became difficult. The pregnancy turned the rape into a "sure-nuff" nightmare. Suddenly and without notice, the entire fiasco shut down all flickers of hope and light in the Lighthouse, for me. This was not supposed to be happening in the church, especially in a Christian home with two loving parents and Jesus.

My mom, Lady Prunell, soon caught on and was highly embarrassed. Again, I wasn't the priority. Jewel and the situation had to be managed amidst many other considerations. What would people think? My daddy could manage his own home. But the pregnancy would undermine the confidence of people who looked to him to lead them. The last thing Bishop Prunell needed was to have to explain his twelve-year-old daughter's pregnancy. What did that say about my mother, the virtuous and wise First Lady? The entire situation was a mess. Sooner or later, my parents might have to answer questions about who the baby's father was. Daddy was always the main speaker besides the Presiding Prelate and the other pastors on the Board of Bishops at the national conventions, because he could preach. He was a big whig in the denomination. Stuff like this could've made folks cut him back. My son and I were never the only lives to consider. Something had to be done. A baby under those circumstances really complicated matters. The baby meant things had to be simply swept under the rug.

So the sweeping began. For five months, I covered "it." No one was to know. While Chase was growing inside of my womb, we were skating through reality with willful blinders. If I kept a journal of meaningful, purposed dialogue about the rape and pregnancy with my parents, it would probably be four lines long.

Once we couldn't hide the pregnancy any longer, I went to my mother's baby sister, Aunt Beefi, down south. I went to "help" her. At least this was the excuse we gave people. I helped her use her Kleenex, eat her food, and keep her company. Meanwhile, I kept thinking my life was over. I wondered if I would be able to go back to school and knew it would be almost impossible to catch up. I was an A to A+ student. I missed the holidays and being home with my brothers and sisters. My mom and dad had to carry on the ministry and take care of the rest of the family. Although they spoke to me almost every single day by phone, I couldn't come back until: Until the baby was born. Until seemed like a lifetime.

Suddenly the smell of grits and bacon on a Saturday morning had new meaning. I had been jolted out of the liberties of unfeigned adolescent joy overnight. Even the grits that I used to love had become my enemy. Everything in life became indigestible. My father, who had once been my hero, came to see me one time that I can recall. Now, I know that solitary trip was probably to arrange the birth of my son, and everything else that followed.

So my Aunt Beefi became my favorite person in the world. I slept in her bed and she held me. This baby was messing up our lives and inconveniencing everyone. I didn't want a baby. I wasn't a loose girl. I had never even kissed a boy before. How in God's name did I end up in this predicament? Somehow, I ended up stuck down south where Aunt Beefi and I had to sit in the car and wait in scathing heat at the gas station store for about two hours to purchase cheese for the macaroni while staring at the sign the clerk put on the door, "be back soon." Or if Aunt Beefi felt like taking a ride, we'd drive twenty minutes down a one-lane roadway passing a bunch of cotton and tobacco fields with outhouses to reach the nearest grocery store for the secret ingredient: a real tangy mustard.

I began to hate myself and everything about me. I hated the sweepers. I hated that I had something within me that made me have cravings. I hated using toothpaste, which all of a sudden made me nauseous. I hated not being able to fit into my clothes. I hated living in fear and never wanting to sleep alone. I hated every creeping sound at night that woke me up. I hated my tender breasts. I hated the change in my odor. I hated the fact that my hands would automatically rub my belly. I didn't want this baby to think for a second everything was all right, because it wasn't.

Playing in the marching band and being on the mathletes and debate team seemed like a past time at twelve years old. There was no way I'd be able to manage all of those activities with a baby. We all knew Momma's policy: She was only raising her own children, and nobody else's. Caputz. Finito. That's it. No discussions. If we wanted to live like the world and have babies before we got married, we sure could. We just had to do it someplace else because no grandchildren were ever living in her house. Grown folks had their own address. My presence at Aunt Beefi's seemed to indicate that Momma meant exactly what she said. Even though I didn't do anything wrong I was still looking at the tobacco fields while the rest of the family was at Coney Island, barbequing, and hitting the beaches.

Needless to say, when I went into labor, I screamed the house down, but my mother still wasn't on her way. By then, I truly resented her. She is the last person I expected to just go with the program. She had eight babies herself. She was supposed to show me how to do this. My resentment didn't do a thing for the birth pangs. Adam should have never eaten the fruit. I screamed and wished I would die. I had been warned that dry labor would be more painful, and since I was so young, I might have some other issues as well. I had a false alarm when the water broke a few days before Chase was born. Before I knew it I had a son, a baby boy.

Delivering Chase was so-words cannot express-that I vowed I will never have another baby again. I couldn't even walk straight for a few days. This is when my aunt told me I still had to stay for a few more weeks. I needed to be under the doctor's care. I really didn't care at that time. If I would have never seen the light of day again, that would have been fine with me. Every time I opened my eyes, the situation was still there. There were no answers that worked. Although I didn't want to be a mother, I didn't want the baby boy to suffer. He was here and he needed love and care. All of the Sunday school lessons kicked in. So I hoped Aunt Beefi was going to take care of us until I could do it on my own. Or maybe Momma would let me bring him home and help me take care of him. The thoughts kept rattling through my mind: If we didn't do it, who would? If we didn't find a way to love him, who would? What kind of a life would he have without his mother? The way I needed my mother, he would surely need me. Somebody had to take care of my son.

Aunt Beefi took care of the baby night and day. After the doctor's check-up, I knew I was going back home. Somebody had to do something. If not, I'd stay with Beefi. I was sorry for whatever I did to make this happen. What about the baby? My aunt said she would try and do something. It seemed as if no one cared about what I wanted. After all, I was a child, and was to stay in a child's place. I remember sleeping endlessly. My aunt kept my son and said she would keep him until a decision was made. So there we had it. I had the best situation out of the worst situation. I didn't have to take care of my son, yet he was getting love and good care. Even though I didn't touch him for about the first three weeks of his life, I listened to him and watched him. He was cute, tender and precious. Since God let him live, there must have been some purpose for him. We didn't have a choice but to step up to the plate and do the right thing.

Just as I was opening up and overcoming the fear of responsibility for another life, my aunt discovered my Dad wouldn't allow me to keep the baby. Just when I was growing comfortable holding him, we were ripped apart. Things had to go back to normal. Aunt Beefi complied, and my son was gone. I went back home, and was told to forget everything. Yup. That was the approach the sweepers took. Erase everything in my mind, and go back to normal. So they thought. But things would never go back to the former place of equilibrium. The daily routine that ensued for an entire decade after giving birth began immediately. Not one day passed without me waking up and wondering where my son was. Nothing would stop the wailing in my soul. And few days passed in which I did not cry wanting him to be close by. Was he with someone like his father? Someone who would abuse him? God kept my mind, just like I asked him to, over and over and over again. My silent cry was, "Lord, please don't let me lose my mind."

I tried to fall in line and be the model PK (pastor's kid) daughter, at least as much as a daughter who hated her parents could. I hated my parents for caring more about the ministry than me, and even resented my sisters because no one stood up for me. I was different and knew things I wasn't supposed to have known at such a young age. But since the rug was back in place, and the sweeping broom put to rest, I withdrew. Isolation served as the building blocks for constructing a divide between the family and me. Although I went back home, I only returned to the house. Things were never the same and the house was no longer a home.

"So, what are you going to tell your son if he asks about his father?" Noey and Danne asked on what seemed to be our daily conference call.

After a few seconds of consideration, I had to be honest. "I don't know. What could I tell him? I don't even know if that man is still alive, or if my parents ever let him know I was pregnant. Whenever I try to get information from them, they don't want to talk about it. I really wouldn't know what to tell him."

"Your parents are a trip," Danne proffered.

"No, they are old-school. They did what the old folks did, tried to keep everything 'hush hush,' and keep what could be kept, so the world wouldn't be turned off from the church." Regardless of the real truth and nothing but the truth, they were still my parents, and my only parents. I wasn't going to let anyone else touch them at all. They haven't been perfect, but they have always loved me.

The automated Jewel defensiveness didn't move Danne. She responded with focus, compassion and concern. "Listen to yourself. Your life has really been affected by this, Jewel."

"Who you telling? I've lived it!" I struggled to keep my emotions and temperament in check. The girls were not the enemy. The syndicate had my back. "I don't know what to say to Chase, other than your dad may not even know you exist. I don't want to tell him about the rape. That's not on him, and I don't want to make him uncomfortable and run away from dealing with me."

"Just pray and ask God for wisdom. Maybe you should give him things in stages or maybe you shouldn't make him go through issues of being a rape baby so soon after just meeting him. You know me, I'm going to say to bring it to Jesus, cause He knows all things." Danne must be Jesus' favorite, because she always has

Him in the forefront of every discussion. But I didn't just hear Jesus again.

"I can't stand the term 'rape baby.' I know he came as a result of a violent act, but he had nothing to do with that. I have to see him as completely separate or I'll never be able to love him for who he is, irrespective of how he got here. I know you didn't mean any harm by it Danne, but please, don't any of you all view him as a rape baby. He got caught up in the shuffle. He's my son and His name is Brandon Chase." I hated to be confrontational with the girls, but I had to check them.

Danne retorted with a hint of sarcasm, "Alright, I'll take that. Look at the mother defending her son and she hasn't even seen him yet!"

"All I know is I am so nervous. Can you believe he is a grown man now?" While I was doing the candid thing, suddenly I felt a quivering in my stomach. "Oh my God! I just thought about what my parents are going to do or say if they find out I've made contact with him."

"Now you know I'm for the giving the parents respect thing. But this isn't about your parents and what they think. K? You have a son out there. Parents don't override your own children. You are old enough now to make your own decisions and you need closure. You need some questions answered. At least I want to know some things. Please girl, you are definitely better than me," Noey prescribed.

Even after all of these years, a flood of emotions rushes through me when I just think of what happened. Others have come through the same fire and they learn to manage, but I never have. I simply cope, digress and divert. "Look, I can't sit on the phone all day, I have a few more appointments, and I'm about to bust out crying in my office. All this time has passed and I am still breaking down. I'm nervous; don't have a clue about what I should say. I'm still hurting and hope he hasn't hurt like I have.

I gotta go. The last thing I need to be doing is having a moment in my office."

My patients would probably never think that a Black doctor who could afford a NYC upper west side pricey commercial lease was ever a pregnant teenager. No one would suspect the sordid past unless I disclosed it. Success has been the respectable mask for the pain. Once I returned home without my baby years ago, I put all my energies into my studies and put up emotional walls to everyone who wasn't "there" for me. I knew my entire family loved me, but I had to have someone to blame. If not, why would I be living with such guilt and agony? I know they weren't perfect, but they did love me. Now, I had to focus on loving me. Prayerfully, reaching out to the man who once relied on me to grow, would bring some fulfillment to my life.

CHASE
Better Late Than Never

It was time to launch out into the deep. All of the prayers, books and syndicate coaching for the highly anticipated moment would finally be put to the test. I looked at the number, time and time again. Brandon Chase was expecting my call. Now was the moment of destiny. *Lord, please help me to get through this.*

"Good evening, may I speak with Brandon Chase please?" I asked with a crackling voice.

Chase responded, "This is Chase. Who's calling?"

With queasiness akin to a passenger on a ship tossing in a violent storm, I continued with a detached professional demeanor, "I understand you've been in touch with Mr. Michael Diaz, a private investigator."

"Yes, he told me my mother is looking for me," Chase answered with a warm inviting tone.

"Well, Chase, my name is Jewel and I believe that you are my son, or at least the woman who gave birth to you." Already fumbling over each word, I could not believe I was so nervous.

"Wow. I don't know what to say. Ok. I mean I was sort of nervous and didn't know what to expect, but this feels good to hear your voice. I always wondered what your voice would be like." Listening to Chase speak seemed surreal.

"Really?

So you've wondered about me?" My heart was soothing in the warmth and reality of hearing Chase say he thought about me.

"Of course I have. When I found out what happened to my mother, I wanted to get to know you one day. I'm glad this day has come." Chase was certainly a gentleman. After waiting a few moments for a response, he continued, "Hello?"

"Yes, I'm here. I'm sorry. I'm just a bit choked up, hearing you say you thought about me. I've thought about you just about every day of your life." If he was putting honesty cards on the table so soon there was nothing for me to lose in doing the same.

"Wow. There's so much I'd like to know about you, Jewel. I hope you don't mind, my wife wants to say hello." And, he was bringing family into the equation as well. This was going to work out well.

I responded as if I was really attentive, although my thoughts were twenty miles ahead. "Oh, you're married?"

"Yes, I've been married for almost two years now to a beautiful woman, even though we've been together forever. Actually not forever. But close to it. My wife's name is Evey. And, you also have a granddaughter, Ruth."

"That's beautiful." I knew I would have to hang up soon because so much was flushing down the emotion gates and I didn't want to do or say anything to mess things up. I couldn't believe at forty years old I already had a son who was already married. I had still been hoping to settle down and have my first baby, at least in the eyes of the rest of the world. All of a sudden, there's a granddaughter on the scene.

All of the good news was a bit overwhelming but certainly welcome. "This is truly a miracle. We've prayed for this. This connection. This is exactly what we had been praying for," Chase admitted.

Trying to mask the weeping over the phone, I kept the ice-breaking conversation going. "So you guys are Christians?"

"Yes we are. We truly love the Lord. I've always hoped that one day I'd be talking to you. When is the day we'll get to see each other, Jewel?" Chase inquired.

"Chase, as soon as it is agreeable to you. I can afford to be away from the practice for a few days." All of the preparation in the world could not replace the actual joy of speaking to Brandon Chase. We were blissfully in the midst of the longest conversation we had ever had with one another.

Chase kept digging. "So you're a doctor, huh?"

"Yes. How did you know?" With Google, Yahoo and public records, if Chase was Internet functional he could have done his homework.

"God does reveal things to me, but Mr. Diaz told me." Duh. It was like me to over-think the simplest thing. "Evey is a high school guidance counselor and I am in the ministry full-time. I'm a prophet and elder, just like my father."

What did that mean? Is the man who raised him a prophet? Did God reveal to him that his natural father was a prophet? And if so, did God show him the rest? My mind was racing with questions and instantaneously feeling crippled by that one remark. I thought out loud. "What in the world…" And then I caught myself. With the thoughts still racing, I didn't want to close the door of a brand new relationship with panic and worry. "I'm just so glad we finally got in contact with one another. Can we concentrate on us?"

"Jewel, I've been waiting for so long and I want you to know that I already love you."

Is this man trying to make me pass out? He loves me. Even after I abandoned him.

Chase continued with poise, as if he had practiced how he would reach me over and over again. "God spoke to me a long time ago and told me, 'your mom loves you but could never take care of you, forgive her.' So I've never had any ill feelings toward you. I just wish things could have been different growing up. But I've had a good life. Really, a great life. And the way God works, I'm sure it's about to get better as we get to know one another."

My God is really fierce. Wow. He visited Chase years ago and caused him to intercede for me and know my heart. Imagine all these years of misery and guilt, and he has known that I loved him. I just listened.

"I hope you know that you can let everything go. God wants to heal your hurt. The enemy can no longer torment you. I have nothing but love for you."

I'd spent so many years crying and feigning happiness, I'd mastered weeping silently so that no one would hear. But I wasn't prepared for all of this.

My son ministered to me, "You can let the walls crumble and fall now. You've been in a place of safety all along, but wouldn't allow God to fully come in and comfort you. You've blocked out your own happiness, because somehow, you felt you didn't deserve it."

Before I knew it, my hands were up in the air. Just like that! Years of bondage, shame and disappointment were dismantled. With a few words from the seed that the enemy thought would cause my mind to be eternally gripped, I finally saw liberty. I finally had the strength and courage to forgive myself.

"Chase, I hope you can understand I have to go now. Please let me know when I can see you; I can leave as early as tomorrow." The truth was I wanted to leave at that very moment and never look back.

My son was prepared to make things happen between us. He took charge with instructions, "Well, pack your bags. I'm going to book a ticket for you tonight. I've been ready to meet you."

In one day, years of pain were wiped away. I've heard it time and time again from the whooping preachers who lean back and hold their ears with an accompanying cascading organ. I've gotten caught up in the hype and shouted and danced and fell out believing it. I had to believe it. I had to think that what was not evident would one day be substance right before my very eyes. But this was different. Although I had seen some measure of freedom before, this was different. I felt as if a dagger that had been in my heart was taken out without me feeling one thing.

Brandon Chase, the child from my adolescence who I yearned to meet for twenty-eight years wanted to meet me. He forgave me, and loved me.

I heard the dial tone and with the same eyes, saw clearly again. Finally, things were coming together. Hope with a deferred end was a hope well spent, and not lost. There was so much to do. I did not want to repeat any mistakes. I had to call Mom, Dad and the siblings. This was a taboo topic. We never discussed the prophet, the rape, or the baby. Frankly, I felt they never had the right to even ask. They did what was best for the family and the ministry, not what was best for me. So we agreed with the unwritten modus operandi. None of them dared to ask me one thing. They forfeited their rights to act concerned about Jewel. The coping rule was I got me, and so does God. He gave me die-hard friends who thought of me. That had been my attitude.

All of the mumbo jumbo didn't change my obligation to consider the family. *Lord, I need your help and guidance.* I don't need any opposition before I go and meet Chase for the first time. It was really happening. I was getting ready to see my baby.

NOEY
The BIAP-Black Italian
American Princess

Noey is always on time, so I needed to hurry up to make the flight. Noey and Danne are the top friends. If I had a best friend kit, and could have made anyone in the world I wanted, they would have been the outcome. Those are the two who understand me and are always in sync with Jewel. Between the two of them, they can finish my thoughts and know my tastes and predilections. We may not always agree, but they always know where I'm coming from. But, those good biddies will also give me a tongue-lashing if need be.

So naturally, Noey and Danne dropped everything to make sure we didn't miss the moment-our moment. Heck. They spent more than enough yak yak hours without earplugs as confidantes to own the moment too. I didn't even have to ask either of them to do what they always do: be there.

"Danne, I just spoke to Chase and he's flying me out to meet him tomorrow."

"He's flying you? What a gentleman. I'm going, too."

Laurel, Chante, and Aliyah each have their different relationships with Danne, Noey and me. But everyone knows "don't even think about it" when it comes to the three of us. We are like the negro on frijoles. Although I wasn't nervous at all, wonderful got better when I knew either one of my best friends in the world would be with me.

Noey is a homemaker and is my cut buddy if I ever decide to be irresponsible and take off work. That's usually when Noey and

I hang out. She escapes from the kids and I escape from the office and we do lunch, the spa, or the mall.

Noey's name is unique. Her parents just knew they were having a boy, so they were deliberating between Joel and Noel. When she popped up, she shocked both parents who hadn't prepared a girl's name. So, her mom decided to call her Noey, because had she been Joel, the nickname would have been Joey and Noey was a combination of the two. Nowadays, Noelle or Joelle would have worked.

Noey is the only biological child of her two parents, who have been married for almost thirty-five years now. She is definitely the love child of her West Indian father, who is still fine as all get up, and her petite Italian mother, who is an impeccable beauty. They met at the Metro Church, a mega church in the heart of New York City, when the ministry was in its infancy. Noey's dad was the minister of music, and her mother was the choir director. Back in those days, the praise and worship style wasn't as popular as it is now. Ms. Paterno was the one who would lead the "song service" and Mr. Persaud noticed her. Although the church was intimate and multi-cultural, it was still a bold move for them to hook up. Ms. Paterno was fourteen years younger, and had never been married. Mr. Persaud had two children and just lost his first wife. So when they fell in love, they had to fight for their relationship. The Paterno and the Persaud Christian families agreed on one thing. They were not going to support an interracial marriage. Ms. Paterno was a precious Italian girl who had no business with a black man, especially a West Indian. Furthermore, she had no business thinking of being with an older man who had just lost his wife. Yet, the marriage worked out. Those two are still fresh to the point of embarrassing—real embarrassing-to this day.

Noey is the youngest and only girl of the three children both of her parents have together. Needless to say, she has always been the spoiled brat. Noey never moved out of her parents' home until she got married. When she was going to college, her dad told her she had to pick a local school because she wasn't leaving his house until she got a husband. That was it. Living on her own was not an option. Since she and her mother talk about any and everything all day long, every day, she didn't mind staying at home. Her home life was like a dream to me. She grew up as a light-skinned mixed Black Italian, knowing the value of two loving parents raising their children in a Christian home. Understandably, she has a loyalty to her parents that I comprehend, but just don't have. The misgivings about what role our parents should play in our lives are a common bone of contention between us.

I could have related to Noey's outlook on life up until the day my innocence was taken from me. I cannot imagine talking to my parents about much of anything, more or less everything. Not my parents. I love my parents, and still wouldn't trade them. I know they have always loved me. They did what they thought was best. Isn't this what I have to believe? All of my other brothers and sisters feel we had an excellent upbringing and can't understand me. They are all married with children, educated Americans in the corporate world, living the American dream. I love all of them, but the family just doesn't have that seat of influence and guidance in my life. I could not trust any of them when it mattered. I could only trust my girls who have never let me down.

"Thanks for taking me to the airport. You are always there for me. I don't take you for granted."

"Girl, shut up. You know I like any excuse to get out of the house."

"Who has the girls?" Danne and I are the godmothers to the two princesses, Lissa and Leah.

"My father. You know I've got to call him first, because if anybody else has his grandbabies before him, I'm in trouble." Mr. Persaud is an out-of-control grandfather. I don't think either of those girls ever needed a rocker or bassinet. Their grandfather's arms were where they slept for the first few months of their lives. He's retired and had been waiting for Noey to have some babies. I love it, because with Danne and my schedule, all we have to do is show up and smile for their momentous occasions.

"Did you tell him why I'm going?" Noey's parents are the ones with whom I tend to check in. They are so loving and consider me to be a daughter.

"You know I did. My father wanted to know if your family knew. He thinks this is great, and God is in it. But, he doesn't want your folks to be offended by the way things are done. So, although I could have told you this myself and you still wouldn't listen to me, I'll be integral enough to tell you what my dad said. He said you better warn your parents." What Mr. Persaud thinks, matters. He has a great marriage and family life, so he must know something.

"It's not that I don't trust your judgment, BIAP. You've been sheltered and you have no clue. That's why you have the Brady Bunch approach to LA Riot problems. When it comes to the parents and some issues in life, your outlook is skewed."

"So because I haven't been damaged, I can't relate? Is that what you're saying? Because I happen to know that since I haven't been damaged, that's why I can help you because I'm not operating out of hurt or resentment. I'm the one that's at a proper equilibrium in my emotions dearheart, okay? Don't get it twisted sister. Anyway, are you nervous?"

"No. I know I've had a lot of insecurities about meeting Chase, but somehow, like your dad said, I know that God is in this. I'm excited and I just can't explain it. I guess the words Chase spoke to me let me know that he is okay, and that alone lifted such a weight off me. And, it really shouldn't have been this way. I can believe God for everyone else. I mean when it comes to anyone else, I've known that God has it. But with Chase, I just don't know why I've always felt such a void."

"Well, that doesn't mean you didn't trust God, Jewel. That's a mother's love. You never had any type of information. Your parents wouldn't even talk about it. You don't just carry a baby for nine months and then move on, especially after some quack raped you. Please! I can't imagine giving up my girls."

"I guess you're right. I just never really considered myself to be a mother. I was an incubator. I wasn't able to express any warm feelings toward him. I cared about him. There was an unwanted bond. At least that's what I can remember. Just when I was starting to love him—"

"Jewel, pumpkin, focus. Let's stay in the here and now. Please don't try to fix and work everything out on this trip. Just embrace the now. Do not obsess, Jewel. You can't re-do or change anything about the past. Okay?" Noey always shoots from the hip and like a true cowgirl, whips the words out of the bolster and shoots truth at you before you even know you've been hit.

"Okay." I looked at her and thought about how much we looked alike. When we were in college, people used to mistake us for one another. I used to be gassed because I'm four years older than she is. We wear the same shoe, dress and bra size. She is a hot tamale, so if I have an event where I need to look spiffy, I hit her up. I'm so much more conservative and she knows how to jazz it up.

"And when you get back, we'll have to re-visit this issue of you dating and getting married so you can hurry up and have more babies, okay? Now that you've found your son you can stop punishing yourself and trust somebody long enough to say 'I do.'"

"You are seriously bugging. First of all, in case you didn't notice, I'm forty and there is no husband in sight. Anyway, you know I'm not ready to ever be pregnant again. Maybe I'll adopt down the line, but pregnancy is not for me."

"Whatever. I keep telling you that what you experienced was not normal. You can't compare what you've been through to what most of us experience."

"I know that. I'm a dag on doctor, remember?"

"So then, Dr. Prunell, why can't you comprehend that you were traumatized and you can be happy being pregnant? Can I still hope that you'll be healed? What if the man you marry wants a child?"

"We can adopt. If anybody marries me, he'll have to notice that I'm a busy doctor who is still working out issues; and I thought we were focusing on the now? You all the way up on Future Lane." The last thing I needed to do was to start obsessing over the gray hairs that I now have to rinse to hide. Even though my body is still intact, I can see the signs of my youth dissipating. I am officially very middle-aged and never shared my body with a man during my youth.

As we pulled up to the curb, I leaned over and kissed Noey good-bye. My younger sister wanted so much more for me. She knows the benefits of sharing your life with another and loving freely. I know she wants that for me too. What I just wasn't able to admit is I want to be able to be married and have more babies. Despite all of my insecurities, I know that one day, I'll have it. This visit to confront my past was a big step in that direction.

"Don't forget to call! I need to know every detail okay? Don't play yourself!"

I snickered. Homegirl is a trip. Noey is so much stronger than she thinks of herself, although she often doesn't see it. She esteems my professional success, intellect, dedication to the ministry, and personality. My gab gal thinks I have it going on. My career plans worked out just like we talked about over and over again back in the day. Hers didn't. Her life is "off-schedule." Noey never intended to be a kept woman with a super-duper fine well-built Christian husband and two beautiful daughters. She thought she'd be on the marquis somewhere on Broadway by now. But we all know that life isn't always what we plan or expect. Sometimes dreams are deferred and we learn to have peace with the now.

SNARES ON THE STAIRS
Surprise Secret

I knew Danne would probably be the last passenger to board the aircraft. She is always right on time, not a second earlier. "What's up dawgs?"

"Not you getting here without them having to page you first," I teased.

"You know I had to drive like a bat out of hell to get a parking spot and check in. Thank God I made it."

"God forbid you gave yourself some time by getting up a little earlier. The plane doesn't wait for celebs, darling," I stated with a deplorable rendition of a Zsa Zsa Gabor Hungarian accent.

It was too early in the morning for Danne. Her retort was cutting, Harlem style. "To think, if I stayed home and did what mattered for my own interests right now, I wouldn't have to be hearing this."

"You're right. And you'd still be late today with someone else probably complaining underneath her breath. But you are right. I love you enough to tell you to your face but it's not like you don't already know you're critically late all the time. Thanks for coming, even with your late self. I'd rather have you late than never." Danne half smirked, laid her head back and closed her eyes. She was a professional at ignoring me.

Like clockwork, as the flight crew began to check each aisle, I decided to call the parents. "Wait a minute, let me try and reach my dad before we take off. I know it's wrong, but if I call him right before we have to take off, I won't have to get stuck in a drawn out conversation with him about this right now."

With her eyelids slammed shut, Danne "broke" on me. "That is so shady, it's not even right."

I didn't have time to rectify anything. The Prunell family has mismanaged this situation from the moment everything happened years ago. Somehow, we needed to break the cycle. Truthfully, I didn't have the guts for a full-fledged confrontation and an unofficial deposition from my parents about the decision to see Brandon Chase. So I took the easy approach. "It is what it is. Shhh, his phone is ringing."

After a few rings, my father picked up. If Bishop Prunell kept his daily morning ritual, he had to leave his personal trainer in the basement home gym to answer the call. Before he could get a word in edgewise, I stated, "Daddy, I really can't talk too long right now, I'm on a flight to Mississippi. But I just wanted to let you know, I found my son and we are going to meet him today."

"What? How come you didn't come to me to discuss this? Who's the we?"

"Dad, it's all good. I already spoke to him. Don't worry, Danne and I are going together. I'll call you when I land."

"I can't believe this. Please call me before you see him. Now I have to raise this with your mother." The tone and choice usage of the words "raise this" took me back to the days of my youth when I wished sleep was eternal. I had to fight to escape the feeling of rejection and rejoice in the now.

"That's up to you, Dad. I'll let you all know what's going on when I get back."

"Jewel, call when you land. Now that's an order."

You would think that after all these years, with all that I have accomplished through God's grace, that my father would have stopped talking to me like I had better get outside and help my brothers rake the leaves and put them in large black trash bags. In many respects, my dad has gotten so much lighter over the years. He's a "wuss" when it comes to his grandchildren. They run him ragged. Sometimes I can't believe this is the same man who made his own children get up in the middle of the night if the kitchen wasn't cleaned the way my mother wanted it. His philosophy is he's grandpa, not daddy. His job is to spoil his grandchildren, not raise them. And so he does. My nieces and nephews can get anything out of their grandpa, and grandma for that matter. But the authoritarian never changed with his father role. He doesn't care how old we may be, we are all still subject to his authority. Especially Jewel because I'm the only daughter without a husband.

"He said to call him when we land." I fought hard to hold back the tears, but failed.

"What you crying for? Are you upset?"

"Not really. I just don't feel like having to discuss anything with them, that's all. That's the culture that we've existed with, and I'm not sure we can handle anything else, especially right now."

"Well, you know how I feel about it. Do what you need to do to get through the moment, Jewel. If that means you call them later, or wait till we get back home, so be it."

"They can't control this part." That's what I thought my father's response indicated, so that's what I told Danne.

Danne, however, was willing to give my parents the benefit of the doubt. "I may be wrong, but I don't think your parents were about control. They were about doing what they thought would protect you." She was probably right.

I let my tears continue to speak for me. "You're probably right. These tears are also tears of joy. I'm about to see my son for the first time. God answered my prayers. He allowed both of us to live long enough for us to meet again. I'm happier than I've been in, I can't remember how long. I've waited so long for this day, and there were many days that I wasn't sure if it would actually happen."

This is the day that the Lord has made. I will rejoice and be glad in it. While I had the daily affirmation to make the Soul know that the Spirit Man is in charge and will be glad in the day, Danne was sleeping so hard that she began to snore. I just continued to think. *Maybe I will call my dad back before I see Chase. Silence and living as though Chase never happened hasn't worked.*

The flight to Mississippi was both the longest and the shortest flight I ever took. It took too long to land to get to see my son and it landed too quickly to have to figure out things with my parents. Danne and I had until evening for Chase to meet us at the hotel. The day was wide open, so we had enough time to unpack and rest. Danne, who never unpacks but lives out of her luggage when we travel, wanted to hit the streets and see what the back woods of Mississippi had to offer.

"I'm going to settle into my room first and try to reach my parents," I told Danne. The Prunells needed to have a private conversation.

"I'm going to find somewhere to eat. Then we'll catch up." I knew Danne would be gone in a heartbeat and would commingle with people as if she were a townie. Give her a piece of wood and a rock and Danne would see fire, ammunition, and materials to build a house. Girlfriend can thrive anywhere.

As usual, the learned desire to be alone and withdraw started to kick in. Although I had no appetite, I needed to stay in motion. So I sent Danne a text. "Actually, why don't you pick us up something to eat. I really don't need to be alone right now." I was aware but felt powerless over the horrible pattern of behavior that kept me in a "slump." Sleeping or anything that resulted in avoidance had become a way of life for me for such a long time. It wasn't until the church grew and formed cell Bible study groups that I realized how non-functional I had become and called it living. The cell leader of our group, Dr. Tangi, is a psychologist whom I have been seeing professionally. I could hear her voice over and over again in my head. She would speak spiritual truths of faith in the unseen and what seemed impossible, and "in your face" truths about depression. So, equipped to recognize the signs, at that very moment, I had to fight the urge to withdraw and shut everyone else in the entire world out.

Well, almost everyone. First things first, I needed to text Noey to make sure she checked on Aliyah. Somehow, I couldn't even deal with my drama without making sure Aliyah was good. Even though Aliyah was two and three-quarter trips, she was still my girl. Although she was about seven years older than me, she was the younger sister I never had. There was a special endearment that we had for one another that no one else in the crew had for Aliyah because of her temperament and asinine requests. Noey didn't have as much tolerance for Aliyah's demands to please pick up Boston Market spinach, Kentucky Fried Chicken biscuits with Panera Bread soup. Noey told me I created a monster by catering to her idiosyncratic whimsical requests. I know I did. It's just that I figured she had a raw hand in life and for her to be sane and love God after all the hell she's lived through, visiting three different fast food restaurants to get her exactly what she wanted wasn't that big of a deal.

Next, I had to tackle the invisible elephant in the room: My parents. "Hey Mom, what's going on?"

"That sounds like a question I should be asking you. Your father says you're in Mississippi."

"Yes, Danne and I are settling in as we speak."

"How long are you going to be there?" My mother is not the type who would let you know what she already knew. She wasn't going to let me off the hook. It was obvious she was going to make me spill the beans.

I answered her question nonetheless. "Just for a few days. I'll be back in the office by Monday." Why did I feel six again? One thing I realized, my parents would never change. "Look Ma, I'm sure Daddy told you why I'm here, and I'm already feeling like I need to focus on what's going on here. I just wanted to call and talk to you guys like he asked, out of respect."

"Out of respect? You guys? Jewel, I don't know what we've ever done to you for you to be so distant. I hoped that if this day ever came, you would have come to us. Your father and I are not 'you guys.' I mean, you don't even talk to your sisters or your brothers. But as long as you are okay, that's all I'm really concerned about."

I was on the bridge again. Why in God's name would I involve my parents in reconciling with my son, the grandchild they gave away? I had no reason to believe they would even want me to find him. The Bishop Larry and Lady Caroline Prunell revolve their lives around the church and their grandchildren and Chase has never been part of their hearts, more or less agenda. Chase was an accident from an incident that was never supposed to happen and was to be forgotten. Or did I miss something for the past twenty-eight years? Yet I responded with an unspoken but loudly heard restraint, "I'm good Mom, I really am. And, I do talk to my sisters and brothers. Just not about this."

There was a wall of silence and separation between us ever since I left home and went down south with Aunt Beefi for five months and came back home, many years ago. No one-not one of the Prunells-ever asked me a question or said anything to let me know they cared. And somehow, they all knew I knew some things that only grown-ups were supposed to know. Somehow, I felt used and tarnished way before my time. The blaring silence sort of said we love you enough not to even address it. What happened must have been that bad.

"I'm not trying to fight you, Jewel. I just wish I could reach you and help you," my mom said with a consoling voice.

Consolation was too late and I needed to move on. "Where's Daddy?"

"He's in prayer," Mother answered. Lady Caroline, determined to get her genuine two cents in, continued, "You know what happened to you happened to us as a family. We did what we thought was best, and apparently, it wasn't good enough."

"Have I ever complained to you about it, Ma? No, I haven't. Please stop it."

"You've never complained but you punish us. You shut down and that's that."

"Ma, I don't mean to punish you. I didn't set the pattern of our communication, or complete lack of it. I'm not the one who fixed a bad situation by wiping out my baby's life. All I'm trying to do is live for real now, and it has been a struggle. Tell Daddy I'll get back with you all later. And if it hasn't gone down the grapevine yet, I'd like to bring this to everyone else myself, when I'm ready. Please."

"Jewel, I love you. Your father and I always have. We just hope you're prepared for what you're about to encounter. We don't know all what you know yet."

"Well, what is there to know, Ma? Please if there is something I need to know please tell me," I pleaded while rolling my eyes.

My mother took a deep breath. "Baby, if you found your son," and there was a pause, "You'll probably find his father. Are you there?"

"I'm here." I wasn't ready for that. I thought the locater said Chase wanted to know if I knew about his father. I completely misunderstood what that must have meant.

"When all this happened, Prophet Swanson and his wife wanted to keep their marriage together. His wife wanted to take the baby herself, but your father was concerned about Prophet Swanson's judgment and the boy being mistreated. So, they arranged for his sister to take the baby. I'm almost certain he's been raised by that family." My parents gave their grandson to the family of the nut job who raped me. The news was beyond unbelievable. "We saw how you responded to the baby so we figured it was best to try and do what we originally thought was best. That's the only reason we sent him away."

"I was twelve years old, how did you expect me to react? Why couldn't you try to keep him in the family?" By that time I was yelling. I finally said what I wanted to say to Caroline. I was reverting back to the old and weary should-have, could-have, never would have, past. I was all the way into "if only things would have been different."

"Jewel, would you have wanted to see your son and call him your brother? We didn't think you could cope with raising him. You didn't even want to touch him. You were only a child and shouldn't have had to worry about being a mother. Your dad and I prayed, and we gave him to his aunt. He was with someone who seemed like she would care for him and love him. And don't think we don't think about him. We wanted to check up on him, but didn't know how that would affect you. And you are our daughter. We failed you once, and didn't want to fail you again."

I wanted to flip on my parents. But I just couldn't. We've never had this much progress in just talking about this situation. I never realized my parents thought they failed me. They couldn't have fixed it. They would have had no way of knowing what would have worked. They could have kept him, and I might have hated him and my parents. Who knows.

"Ma, you didn't fail me. I know you did your best. You really did, and I've always known that. It's just that somehow, this might have been easier to deal with had I had somewhere to lay the blame. And really, the only blame should be placed on the devil. He is the only driving force behind what that man did to me." By that time, an impending headache was trying to creep in and complicate the day.

"Jewel, remember that it was the devil. And you've got victory over the devil in your worst and weakest state. So please, whatever you do, remember it was not flesh and blood that tried to make you lose your mind; it was the devil."

"Tell Daddy I'm okay. My son's name is Brandon Chase, and whoever raised him did enough to make sure he knew God, cause he knows Him. That much I can tell."

"I wish I could be there with you."

"God is with me. And so is Danne." This was the most progress I've ever had with my mother about this entire situation. Now, I have to prepare my heart to see the family of the man who raped me. Only women who have been single well into adulthood would understand "the feeling." Although grown single women may lead content or happy lives, there are those moments when a sister would love to have a companion connected to such matters of the heart. In our syndicate, we've learned to hang tight with one another. Although a girlfriend certainly can't replace a man, we learned to be there for one another. I needed Danne to help me face the horrors of my past.

DANNE
Sister girl

It's funny how Danne and I met. She was hilarious. We were both on a flight headed to the same gospel music industry conference. She's an indie label owner and was sitting next to a hoity toity sister who did a piece of carrying on. Danne decided she was going to try to put up with her, while I kept thinking *I don't know how she could put up with such a snob.* When the sister asked her to make sure she didn't touch her seat at all, Danne said, "How about you get up and move now," as she touched all over her seat. I burst out laughing. Sometimes I wish I could get away with stuff, and I admired her demeanor in putting this "wanna be on my own private jet yet got to ride coach" sister in her place. I didn't speak to Danne then, but ran into her again at my girlfriend, Kamoi's new artist showcase which my practice helped to sponsor. I told her that I observed her keen sergeant-at-arms behavior on the flight, jokingly, and we connected. Ever since then, she's been my alter ego and has pushed me to be a better me. Danne wouldn't dare miss the biggest moment of my life.

"You know you are top dawgs when you know exactly what I like on my sandwiches. Black olives, sun-dried tomatoes, red onions, loaded with fresh spinach and a light vinaigrette does it every time." The gab gals and I know the intricacies about each other in ways that make us more like sisters.

"And don't forget to give me back my money, cheapy," Danne responded. She's right. I make so much more money than she does, but she's always spotting me. And every time I try to pay her back, which isn't often, she finds a justification for me to put the change elsewhere. It's good to have a friend that gives of herself, not based upon my ability to handle a bill.

"Whatever. I hope you aren't holding your breath for the change. Anyway, my mother and I spoke. It turns out that they have known where my son was all the time."

"Oh Shoot. You've got to be kidding me!" Clearly, Danne was as shocked as I was.

"Nope, they just didn't know if I could handle knowing where he was, if I wanted to connect and all that," I stated with a flippant matter of fact, please pass the salt, sarcastic delivery.

"So where has he been?"

"With the man who… raped me. His sister. So, his aunt raised him. At least that's what they know, or what they told me, I don't know. My parents are not certain, because it sounds like they've never even checked up on him." As I stated those words "never even checked up on him," nothing could be clearer in my mind that my family didn't care about my son.

"Wow. Wow. I don't know what to say. This is a wow moment. How does that make you feel?"

I had to think for a few seconds and began to respond, "I'm already here. And, I don't want to disappoint him. But had I known before, I probably wouldn't have come. Just the thought of seeing this man responsible for—"

Danne cut me off to break the cycle. "Jewel, this isn't about him. Stop giving him power over you. This is about you and Chase, isn't it? C'mon. He stepped into your life for a few days and you've got to cut off the power he's had over you all these years. You can't undo it. It is what it is. You've got to let all this stuff go and live now."

"I am living. I'm here ain't I?" I knew I was being defensive, but so what.

"Okay, I'm not trying to take you there. You just need to see beyond this. This yoke was destroyed a long time ago through God's anointing. You keep letting the devil gather up all the crap in your mind and keep taking back the shackles. You have authority over your thoughts and what you say and what you do. Some people die bound, but you know too much for it to go down like that. It's up to you."

"So what am I supposed to do? Tell me what to do."

"I can't tell you what to do. I can tell you who you are in Christ Jesus; then you'll know what to do."

"I just want to be truly happy. I know I can't go back to where I was before this happened. But, the feeling of just being able to trust and love, and not be afraid; I want to know that again."

"And this is going to happen if you just get the lesson in all of this. Just be you and stop over-thinking everything. Stop being analytical about things that can't be rationalized. You can't change the past at all. The past is over and done with. Period. See it for what it is, and cut off everything in the past that stops you from enjoying the now. The man raped you and hurt you, twenty-eight years ago. You were traumatized. Are you going to give him twenty-eight more years? He lives in your thoughts and you've crafted your life around him and what he did to you, and he hasn't earned that place at all. Focus on what is tangible and what you can control. Remember, all that heebee jeebee stuff your son told you may be true, but he is still a man who had to grow up without his mother. So now think of him. You are a wonderful human being. Let him know the real you, and let God use you."

"I hear you. I heard every word." Danne is always in my corner and won't let me be a big baby. Those words were hard to swallow, but I needed to hear them and let them register. It's not as if she didn't have her own baggage; she just doesn't live in an experience like I do. She told me it's because she goes to church and stays in the presence of the Lord. She is constantly being inspired by the Word of God. *Father, help me to be more faithful and focus on you. You have given me abundant life. I know there is more for me. Please help me to do everything I must to forgive. I will forgive. I will let all of this go. It has held me long enough. Heal my heart, Lord. Heal my hurt Lord. I want to trust you fully. Lord, I need to be free to love. I can't go on in the state that I am in. I need to be free from this. I've carried it too long.*

I guess my silence concerned Danne. She asked, "You okay?"

"Yeah, I'm just talking to the Lord," was the truthful response.

To think, Danne is concerned about me when she has so much on her own plate. Danne is a carefree and brilliant thinker, mover, and shaker. Many would classify her as an underachiever considering her natural ability. She could have been a Mother Theresa or Condoleezza Rice, some phenomenal woman who would be a notable figure in world history. However, Danne is true to herself and uses her talents, skills and know-how to make her mark in the gospel music industry.

Danne wears fifty different hats at the record label. She's always busy at the studio, doing interviews, at every festival and concert she can think of, and she visits so many of the small retailers. Promise Records has its own in-house management, booking, promotions, manufacturing and distribution and retains three artists, two of whom are very successful. Bishop Chauncey Deuce and the Voices of Zion Cathedral is the first artist who put her on the map. Since Aliyah used to work for the Bishop, when he wanted the choir to record, she hooked Danne up with the whole deal. Danne had been talking about doing her own thing for years, after having worked for RCA since she was a high school intern. She climbed the ranks at RCA, but wanted to do gospel when she got saved. Bishop Deuce could have gone with just about any label, because he pastors almost forty thousand people and is on television, radio and the Internet all over the world. But, he really can't hold a note, and pretty much knows it. This music artist thing was a maraschino cherry on top of the cake for him. Danne assured him that her label, which wasn't even formed at the time she landed the deal, would shine and let everybody experience true worship.

Then Danne landed Heaven's Gate, a three member white rock Christian band. She originally signed them because she wanted to break into the Christian music market, but didn't know that they were a real pot of gold. These cats look like they'd be working at a meth lab in some Middle American suburban basement with expensive funky haircuts and rich blue denim skinny jeans. But, when it comes to just being yourself in pure worship, these boys are it. They love Jesus and love life. This group showed Danne and the rest of us just how limited we'd been in our own niche. They didn't do the bling bling thing at all, but had financial planners to handle all of their business. Two of the brothers, David and Katon, both signed celibacy covenant agreements and married by the time they were twenty-two. Evan, their friend and third member of the group, is nineteen; they keep a tight grip on him while they're on the road.

Promise Records has the "star" of the label who sells records to her family, friends, and a few people who love her. Evangelist Sandra Brown-Deuce is Bishop Deuce's wife. Girlfriend is highly anointed and sings her rear off. But, she is a monster. When she did her first showcase, she came back and told the church she was a worldwide gospel artist. She is drop-dead gorgeous, considerably younger than her husband, has great fashion sense, but alienates most of the women at the church. She is so anointed that someone has to carry her Starbuck's coffee cup up to the pulpit, with her pocketbook, coat, and uh, no bible. Everyone she meets, who talks to her more than twice, is her "son" or "daughter." Nice-nasty is the best way to describe her personality. She is Danne's worst investment from a business perspective and demands the most attention. So, Danne and Evangelist Brown-Deuce are always going at it. From her demands to fly first class because the other artists who chart Billboard bring in tour dollars, scan g-money in road sales, and millions in Internet sales, to her constant diva lateness for every single performance, Danne sometimes wants to pull her own and Evangelist Brown's hair out. To get her goat, sometimes Danne will call her Sandra, which is a sign of disrespect to her First Lady. She is one of those caught up with titles yet lies, gossips, and starts forty-two percent of all the drama in the church. Of course, since she is the hot-to-trot first lady, she is rarely challenged and free to be the star of the ministry.

And, if this isn't enough, Danne is the primary caretaker of both of her parents, Mr. and Mrs. Ware. They've been married for fifty years and refused to move in with Danne. So, Danne had to move into their building, bought two adjoining apartments, knocked out the walls, and made a Manhattan apartment house, fourteen years ago. The Wares insist on being financially independent, and dwell on the fact that they don't need help. Yet, they need a ride everywhere they go, lose keys every other week, forget appointments, and the list goes on. So, Danne manages their schedules and daily activities as well as her own.

Danne's outfit keeps her nice and comfortable, although she could have made so much more money in a major music corp. But, Danne loves gospel music, and with her convictions, would have it no other way. She invests so much time with her business and parents that her personal relationships often suffer. I'm not sure the commitment is the root of the issue more than her proclivity for around the way brothers from Harlem. And, those brothers say they're comfortable with a sis with her own dough and independence, but typically don't like it when down the line, they find out her kitchen renovation costs more than their yearly salary. Danne doesn't mind dating down. She doesn't mind dating a brother that doesn't have a college degree, or a professional career. All she cares about is dating someone who she can have a good time with, who enjoys life, likes to laugh, and keeps a job. And it goes without saying, he has to be a Christian. She can't stand churched-out brothers who shout without missing a step, have the look, can hoop while preaching, but have no self-control, scruples, or integrity. She prefers a man who will honor a woman and value her for who she is and what she brings to the table.

Yet with all of Danne's commitments and responsibilities, she is always there for any one of us, at the drop of a hat. The fact that she is a voting member of the American Music, Grammy, Dove and Stellar Awards does not interfere with her syndicate activities. Regardless of whom she may hob-knob with, or sit next to at a gala event full of celebrities, Danne makes things happen for each of us, down to remembering the black olives on our sandwiches.

GHETMO NONSENSE
Image In An Orange Jumpsuit

Leave it to Rashaun to cut up right when Danne and I were getting ready to leave to meet Brandon Chase for the first time in twenty-eight years. He gave us a piece of ghetmo–can't get mo ghetto than this–in accosting Aliyah while Danne and I were long distance. As we were preparing to leave the hotel, I noticed a number of messages from Aliyah.

Because of her health, there was an immediate alarm. "Aliyah, I got your emergency text. What is going on? I have to leave for an important appointment in about ten minutes, for real."

Only in extreme situations could we truly attest to the fact that Aliyah is from the streets. During these times, she may be likely to revert to her old man language and go there. "Jewel, he jumped on me. I can't believe that [SOB] jumped on me!"

"Aliyah, who jumped on you?" I yelled. "Who jumped on you?"

"Rashaun."

"Aliyah, what do you mean by 'jump on you'?" In the world where I grew up, I could not conceive of what I was hearing. Sons don't dare jump on mamas and live to talk about it, so extreme clarity was imperative.

"What do you think? He tried to get at my bankcard. I told him no, and he tried to get my wallet, anyway. So, I pushed him away from my pocketbook and he slammed me to the floor. He took my card and threw my pocketbook at me," Aliyah explained.

I thought silently, *Lord Jesus help me.* Immediately, I imagined sitting in an orange jumpsuit with a puffed up jail-look hair-do, with bright red lipstick, locked up in a federal penitentiary for women, in a one-on-one exclusive interview with Diane Sawyer, or a 20/20 correspondent with headlines, "Abusive NYC Doctor Whipped Troubled Young Man Into A Paraplegic State."

Rashaun took the female emotions quotient to the outer boundaries with this one. "Where is he right now?" I wanted to do a karate move through the telephone.

"He's outside in the living room. I had to lock my door so he couldn't get at my cell phone."

"Open your door and give him the phone."

"I'm scared! He's out of control."

"Aliyah, give him the phone right now."

"Rashaun, this is Aunt Jewel. I just spoke to your mother—"

"She's trippin right now. You know how she is—"

"Rashaun, I believe I was talking. Don't you ever interrupt me when I'm speaking to you. You got that?"

"Look, I ain't got to take this [s***]."

"You are right, you don't. You don't have to eat pizza in jail either. And your mother doesn't have to have herself barricaded in a room shook from you. Now you know it's not going down like this, right? You do know you went too far don't—"

"You don't even know what happened—"

"Rashaun, I told you before. Don't interrupt me. What you don't comprehend is that you don't run anything. I know you've been disillusioned to think that nobody can tell you what to do, but you better hear me before you end up with an orange jumpsuit on. Trust me. I'm two seconds from making you understand. I'm not your momma and I will knock you all the way out. I just need you to listen and hear me real good. I'm not going to repeat myself. Are you listening?"

"Yes."

"Okay. I need you to pack your bags for the entire weekend, and don't forget one thing, because you are not getting back in your momma's house until I get back. When you are packed, get on the bus and go to my father's house. Do you know how to get there?"

"No, that's okay. I'll go by my friends."

"What you don't seem to understand is that we are not negotiating with you. You don't run anything and you're not going to do whatever you want and we have to live with it. You either follow my instructions, or you are out for good. You have crossed the line when you hit your mother."

"First of all, you wasn't here and she ain't my mother."

"Well, Rashaun, whether you like it or not, she is your mother. She's your mother when you want the new Jordan's and when she hooks you up. When you need to be there for her or can't get what you want, all of a sudden you play this card. So if she's not your mother when it's convenient, then we're going to work with that concept. You are not going to keep manipulating your mother and holding her hostage to the past. I know you're angry, and if anyone can relate, I can. You have every right to be angry, but she cannot undo your past or hers. So you gonna jump on her because you want money? We know what the issue is, and you are not gonna jump on her and think that it's okay. So get your stuff right now and if you're not packed and at my father's house when I call there, I'm calling the police. Now put your momma back the phone."

Rashaun took his tone from ten all the way down to one and attempted to communicate again and said, "Auntie Jewel."

I shut him all the way down. "Look, you don't have an ear with me when you threw your mother on the floor. You could have called me earlier before it got to this, but you blew it. You hit your mother, Rashaun. You can't hit my girl and have anything to say to me right now. Get your stuff, and if you don't want to have police officers assist us with you, work your way over to the Bishop. And I better not hear one word of complaint from my momma about you because the next step is the police. And you know I'll do it. Now give Aliyah the phone!"

As soon as I could hear homegirl breathe, I said, "Aliyah, he's getting out for the weekend. I'm going to call my dad and let them take him for the weekend. Don't cater to him; let him go. We need some intervention if he's to the point of knocking you down on the floor. He knows you have AIDS and can hardly walk."

"Jewel, I don't want all of that. He's hurting, that's all. I keep messing up and he's tired."

"Aliyah, and so are you. And you keep playing into his manipulation and control. He needs to find another way to express his anger and frustration. You have Tysheem to take care of. I'm going to call Noey and ask her if Jayden can come over there right now until he's out of the house. Unless you want me to call Bishop Deuce or someone to handle this." I knew the Bishop Deuce thing would trigger some cooperation from Aliyah. She wouldn't want anything to ever escalate to having to trouble the Bishop or church staff.

"No, I don't want you bothering Bishop with this. He has too much on him already."

"When I get back, we're going to have to get your leadership involved, or Rashaun is going to have to go into some sort of program. He's cutting school, smoking weed, and God knows what else, and now we have to add 'putting his hands on you and got you crying on a phone locked up in your own house.' All of this from him? I don't think so."

"Okay. I don't like it, but I don't know what else to do." Aliyah sounded weary and I could tell she needed much rest. The last thing she needed was ghetmo drama.

"Pray. Tell him you love him, and stop cursing him out. He hears and digests every single word that comes out of your mouth. You are sick but you are not the only one suffering through this condition. Every time you hurt, he hurts. He loves you and can't stand watching his mother suffer. He just doesn't know how to deal, girl. But don't worry about this; you'll survive this. This is a light thing. Just let him go for the weekend and let him think about what life is going to be like without you if he keeps clowning."

Danne and I had to take a breather after all of that. We had to appreciate God who knows all things because if we were home and got that call, there probably would have been some bloodshed and we would have been in the orange jumpsuits. Danne could not comprehend how Rashaun could cross the bounds of decency. "That negro jumped on Aliyah? Doesn't he know that she cannot have stress at all, that she is fighting for her life?"

"He knows that, but he can't help himself. Everyone handles grief and abandonment differently. He had a father for a few seconds, and now BJ is in jail until God knows when. Aliyah is shady all day long when she's home if she's in pain and in and out of the hospital every other day. He is the one living with Aliyah, and we all know she isn't a piece of cake. And when he aggravates her, you should hear how she speaks to him. He just got his mama back–what is it, not even ten years ago–and in his mind, she is dying right before his very eyes. We believe God is going to heal her, but he may not be there. He probably thinks we are all crazy. And, if you think about it, Aliyah has completely alienated the boys from the rest of their family, so she is all he's got. There is a whole lot Rashaun is dealing with right now."

"Yada, yada, yada. He is a teenage boy who jumped on his mother, who is sick with AIDS who dropped three dress sizes in the past year, because she wouldn't give him what he wanted." Danne had no problems deducing the facts to the bottom line. "He better be lucky we were not home and we know Jesus."

"And, he is angry and he is pushing her away and most boys his age are sick of their parents under good conditions. We've got to bust him, but understand what we are dealing with. The boy is hurt." The New York drama had us messed up in Mississippi time. The last thing I wanted to do was to begin with a bad impression. As I looked at my watch I told Danne, "We're late. We better get downstairs."

While on the elevator, I shot a text to Rashaun to put his mind at ease. "Your mom isn't throwing you away. We all love you. We will work it out. I know it's hard, but trust God. Now hurry up because I don't want to bust you up when I get back!" With that text and Jayden leaving work to show up at his front door, Rashaun knew the crew was on the case. Aliyah was weak, but she wasn't alone. Girlfriend had quick responsive reinforcements in the syndicate.

Danne shifted gears. The gab gal crew discussed this day in faith many times. "This is it! We're not going to let this high-end drama dampen the day."

"Okay, let's do this." All of a sudden, I felt a bit weak and overwhelmed. "How do I look?"

"Great. You know you bring it." Danne gave me the smile and "thumbs up" to let me know all was well.

"This isn't a 'bring it' moment. I mean how do I look for him to see his mother for the first time?" I wanted to make sure I looked suitable.

"C'mon let's go and don't start carrying on. You are who you are and you look like who you are."

DREAMS DO COME TRUE
The Little White Sock

When Danne and I got off the elevator in the main lobby, we walked outside the main entrance and my legs started to feel like lead. I saw Chase holding a toddler in his hands and his wife pacing back and forth. He turned around and I saw his face. I've always wondered what he looked like. Did he look like me at all, or look more like my father? I am the spitting image of my mother. I really couldn't remember what his birth father looked like. The trauma must have caused my psyche to block his face out of my mind. I just remember his image, and his big body sweating on top of me. I've always hoped that Chase didn't look like his father. A real concern was how I would react if I saw the pedophile one day, and was abruptly cajoled out of the protective place in my psyche where I did not see his face. I was hoping not to have that experience in seeing Chase by seeing his father's face in him.

All of a sudden, I didn't care what Chase looked like. I could hardly see anyway with all of the tears in my eyes. They came gushing from a different place this time. They were tears of overwhelming joy. My son came toward me and said, "Hello Jewel. Can I call you Momma?" He leaned over and hugged me. *This is what I have been waiting for. OMG, this is what I've been waiting for.* I could not stop crying. Something was breaking inside of me. There was an exchange going on: mourning for the oil of joy; sorrow for contentment; shame for confidence; pain for healing; and disappointment for hope. Years and years of heartache were answered in this one embrace.

Chase smelled good. His scent was nothing like the little white sock that I hid among my things and kept for years. Every now and again over the years, I would hunt for the sock to smell it, hungering for some connection to the baby boy who was gone.

Chase looked good. It was twenty-eight years since I held my baby, but here he was in my arms again. I held his face and wanted to fall to the ground and just get prostrate before the Lord. People were looking at us but I didn't care. He was weeping and his wife started crying and Danne, of course, offered, "Let's all move to the lounge or something," a skilled attempt to intersperse etiquette into this emotional soirée.

Chase and I all started to walk back inside to the lounge area, but I couldn't let go of Chase's hand. This young man, my son, was holding my hands. I couldn't tell whom he looked like. I guess he looked like himself. When he was a baby, that's what Aunt Beefi used to say, "He doesn't look like any of us. I guess he looks like himself." Twenty-eight years later, I could finally concur. For the first time in my adult life, I was speechless. I just kept looking and smiling.

Chase offered the first words of dialogue. "This is my wife, Evelyn, and our daughter, Ruth."

"Hello. I'm glad to meet you," I spoke as I checked out his wife. Evelyn looked a bit older than Chase. She looked old enough to be one of my homegirls. She was petite and cute. Suddenly the striking oddity of having a child at twelve hit me in the face when I saw his wife. We really weren't that far apart in age. I stopped to give Evelyn a hug. I tried to touch the baby's hand, but she pulled back. That was understandable behavior for a child who had just met her grandmother for the first time. Then I said, "I don't mean to be rude; this is my best girlfriend, Danne. And Danne, you know who this is."

"We've been waiting for this time. God is great, isn't He?" Danne is always going to bring the conversation into proper perspective. God is good and this is His doing."

"He sure is. Only Jehovah can do something like this." Chase looked at me and said, "Do you know I dreamt about you when I was six years old?"

"Really?" I'm not used to being short on words. I just felt like feasting on every glance, every word, and not missing a gesture. I didn't want to hear me, I wanted to hear everything Chase had to say.

"Yup. I dreamt a woman had my yellow blanket and kept looking for me. There was a panic in you. So I told Aunt Catherine and she said I must have been dreaming about my momma."

I still said nothing.

"She said if you keep dreaming it, ask God to show you what it means. So, I asked God to show me what it meant. I heard a clear voice say, 'you're momma loves and misses you and one day she'll show you herself.' From that moment, I wouldn't let anyone get in your place in my heart."

"And you've always had a place in mine." Chase and I were finally able to share with one another. "I don't remember a yellow blanket, but there was a side of a pair of white socks that I kept with me for years. That's all I had to hold onto, while trying to hold onto the memories. Do you have any questions for me?"

"All I want to do is get to know you. I've been loving you, and God already let me know that you've longed to show me your love. Can we spend a few minutes alone before we go to eat? There's something I have to tell you, Jewel."

"Sure." Evelyn, Ruth and Danne decided to go and get the cars so we could get ready to go to the restaurant.

Chase leaned over and kissed my check for a long time. I had locked myself down from love and affection for so long that I almost didn't know what to do. I think this was the first time I just let a man hug me without being tense. "I want you to know that I've had a good life. My aunt, Catherine raised me, and never let me call her Mama. She told me she wasn't my mother, and she knew you'd come looking for me one day. I've also always known

Pop and my mother, I mean, Ms. Edie and I know that might be uncomfortable for you."

I just displayed what I could muster–an uneasy smile. There wasn't anything that I could think of that would be edifying, so I chose to say nothing.

"Pop told me that he did you wrong."

"Did me wrong? Really. Is that how he described what happened?"

"Well, he didn't use those words. I don't remember exactly what he said. But it doesn't take a genius to figure out that he would have been in jail today if he did what he did to you to a twelve-year-old today. I mean, I know you had me when you were twelve and he was married to Ms. Edie. And that is why we never contacted you. They didn't know if you wanted to have anything to do with me under the circumstances."

"Well, a day never went by that I didn't want to know. I've grieved day after day, hoping that God would keep us both so we could know each other one day."

"Well, there is more. I have brothers and sisters, and Evelyn and I stay in a house on the back of Pop-Pop's house. We all live on a seventeen-acre lot."

I was on the bridge again. Oh shoot. This oink oink gets to know his son, his daughter-in-law, grandchild and I've been tripping most of my life from guilt over what happened and what he did to me. My relationships with my own family have suffered while the rapist has been blessed. Wow. I turned my head.

"And, I'm his assistant at the church."

"Whew. There isn't anything I can say other than I'm glad you've had a great life." I really did mean that. I'm glad Chase is a good man despite how he came into this world.

"Jewel, I mean, Momma, I know this is a lot to ask. I want you to come to church with us on Sunday, and to meet Aunt Catherine."

"Is Prophet Swanson going to be there?" I had to know what to expect.

"I suppose. He knows you're here, so depending, he just may not. He may not be ready to face you. I'm really not sure." Chase took my hand and squeezed it firmly. He pulled me to him and said, "Whatever you choose to do, I respect it. I'm just glad you're here. You are so beautiful. I can't believe you're my momma. You're too fine to be my momma!" My mother's words were realized. Remember it was the devil who tried to destroy me. Forgive.

The entire party went to eat and Evelyn didn't say much. She is a real southern gentile woman. And my son appears to be a real fine man. He inherited so much I didn't anticipate.

I put Danne down on the private talk as soon as we got back to the hotel room. "Look, if you want to, we can break out tomorrow. But, I don't think you should make any hasty decisions. Sleep on it because something great is happening, and we can't let our flesh mess up what God is doing." Danne's sound advice sank in.

That night I lay down and thought about all of the emotional walls that caused me to not trust my own family. Like my mother said, we all suffered. She was embarrassed when she had to explain why she had a twelve-year-old pregnant daughter. She was hurt for me. My dad did feel like he failed me, being all things to all men, but his own daughter was violated in his own home by his ministry guest. And all of these years, Chase has known and loved his father and even Edie forgave her husband. I'd been in emotional bondage and people have been living. Everything was going to have to change.

AUNT CATHERINE
Spiffy and Spunky Salve

Danne and I talked and decided to ride out the weekend as planned. If my son asked me to meet his family after having lived without me for twenty-eight years, I could grant him this request. After all, I drive through three fast food restaurants to get Aliyah what she wants. It wasn't about me. It was about destiny and Chase. Danne felt I should go this day alone. She'd join me for church tomorrow.

Chase and I arrived at Aunt Catherine's house right in time for a good old country breakfast. Although I have a gorgeous home in New York that could be featured in Decor magazine, it did not compare to the feel of Aunt Catherine's home. We pulled up to a grand Victorian mini-mansion with a huge, well kept, wrap-around porch. If I ever lived in the country, Aunt Catherine's stunning home with the perfect mix of country breeze and updated accoutrements would be optimal.

Aunt Catherine wasn't anything like what I expected. She looked like she could be featured in the annual Essence magazine edition where physically fit seniors look thirty years younger than their actual age. Aunt Catherine had on a Baby Phat velour sweat suit with crystal "bling bling" writing across the backside of the outfit. Homegirl obviously didn't get the notice that she is a senior citizen and is not supposed to be dressed like she's nineteen.

Ms. Catherine acted like I just saw her yesterday and lived next door. "Put your purse down right over there and come give me a hug." So, of course, I followed my instructions. "Baby, you are beautiful. No wonder my boy looks so good. He got your good genes. Or maybe he's got mine!"

I cracked up and laughingly stated, "Hi, you must be Ms. Catherine."

"That's what they call me, and don't wear it out. Now sit down before these grits get cold. And if you've ever had a better breakfast in your life, you better act like you didn't cause this right here is the best cooking you ever gonna have, agreed?"

"Agreed." Aunt Catherine was hilarious and the type of funny that was contagious. I liked her instantaneously. As a matter of fact, I had to love her. She raised my son. God used her to nurture and help mold the character of my son when I couldn't. Aunt Catherine did what my family wouldn't do so I had to respect who she was to Chase. I got to see first-hand what kind of care Chase experienced with Ms. Catherine's "hand." She served me a plate of grits, eggs with cheese, sausage, bacon, fried whiting, biscuits, butter and jelly. No questions were asked, and I dared not act like I hadn't eaten grits since they made me nauseous when I was pregnant with Chase.

"Well, where's my compliment, huh?" Ms. Catherine asked as if I were a food-tasting judge at the county fair.

With my mouth full of the savory country breakfast, I responded, "I'm too busy eating to talk. That in and of itself is a compliment, Ms. Catherine. This is the best."

"Child, now don't lie. I cook good, but not that good!"

Somehow, I kept feeling like I didn't know what to say. I was following the leads and going with the flow. Walking into the lives of a close-knit family and getting to know them was work. Chase and I had to get to know one another, and that included his family, the family that raised him, the people he loved and who loved him. But, it is worth it all.

"So I hear you're a doctor. What kind of a doctor are you? I need some antibiotics." Aunt Catherine really missed her calling. She could have been a comedienne.

"I'm an internist. I treat mostly HIV/AIDS and some cancer patients."

"Okay, I don't want nothing from you then. Nothing but your love. I declare, I'm never coming to visit your office. Nope. I don't never want to be one of your patients." I was in stitches again. Meanwhile, I kept looking at Chase. My parents would love him. Everybody would. At least I hoped they would.

After breakfast, Ms. Catherine showed me a litany of pictures of Chase during his boyhood. I had mixed emotions. The reality of his life without me was right before my very eyes, yet I got to see him smile at four, five, six, seven, and at all of his birthday parties until he was eleven years old. This just wasn't fair. But all of these missed days and birthdays could not be undone. The pictures provided the closest glimpse into what kind of life Chase had with Aunt Catherine, his siblings, his father and his mother, Ms. Edie.

Chase narrated as we perused albums, shoeboxes and scrapbooks. "I preached my trial sermon when I was twelve, so I couldn't be no preacher and still having backyard birthday parties with party favors."

Hoping that I could hear what his voice sounded like back then, "Do you have a tape of your trial sermon?"

"I think Pop Pop does. I'll have to see if we can find it."

The mention of "Pop Pop" from Chase's mouth was like a knife in my heart. I had never fathomed in all of my thoughts or delusions that Chase knew who his father was, and if he did, if he knew he raped me, that he would call him Pop Pop. And here it was, Chase didn't just say Pop Pop, but knew and loved Pop Pop. I immediately had to hold onto words of power. I thought, *Lord, help my heart. Help me to see with your eyes and hear with your ears. Help me to have your mind and your outlook. God, that is the only way I can survive this. Your love is enough to see us all through. I want to love right. I need to be free.*

Ms. Catherine doesn't miss a beat. Whether it is her quick wit or discernment, she knew exactly where I was. "Call on Him, honey. It will take God to help you through this. I'm a woman, and I can see your pain. I've always felt your pain. That's why I wouldn't let Chase think I was his momma. He's always had a momma, and it wasn't your fault you couldn't be there for him. No one could take your place. I raised him to know that. Didn't I Chase?"

"Yes, mam."

"And he got a whole nother family out there. And they got to be good peoples. Cause God knows if it was up to me, Delayne would've had a bullet in his butt." I could feel a fluttering in my heart and soul. Step by step, Ms. Catherine's tenderness and humor helped.

I walked to the back door and looked at the beautiful yard. I can't remember the last time I looked at a yard and really saw the beauty in it. "Do you mind if I look at your garden?" Something needed to break the mounting pressure, and a wisp of fresh air seemed like the perfect answer.

"Are you asking? Don't you know how to act like you're one of the family? Help yourself. As a matter of fact, let Chase help you out. He's the one who did most of the sweating out there. I could act like I had on some gloves and between romance novels decided to plant the flowers of the season. Truth is, that garden is a result of a hit or miss punishment project. We figured it out piece by piece and to tell you the truth, God waters it and keeps it the way it is." Ms. Catherine spoke as she opened the huge white French doors that opened to the garden.

"Punishment project?" I asked Ms. Catherine.

"Yeah, he'll fill you in on the details," Ms. Catherine responded referring to Chase.

While Chase and I walked outside, I understood the loyalty southerners have to the south. I could have stayed out there all night. The yard had the feel of a comfy but stately country quilted oversized couch as opposed to the finely manicured landscapes that are more like a fine antique chair overlaid with 24-karat gold. You could put up your hair and just let yourself go. As we entered the garden, and had the pleasure of viewing ornate white, plum, red and the most unique orange-colored lilies, I knew Chase and Ms. Catherine had a bit of heaven on earth. Chase's garden had makeshift borders, which gave it a distressed character. I asked the same question but directed it to Chase, "Punishment assignment, huh?"

"And I got the lesson." The way Chase owned those words, you could tell that he did.

"So what happened?" My inquiring mind wanted to soak up every detail.

So Chase began to tell the story. "One summer, Pop Pop took the youth from the church to Camp Wannakee for a week. I had to be, uh, somewhere about fourteen. By that time, Aunt Catherine had let me go visit Pop Pop and 'em all the time. But this was the first trip that she let me go overnight without her. She never wanted Ms. Edie to mistreat me, cause then she'd have to handle-up on her. Anyway, Corey, Chris and I always hung together, so we were pretty cool and excited about the camping trip."

"Who are Corey and Chris?"

"Oh, well you wouldn't know. I have seven brothers and sisters. Corey and Chris are my brothers and Christine, Charmaine, Ceda, Cybil and Candace are my sisters. Corey and I are the same age and we are the babies."

He sure as heck is a part of this man's family. OMG. There were so many layers to what Ms. Edie and I both experienced. The prophet had me and his wife pregnant at the same time. She was probably miserable back then too. I wondered how she must have felt carrying baby number seven for her husband while finding out that he had a twelve-year-old whom he raped carrying his baby, too.

"Well, there were only two hot girls on the trip, and we were all trying to pull one for ourself, you feel me?" Chase has such an endearing grin. I could tell he probably had an easy time with the ladies growing up.

"So, Chris and I wanted the same girl—"

"Isn't Chris your older brother?"

"Yep. He was the same age as Evelyn. They were both nineteen, but I knew I could pull her. She was mine," Chase stated with confidence and a tinge of arrogance.

"And this must be the wife," I supposed.

"Bingo. I can see how you've been so successful, Dr. Prunell."

He's definitely got a hint of the smart aleck gene in him. Maybe that's what he got from me. My mother has that thing in a raw way. Sarcasm should have been her middle name.

"So Evey, that's what we used to call her, was checking both of us. You know, I had to get a one up on Chris cause he was older, and she would see him all the time at the church. I needed an edge on him to show her that I could handle her. See. So when we had the swimming competition at the lake, I held Chris' legs and pulled him underwater for a few seconds to tire him out, cause I knew I had to cheat to beat him. If I beat him, I would be the man. Evey would notice me."

"So what happened?"

"When I pulled Chris under water and took off swimming, he never came back up. Everybody was screaming and I thought for sure it was cause I was winning, but when I got to the finish line and saw all the commotion, I realized something was wrong. They had to go diving to fetch him out of the water. Chris had passed out cause he couldn't catch his breath. Pop Pop whupped me, and everybody was mad at me. Ms. Edie thought I hated my brother but everyone else knew what was up. They knew it was simply over Evey."

"And so when Ms. Catherine found out," I uttered to help Chase along with his story-telling.

"I got whupped again. Then she told me what the purpose of water was. It wasn't to kill my brother by playing games, it was to bring life to things, and to let the water creatures have a home. So, she wanted me to see it demonstrated, and that's how we got the garden. I was on punishment for the rest of the summer because of the accident, and this is what came of it."

"Well, it is absolutely beautiful. Actually, breathtaking. I could stay out here all day. That was a constructive punishment. Ms. Catherine is a wise woman."

"Yes, she is. She saved my life."

I refused to let the guilt thing survive this victory. The battle to fight the instinctual guilt had to be won. "She saved my life" meant his life needed saving but from what? Not having a mother. I've cried out to God out of a womb of emptiness for years for my son. The only thing that had kept me was knowing that God answered my prayers time and time again, and He would do it for me again and again.

I don't know if Chase sensed my struggle, or if he is just that sensitive. Yet, he clarified, "I don't mean to make you feel uncomfortable. I'm just letting you know that Aunt Catherine has really been there for me. She was the closest thing to a mother I had, and when I got a little older, Ms. Edie, too. It isn't a statement about you."

"One thing I've learned is that you can rehearse something in your mind a thousand—no probably a zillion—times and it won't change a thing if the performance of it is already over. It doesn't make sense to keep having rehearsals after the final performance. I've never lost hope and had to learn to rehearse for this performance, when we'd be talking, and I could smell you, and touch you, and see you alive, with a great heart, a great spirit, and all of this right here. I do regret the way things turned out. I have to be honest. I wanted to be with you in all of those pictures. I wanted to take care of you, and hug you, and kiss you, and tell you that I loved you. But that's not what happened. Since things went the way they did, I'm glad Ms. Catherine was who she has been to you. It's almost like she's been your Jochebed to Moses. God had the right one on the scene to love you the way you needed to be loved. I asked God to take care of you. As if I really needed to do that. You're His and have always been. And, I'm not even going to sit here and tell you it's not difficult for me, but it is what it needed to be. I am really okay with all of this. I'm just glad that you're alive and happy."

"You don't know how much, oh man, how good it is to hear you say that. When I was little, every time I'd see you, you were travailing. I've always felt your pain."

"I can't tell you how many times I've fallen out in church, hollered, wailed, and just praised God so the pain wouldn't stop me from living. It has been a fight. A real fight. But what matters most is you."

"I'm sorry I caused you so much pain."

I wasn't ready for that one. When I carried him, I don't think I saw him as the enemy. I just knew he was a serious problem. He was the reason I had to wear sweatshirts during the Spring. He was the reason I was the only kid in the doctor's office for pre-natal visits who wasn't kicking my legs on the chair waiting for my mother's visit to be over. I was there looking like a watermelon was crammed into my belly. As a matter of fact, I don't even think I had pre-natal visits until I went down south to live with my aunt. He was the reason I couldn't play with my brothers and sisters because I just might have hurt myself or hurt him. He was the reason I couldn't go to the grocery store with my mother anymore, because she didn't want anyone to see me. He was the reason I vowed—and have had no problem keeping it—I'd never be pregnant again. Never. I didn't want to ever see all of the strange looks from people who must have been wondering who I was and where I'd been to be pregnant at an age when I should have only been jumping double-dutch, playing hopscotch, or snatching jacks from a smooth outdoor surface. I didn't want to ever feel the shame and disgust from carrying a baby who ripped my heart out when he left.

Deep down inside, Chase's existence had been the reason why I resented the way my parents embraced all of my nieces and nephews as they came. The seed from my womb wasn't fruit. They rejected him. I knew why, but he was still given away. Chase couldn't be part of our family. He was the reason I would never wear a low cut shirt. The preachers never had to be a clothesline preacher with me. They didn't have to worry about my treasures. My hips and my broad upstanding backside were not an issue. Not over here. The figure distracted a powerful preacher and made him do the abominable: rob me of my innocence. That had to be the conclusion I settled with, because had it been another reality, somebody would have called the police, and not protected the "mand" of God or his ministry. The pain Chase spoke of was because of his father, not him.

"Chase, you had nothing to do with how and why you are here. You and I have had to deal with the hand of life that we've been given. That isn't on you. You had nothing to do with that. I have to be honest. I didn't always understand that, especially when I was much younger. But I know, and have known for a long time, that you had some purpose. The void in my life was because I was," and then I stopped myself to be careful not to ever allow my son to hear me say what really was. "You were conceived and I was confused. But you were the closest thing to a love child that could ever be. Despite all of the conflicting emotions and pressure and all of that stuff, love prevailed and my heart could never let you go."

"That's really deep. Are you just saying that, or do you really believe that I am your love child?" Chase was definitely Jewel's son. He wanted to know the real deal.

"You were my love child," I confessed with tears rolling down my face. "Most babies are conceived in love, or at least some hot passion. When it came to you, love overpowered all of the negativity and time couldn't kill the love I've had for you. I mean, look at how blessed Evelyn is to have you. Imagine her life without you. Imagine Aunt Catherine's life without you. Your brothers and sisters. Seeing you let me know that the pain was worth it all, and Chase, you didn't cause any of it. It was the devil." I know it was the devil that used that incident to destroy the rest of my life. Travail helped me to get to this point, and now the door of rape that the devil used is shut. He meant to keep me from being free and giving God all of me.

"I love you, Momma," Chase said as he leaned and hugged me.

After chatting all afternoon, Evelyn offered to take me to her beauty shop and do my hair. I didn't want to insult her, but didn't want a BAPS crunchy six hairstyles on my one scalp hairdo. Based upon Evey's hairstyle, this conclusion was a reasonable presumption.

"Evelyn, I'd love to, but then I'd be in trouble with my hairdresser when I get back home." That was a close escape from giving Danne roasting material for the next fifty years.

"Well, let me do something for you," Evey offered.

"Okay, I'll let you take me shopping as long as I can pay the bill. How about that?"

"That's an offer that I don't believe I'll ever turn down, provided it's alright with Chase."

It was weird shopping with a daughter-in-law that I just laid eyes on a few hours ago, who is only seven years my junior, who has known my son for most of their lives, and whose taste couldn't have been farther from mine if we tried to make it more disparate. She definitely wasn't feeling my modest conservative flow, so I bought her and my grandbaby whatever she wanted. Chase was blessed to have a wife like her. She had her own mind, yet she knew how to reinforce him without being threatened or the center of attention. This was unusual for a woman who has an outgoing personality and is older than her husband. Aside from her image, she reminds me of a younger version of my own mother.

THE ENCOUNTER
Triumph In The Former
Place Of Defeat

Of course I woke Danne up when I got back to the hotel. It was almost two am, but she knew we'd have to strategize for tomorrow.

"I walked into his world down here and it has been overwhelming. I can't wait for you to meet his Aunt Catherine; she is off the chain. I loved her within five minutes," I told a sleepy Danne.

"So we are still going to the service tomorrow? Rather, in a few hours? Are you going to go to the church?" Clearly, Danne was speaking while trying to fight falling asleep.

"I think it will be good. So far, everything else has been good and while we're here, we might as well just go all the way." The outlook had to be hopeful. Dr. Tangi wanted me to be a good Christian and learn to see with eyes of faith. I would see the glass half full.

"You might as well go all the way. Are you ready to see him?" We both knew the "him" Danne was referring to was Delayne Swanson.

"No. No, I'm not. I don't think there will ever be a day when I want to meet him. But, I'm not focusing on him. I just want to be there for Chase, meet his step-mother, and the rest of his family. I'm sure they're going to be there. Have you heard from Rashaun or Aliyah?"

"Both of em. Aliyah is being crazy. I listened to her rattle for about an hour and fell asleep on her. But Rashaun called earlier and said he wanted to go home. I played good cop and let him talk about Aliyah and you like a dog. Then I busted him out and told him to grow up and stop his mess. I told him he's still my nephew and all that, but he better hope I forget he put his hands on his mother by the time we get home or I'm going to jump on him."

"What did he say?"

"He started laughing talking about I know he'll hurt me and he wouldn't even let me play myself like that. So, he was in a lighter mood and wanted to know what's going to happen from here."

"I'm going to finally take him. Aliyah asked me to take him a while ago, but I'm going to ask her to take both of them, because I don't want Tysheem to feel rejected and really, she needs to rest. So, until she stops going in and out of the hospital, they both need stability. And you know she's not going to let him go to that family of hers."

"Better you than me. I'd kill Rashaun. Now Tysheem, I'll take him to the moon with me. But that Rashaun?"

"I know I need to take him. When I was in the garden with Chase, I saw it clear as day. I'd rather not have to take them, but somebody has to. Being in Ms. Catherine's garden and seeing my own son helped me to see that."

"Okay, Jewel. Get out because I don't want to be sleeping in church. At least not in this church service; I don't want to miss a beat."

Even though I knew we were only going to be gone for three days, somehow almost half my wardrobe ended up in Mississippi in three suitcases. Danne, Noey and I always road trip together, and they swear I over pack. I usually have one bag with casual clothes, one with footwear and pocketbooks, and one with the real gear. Thank God for my usual overflow because I couldn't figure out exactly what I needed to put on to go to church. Nothing seemed to be the right suit or outfit. I tend to like the quality casual look, where I don't have to suit up on a Sunday morning. But, I was not sure what kind of culture this church had, and I certainly didn't want to stand out and bring attention to myself.

So I opted to go with a timeless look: a twenty-year-old royal blue Chanel suit with velour-cuffed sleeves.

"You look lovely girl."

"And so do you! When did you get that hot blouse? Why didn't you get one for me? What's up with that?"

"Look, cut it out. If, and only if, I find another one, then I'll get it for you."

"How about I'm going to motivate you to find one, cause you gonna leave that one with me when it comes off your back today. Okay?" And, I knew she'd give it to me. Sometimes I wonder why Danne even puts up with my craziness.

Danne and I did the GPS thing and drove to the church ourselves. We didn't want to have them waiting for us; we know we are always late for church on Sunday mornings. I'm late because I'm always tired from chilling with some one of the syndicate from the night before, or staying up late watching movies or one of the church channels. Every now and again, it's because I had an emergency situation. More often than not, it's just me being straight-up trifling. Danne is always late because she can't stand all of the spiritual gymnastics that go on before the Word is preached. When the worship leader yells, "Hallelujah," exactly two times after every song when she feels the anointing, Danne says under her breath, "She needs to sit down and stop playing." We both have a disdain for twenty references to honoring the pastor but Jesus might only get daps three or four times. So, Danne traditionally gets to church right when the choir is scheduled to sing before the preacher, who is usually my own daddy, gets up. But today, we did our best to get there on time.

When we hit the parking lot, my stomach started turning. No tears, just uneasiness.

"Can we wait a minute?" I needed more time and there was no need to try to play cool. At least, not with Danne.

"Of course we can. If you want, we can go get some breakfast somewhere. We don't have to do this. You know me."

"No, I don't want to be too late. Service was supposed to have started fifteen minutes ago. They've got a lot of cars out here. They must have a bit of people at the church. I don't know why I presumed it was probably just a few people in the church."

"I know why. Who would think a whole bunch of people would follow a pedophile rapist?"

I almost cringed. We don't say it. We know it, we think it, we've talked about it, but we rarely called it what it was. Lately, we've been calling it what it was. A rape. Prior to finding Chase, we followed the unspoken modus operandi and didn't audibly say "rape."

"Just give me a few minutes. I just need five minutes. I have to time this or else I just might not go in." Who would think in their wildest dreams that anyone in her right mind would be sitting in a car in a church parking lot, about to face the pastor who everyone else sees as a man of God but was once a pedophile rapist? I was about to see Chase's brothers and sisters, some of whom are older than I am. I had to talk to the Lord. "Lord, please cover my mind. Help me to see you in this. Help me Lord. Father, I'm asking you to help me. Heal me. Heal my hurt. Help me to let this thing go."

As Danne and I walked to the two glass double doors, some fine brothers were there to open them. They handed each of us a program and did the usher thing and directed us to the back of the sanctuary doors. All of a sudden, I had to use the bathroom. I had the runs. Danne kept reminding me that breaking out was a viable option. I didn't have to face Delayne Swanson if I wasn't ready. I looked at myself in the mirror and thought of the things I didn't have the courage to do because the man I was about to see climbed on top of me one night in my youth. Something had to happen, one way or the other. I just needed to do what my mother taught me to do when I was carrying Chase. I'll never forget when she said, "You can feel one way, but don't ever let the enemy see you sweating. Get yourself together and hold your head up. You can cry when you get back home." That would be on one line of the non-existent journal. In spite of a difficult past, I was still here, and God has certainly graced me and made me who I am.

I had to let God know I was grateful. *Thank you Lord. You've always been there for me, and I know you'll see me through this.*

Chase was looking out for me. As soon as we came in, Danne and I filed right into the back of the sanctuary. Evelyn immediately turned around, saw us and came to the back of the church with a huge smile on her face in one of the new outfits we had picked up on our shopping trip. She hugged me and shook Danne's hand. She asked us to come up front. I insisted that we stay right there, we were fine.

All of a sudden, my breathing was stressed. I needed to calm all the way down. Evey seemed a slight bit disappointed but went back to her seat. That's when we started to see glances from all over. We had no way of knowing if it was because we were new faces, or if we were the new faces that Chase's brothers, sisters and their huge family expected to see.

The entire church was up on their feet, clapping and singing praises. I didn't want to stand up because from where I was seated, I couldn't see up on the pulpit too well and wanted to keep it that way. After spending all my life in the church, I had enough sense to know that I shouldn't come to church and be bound with the cares of life. God has been too good to me to conduct my behavior based upon people and not wanting to be seen. The choir began to sing one of Jonathan Nelson's songs, *My Name Is Victory*, "I know who I am, God wrote it in His plan for me…My name is victory." I needed to hear those words. One hand went up in the air. Then another went up. My eyes closed and I just focused on God. He deserves all of my attention and all of His glory. After all, without Him, I wouldn't have survived, and Chase wouldn't be the blessed man that he is, and the list goes on and on. Before you know it, tears were streaming down my face. The presence of the Lord was there. In the same building with walls lined with canes, wheelchairs, and crutches, there was a heavy manifestation of God's presence. Clearly, miracles take place by faith despite the fact that the pastor committed an abominable act almost three decades earlier.

As the service moved on, I saw Chase smiling at me. I smiled back. There was a choir stand full of singers and I knew Jesus had some singers in the South. I didn't notice anyone who could have been Chase's father on the pulpit. It had been twenty-eight years. Then the announcements started. They announced Elder Chase Swanson was going to be preaching this morning, Prophet Swanson was in the house, but there is a Word from the Lord. Seemed like the Lord knows what He's doing. The nerve of me to not trust God totally and completely.

I soon found out that Chase can preach his neck off. His vernacular is totally different when he's preaching. He sounds like an educated old bishop who's been preaching for forty-five years and he's a young man. People were falling out while he was preaching. The anointing of God and His presence was so great. Chase preached, "My Womb Can Handle This." He talked about the womb and worked the Word of God until everybody knew that there are some things that are within us that we have the assignment and power to cultivate, nourish, and bring forth through great travail, and great pain. But when that thing lives and fulfills purpose, the pangs of birthing become badges of honor and strength. I fell on my face weeping. My womb had birthed a man of God. He was being used to bring healing to many who dared to believe. The church walls were lined with canes, walkers, crutches and they even hung up a few wheelchairs. I just carried him and prayed for him over and over again over the years. And look at what God was using Chase to do for Him. Before I knew it, Chase was off the pulpit, praying for people and eventually came to me. He hugged me and I felt him praying for me. I stayed on the floor for quite some time. I refused to get up in shame again.

It was over. My Womb Could Handle This. The country church was not a "sit and clap after the Sunday inspirational speech" church. I knew I looked a hot mess but I didn't care.

After service, Danne and I made a B-line for the door. Evelyn ran to us and asked us to wait. Chase came to the back and so did Aunt Catherine.

"Are you getting used to me calling you Momma yet?"

I just smiled. "Momma, I want you to meet my family. I asked them not to introduce themselves, I wanted to give you space to choose for yourself."

"I'm okay with that." Chase started waving for people to come to where we were. One by one, I met his brothers, his sisters, aunties, uncles, and there couldn't have been another baby cousin or whoever left. I used to think my family was big, but we don't have nothing on the Swansons.

Then Ms. Catherine popped the million-dollar question, "Do you want to meet the old fart?"

I knew she was referring to Delayne Swanson.

"He's in his office and he wants to talk to you," Ms. Catherine continued.

I looked at Chase. He was waiting to see my reaction. I paused because I really didn't know what to do. "What else is on the schedule for today?"

"I figured we'd go out to eat," Chase said matter-of-factly.

"Well how about we all go out to eat together. Everybody. Can we do it like that?" Then at least I would see him first, and not have to have the one on one. I needed to take this in stages.

"Whatever you say. Momma, I'll drive you and Ms. Danne."

I put my shades on. I knew my eyes were probably red and half-swollen from weeping the entire service. We went into our cars and all seemed to be waiting. I saw a frail old man get into a car with a healthy looking woman. That must be them. I wasn't ready for that. He was still big and fat in my mind all of these years.

When we got to the restaurant, there were about eighty in the party including children. We needed a separate room. The frail man was "Pop" to everybody, including his wife. Ms. Edie fared well for her age. I sat across the room trying to eat but had no appetite. Chase was securely and very much a part of this huge family. My grandbaby was going from lap to lap, getting and giving much hugs and kisses. Danne and I would have won the "can't-believe-them-two aren't-saying-one-word" award, had the people who know us witnessed our silence. I just smiled and picked at the food. I glanced over at "Pop" and Ms. Edie every now and again and wondered what must be going through their minds. It wasn't that difficult to look at them. They looked like normal people.

Evelyn poked me and leaned over and said, "You don't know how much you being here with us means to this family."

"Thank you. Actually, it's an honor to be here with you all." I said to her in a soft tone. This was a good time to take a run to the ladies' room. As I entered and began to try to fix my make-up, Ms. Edie entered. I was stunned.

"Hello Dr. Prunell. I'm Ms. Edie, Chase's mother. I figured I'd come in here so we could at least talk privately.

"Ok."

"I just want you to know, I wish I could go back in time and change some things. But, I can't. Maybe this wasn't a good idea. I don't know what I was thinking."

"Probably what I've been thinking. How do you work your way out of this when you know that all of the people involved love God and there is so much hurt?"

"Good answer! I'm so sorry. I don't know what to say, but feel obligated to say something, baby. I'm just so sorry! I've wondered what you were like. There were days when I wanted to walk away. For our family. Because of you. A child. Had you been another woman, then it still wouldn't be right, but at least if it was some woman that he fooled with, I'd know it was just sex. But to take a child? That wasn't right. I couldn't understand how he could do such a thing. The man that I had known, it just didn't make sense. But I had to trust God. Everyone told me to go. Once you get with a little girl," Ms. Edie tried to finish her thought.

"He didn't just get with a little girl as if I were giving it out. He forced himself on me, Ms. Edie. Your husband stuck a pillow over my face while he did what he did. Then you people ended up with my son." I was beginning to get irate, knowing I could not–no it was not an option–lose my composure. I wasn't going to allow them to dance around the reality of what transpired. It was clearly pedophilic rape. This was another bridge moment, and I felt myself dangling off the edge. There was a huge inner battle to keep my words purposeful and effective for the relationship I was trying to build with Chase and not to offend his mother.

"When we found out about Chase, it seemed like nothing could get any worse. It was so embarrassing for us. The people were discouraged. You know, when you are in leadership, we are supposed to be above all of this. I've wondered time and time again how you've fared in all of this."

"I'm okay. Thank you. I'm ready just to let all of this go. I've got to. I've been messed up long enough. I must have played this whole thing out a million and two times. And you know what? Nothing changes. Things happened just the way they did. The past cannot be re-written. I've just got to learn how to live without this being the focal point of my life."

There was a brief and awkward silence.

"Your parents, how are they?" Ms. Edie asked.

"They're pretty good. They are still laboring for the Lord and all is well."

"What can I do? Is there anything I can do?"

I wanted to tell this lady I don't know what to do and her question was twenty-eight years late. I was ready to leave. I remained silent while searching for a suitable answer.

"My husband didn't come out the entire service. And, I know there's some things he needs to get off his chest."

Danne, the true dawgs, came to the rescue. I felt my sarcasm gene about to kick in, although I did have enough sense not to actually release the thoughts that ran through my mind. This man needs to get things off of his chest twenty-eight years after he got his oats off. I did want to heal, but there was a very huge part of me that wanted to know that somehow, he suffered. He didn't go to jail, he still had his family, and most of all, he had a strong bond with *our son*. It just wasn't "fair." He has known Chase all of his life, and I was the outsider. In all of the pictures that captured indelible moments of Chase's childhood and life, the great prophet was there. Even though nothing about this has been a competition, it seems like I've just been the scrub in all of this. Where was the justice and equity in all of this? Life just isn't fair.

"I need to go back to my room and make some calls. How about we meet later this evening? I promise but can we do this later, I need a few moments."

"That is certainly understandable."

We arranged for Chase, Ms. Edie and the man who spent twenty-eight years in my mind as a rapist to meet at the hotel later. Danne grabbed our stuff as I exited without a proper departure. I knew I really wasn't mad at Prophet Swanson. I was mad at everyone else's ability to live past that dark period of all of our lives while I had been stuck.

Danne knows me well enough to know when silence is golden. And this was a 24K moment. I went back to my room and slept. I needed an escape to refresh and calm down. I knew God did something in me earlier in the service, and the entire weekend was breathtaking. I didn't want to blow it. I knew what I had to do. I had to forgive. I had to look him in his face and know that God had already forgiven him for what he did to me, and he still mattered to God.

The wake-up call came and I needed to freshen up. *Lord I'm strong in my weakest state through you. Strengthen me oh Lord. Strengthen me. Help me to not live in the me, me, me, mode. Help me to see you. Help me to see your righteousness in others. Help me to forgive. I want to be free from all of this.*

I went downstairs early so that I could already be seated in the lounge. I know enough about power moves to know that would have me on the up and up, even as I struggled not to succumb to the pressures of being in the presence of an attacker. Danne and I had a text plan, where I'd send the draft, "7 secs" if I needed her to rescue me. Pastor Swanson, Ms. Edie and Chase walked in. Now was the time to test all of the years of church, Sunday school, and personal intimacy with God. I had to fight to be responsible for the words that came out of my mouth. I stood up to shake their hands. Chase, by now, had grown accustomed to hugging me. He kissed me on my forehead and held me for a few moments. Things were quite tense, and Chase was determined to break the silence.

"Does anybody want to order anything?"

I replied, "No, I'm good." I decided to let them set the tone and pace, and I'd follow suit.

Pastor Swanson spoke up. "Dr. Prunell, I've tried to figure out a thousand times what I could say to you to make up for what I've done to you. There are no words that can do that. I asked God to forgive me. I know He has. All I can do is ask for your forgiveness. I would have come sooner, but obviously couldn't contact you. I am sorry. I never should have—"

Prophet Swanson stumbled for words while I looked at a man who had endured inner turmoil and shame. I didn't want to see that. I wanted to see something that would give me the right to flip out on this piece of work. I wanted to see a man upon whom I could release years of frustration, inadequacy and insecurity because I couldn't reconcile—no matter how hard I tried—how this could have happened to me. I lived with a void that was his fault and wanted to be able to shift the blame. But this was not the case. This isn't who I was looking at before my very eyes. The guilt had been shifted thousands of years ago through Jesus, and I had an obligation as a Christian to let it go. I just sat there and looked at him. I would have never chosen him, but he was the father of my son.

"I need to forgive you. So much has been held up in my life, because I couldn't forgive you or myself, or my parents, or any and everybody. Please, sir, know that I forgive you." Somehow, a sex offender commandeered a level of respect. Respect? Yes, respect. I had to make myself respect a man who put a pillow over my face to stifle my voice from being heard so he could get what he wanted. The man who did an incredible job raising my son was not what he did to me. By taking accountability for the wrong he did, he was in a place with God as if he never did it. And, God allowed him to live the results of being in the place of grace with God.

"I tried to figure out a way to let you know that I accept full responsibility for what was done, for what I done, but I knew I shouldn't have had any communication with you."

"Actually, I don't know if you remember, you apologized profusely right after you took that pillow off my head…that was after you did it again." Maybe, I shouldn't have said that. That information may have been too vivid for Ms. Edie and Chase. Even for Swanson. Certain things I can remember play by play, and other things are completely blocked out. I just know I had hated this man for changing the course of my life, and living with a void for my son, which no one thought I was supposed to have for a "rape" baby. The hard part would be letting go of that hatred and learning to live with a clean slate.

"And, I owe you an apology. I hated you over and over again, my thoughts fed the hate, my prayers fed the hate that crippled me. I'm sorry that I've hated you. I've really hated you, and it has made me untrusting and bitter. I didn't want anyone who could ever have the potential to do what you did to me. You were a man of God. Had a church. And a family. If you did that to me, then anyone could. No one could be trusted."

No one said a word.

"You know, if I had just seen you on the street, I would have passed right by you; I wouldn't have recognized you at all."

Ms. Edie interjected, "My husband never been the same since this happened. You know, he was into some private stuff that entertained the devil and lust and it affected our marriage. When this happened, he knew he had to cry out to God and if we didn't have all them children, I would've gone. But, God saw us through and when your father let us know about your condition, my husband knew we had to take responsibility. So Aunt Catherine being that she didn't have any of her own and things weren't too stable with us, agreed to take Brandon Chase and raise him so that way he could be part of the family. I mean, I was having a baby too at the time. It was a lot."

Ms. Edie kept on talking. Maybe this was an opportunity for her to vent too.

"So then my husband had to get some accountability to somebody other than hisself. I told him he had to come off the road or else. And he had to stop watching that porn and stop socializing with them demons who had orgies and cheated and all of that hoing. There was no other way he was going get free and look at what his flesh problem had done."

Interesting. Rape and pedophilic behavior amounted to a "flesh problem." Nowadays, it's a mere "proclivity" that the good old boys use the Bible to preach and justify their obscene lifestyles that affect their entire family. At that very moment, I looked at my son who had to listen to us talk about how much his existence was a problem for everyone.

"I've heard a zillion messages about how God uses our mess for a message, and how to make lemonade out of lemons, and all of that. But looking at Chase right before my very eyes, I can see it for myself. And to be honest with all of you, I'm not glad what happened, happened. I'm glad that since it did happen, at least we got Chase out of it. He's the only good that has come of this." I held my son's hand. It could not have been easy for him to listen to the conversation.

"This is the one thing I asked the Lord to do for me before I leave this earth. To give me a chance to make it right." Somehow I could sense the genuineness from a man that I spent years loathing.

"Sir, I don't know if you can ever make it right. I don't know if that is possible. But this has to be overcome and forgotten. You know, I have been so willing to love the unlovable, help everybody, be there for anybody, and don't have a lesser obligation to love you because I was the recipient of the damage. So as much as is within me, I forgive you. Jesus died for all of us because we were all born in sin, and shaped in iniquity. Then we all fail to please God and it is our job to repent. We want forgiveness for our misgivings, shortcomings, and downright sins, so to be like Jesus, we've got to love like Him and have mercy and forgive. This will never be made right but we can be made whole. Only God can do that, once we do our part. And, I see how much I need to do this, so I can live for real. And you, Prophet Swanson, Christ died for the offender just like he did for the offended. It's the same blood, love and forgiveness of sins. So long as we have received it, we are both His." This was difficult for me to confess. All of the years I wanted Swanson to hurt because if there couldn't be any resolution that would bring justice, at least there could have been some equity in the emotional toil. But nothing that could have happened to Mr. Swanson would change the facts or really change me. A real acknowledgment of wrong may have made it easier for me to forgive for real, much sooner. But clearly, this was really about me becoming free. God knows how many times others have had to forgive me for the wrong I have done.

"And, Ms. Edie, I admire the job you all have done with Chase. The day I knew for sure I was pregnant, you were the first person I thought about." I was about to get real emotional. I remembered the panic and pressure as if it were yesterday. "I thought about what my mom would feel if another person had any of my daddy's children. And even though it wasn't that type of situation, I thought of the shame and hardship you would feel if you ever found out about Chase. In the strangest way, I can't explain it, but I felt so guilty." As a woman, I had to give Ms. Edie her kudos. Who else would have put up with my son and really loved him?

"You are a remarkable woman to have taken my son and loved him. Most women would not have been here talking to me today. And that is not weakness. You had to be strong to live through what you lived through and still be a family. I admire you and Ms. Catherine for that. And, you all seem to be close. You all have been there for each other. I'm glad he grew up knowing his family and being loved. I'm glad we had this opportunity, and Prophet Swanson, please know that it is well with me."

I needed to say whatever Swanson needed to hear so that he didn't continue to suffer from guilt, if he was even still there. He would have to forgive himself. There is truth to not even wanting your enemies to suffer as you have. And, he wasn't the enemy. God restored him years ago. None of us should still be locked into the past.

Before that meeting, I could not imagine how all of the women I had seen go through utter madness in Christiandom could stay with their husbands. As a pastor's daughter, I've had the knowledge of a lot of infidelity, betrayal, and disrespect from men who mounted the pulpits and glossed over it, justified it, and perverted the Bible to justify their behavior and take no time for reproof, correction, and restoration. These men of God, the master pimps, tricks, and whores, were the "anointed" ones, good men who just "made some bad decisions." Over and over again. They bragged about orgies. They were worse than the drug dealer on the streets. Church people bought the hype and God's government went out the window. Too often, I'd seen the bishop divorce in January and re-marry his secretary in March of the same year. And, the selfish men walked away from their children and their responsibilities to be with another woman, or man. We've seen affairs with extramarital children, left and right. We've seen drug use, and alcohol addiction from the leading and most celebrated celebrity preachers. We seen men beat their wives and deny it. We've seen them beat their wives and say "so what." We've seen hatred toward the wife, who is "tearing down" the Bishop, the Apostle, or the Man of God because she didn't pray enough, wouldn't act like the whores in the porn movies the men of God use for daily entertainment, should've lost weight after popping out baby after baby, or backed up her age after investing years into a marriage. We've seen homosexual affairs and down low raping and turning out of young boys by the leading men of God. And I'd *known* being raped by a man of God as a child to have a child, and never have the opportunity to know my own baby before now.

    These same men, would counsel and cover-up for one another. All of the casualties were completely expendable. The children could amount to a monthly check from the church's treasury to a third party, so the wife wouldn't be able to track down payments for unknown side children. The boys would spend years trying to be delivered from the taste of perversion they were introduced to from men of God as their initial entry into sexual relations. The girls would become silly women, or women like me, Tamars, who would remain desolate because they were wrongfully desired, used, abused, rejected, then despised. We became an embarrassment. Our total existence and worth in the backroom discussions never included our individuality, our worth, our promise, or our purpose as God's seed. We all too often became the problem, or the devil's mess trying to take down or cause a man of

God who "made a mistake" to be exposed. "We," real people who God is concerned about, became de-personalized "situations" that needed to be managed. The Word of God wasn't the guide. The "wisdom" of defiled corrupted "wise" men chose the path that many of us would take. Years of observing this vicious cycle helped me to remain faithful to God and not let one of these jokers gain my love or have a place in my heart. Except one.

XAVIER JOHNSON
Square Head, Big Heart

When I first returned home from having Chase, things were the same, but never the same, at the same time. Everyone tried to act as if nothing happened, and no one ever mentioned a thing or asked a question. Even when I tried to ask my mother about Chase, she told me, "That's over with. Try and forget all of that ever happened. You can still have a childhood." The family was getting ready to go to a convention and somehow I couldn't connect to the annual fervor. The new clothes were meaningless. So was the excitement about what songs our youth group was going to sing the night my daddy was the keynote preacher. And so was catching up with some of the other kids we only saw during conventions. I didn't even want to go. But, Ma was surely not going to leave me with anyone.

It was at the convention where Ma noticed my desire to be left alone. How much did everyone in the other churches know about me? We had already been well connected to the game of telephone, passing along other people's business. Now, I was certain that the gratuitous smiles, uneasiness and stares evidenced my own turn on the church-world gossip line. I left as an embarrassment and returned in shame with a void and nowhere to turn to fill it. So, I didn't have to sing in the choir. I was tired. I slept. I didn't want to process being left back and having to re-do my first year of junior high school all over again.

That year, I somehow began to think I must have been adopted. Just as Chase was going to be with someone else, maybe I was displaced from my real mother and father and wound up with the Prunells. Although I looked just like my mother, maybe

I really belonged to my aunt and that is why I had to go be with her when trouble came. I yearned for my aunt who had been there for me through false labor, and who kissed me and told me that she loved me every single day. My mother found out this theory of mine under the most inopportune circumstances. When she wanted me to get dressed more quickly for service one night, I told her to please send me back to my real mother. She insisted that she was my real mother, and I didn't believe her. Needless to say, much laying on of hands and prayer took place for me so that the devil would stop tormenting my mind.

When I saw how wounded my mother was from this revelation of mine, I felt sorry for her. Maybe I was confused. This warranted a stick close to me strategy from my mother, Lady Prunell, reinforced by a notable yet unflattering run-in with Xavier, the convention comic.

Xavier thought he was cute, and probably really was for a ten-year-old Bishop's son. He was the youngest of five, and his dad and my dad were both on the board of Bishops. Hailing from Wilmington, North Carolina, he was quite bamma and country in our book. After all, we were from the best city in the world, New York City. So with undue pride, our youth group tended to slam Bishop Johnson's youth group. Even though they killed us with the singing and the shouting steps, we still had to act like we were on top. So, in one of our snapping fests, I snapped on Xavier's clothes. He snapped right back and went for the jugular.

Xavier Johnson looked me right in my face in front of a bunch of convention kids and said, "Don't you worry about my clothes, at least I can fit in mine!"

I retorted, "So can I, squarehead!"

"No you can't, your big fat butt has that skirt lopsided!" Xavier did not fail to demonstrate with perfected mockery by sticking out his backside and leaning over, to embellish how my butt looked. "With that big belly when you was pregnant, you might have been even!"

I looked at Xavier Johnson and can't remember all that ran through my mind. I do remember the first instance of wanting to literally snatch someone's eyeballs out. Before I knew it, I lunged at Xavier, and don't know how much damage I did. It was immeasurable, because two of my brothers, Harris and Ford, went to town on Xavier. Xavier was obviously not aware of the covert plan to ignore and erase the entire fiasco from the Prunell family reality. His words were the first words that penetrated the façade that had been protecting the big dirty secret. They were embarrassing, hurtful and went below the belt. So I went for him below the belt, literally. I kicked him where it hurt.

In true Prunell form, I was chastised for my unseemly behavior, especially for a girl. My mouth, my mouth, my mouth. Xavier didn't know better, he was just a kid. I knew that. His words just triggered the reality of my pain and confusion. So, next to Ma all day every day, was my station. I overheard my mother telling my brothers this was none of their business, and to stay out of it. She warned me not to discuss this with any of my brothers—ever—she did not want them getting into any trouble over me. She was determined that none of her sons would ever be in jail, and apparently, Prophet Swanson wouldn't be either. Meanwhile I was mentally locked down, I kept getting the unwritten message of my worth, particularly compared to my other siblings. I put Xavier Johnson into a box in my mind: He got on every one of my nerves.

Years later, about seven years ago on my thirty-third birthday, my father woke me up with a phone call. "Happy Birthday! You know I love you don't you?"

"Of course I do, and I love you too." My dad has always tried to show me in his own way that he really loved me.

"You are officially thirty-three today. What are you going to do?"

"I'm going to work, Dad." I thought, *duh, we've been through this year after year. Doesn't he know the routine already?*

"Why don't you take off and do something for yourself?"

"I'll do something with my friends on the weekend. You know I like to make my birthday a month-long celebration. You all can do something for me later."

"I'm your father, Jewel, and I am concerned about you. Don't you want to get married?"

"Of course I do, just haven't met the right one yet."

"You may be too picky."

"Maybe, maybe not. I just may be dealing with the reality of statistics. I'm not the only thirty-something year old waiting for a good Black man who is really saved."

"I have never interfered with your decisions for your life." I immediately thought. *This man must have amnesia.* "But maybe you need some help. How about I find someone for you?"

"You know what, Dad, I'm going to take you up on your offer. How about you do just that. Make sure he is disease free, got decent credit, has a proven work history, and is really saved. Even if he doesn't have teeth, we can buy that. Oh, and I'd prefer a man without a bunch of kids, and who doesn't support the doc syndrome."

"No kids? That's going to be difficult at your age."

"I didn't say 'no kids.' Maybe one or two. But I can't do the five kids from seven different baby mamas, drama. Nope. I'd rather be alone."

"And what, may I ask, is the 'doc syndrome'?"

"Never mind Daddy. I just don't want anyone who is interested in sitting around in the back rooms or restaurants with a bunch of clergy."

"What kind of request is that, Jewel? Should I be offended by that? I'm a Bishop."

"I'm sorry, maybe I shouldn't have said it like that. I'd rather be with someone who loves God but has another profession."

"Another profession? What's wrong with a good Godly man?"

"Daddy, there are good Godly men who are not clergy. I just don't want anybody who holds a microphone and wants to call themselves a preacher. That's all."

"What's wrong with preachers, Jewel? Your brothers preach."

"Absolutely nothing if that's what you want. I can't live with someone who has a doctrine for not living what he preaches. And, the record doesn't look good from what I've seen and you know it, Dad. For some strange reason, I am under the very Biblical impression that men of God are supposed to have a standard."

"We are human too, Jewel. We have to walk with God too."

"It's not that I can't handle your humanity, Dad. I can't handle the sin that is cloaked as humanity. I can't handle the arrogance, and repeated wickedness, that is called humanity with people's lives being destroyed. Don't get me started."

"I can't believe I'm hearing this. I had no idea you had such disregard for God's people."

"I don't have disregard for God's people. I have disregard for nonsense. Come on Daddy. Let's be real. Look at your board of Bishops. You know what we know. Men cheating on their wives left and right. Having extramarital babies. Preaching so they can maintain their lifestyle and running neck in neck with their 'doc' brothers. Homosexuals. Orgies. Alcoholism. Flying in fresh bootay everywhere they go to preach with offerings that God's people give by faith, believing they are supporting the work of the Kingdom of God. But they all love God and have struggles. Do you personally know any of the casualties to their struggles? You're listening to one of them, Daddy. The people have names. And where is the repentance? Where is the Godly sorrow? After twenty years of whoring, when is enough, enough? When will a leader, a man of God stand up and hold these men accountable so that this vile behavior will stop? When will arrogant apathetic men stop making excuses for one another and remove your friends from leadership until they have repented and their lives have been restored? When will God's way be more sound than your counsel of how to handle all of this mess so that this will finally stop?"

"It sounds like you've thought about this quite a bit."

"I've more than thought about it. I've lived it, Daddy. I'm not saying everyone is there, but you know good and well there is a sick Godless culture where the robed and collar-wearing cover each other's mess and it is dead wrong and you know it. I'd rather be with someone who isn't so deeply entrenched in the church that they bite this bullet. There are men out there who believe the simplicity of the gospel and live by the Word and want to please God, and do not find eternal excuses why God loves them despite their mess, so feel free to stay in their mess. It takes time to book tickets for a girlfriend to meet you after you preach, Daddy. That's not a good man who has fallen or has a struggle. That is a straight up clown defacing the very God who has given us the victory to overcome sin. It's not me, it's just too many Sunday school lessons talking, that's all."

"I'm listening, Jewel and I'm hearing you. I am *hearing* you."

"Good."

"I guess I'll have to take what I can get. This is good. It breaks your mother and my heart to see you are the only one who is not married and has no children."

"Thanks for reminding me of that on my birthday. By the way, I'd rather be right where I am, just as I am, than to deal with being with someone that I love but really don't like."

The two of them are so oblivious. I know they wanted me to be happy. Fortunately, we had the same aspirations for me to have a family. That has never been the issue. They glossed over Chase's existence and my void from not ever having his love or being able to give him a mother's love since I returned home six weeks after his birth.

The first Mother's Day after I had Chase was the third most miserable day in my life. The first was the day he was conceived, and the second was the day he went to his new family.

My dad had learned years before, not to play himself on Mother's Day. My mom was a supportive pastor's wife. She cleaned the house, did laundry every day, did the girls' hair every day, did all of the shopping, cooked a real dinner every day, and taught at the church. She didn't ask for much attention for herself at all. In fact, she rarely wanted to do anything without us because she never really trusted other people with us. She wasn't into this new age ministry foolishness, where mothers have adjutants raise their children while they run around preaching and seeing about church people first. Not my mother. Our throw up or oops could fall on her clothes any day. We were Caroline Prunell's babies and she was careful about who she would allow to be around her babies. Because of Caroline, my father's children were cared for and not just raised.

Accordingly, we could count the babysitters we ever had on one hand. So, Mother's Day was a big deal in my family. My father better not give Lady Prunell the gift that he really wanted, like he mistakenly did one year when he gave her a barbecue grill utensil set. Or, when he gave her a new vacuum cleaner. Bishop Prunell learned the hard way, remember the wife on Mother's Day, or else. It was the day we all had to think of Caroline Prunell because she always put my father and each of us before her own needs. As long as we were good, she was good. You would never find my mother laced, face beat, while any one of us looking like who caught the rat. We weren't eating hot dogs made from meat scraps while she was sitting somewhere hob nobbing with other ladies and upper crust clergy. Impossible.

So on Mother's Day, we all bought Ma a gift, wrote out our own cards, and Daddy did the same. We also got Nanna and Grandma greeting cards. My first Mother's Day I ached and ached. I was only thirteen, but I still yearned for my son. We showered my mother with gifts, while she thanked God for all of her children. This was the day I realized I was going to live an indefinite façade. My parent's obliviousness spread to the entire family so much so that when my brother Harris had his first daughter with a college sweetheart he would end up marrying years later, after my parents' got over the shock and reproved him for "knowing better," the entire family went full gear into preparing for the first grandchild. The first. I too, was delighted to know we were going to have a new baby in the family, but certainly my niece wasn't the first. I learned to celebrate all the arrivals of my siblings' children, be a happy bridesmaid, attend all the weddings, do all of the holidays, and constantly show up unmarried and "childless." I learned how to truly enjoy their company, fight back the tears of loneliness, and wait until I pulled up to my admirable home and sit in my successful doctor's car and cry. I used to wonder if my son was functioning well without me. Yet, in the eyes of my family, and true to my reality, I was single and childless. So, I had no problem letting my father take the reins and arrange a suitable relationship for me.

My father's choice: Xavier Johnson. He and Bishop Johnson were still bosom buddies, and Xavier was the only son who hadn't married yet. He obviously forgot about Xavier's comments to me years before, which probably never even registered with my father. Because the pregnancy and Chase's existence were taboo and never discussed, I didn't bother to take my dad down memory lane. I didn't feel like a sermon on being trifling and the need to get over it. He told me Xavier had re-located to Connecticut, so he was only two and a half hours away. He gave the gentleman my number, and I should expect his call.

Xavier and I spoke for about three hours the first time he called. I started out as nice-icey as I could be, but Xavier wasn't having it. He busted me out in a few seconds and put our adolescent spat in perspective. He remembered. And now he talked the right talk and said he walked the right walk. We talked for hours almost every night for almost one month. He was in seminary and employed as a state caseworker for troubled youth, so he seemed to be a miracle. He had no children, swore he wasn't a homosexual, had his own place, own vehicle, and was the youth pastor at the church he attended. He even confessed that he had a prior promiscuous life and used to be a player, but that was over. One day he had to meet me, he had to see me after all of these years. I was still cautious, but agreed. Maybe Daddy found a good man of the cloth for his daughter.

Xavier got off of the train and I looked at him. He was the exact same image of a man I dreamt about years earlier, who I knew I was made to help. He had a big square forehead, a nice physique, far from a six-pack, but quite put together. Overall, he was acceptable. After much talking and communication over a few years where he insisted he loved and respected me, the first allegation of another woman popped up. By this time, he and I were so emotionally close, and I was dependent upon him and wanted to see the best in him. So I "forgave" him until a few months ago when a baby popped up. This was another one-night stand. He would not go down as playing Bishop Prunell's daughter, or any other woman because after all, he wasn't a womanizer or player. He is just another man with a "flesh" problem. His only fault was his weak flesh as a fornicator, which could certainly be understood for a young single man, and according to his twisted doctrine. So that was the end of Xavier, who begged for continued companionship. Xavier could not comprehend how I had no desire to have any type of relationship with him, because he lied for breakfast lunch and dinner about his friends, cousins and co-workers who all turned out to be women who he turned to, to meet his needs. Again, I was left holding the bag from a ruthless preacher. My daddy was fired from ever choosing a mate for me, and I never bothered to tell him why. He just wouldn't get it.

My head divorced Xavier emotionally, but my heart never did. He became the friend I wanted to get rid of, but never did. Xavier was still the one who would know exactly what to say at the right time. Although I had "friends" in college, and a few boyfriends down the line, I knew none of them was marriage material, so I never invested in the relationships enough to work toward longevity. Xavier got past the walls and I could not explain how. Even though we weren't on speaking terms, I realized that if I could forgive a pedophile who was accountable and repentant, I had to truly forgive Xavier too. Xavier wasn't what he did to me, and what he did, wasn't directed to me. He had issues that I couldn't see, because I couldn't see him. All I could see was the man Xavier presented as himself, who was a mere fragment of the real man.

NO MORE ABANDONMENT
A New Beginning

Danne and I sat up all night, irresponsibly, discussing how much we actually couldn't believe how things turned out. I saw the man who had been locked in my thoughts as an evil beast, and saw that all of that was only in my mind. Prophet Swanson had been living for years with the grace of God and raised Chase to be a wonderful young man. We both had a condensed week before us, and needed rest to be our best on Monday morning, but couldn't help see how good God is, and how much we really needed to grow in Him. I had owned the pain of a man putting a pillow over my face, taking my innocence and having Chase taken away from me. That pain was fed with continual guilt and rejection, revisiting every single incident I could recollect, and then allowed the pain to run rampant in my life.

Danne could relate, as she periodically discussed the similar emotions and wounds she suffered from having an abortion when she was seventeen years old. But Danne refuses to live in her past. She could get up and shake things off. She trusted God to do what she knew she could never do.

The next grown-up thing I had to do was to see Chase in a few hours and leave him again. In a very real sense, I had to leave this utopia that I found in connecting with him for the past few days and go back home. But this time, things would be different.

Chase broke down at the airport. I wasn't expecting that.

"Where do we go from here? When am I going to see you again?"

"Chase, not one day in your life has gone by when I haven't thought about you." He would probably never fully understand how much that was true to the point that I wouldn't enjoy anything else for long. "If it were up to me, I'd be back this weekend." I began to tear up. Really, I was so happy to see him, I didn't even want to go back home. I loved my family, practice and home, but all of that I would walk away from, for my son.

"Chase, I think it would be best to follow your lead. Whatever you are comfortable with."

"Please let's try and talk every day, *Momma*." There goes that word again. It feels like passing the state boards to the twentieth power. The fluttering in my stomach was good this time. "I want to come and see you soon and meet my other family."

We hugged and I walked away. It wasn't abandonment this time. It was the beginning of the rest of our lives. We would have the opportunity to get to know each other. Now, I would have to face my family, Chase's family, and hope they would accept him—the one grandchild who had been zeroed out. This feat would warrant discussion and require breaking down taboo walls.

WHEN THE COOKIE CRUMBLES, THE CHIPS FALL WHERE THEY MAY

Paid Too Much To Play With It

Noey is faithful to the airport runs, or any run where she can strap up the mini-queens and go. Lissa and Leah don't look anything alike. One looks like Jayden, and the other like Jayden's sister. Noey completely lost the gene war. But, the two little women act like pristine ladies in waiting and their over-the-top momma.

We spotted Noey, and once we saw her, we knew what the babies were wearing because she insisted that the three of them coordinate. I kissed my god-babies, and for the first time realized that what I experienced wasn't just a circumstantial healing that changed once I got back home. I didn't kiss my god-babies this time with a godmother's love, thinking how privileged they were to have their mom, all while yearning out of emptiness to be able to kiss my own son. I had just kissed my son. In hugging the babies, I realized that even my former kisses had been coupled with pain.

Rashaun was acting shady, I guess he figured I would still bust him up for hitting his mother. "Come here, boy. Give me a hug, and get my bags." He tried to act as if he wasn't relieved that I wasn't acting salty, as if he wasn't on edge at all. He loves to try that macho stuff with me, and because of his manhood, generally, I don't touch that. I let him handle things the way he thinks he should. I had to figure out what to do with him next and see if Aliyah was still on the same page. She is growing too weak to deal with his acting out through foolishness and drama, right now.

Danne was getting ready to do a photo shoot in Manhattan, and Noey and I were going to our neck of the woods, Long Island. I thanked Danne for everything and the rest of us went home. I was already running behind schedule, and after a couple of days out of the office, that was not good. Knowing Aliyah, I couldn't even call her, because five minutes amounts to five hours with her. She has no concept of reason with other people's time, unless it involves Bishop Chauncey Deuce, the "mand" of God. Rashaun would have to sit with me in my office all day.

Of course, my mother blew up the cell phone, wanting to hear from me. I couldn't handle three mountains at one time: Aliyah and Rashaun, Ma and 'em, and building a relationship with Chase. Chase was a priority to me. I wanted him to know that I am never too busy for him, and will make any accommodations necessary to have a great relationship with my son. And, after thinking the entire plane ride home, I couldn't afford for any potential craziness with my family to upset my emotions with Chase, although I hoped for the best. God already worked things out beautifully between us, and I wanted to keep it that way. And, my mother was certainly not going to be in favor of me taking custody of Rashaun and Tysheem. She had already repeatedly admonished me over the years that I was so busy taking care of my friends and their children that I would be worn out by the time I had my own. What she failed to realize is that nine months of pregnancy made me think that I already had my own: I just hadn't known him. Yet, I didn't want to be insensitive to my parents' feelings. I know they were on needles and pins. So, I did what I always do. I made a diversionary move. I called one of my siblings and gave a check-in phone call, and told them to call the parents and let them know I'd call them as soon as I got the chance.

By the time I arrived at my office, there was a delivery of flowers with the message, "To Momma, it was great seeing you this weekend, love your baby boy forever, Chase."

Helen, our office manager asked, "What kind of a weekend did you have? Not you playing frisky. And the catch was smart enough to try and disguise himself in the message. Tell him your staff is nosey as hell, he can't get past us."

I shook my head and grinned at Helen. She is a wonder in her own mind. She is a beautiful Greek woman who fits the description, "hot seductive mess." Helen is about the business, but would not miss an opportunity to induce anyone to have illicit sex. "Now, you know me better than that. Actually, the card is from my son. You just didn't know I had one."

"You have a son?" Helen asked while gasping.

"Do we have time to discuss this now? I have so much on my plate, I can't afford to talk to a billboard right now that will publish all of my dag on business. I promise, I'll let you know the dirt later. But I do have a son." That felt good. I'm opening the closet door and one by one, people will eventually know I have a son. I'm the best person to put the news in proper perspective. The real shock will be when they find out how old he is. I certainly don't fit the stereotype of the girl who had a baby at twelve.

"Ok, you better not forget, cause I will come and get your business right from your own nostrils."

All of my colleagues always said I was too commonplace with the staff. I've never had the hierarchy mentality in the medical profession and especially the church. As long as the person performs, she's all right with me.

I took a few minutes to call Chase. "Chase, I can't talk for long, I'm swamped at work. But, I just wanted you to know that I got your flowers. They are beautiful. You are so considerate."

"I just wanted you to remember me all day when you see them. I miss you already."

"I miss you too. I do have to go now, but we'll touch base later. Okay? Send Evey and Ruth my love, please."

In one weekend, just about everything shifted in my life. I had an actual relationship with Chase to look forward to, and had to assume responsibility for Rashaun and Tysheem at the same time.

I'm glad Rashaun got to see me in action at the office. He needs to know that his mom is not a drug addict on the streets anymore. She has allowed God to transform her life. I could see so much of his own pain and rejection. I kept telling him all day, this could be you one day, if not medicine, you can still have your own business and help other people and make plenty of money.

After a long day at work I was ready to crash so Rashaun and I hit Aliyah's spot. She, of course, was in great discomfort so she put all type of decency out of the window and was lying butt-naked on her bed. She had boils on the inner thigh, so did not want to put on any clothes. I, in true form, flipped on her for being so incredibly irreverent of her two sons. "Do you think they need to have memories of their mother lying on a bed butt naked? Put a sheet over yourself."

"They shouldn't care, I'm suffering, Jewel. You don't know what it is like."

"You are right, I don't know what you are going through. Whatever the heck you are going through you can go through with a sheet on yourself so your kids don't have to smell and see your business. You don't know what they are going to have to go through processing that! Even though you are suffering, so are they!"

So I won, and she covered up her nakedness in front of her impressionable sons. Aliyah and I continually fight over her behavior. When she is up and feeling good, she is all good. When she is really under the weather and suffering, she carries on. I am not her doctor, I am her best friend. She knows this, so she takes it, although I try to reserve the blows for absolute necessaries.

"So, what are we going to do with Rashaun?"

"Just let him come back home. I don't want him in the system."

"Neither do I. That was just a threat. I'm thinking it would be best for me to take him right now."

"If you take him now, after a fight, he's gonna think I don't want him and put him out. He doesn't need to think I hate him."

"So how are we going to manage this then, because he can't stay here. He resents you, no matter how you look at it, and I don't think he meant to hurt you when he hit you. He just doesn't know how to handle watching you like this. In a way, you're getting ready to leave him again in his eyes."

"I'm not going anywhere. I'm not dying from AIDS and he knows that." Aliyah has crazy faith. She is a faith landmine, waiting to erupt and blow up all doubt.

"Okay, so then let's talk to a social worker and set up some counseling. He definitely does not do well here, because he knows you don't have the strength to stay on top of things. He's been cutting school and we need to do something before he goes out there for real. Until you get better, I want to take him."

"No. I asked every one of you before, but no one would take him. Now, he just needs to come back home. We'll make it."

"Aliyah, I'm not just thinking of you. I'm thinking of him and Tysheem."

"What does Tysheem have to do with this?"

"When is the last time they didn't eat pizza or Chinese food? They are taking care of you. That is not fair to them. They need to be in school, and you need real care."

"I don't need no care. They do whatever I need them to do."

"Aliyah, I'm not going to fight you; you are their mother. Think about it. They need to be involved in your care, but not responsible for it. They need to see you, but they also need a stable life. Rashaun's only had it for the first five years you got him back. Now, if you want, you can come move in with me too. I'll fix up downstairs for you and with your Medicaid, we'll get an aide. That's a no-brainer. If you don't want to leave, think of the boys. I know I wouldn't take them before, but after seeing my son —"

"You went to see your son? When did all of this happen?"

"It's a short sort of medium long story. I'll put you down later, but I did meet my baby. He's twenty-eight." Hearing myself say those words seemed so surreal.

"I can't believe you didn't tell me. Oh My God, Oh My God, isn't that just like Him? I told you God was gonna do it for you." My girl started weeping. The whole crew knew this was the "thing" about me. Yearning for Chase wasn't a secret to them. They knew even when they wouldn't verbalize it, I never felt complete without him. "Jewel, I can't, nope, I can believe it. You finally met your son. What is his name?"

"They named him Brandon Chase. They call him Chase."

"What kind of a name is Chase?"

"The same kind of name Rashaun or Tysheem is."

"You just met your son and you feeling yourself already? Don't trip. My boys have fly names."

"Yeah, I know. In the ghetto," I whispered under my breath.

"You betta be lucky I can't jack you up cause I'll show you ghetto." We both smirked. So I fell asleep at Aliyah's talking to her half the night about Chase and his family. She could definitely school me on how to step into a child's life after being absent since birth. Although Chase is a grown man and doesn't need to be raised, Aliyah's advice was irreplaceable, "Get up every single day early and ask God to show you Chase, where he is in his spirit, and what he needs. God will let you know everything you need to know. Only God can do this, girl, only God."

"Okay, like I said with Rashaun and Tysheem, I'm going to get them some counseling and you and I need to go see a social worker."

On the way home, I thought of how I had lived the perfect life externally. While I had learned to hide the pains from my past, I lived to please everyone else. Jewel had been successful ever since she had to repeat a year in school. I was determined to never have to repeat anything else ever again. So, I aced everything—tests, class grades, state exams—everything. I hated school and did not want to spend an extra millisecond doing the inevitable. No one could exist in the Prunell household and not do well in school. So, my best academic performance ensued the year I was left back. I was "skipped" back to my right grade by the time I went to high school. Schoolwork became my best friend. I was embarrassed to be with the younger kids and became withdrawn. By the time I got back with my "real" classmates, I was out of the loop for too long. I would sit, laugh and cut the mustard with my friends, but I wasn't into what they were into. Jewel couldn't care less about looking cute and trying to pull some of the very boys that were into me. I knew what they wanted and didn't want to have any parts with that. So, I couldn't comprehend the beauties and the brains hooking up with all the guys, who played the women like a good fiddler in a country tavern riddled with haystacks and canning jars as mugs for inviting décor. Their reports of sexual escapades and all of that could not have been more nauseating. Mitchell, Izzy and anyone who tried to get with me realized that their charm didn't mean a thing with me. I didn't think hands moving up and down my legs were cute. That stuff made me feel uncomfortable and downright nauseous. I was not a cheap thrill who would end up being a notch on a player's belt. Frivolous attempts to play out of bounds were irresponsible and unwelcome.

I knew I wasn't normal and didn't want to be normal, at least not the kind of normal where I would de-value my own worth for a hot lay. I already knew what it was like to be scared to the limit of a breakdown because sex amounted to an unwanted pregnancy. I had to fight to keep what little worth I felt I had left. Knowing how much I suffered from no one recognizing and assisting me through the trauma, I felt for Rashaun. I did not want to see him suffer the same way. He was born into a fight against generational tendencies.

Aliyah had been smoking weed since she was about nine years old. She grew up in the Chicago ghetto. The drugs and street gang scene was similar to the one Florida and James Evans fought to keep JJ, Thelma and Michael out of, full of hard working Black folk. Aliyah's father was the mack daddy of the neighborhood, at least according to her recollection. He was a grown man, who still lived with his mother. He had a number of women, and Aliyah's mother was just one of them. She was his main woman, but he did not, and certainly would not mess up his game, by ever marrying her. All Aliyah remembers is sleeping in the same bed with her grandmother, along with her sister and brother, while her pops had a bunch of his friends over and they shot up heroin and snorted cocaine. He hustled during the day and always had sufficient dough to throw a drug party. Aliyah's mom was a straight fiend, and so was her uncle, cousins and most of the druggies she saw only when it was up and popping.

Ma-D, Aliyah's grandmother, didn't participate in the drug fests that took place in her living room. She would lock up her bedroom door with the children inside, and attempt to stifle the pungent smells of PCP, heroin and cocaine that seeped through the hallways and doors. Ma-D did her goodly duty: she made sure the children in the house ate, had clothes, bathed twice a week, and attended school just enough to avoid a visit from the truancy officers.

Aliyah was cool with her lifestyle while she was living in the thick of it. She had the father who when people saw him coming, they stepped out of the way and let him go first. He was the man, and so she was hot stuff herself. She slipped into the party, which often had an orgy component that goes hand-in-hand with drug addiction. So, Aliyah's "first" took place while her uncle sexed her at twelve years old, right in the presence of her Mac Daddy father. After a while, her cousins, and a bunch of grown men would take their pick with her, or the other women who were so "stoned," they couldn't have known what happened. Before Aliyah knew it, she was getting high on marijuana every day. In her mind though, that wasn't a drug situation: It was just weed, and everybody does weed.

Before Ryan White, Oprah's town hall meeting on AIDS, or any national public awareness of this disease, Aliyah's pops kept getting sick. He was in and out of the hospital, alongside her mother. All Aliyah remembers is they were quarantined on the same floor in the hospital. Her last time seeing her mother alive was when a nurse told her to put on all of this protective gear, and screamed at her and told her not to assist her mother going to the bathroom. Aliyah had been living with Ma-D since birth, and really hadn't bonded with her mother. When her mother died, Aliyah was saddened. One year later, when her icon-in-her-mind daddy died, she lost her mind. This was when all hell broke loose. By the time she was fourteen, she was a professional drug addict. She had been a first-hand observer of how to do everything necessary to perfect a high, and maximize the use of supply. Ma-d couldn't find her, and when her brother or sister spotted her, she would hide underneath cars and run and tell her druggie companions in the street that they were trying to mess with her.

Raheem was a drug dealer who came to her rescue. He was only a few years her senior, didn't do the drugs, but thought she was cute. He told her if she would do some tricks for him, she would never have to worry about getting high. He promised to keep her laced. So, Aliyah began to turn tricks. And, like her mother, she was the top ranked ho for her man, Raheem. Many pregnancies and abortions later, she finally decided to keep Rashaun. By the time Rashaun was born, crack was the addictive drug of choice, and Aliyah was on it, and on heroin. She gave birth to Rashaun and called Ma-D from the hospital and told her to come and pick him up. By the time Ma-D got there, Aliyah was back on the streets. She couldn't wait to be back with Raheem who not only said he loved her, but showed it. He kept all those hos in check for her.

Until Giselle showed up.

Before "Latina" became the correct way to address women of her origin, Giselle, this "Puerto Rican" chick who was really from Santo Domingo, kept catching Raheem's attention. Aliyah wasn't having that. Nope. Nada. Giselle was trying to out-do Aliyah and she did not respect the process. Didn't Giselle know that Aliyah just had a baby for Raheem? Or at least that is what Raheem and Aliyah concluded after her unprotected daily intercourse with a battery of potential sperm donors. Giselle had that long hair, and light skin. She was in style at the moment. Aliyah knew how to put an end to the madness. She enacted her master plan, and put an end to the situation all right, be it an unexpected end.

After slicing Giselle's face with a razor blade, which made Raheem beat her down to a pulp like a wet food stamp while declaring that Giselle looked better than Aliyah, Aliyah was done. She finally got sick and tired of being sick and tired. When Raheem dissed her the way he did, Aliyah determined it was time to get out. After escaping the streets, statutory rape, and all of the potential and literal contacts with AIDS, Aliyah decided to take this crazy church lady up on her offer. She remembered the nuisance church lady who often told her she didn't have to live this way, and God knew all the pains of her past. So, after looking at her swollen crackled frostbitten feet, Aliyah decided to try Jesus. Raheem wasn't worth it.

Aliyah went to find this lady who said she owned a beauty shop. She walked into the shop; the church lady was running her mouth and doing hair. She also had a television set with a video tape of Apostle Merriweather preaching. The church lady saw Aliyah and told her to go in the bathroom and clean up. Aliyah was already captivated by Merriweather's message. He was hollering with all these people talking over him saying, "preach Apostle" or "you betta say so", and hollering back and forth. Shoot, for a split second, Aliyah thought the man had been one of her tricks. She soon realized he couldn't have been, because one thing about her is she never forgot a face. This man was yelling at the church people, telling them to get off their high horses and pedestals, and get the drug addicts and the prostitutes off of the streets. He was telling them they had to make room for the streetwalkers because everybody was once in sin and somebody prayed. When they prayed for Jesus to save men's souls, he was going to bring people from off the streets right into the church to do what they wouldn't do. God was going to raise up people who had already seen hell just in living right here on the earth, people who would dare to believe God and use them while the hypocrites kept warming the benches. "You might as well move over. There is somebody right now, who is getting ready to come and take the space you are holding up. They have seen everything there is to see, and when God is through with them, they are going to be God's best weapon against the devil." Aliyah was already in tears. He must have been talking to her. God must have been showing Himself to her. She immediately wanted to know where to find this man so he could teach her how to fight the devil. The church lady told her that was her pastor. She told someone else to take over the perm, and in the middle of the beauty parlor, prayed for Aliyah, spoke in all types of tongues, cast the devil out of her, and told her, "Your life will never be the same." Aliyah held onto those words. She had seen her last day in the streets.

Aliyah went to find Apostle Merriweather. He instantly took her under his wings as if she were his natural born daughter. He was the first man who did not, and never would, value her for her pu-pu power, or expose her to harm. He covered her, protected her, and showed her a new way of thinking and living. Aliyah never did rehabilitation, and never went back on the streets or drugs from the day she searched for and found the church lady. Jesus was her rehab and gave her greater fulfillment than any type of high she could get from drugs or the streets. She had been so amazed by the power of God in destroying the entire craving and need for drugs, which she depended on for most of her life, that she immersed herself into the church. Whatever God did for her, she wanted to help and make happen for others. So then, it is easy to comprehend Aliyah's radical approach to living for Christ. She never missed a church service, prayer, or any special meetings. She was never late either. She wanted every drop and had to make up for lost time. This thing was too serious to play with. God was real, and God was too good.

    The church lady began to teach Aliyah what most grown women already knew. She permitted her to wash hair in the salon. Aliyah was happy to do it for free. She would get to watch tapes of the Word all day, have heat, sleep in the back room on a couch and have meals. She was doing something respectable, and she was grateful. Sticking to a routine was challenging, but she was working it out. Once the church lady found out Aliyah had a child, she said you've got to get him back. Aliyah wasn't certain that could happen because Ma-D and her younger sister, Quinaisha, had joint custody of him. The court had completely severed her parental rights after years of neglect and never showing up in court. Besides, her family knew the girl who was smoking, was fresh and was giving trouble from the time she was nine. She hadn't spent one complete day with Rashaun since he was born, and they didn't even believe she was saved and clean on the few visits she made to the same apartment Ma-D had since Ma-D was a teenager. The church lady assured her, "If Jesus made the way for you to get back to God, then He's made the way for Rashaun to get back to you. If you want him, ask God, cause you'll have what you say, so long as you live right, and it is His will. God gives you the authority to speak to situations in your life and all you have to do is watch God work everything out."

    Aliyah began to fast and pray. What it took church people twenty years to get, she got in a few seconds. Aliyah believed God would do it for her because she had seen him deliver her from heroin and crack with ease. She also had nothing to lose in trusting God. Church people, in her mind, play with God and take Him for granted too much. So, after much fasting and prayer, Aliyah went to see Ma-D. Quinaisha had left Rashaun with Ma-D, and started in the generational path of drug use. She was a functional user, but a user nonetheless. Ma-D put Quinaisha out, and she was tired of raising children. She was ecstatic to see Aliyah this time. Ma-D suggested Aliyah start to visit more often to spend time with Rashaun. Before you knew it, Aliyah was spending the night and taking Rashaun to church with her three times a week. He was going to know God so he wouldn't ever see the days her father, mother, uncles, cousins, and now younger sister saw. He would not go in the path of his forefathers. He would serve the Lord.

After a year and a half of consistency, Ma-D suggested that Aliyah take Rashaun, against the will of the rest of the functional yet addicted family. Aliyah was ecstatic. Although Ma-D berated her, told her she was good for nothing, and not doing anything with her life because she spent all of her time at that church running behind them corrupt people, Aliyah remained humble. She kept her eyes on the prize, getting Rashaun back. The same Ma-D, who questioned Rashaun from A to Z about everywhere Aliyah took him, what those church people said to him or did to him, and reported every move Aliyah made to the family who she respected, all of whom were functional drug addicts, wanted Aliyah to get custody of her son. Aliyah trusted God. She wasn't concerned about things she didn't know about. She was just learning the advantages of abandoning the sink ho bath method and soaking in a warm tub with bath salts every single day. She was primarily concerned about what she did know: generational curses and growing up in a household that manufactured professional drug abusers. Unbeknownst to Aliyah, Ma-D had already been petitioning the court to find a suitable home for Rashaun. She was sick and knew she was dying. Ma-D had been to court numerous times and told the judge she felt Rashaun should go with his mother, Aliyah, who was now clean.

Without any forewarning, Ma-D passed away. Aliyah had been completely oblivious to Ma-D's diabetes, and didn't think that it was serious enough to cause death. Aliyah didn't know what to do, but surely Apostle Merriweather, the church lady, and Aliyah's church family took care of everything. It was at Ma-D's funeral that Aliyah's family actually witnessed who Aliyah had come to be. She had honor among the saints. She had love and relationships with strangers that she never had with her own family. Aliyah had enough clout to have Ma-D buried as if she were Princess Di. Ma-D's funeral made a clear statement to Aliyah's family: there was honor for a woman who spent her entire life in the projects raising three generations of children, even if she cursed them out, told them they were no good, and let them use and sell drugs. Shoot, if Aliyah was jumping up and down, running in place with fancy footsteps with her hair flopping from side to side for the entire funeral acting as if this was a party, then there must have been something to this church stuff.

Only, Aliyah knew her peeps-her own family-and their motives. She was careful to let them know there were benefits that come right along with serving God, but God can't be manipulated or pimped. They weren't about to start coming to church so they could milk the church and its people, and infect the church with their vices. Either they wanted God, or they would stay where they were until they were ready to let God take control and be Lord of their lives. Didn't they see that all it took was one decision? Just like that, God transformed her and He was waiting to do it for them. But the Lewis family as they knew themselves, was not about to make the church their ballpark for the next round of games. Aliyah didn't realize that her family trying to work her church family wasn't worth her energy. The fight over Rashaun would quickly take precedence.

Aliyah decided she would not stay in the apartment and only real "home" she had known in her lifetime when Ma-D died. Although the projects were the breeding place for Ma-D to raise three generations of Lewis', she knew she needed to get Rashaun out of the very atmosphere and condition that successfully kept all three generations of Lewis' in the life of drugs and perverse sex. Quinaisha and Aliyah's aunts and brother were not going for her plan. They wanted to have oversight of Rashaun, and Quinaisha was quick to remind Aliyah that she and Ma-D had joint custody of Rashaun.

Aliyah and the church family prayed. The Word of the Lord came. "You will prevail, hold your peace and I will fight your battle." This was one of those services where Aliyah, according to the ministries that teach people to make money and that losing such composure is the flesh or influence of the devil, praised God like David did when he danced out of his clothes. Aliyah shouted for almost an hour, and her infectious praise must have been beneficial for some folks who never hit a gym or exercise apparatus but must have lost five pounds dancing. Church folks have a way of praising themselves into believing the impossible, or believing the impossible so much that it ignites an unquenchable desire to praise God for His goodness.

At the first court date, the presiding judge sent the case back to the judge who had been over the case when Ma-D was petitioning for alternative custodial arrangements for Rashaun. The judge felt that the other judge would have a better grasp of what the family situation was and did not want to start a new mountain of investigation and testimony. At the first and only court appearance in front of the original judge, the judge only wanted to know one thing: was Aliyah still clean and could she provide a home for Rashaun? Aliyah submitted to a drug test, and the church lady told the judge she owned her own shop, Aliyah was an assistant, and she provided complete room and board for Aliyah and Rashaun in exchange for her services.

The judge said he would issue temporary custody to Aliyah conditioned upon her completing parenting classes, and passing drug tests. He said this case was a no-brainer. Although the state had severed Aliyah's parental rights in the past, if the same woman who had custody of Rashaun petitioned the court for alternative custody arrangements for him suggested that Aliyah have him, it was a done deal. Had Ma-D not initiated the case before she passed, the judge stated he might have had other considerations. But, in his years of experience as a family court judge, he found that the only time people reverse themselves is when there has truly been a change. Aliyah was humbled because that day wasn't just a day when she re-gained legal custody of her son, and in the eyes of the law would be viewed as his mother, but it was officially on record in a court of law that she was a respectable human being. Jesus didn't just redeem her soul, but her stature among men was being restored. This time it was with true integrity and respectability.

Aliyah didn't stay in Chicago after her custody order was finalized. She wanted to completely sever all ties with her past. She couldn't afford to be undermined as a parent. So that is when she took Rashaun and made her way to NYC. The only way, Aliyah thought, she would be able to form a genuine bond with him was to get him away from all of the negative influences of their family. So, they hopped a bus to Harlem and never looked back. No one in NYC would ever know their story, unless they disclosed it, because she was brand new, and so was Rashaun. They have always fought like cats and dogs, but no one from the outside looking in would imagine that Aliyah didn't know Rashaun until he was four, and gained custody of him right before they landed in New York. They acted like he supped from her breast for the first year of his life and had been cradled in her arms for hours night after night.

The breakdown in their relationship according to Rashaun and Aliyah started when she began to be sick. Rashaun knew drugs in the womb, rejection since birth, instability and confusion at Ma-D's until the two of them were united. Then when there seemed to be some normalcy for Rashaun, came a stepfather in jail and a mother with AIDS. Rashaun was not only bitter, but fearful of what would happen to him if something happened to Aliyah. Rashaun needed counseling. I urged Aliyah that he could not go on as if his concerns weren't real. I lived a life where all of the love, mashed potatoes, brown gravy and steak could not answer, bring reason, or cause the necessary re-adjustments for my emotions, behavior and corresponding life decisions.

Although Rashaun was a completely different human being dealing with different circumstances, I could feel his pain. Danne would constantly remind me that I can't be all things to all men, and shouldn't take on Aliyah's burdens as my own. I had to be careful of not being captive to the savior complex. Yet, I couldn't sleep at night knowing that God placed people in my life and that I had keys, and wouldn't use them to help them, even to my inconvenience. The fact is, if Aliyah dies, Rashaun will be displaced, again. I remember cringing countless nights, not knowing if Chase was in the system. Someone other than his natural mother nurtured him with love. How much more should I be able to give to Rashaun and Tysheem? Aliyah's children will never be in the system. They will not have to go back to live in a culture that she fought so hard to sever from their existence. Never. She had family like Jesus did. His brethren weren't just the ones that came out of Mary's womb. Aliyah and I had the same Father, and what she was in need of, He could count on me to help her with, if it was within my ability. I needed her just as much as she needed me. I needed to see her blind faith and witness her accomplish more than the double PhD saints could in five seconds. She needed my practicality, wisdom, discipline and ability to teach her basic life skills. Our friendship was completely unexpected for two polar opposites, but it was one that was set in stone.

I'M NOT A LITTLE GIRL ANYMORE
No More Shame

The hours I spent in my own bed weren't long enough. But, the sunlight wasn't an intruder today. It was welcome. Today was another day. And, I was anticipating what could unfold today. *This is the day...I will rejoice and be glad in it. Lord, I thank you so much for today. I am sorry I wasted so many days, thousands of days, looking at the glass half-full. By faith, the glass is full and has everything I will ever need. Thank you for forgiving me and giving me endless days before me. I commit to making the rest of my days, days of hope. Help me to optimize each day and to see your promises fulfilled, so that your glory can be seen in me. I love you, Lord, and thank you for the journey from faith to faith. Lord, I trust you, and want to trust you more and more. Thank you for today!*

I knew it was early, but took a chance to call Chase. I didn't want to go through another busy day without talking to my son. "Good morning. I'm sorry to call so early."

"It's okay Momma. I'm up at at least 5:30 every morning. I'm almost ready for my second meal by now. How are you?"

"I'm well, Chase, and actually hearing your voice makes me feel wonderful."

"Well, get used to it Momma. Evelyn and I were talking, and we want to come up to you and pay a visit."

I wasn't ready for that. I haven't even spoken to my family yet. And, presenting a son who was never acknowledged might be a feat. Oh yeah. I'm living with a full glass. "Okay. I really enjoyed visiting you and was thinking of running down to you as much as I can for now, but if you all want to come up to visit, that will be fine."

"Great. How about this weekend? "

"Sure." He readily accepted me into his world, I should do the same, even if it might include Rashaun, Tysheem and my family. One thing was for sure, I wouldn't be able to avoid my parents much longer and needed to give them an opportunity to prepare to meet their grandson. "You're welcome to stay at my house."

"No, we wouldn't dare. We'll be fine at a hotel, someplace close."

"Chase, you'll do no such thing. You, Evey and the baby will be more than comfortable here. I have a loft with your own bathroom, mini-kitchen and sitting room. You all can have as much privacy as you need. Please, I'd love for you to stay here."

"I didn't know you were rolling like that, Momma. Wow. Ok, we'll save some money and get to spend some quality time with you. I'll get back to you with our flight information."

"Great, I am so excited. Love you Chase."

"Love you too, Momma."

A few days didn't seem like enough time to make everything perfect for Brandon Chase's arrival. I would need help, and it could only be from a friend or family member. I could never allow anyone to have keys or access to the alarm codes to the house. Although Chase's father raped me right under my father's nose in the family home, I still take precautions and have never felt completely safe. So, I never had any staff because they wouldn't have access to my personal space. I never use parking garages, use drive-thrus while in a car by myself, or leave my doors or windows unlocked. I don't do staircases in public facilities, or enter an elevator alone. I don't do hotel rooms close to the elevator, or exit an automobile without my hands firmly secured into my key rings with mace spray. I don't use public bathrooms, and in case of an emergency, have my mace key ring in my hands. The absurd standards I've adopted probably haven't stopped any intruders or potential attacks. But they have helped me to stay sane and know that if something did occur, I would be prepared to fight.

Telling my parents that Chase and I found each other was not going to be easy for anyone. I pulled up to my parent's home and sat parked in the car. They have done so much work on the house to keep its character, and the home still is quaint after all of these years. I really should visit them more often. After all, this is the house that I called home until I was 30 years old. I went to college, medical school, residency and still stayed home. When the rest of my siblings were going away to college, marrying, and starting families, I was a stable face in the Prunell home. I didn't ever want to leave this house and live on my own. I thought I'd stay there until I got married. But, as marriage did not take place year after year, and my siblings kept enquiring about when I am going to move out, I decided to stop their useless conversations.

I didn't get an apartment or buy a house in the neighborhood. I bought a home that I could be happy with if I never moved again. My home was waiting for me. The sale-by-owner transaction took place in forty-eight hours. I drove past the home one day, and knocked on the door. The previous owner had no relatives and was dying. She said she and her husband raised her family in that home, and she wanted someone who would relish the property to have it. I was in a wealthy neighborhood, so was stunned to hear a low asking price of $800,000. Nothing in that neighborhood went for less than two to three million dollars. So, at that asking price, if nothing worked, it was worth me gutting the entire home and re-building. But, I had to do no such thing. Except for a few aesthetic changes, the lonely widow had the house in mint condition. She moved to a nursing home and I moved into the blessing. It became a haven for me, and a place where I could live in solitude and peace.

This wasn't going to be easy for my parents and for me. We never ever discussed Chase. Now, Chase was on his way to meet them. At least, I hoped they would want to meet him. He is my son.

"Hi Ma," I yelled hoping to trace my mother's whereabouts in her own home.

Charelle and Riley were gallivanting through the living room. To see my parents with their grandchildren was so amazing. Their second generation babies could do no wrong, even though they did the very things for which we would get our heads cut off. Grandparenthood is surely a different world from parenthood. My mom watched all of her grandbabies until some one of their parents would pick them up after work. Both of these were light-years apart in personality, but both blissfully in their terrible twos. I hoped we could get through the conversation before other family came over to get them. If this situation followed true Prunell protocol, everybody already knew and was speculating about my trip in a syncopated rhythm. There was probably a consensus about how to handle this situation and I would be apprised of it. I spent a few seconds with my precious nieces, as much as they would allow me to interrupt their pre-track star traipse through Daddy and Momma's house. Watching them was hilarious. The two of them reminded me of how things used to be when we were much younger, running in the safety of the Prunell home as long as my mother wasn't looking.

"Well, little lady, it's about time you showed up." When my father used that type of lingo with me, I knew he was going to go the hard route.

"I'm sorry, Daddy. I know I should've showed up earlier, I just had to settle in and take care of some things before I made it over here." I had enough sense not to mention Aliyah, because that would steer the conversation off the cliff before we got started. Although my parents loved Aliyah, they couldn't appreciate my loyalty to her and her children more than my relationships with my own siblings, nieces and nephews. They measured the parties I threw for my godchildren and extraneous nephews and nieces, trips we took, and kept a pretty accurate score sheet. Aliyah, Danne, and Noey always fared above the blood siblings, and that just wasn't right in their eyes. I admired their protectiveness while I resented it at the same time. Chase was twenty-eight and wouldn't know Grandma's hot chocolate, snacks and full-scale dinner before he ever made it home from school each day like all of the other grands. He wasn't even part of the family.

My mother was overly consumed with monitoring Charelle and Riley. "Hi Ma."

"You ate yet?"

"You know I didn't. Why would I eat when I knew I was coming over here?" Everybody and their grandmother know that my mother throws down in the kitchen. She is a fabulous cook. "I'll pack me a plate on the way out. I just wanted to stop by."

"Now, you're not about to short-shrift your mother and me. Sit down and take your coat off. There's some things we need to discuss."

With all of my professional accomplishments and relative independence, whenever I hear that authoritative tone in my father's voice, it automatically repels me back to my childhood and causes an uneasy feeling in my stomach. This was a good time in my life, a happy time. Things have changed, literally, in one day. I could not spend time unraveling the past and making everyone else understand. Chase and I had been without each other for most of the days of his life. My family would have to get on board and accept Chase. This is what I needed.

"Caroline, we need you to come in here," my father almost yelled. By the time my mother was seated, I coached myself—as I had learned to do over the years—to lift my head and look directly into my parents' faces. "Jewel, is there something you need to tell us?"

My sarcasm trait was trying to manifest its dominance and spew out an answer that could make this entire situation ugly. I immediately thought, *should I have to tell them anything in light of the fact that for years, there was so much that they should have told me?* Thank God for the fear of the Lord and enough good sense to think before I respond. "Yes, Daddy. I hired an investigator to find my son, and he did."

Then came Ma's lovely salty words, "We already know that much. At least we were afforded this information while you were on your way to see them people. Thanks. We feel special." See where I got the sarcasm trait from?

Daddy knows how things end up when Ma and I are left to communicate without intervention. He took the steering wheel again. "Jewel, what I'm getting at here is why didn't you come to us first?"

"Dad, I don't want to get stuck in the logistics. None of us will ever win if we go there."

"Win? This isn't about winning or losing. We are not against you, we are your parents."

"And, with all due respect, I am grown. I am also a mother. I made a parental decision to go find the son that no one in this family ever acknowledged existed. Okay? So, I'm sorry I didn't come and consult, or ask, or notify you that I wanted to find the child that you all took away from me and never ever told me anything about." I felt myself trenched in defensiveness and was fighting to hold back tears. All of the restraint wasn't working. Angry at myself for breaking down, the tears came. "I don't want to be here. I just want to move on and be happy about Chase."

With an astonished look on his face, my father said, "I don't know what to say. Your mother and I never looked at the situation this way."

"This is more than 'a situation' Dad. We're talking about my son's life. Actually, we're talking about your grandson. Your first grandchild. Ameena is not the first. Remember, I carried Chase for nine months."

"Now wait a minute, honey," for some reason, my mother always fared worse than anyone else with this. My mother, of all people, should have known where I was at twelve and has never been able to understand me. She, albeit unjust, was always held to a higher standard. I needed her, if anybody, to know my pain. "We can see you're upset here, but you're not about to beat us up. We did the best we could. What we thought was right."

This conversation needed to stop. We were getting ready to dive headfirst off the cliff into steep drowning waters. "I know you did what you thought was right, what was right for you all, and the family, and the church. For me? That's a whole other story."

"What are you talking about? What should we have done, Jewel? You were twelve years old, you were a baby yourself. You weren't mature enough to handle raising a baby. You didn't even touch him much, if I remember correctly."

"How would you know how much I touched him, or didn't go near him? You weren't there with me to know one dag on thing." At this very moment, after almost three decades of playing this over and over again, I realized something: my mother had never even laid eyes on Chase.

My mom spoke with an authoritative tone, "Jewel, I know you're hurting, but I will still knock your teeth down your throat, watch it!" There was a brief moment of stupor. "Beefi told me you didn't want to be around the baby. We understood that."

I looked at my father. He looked like he didn't know where to go. "I honestly don't know what I wanted at twelve. I know I didn't want a baby. I didn't want any of it. But, it was something that happened. And, I did have a baby. I didn't know how to take care of him, especially when my own mother and father shipped me off to someone else to figure it out, or, not embarrass the church."

"That wasn't our motivation, Jewel. We didn't have the answers. When you told us what happened, we took the steps that we thought were appropriate at that time, to make sure you were safe from him, and that he pretty much wouldn't be around other young girls to do it again."

"Uh huh. Most people think of jail, but I forget we're dealing with the church." I was so upset that I couldn't keep my composure.

"And we tried to make sure that you wouldn't be teased or harassed by anyone else about it. That's why we sent you to Beefi."

"Oh, so I was sent to Aunt Beefi so that I wouldn't be teased? When I needed my mother the most, during the worst time of my life, you all sent me away so people wouldn't tease me? Ok. I buy it. Can we call this discussion over yet?"

"It wasn't just you being teased. It was your brothers and sisters, and the entire situation."

"What situation? That you had a twelve-year-old daughter who was pregnant because of your houseguest? Please. Did it ever occur to you two that something took place out of that situation that I could just not forget? Or overlook? I had a baby. Had you taken the time to help me...Oh yeah, I keep forgetting. I wasn't the focus. You might have figured out how to help me and know what I needed. I never hated my son. I was just scared to death of being pushed into a place in life I was supposed to mature into. You could have helped me with that. You were supposed to help me and my baby."

My father looked weakened. I guess I've had an emotional wall up against my mother for so long, I really wasn't concerned about where she was. Although my mother kept me close to her from the day I returned home after having Chase, I couldn't accept her love. She had abandoned me when I needed her the most. Her affection and attention came too late. I knew it wasn't fair, but it is what it is.

"Instead, you all shipped him off, never said a word to me about him, like I could just forget I had a baby. Then, after all these years, I find out you've known where he's been all along. With his father's family. So everybody walked away from this deal okay, except me. His father raped me, and got a wonderful son. You let an anointed lunatic in the house, isolated me from the family when I needed you all the most, and the mode of operation after that was push it under the rug, ignore reality, and hush hush. And Ma, you didn't have to see me upset the picture you all tried to give the whole world that everything was Jesus Joy perfect. Nope, you didn't have to be discomforted by seeing me have a baby. Remind me to set up an appointment with y'all so I can tell you one day about my labor, at least what I can recall after about ten more years of therapy!"

"Larry, I'm leaving, I'm not going to listen to this. We don't deserve this!"

"Sit down Caroline. And be quiet."

"There you go, you won't be disrespected. I can be displaced. Better yet, your own grandson was wiped out of our entire family, but you won't tolerate some crazy words that happen to be the truth. This is still about you, isn't it?"

"Jewel, I know you're hurting. We never knew just how much. I'm sorry."

Something broke when my father said those words.

"We really did think we made the right decisions for the family. And hearing you lets us know there was a better way. We just wanted to protect our little girl from having to have a burden upon her that she never asked for, and wasn't ready for, had we kept the little boy."

"He has a name, Daddy, Brandon Chase."

"Had we kept Brandon, there is the very real possibility that we'd still be here tonight with you telling us we made the wrong decision. But, we should have done more to consider what you needed. We made a mistake. We're sorry."

I hated to show vulnerability, but I needed my father's acceptance and approval. I know he is a great man. I'm the only one in the family with "issues" about my upbringing and my parents. It doesn't take a rocket scientist to figure out why. All of my other brothers and sisters think the world of these two. That's why every single one of their children have been entrusted to their care as grandpee and g-ma. I went to hug my father. He has been the only covering I have ever known and something about this moment brought healing. My mother was flooded with tears, and it could be for a number of reasons. Who knows. I needed to do the right thing and hug her too, although it was killing me to do it.

"Baby, I'm sorry." I knew she meant it. My mother meant it from the day I told her about the big fat man throwing the pillow over me and forcing his gargantuan penis inside of me. She meant it from the days I threw up and everyone knew my life would change forever. She meant it from the days I couldn't fit into my clothes any longer, and sweat suits became my 24/7 wardrobe. She meant it from the time she couldn't stand to see me in that condition. She meant it from the time I came back home and could look in my eyes and see that something had happened that caused me to look like the void I had in my soul, that her best efforts could not fill. She meant it from the day she felt that silence was the best policy. I knew she was always sorry: she was just in a position that she could not fulfill. She was my mother, and mothers are supposed to be able to make it well.

"I know you are Ma. I know you are. And, so am I." My parents were broken. So was I. There were so many questions I wanted to ask them, but elected not to. They were hurting, and hurt just as much as I did. As my father so capably put it, this didn't just happen to me, it happened to the entire family. I didn't want them to hurt any longer.

"Jewel, we never knew how much…how this affected you. Is there anything your mother and I need to know? Or you need to know from us?"

"I can't really answer that Dad. I've never been here before, so maybe down the line I'll need to ask some questions, but right now, I just want to build a relationship with my son. He's not a baby anymore. He's twenty-eight."

"Born at 12:32 in the morning, December 24, after nineteen hours of labor, he was six pounds, two ounces, and twenty-one inches long." My mother completed with what I had to believe was accuracy. I couldn't even remember Chase's birth statistics. "I walked the floor from the moment Beefi told me it was happening until she called back with a good report. All I wanted to know was that my baby was fine. You were so young, and medical technology wasn't the same as it is now. We were so concerned about you having him on your own. C-sections weren't as normal then as they are now." Who would have thought that Caroline would have known this stuff, more or less remembered after all these years. "I just wanted my baby to make it through and be back home. We wanted it to be over."

"Ma, I've never been able to shake Chase. There hasn't been one day that I haven't longed for him. Not one. I can't explain it, but I've needed to love him and to know his love. His father raped me, and I know I'm jacked up because of all of that. But the one good thing that came out of this, is, I do have a son. We've met and he's known about me and wanted to know me all of his life. God has been good to him. He really covered his own son. I've wasted all this time worrying about him, and he's had a good life."

"You haven't wasted time, honey. You were lamenting and the miracle is that you haven't become like Tamar. You haven't been desolate in the king's house forever. As your father, I did fail to cover you. I should've done the hard thing and made Swanson answer to justice. You've continued to thrive and dared to live until you saw the hand of God move. At least you've never given up."

"He has answered to Justice. He has answered to God. We had the opportunity to speak and he apologized. He's never hidden himself from his wife, or children, and I have forgiven him."

"Wow. I'm so proud of you baby. You actually saw him?"

"Yes, and he was so embarrassed and all of that. I met his wife, and Chase's brothers and sisters, and Chase is married and has a daughter. Can you believe it? I am a mother and a grandmother. You actually have a great-granddaughter named Ruth."

"Do you foresee a relationship with them?"

"Definitely with Chase and his wife and my grandbaby. I can't imagine that we'd ever be at our fullest if I limited it to just him and not the people whom he has known for his entire life. By the way, his aunt who raised him is a piece of funny. She is phenomenal."

"So you are comfortable with dealing with the entire family?" Bishop Prunell was in his make sure everything is alright mode.

"I can't say that I am. I'm not there yet, and don't even know if that is best. I just don't want to limit God and what can happen if we all do what is right concerning one another."

"You never know what life will bring. I never thought you'd be ready for all of this, and we'd ever—"

"Ever what, Ma?"

"Know Brandon."

"Hearing that is good. It hurts a bit, but you're being honest, and that's good."

"Baby, I don't want to hurt you another second. What am I doing wrong?"

"Nothing. To be honest, Ma, absolutely nothing. Your frame of reference has only included your grandchildren who have come from all of your other children, and that's the way it has been. Chase grew inside of me and he never really counted. And, don't get me wrong, we know you all thought it was good that way. I don't really need him to count with you today. I hope that he will, and that things will change and that you will meet him. I need you to do this for me, and probably for yourselves. But even if you don't accept him, I'm here to tell you that I have a son, his name is Brandon Chase Swanson, and prayerfully, one day, you'll consider him to be your grandson."

My parents exchanged a "we have to talk about some things privately" look. I know this was a bit much for them to handle.

They would have to see the grandson they gave away, and our family would have to accept Chase. Sometimes I feel so alone, and this was one of those moments. I know I have King Jesus, but it would be nice to have an earthy companion who could stand with me. Because of Jesus, I'm still able to stand.

"Just tell us what you want us to do," my mother stated.

"Meet your grandson. He'll be here this weekend. He's a great human being, and I still can't believe he's my son. And, he can't believe his momma looks like his older sister. All I'm asking is that you meet your grandson, please. And if you want this to be a private matter so be it."

"What is that supposed to mean?" Ma questioned.

"Everybody knows I'm the old maid without any children. You will have a lot of explaining to do with the church gossips so I'm just saying, if you aren't ready to deal with all of that, you two can just meet him until you figure out the rest."

"That won't be necessary. He is who he is, and we won't dishonor you or him. God will give us the wisdom on how to handle this. Just let us know when he's coming in, and we'll meet him whenever you want us to." Well, Daddy has spoken, and Mother always complies.

"I hope you can learn to really love him, and accept him. Since we're talking, I just thought I'd throw that out there." After what seemed like an eternity, my parents and I tackled the insurmountable. This was just a beginning, but so much was accomplished. They have agreed to meet the one child they never talked about. The glass was really full.

My mother hugged me again, long and hard. "Now, come and eat." A momentous night with my parents could only be topped and delicately finished with a good meal from my mother's kitchen. Although we could all cook, no one does it like momma. We are surprised she can still walk with as many feet as she has put in meals over the years.

I heard a car pulling up and wanted to make a B-line for the back door. Whichever one of my siblings was stopping by for food, to check on my parents or to pick up their kids, I didn't want to explain why my eyes were red from crying. And, I'm sure there was a deeply-entrenched continuance in the silent buzz they have had with one another regarding their sister's rape, and the family's embarrassing unwanted pregnancy.

My favorite brother, Harris, came in, "Whew, it's getting brisky out. Hey girl." He leaned over and kissed me. I tried to dodge a direct look, because I didn't want to re-hash anything with any of them right now. "What's going on?"

"Nothing, I'm actually getting ready to go. I think I'm going to take this with me, Ma. I have an early start and a busy week."

"Jewel, we've been avoiding stuff long enough. You were just getting ready to eat and now you want to run. Your brother already knows. Sit down and eat." I've been a professional at playing the since you're not saying anything, I'll act like everything is copasetic game for so long, that I really would have just picked up and left.

"You're right. I was getting ready to jet out of here." Then I turned my head to look at one of my favorite brothers, "Harris, I'm not ready to discuss this with you all yet. But, I met my son, and if you want to, you can meet him too." I looked up and decided to stare my brother in the face. "Okay?"

"Fine." He mocked the black woman swivel neck thang. "Whatever you say, girl. You know I love you."

"Harris, I'm eating, it's been a rough night," with my eyes swollen, "and I love you too. Can we change the subject?"

"That's cool, cause as soon as you leave here you know Ma's gonna call us and tell us everything anyway." As if he had to say that for me to know that. We all laughed because we know how the family network goes down. Ma can't hold hot water with us. She tells all of us all of each other's business. And, we've all learned, through trial and error, how to act as if we don't know until the owner of the biz decides to tell it, so that we can maintain our place in the unofficial Ma dissemination of all her children's business network.

It's official. The whole family at that very moment, would know within a few seconds after I left the house, or could pull out from the driveway, that Chase was coming to town and I actually met his father.

"Just remember this is sensitive for me, for all of us, and I don't really want to talk about it just yet. So much is happening so fast, and this is good, and I want it to stay that way. Comprendes?"

"Comprendo. Just remember I love you and I'm here for you." Each of my brothers, in their own unique ways, has always been there for me. A brother couldn't stand a five-second chance trying to check me out with any of them. Honor and Ford, the two older brothers, and Harris and Justice, used to block all kinds of play from any guys in school or church. They pretty much blocked action for my older sisters, Precious, Diamond, and Sylva, too. Since I am the youngest girl, and all of my brothers have been overprotective, I've always functioned like the youngest in the family, although I am not. So Ma never had to worry about any of us girls getting caught out there. They had trained their sons to shut down all activity for their sisters. And as far as I know, after a while everybody got the picture. Even after my sisters got older and began to date, Daddy never had to do the subtle threatening stuff. My brothers had grown up prepared to pounce on any brother who messed with any of us girls. They were out of control, now that I think about it.

I would never really know if their fervor came from knowing about the silent invisible elephant that never left any room in our home since the incident. I always felt like I was under a microscope, because I had already known what a grown man's "stuff" looked like. And, although I didn't enjoy it, after he put that pillow over my face, I made myself calm down. I didn't want to keep fighting, and make him stifle the breath that was in my body. I've always wondered if that was the biggest mistake I made during the whole ordeal. Did my behavior send a signal that it was okay? Is that why he began to say a bunch of nasty things in my ears while he sweated and forced his way back into my body? Where was he trying to get to? How was I supposed to follow his instructions to calm down and relax? Couldn't he tell from my tears that I didn't want him? And, when he kept riding me like a bull and I couldn't scream or react, did my behavior make him think it was okay? Is that why he stopped and then went back again? Did my decision to try to relax make him happy? Maybe if I didn't make him happy, he wouldn't have done it again. And that could be when Chase was made. Didn't he know that I hadn't even kissed a boy yet? This could have actually been my own fault.

So were the thoughts I grappled with over and over and over and over again while carrying Chase, and for years later. These shapely hips and buttocks had to be part of what he was looking at. My boobs could hardly pack out an A-cup at the time. Swanson could have gone for any of my sisters, but for some reason, he chose me. I didn't want it and I vowed another man would never be happy because of me, and tell me porn movie lines again. So little did my brothers know, I really wasn't interested in brothers beyond a good laugh. I didn't want any interactions that would make boys or men happy, and give me another baby ever again. Although I felt pretty, but my looks proved to be a problem that brought me unbearable pain. I didn't understand that rape was about exerting control and power over another human being. I never wanted to have a child that I felt powerless to raise, and experience already let me know, that my parents wouldn't take care of or help me take care of my children.

Even after countless men, from the sixteen-year-old boys who would appreciate a good old time with a fine cougar, to the older wealthy man who would have a lot to offer a young woman like me, have made efforts time and time again, I didn't want to even try. Who wants to be trapped in some relationship where she would be obliged to take care of a man who she does not want? I'd seen the extreme. I never want to have to just relax and lie there again, for the comfort of a man. Only a husband should have that privilege. Rape and giving birth to a child that I was supposed to forget was enough to thwart any desire for frivolous meaningless sexual contact.

But, now I know better. Years of therapy unlocked truths for me, and helped me to process things. I learned that it was a defensive reaction for my body to react the way it did by releasing all of those fluids from an orgasmic flow. That wasn't consent, it was the physiological response that many rape victims experience. It was simply a coping mechanism. I am well settled that it will take real love for me to go down that road. Only love can make me relax and want to know a world that almost caused me to lose my mind.

WHEN IT RAINS, IT POURS
The AIDS Roller Coaster

Sleep was beginning to be a time for rest and to refurbish my body, mind, soul and spirit. Today, I beat the sunlight. I opened my eyes eternally grateful for another day. Even though I spent years struggling with the aftermath of one dreadful experience, I always appreciated the value of one more day. All of the Jesus teaching caused me to never be suicidal, although I heard the pleas of torment time and time again. I had a firm "no" in response every time. Stephanie Greene gets the credit for that.

Stephanie Greene and I were classmates since kindergarten. She was a quiet girl, light-skinned, tall and extremely developed for her age. She had a short natural haircut; I used to think her mama was trifling and robbed her of cute hairdos because she didn't want to do Stephanie's hair. Shoot, my mother had eight kids, and combed four heads full of hair every single day of the week. By the time we were in 6th grade, Stephanie often missed school. To tell the truth, I never noticed she was a chronic absentee until the day our teacher brought it to our attention.

Ms. King, a fierce Diahann Caroline type, asked us if we knew any information about Stephanie. Then, her mother came into class one day, and told us she kept running away, and if any of us knew why, would we please tell Ms. King, or write it down on a note. I remember thinking everyone is going to be in her business now. Right before the end of the school year, we found out that Stephanie Greene committed suicide. She had been pregnant and her mother made her have an abortion. Apparently, she had an older brother who raped her repeatedly. He then went off to the service, and Stephanie was pregnant. She wouldn't tell her parents any information whatsoever. It wasn't until she died they found out that she was envious of her brother's new wife, whom he married while overseas. She was "in love" with her brother, and decided to end her life.

Mrs. Greene disclosed what must have been painstaking and embarrassing for her family, so that we would never make the same mistakes. She visited the class and told us, "If Stephanie would have just told me." So, the very next year, when I found myself dealing with blood that did not come from my period, I immediately went to my mother and told who did it. Stephanie Greene's mother may not ever know that her openness to a class of sixth graders during her pain, literally helped me not to ever listen to those voices. I knew that suicide is a permanent answer to a temporary situation, and my parents need to know everything.

So today, I was excited about one more day. I was so far away from the days of needing to remember Mrs. Greene's advice. I wasn't fighting to want to live. Life was suddenly real good. So much was happening, and although it wasn't easy, all of the dialogue with my family, and unraveling all of the ties from my past was necessary. At the same time, I was excited about preparing for Chase's visit. This is the day that the Lord has made. I will rejoice and be glad in it.

Just as I began the daily devotion, I found myself in another precarious position with Aliyah. "Why haven't you answered your phone? I'm about to pass out, I think I need to go back to the hospital," said Aliyah in desperation.

"Okay, call an ambulance."

"Can't you come and get me?" Aliyah has no concept of my other commitments and responsibilities. And, most of this is my fault. Although she is this way with everyone, I allow the monster to be a monster. She acts as if she is the leader of some dictatorship and I'm a lowly subject.

"No, but I'll find somebody. Can you get dressed?"

"No, that's why I need you to come." Here we go again. I wanted to be on time today, and leave work about one hour late, cause I always put in extra time. I wanted to get with Noey and have a real fun evening preparing for Chase's visit.

"You know I need you to stay on top of things."

"Alright, I'll be over in a few. Where are the boys?"

"Rashaun already left for school, and Tysheem is right here."

"Okay, I'm going to have to bring the boys over here because I can't do the back and forth thing right now. My son is coming this weekend."

"Do whatever you have to. I don't care about any of that right now, hurry up, I don't feel good!"

Aliyah has it made. She never asks, or even thinks about her kids and their well-being when she is in and out of the hospital. She knows that among Danne, Noey and myself, we have it covered. If we need to stretch beyond us, Chante will kick in dough, but doesn't do the watching the children thing. She has a daughter who spends most of her time with her father and she is definitely not trying to take on someone else's children when she doesn't even really want to spend quality time with her own. Clean clothes, food, money, transportation doesn't even cross Aliyah's mind. She expects us to handle it, and we always do.

Once we made it to the hospital, obviously she was taken care of immediately. I made sure of that. I asked the emergency room physician to call me with all of her stats and blood work as soon as possible. I already know that Aliyah does not take her medication most of the time, she watches healing tapes and stays in church or prays in God's presence for her healing. All of my pleas for her to take medication go in one ear and out the other. Every single death from AIDS that I have witnessed is in people who did not take care of themselves, did not take medication, did not change their lifestyles, or eating habits. But, Aliyah wanted a miracle. She wanted God to touch her body, and if He didn't do it, it wouldn't be done. This ideology was insane, because Aliyah has no problems going to the doctor when she is at death's door and allows all of the antibiotics to re-build her strength. Nonetheless, I admire her faith.

"Aliyah, I've got to go now. Make sure your doctor calls me with the lo-down. I've got to get into the office."

"What you going to do about Rashaun and Tysheem?"

"I told you, take them to my house. I'm going to ask Noey to pack them up today, because God knows how long you'll be here this time, and see if Danne can get them this weekend. If she can't, they'll be with me."

"I think you better get some papers done and I'll sign em. I need to go back to Chicago and be with Apostle Merriweather. I need to be up under that healing anointing. I'm not dying, or going anywhere, but want to do whatever so the boys will be taken care of."

"Well, unless you have some hidden treasures somewhere, you don't have any money, and I know we'll have to do guardianship papers. I'll give my attorney a call today. When are you leaving?"

"As soon as I get out of here. So when you know I'm getting discharged, I'm going to need you to book me a ticket to Chicago."

Jewel is supposed to dish out more money that I'll never see from Aliyah. She doesn't even think about whether I have it or not, or want to give it or not. What she desires is just supposed to be done. And so I don't have to restrain myself from wanting to strangle her, I don't even expect her to repay. "How about please book me a ticket, or can you buy me a ticket, Aliyah. You don't run my pockets, sick or not."

"Please. And, thank you. You make me—"

"Don't play yourself. Just be quiet while you're ahead."

Now, I had to work Rashaun and Tysheem back into my schedule, and try to keep some sort of continuity with their activities. We've done this a zillion times, so it's no biggie. I called Danne's executive assistant to find out what was on her calendar for this weekend. I have to backtrack with her, because she'll be conveniently busy when it comes to Bebe's kids. I've learned to go with the information at hand to strong-arm her into taking care of her vicarious nephews.

"Here you go again. That's why Aliyah is a maniac and thinks she is entitled to everybody dropping everything whenever she needs it. You cow-towing to her makes the rest of us look bad and unreasonable when we tell her no, with her rude self."

"I know Danne. But you know me. The bottom line is that the boys need to be taken care of, and what would happen to them if we all said no?"

"She'd let them stay in that house by themselves with her ignorant self."

"Yes, she would. And, who suffers in the long run? The boys do. So I already hit up Jeenie and know you're in town this weekend, with no majors. So don't even try it. Can you please help me out with them this weekend? Chase is coming, remember?"

"Well, they gonna be with you anyway, cause I'm gonna be with you and Chase, so what difference does it make? And, Chase is coming and I always have Rona and Charles Ware."

"The boys love being with you. You know they always want to see the who's who, love being uptown, can get away, and please let Chase have one visit without Bebe's kids around. He's staying at the house."

"Oh, that puts a whole nother spin on things. You better tell Rashaun I will knock him out if he even thinks he's gonna while-out over here."

"I ain't got to tell him nothing. He knows you will actually beat him down and I just threaten to do it. He already knows who talks trash and who'll put his head in some."

Everything is coming together. Noey, Danne and I have each other's backs like that. We are just a phone call away, bust each other out, but will do whatever it takes to make sure each other's plans are carried out. Even though I have three sisters and four brothers, all with families, I would have to go through hell on earth to get a "no" from most because Aliyah isn't the only person in the world with AIDS and children. What do the rest of them do? Maybe the people are where they are because they are reaping what they have sown and this is God's judgment. If I would hold back, someone else would step in, or they'd figure it out. Harris or Justice might step in, but the cost is too great for their beefing wives who like to keep their weekend schedules and houses neat and tidy. These are the ways of not all, but too many faithful church folk, who go to church, shout, and do me, mines and ours week by week. They are the same people who want a babysitter to get their nails done.

What a way to start a day at work, but this is life as usual. Or, at least what it is becoming. Although Aliyah gets on our last nerve, and I mean there is no room left for any more aggravation sometimes, we must love her. Love isn't just words. Sometimes it requires a giving of oneself more than we might want to give. But I tend to look at it like this: if I were living with a debilitating condition, would I expect God to plant people in my life, who would look past my personality flaws and spiritual immaturity and go the long haul with me? Would it be because I deserved it, or because God has decided to be merciful? So, let me sow what I expect to reap. Let me give what I expect God to give me in every area of my life. Love and mercy.

Millions of children around the world are waking up every single day, after years of seeing their parents sick and recover, sick and suffer, sick and discouraged, or just plain old sick, and must face the reality that their parents are dead from AIDS. To watch a parent die from a disease that often comes with a stigma is no joke. Although Aliyah isn't the only one I know with AIDS, she is the only one who came from the streets five minutes ago and has completely turned her life around through faith in God. She doesn't have a familial support system, and from her take on the matter, shouldn't try to develop one. She is still fighting to see the rest of them come out of the apathetic lifestyle that makes one immune to the effects of drugs. Her utmost concern is that they will see the grace of God present in her life, so they want to follow her—the Harriet Tubman of her family—out. She can show them the way out, and the only purpose for her communications with them is to do just that.

This sure does change the landscape of plans I had for Chase's first visit. Well, if he wants to know who I am and get to know his mother, this is the way it really is. This is who I am.

CLEANING
More Than the House

I don't know what I was thinking when I asked Rashaun to help us clean up. First of all, not only did he not want to help, but when I think about it, he probably doesn't even know how to clean. His grandmother did everything for him before Aliyah got him back, and Aliyah is a straight slob. Whenever the girls hit the road, she knows I cannot room with her. She thinks Noey and I are literally demented and insane for caring about germs and cleanliness. Who cares about all of this type of stuff? Too much brain power and Jesus time given over to germs is Aliyah's take on the matter. After all, she has slept with half of one urban city, walked the street bare-foot, and never had any major issues, at least she thinks, until she got saved. She walks into a public bathroom and sits down, an action for which Noey or I would need resuscitation. I am the first person who ever told her that she needed to put her backside in the tub every day, and do the same for her children. Rashaun got that message so much that he showers for at least one-half hour. But clean up? That's not happening. He, along with his mother, still hasn't optimized time-management skills or basic responsibilities.

"Rashaun, you might be here for a hot minute. Tomorrow when you get out of school, Aunt Noey is going to pick you and Tysheem up and take you to visit your momma."

"I don't want to visit her."

"Are we going to have to go down this road again? Cause you know where it ends."

"Yo, I'm tired—"

"Yo? I'm not one of your ace boon coon homeboys from the street. I'm really not trying to ride you. You must know that you have to watch who you are speaking to, and make your language choices appropriate for the person you are addressing and for the setting. Do you understand?"

"Yes, Aunt Jewel. I already know all that. I just thought I could be me."

"You can be you, but recognize that I am not your friend. I'm your auntie. So be the you that allows me to be me, and be respected. I don't respond to 'yo.' Now, let's not get sidetracked, you have to see your momma. These visits are for you and she needs to see you."

"Fo what? She don't give a [d***]."

"Did I just hear a cussword in my house? Hello! Boy, you'd better watch your language. You are headed to a place in life where that language isn't going to suffice. So you might as well change it now."

"Whatever. Y'all always talking that smack."

"It's not smack. You think God rescued you from generations of drugs for you to be a grown kid? I don't think so. Better yet, the choice is yours, and it's not going to happen because you're not a fool. Anyway, I need you to go and see your mother, if not for yourself, for her. Did you have something else pressing to take care of?"

"No, I just wanted to hang out."

Aliyah's concept of education is making sure the boys have the best gear to wear so that they don't get played by the rest of their peers. Every time I keep the boys, there is such a struggle to get them to value their education. They practically look at having to go to school as going to jail, and homework as penance. Since no one has ever graduated from high school in their family, according to their knowledge, the benefit of education is something that they cannot identify with firsthand.

"Well hang out with your mother tomorrow. You all need to spend time together."

"What you tryin' to say, Aunt Jewel?"

"I'm not trying to say anything other than what I said. Don't read anything else into this. This is how we should live every day. I could get hit by a bus tomorrow so I need to do as much as I can today. Tomorrow is not promised to anyone."

"I see what you're saying."

"And, I'm not going to bombard you at this moment, but you need to start thinking about what you want to do with your life. You're going to be my age in a minute and believe me, I was your age five seconds ago. Time flies, and time can be your friend. You are not going to go the way of your forefathers. You are different, and I'm not going to lie to you. You are going to have to work hard, never give up, and believe that with God, anything can happen for you."

"You believe that? You really believe that?"

"I know you see me as your mother's homegirl, some bourgeoisie doctor who has it easy. I have a mother and a father in the church, a bunch of sisters and brothers, and everybody has houses, a little bit of money and all that."

"Well, do you know whose coming to visit me this weekend?"

"Who?"

I couldn't believe I was about to be transparent with Rashaun. I've never disclosed our family secret to anyone other than my girls, one friend in college, and my cell group leader, Dr. Tangi.

Telling Rashaun could potentially mean making this information common knowledge. "My son, Rashaun."

"What son? You gotta son?"

"Yes, I do."

"Oh shoot. I knew you were too fine for somebody not to have tapped that."

"Rashaun, my son is twenty-eight years old and stop being fresh."

"Ain't you and Mommy the same age?"

"She is a few years older than me. I had him when I was twelve. And—"

"Twelve? Oh my Gawd! Not you!"

"Yeah. Me. I had a son at twelve, and to make a long story short, I just met him last weekend for the first time since he was a baby."

"Wow. Does Mommy know all of this?"

"Of course she does. The point I'm trying to make to you is that I've battled since I was twelve years old every single day of my life to live a good life. I'm good, but God had to do this, and keep my mind, or I wouldn't be here. Things may look good, but everyone who lives long enough has a story. So, you need to know that it doesn't matter where you begin. Wherever you find yourself, let God be God in your life, and it may not be roses all the time, but with God, you will make it."

"So why have you been battling every day if you didn't have to take care of him?"

"Because I had to deal with missing him, not knowing where he was, what type of a life he had, and a whole bunch of regrets. I didn't have to battle every day, but to be honest, that is just the way it was. I guess the best way to describe it would be to imagine having a pain that won't go away, but you learn to live with it. I spent a long time heavy with things that were already worked out."

"So what are you saying?"

"Learn to trust God while you are young. You've got to fight in life, and know that your own life is worth fighting for. You should check out this poem Langston Hughes wrote, something about his mother let him know that life for her hadn't been crystal stairs. It hasn't been for any of us. You've already been through some things, but look at you now! You are fly and got it going on, don't you?"

"Believe that."

"Good. Now, go see your momma, and since you are going to be here for a while, you and I are going to have to agree on a schedule and what you can and cannot get involved in."

"Here we go."

"Look, I just told you I had a baby at twelve. I'm not about to bug out on you, but you better know that as long as you can be real with me, and be honest, then I'm sure we'll agree on what is best for you. And, that would be to your advantage anyway, because you know the bottom line."

"I don't run nothing."

"Exactly. Not until you get behind the steering wheel of your own car. And, that's after you're qualified to drive. While you're riding with me, you and Tysheem are going to be straight. Now, come here." I had to hug and kiss Rashaun. I have to be careful with him though. Aliyah already told me he has a big fat crush on me, yet, I get on his last nerves. But he craves affection and his mother is so cold with him most of the time. She fights with him night and day, and when she can move past that, he doesn't want to be bothered. I know my love and affection can't answer what he craves from his own mother, but he will know that his Aunt Jewel loves him.

I'll let his mother break the news to him that she is going back to Chicago, indefinitely, and that if anything happens to her, they will be moving in.

"Remember to let your mother know you love her tomorrow when you see her. Don't take her for granted."

I decided to eat my own words and call my own mother. It's time to turn over a new leaf in our relationship. I've always been respectful to her, but kept her at a distance–emotionally. Since the day I was shipped off to Aunt Beefi, I never wanted to need her again. Now that I am older and wiser, there is probably nothing she could have done to alleviate the inherent panic that I lived in each day since I recognized Chase's first kick inside my womb.

The day Chase kicked I felt something fluttering. Even though we all knew I was pregnant, the kick nullified all of the mental calisthenics to which silence and avoidance catered. When I recognized what the kick was, life spoke and said it was forming and coming whether I liked "it" or not, or was ready for "it," or not. "It" was real. This was really happening. The pastor's youngest daughter was pregnant out of wedlock. I couldn't sense Chase's voice fighting to be heard. I could only know the big man, whom my father trusted, with a wife and family still was speaking smut into my ears. And what he did, left something behind that wanted me to carry "it," then have to feed "it," and then take care of "it." Chase was an "it." What was I supposed to do with "it?" Who would help me with "it?" Why even talk about "it?" "It" was keeping me up at night, and as "it" grew, making me uncomfortable most of the time. There was no happiness surrounding "it." No announcements that "it" was on the way, and certainly, no baby shower for "it." When I asked anything, I was told, "Don't worry about 'it.' Everything is going to be fine." Ma is the one who paid the most for not being able to help me process "it." If she couldn't help me with this, then she'll never be in a position in my heart to help me with anything else. Years of a good but strained relationship had to change.

Ma probably never had a clue, or at least let me know that she knew, why I didn't want her or Daddy to be involved in my life like the rest of my brothers and sisters. Diamond was the first to marry. When she announced she was pregnant, the earth stopped rotating for a few fragments of a millisecond. I was excited for Diamond, and like everyone else, went overboard. I was so jealous of her joy during her pregnancy, and all of the attention she received. It's not that I didn't want Diamond to experience the joys of pregnancy and motherhood. I just wished I had been in her shoes when I was carrying Chase.

Just like the first grandchild, Ameena, Carolina, the "second" grandchild, was and still is a beautiful gem. I noticed all of the happiness, excitement, and grandeur. Carolina is a tremendous blessing, and I'm probably her favorite aunt. I spoiled her from the moment she was born. All of the twenty-nine nieces and nephews, and I mean every single one of them, have received a regal reception and are loved tremendously. And, their lives shouldn't have been any other way. They are all unique and precious in their own right. The Prunell family is ridiculously close-knit, and I am probably the only outlier. My pregnancy with Chase, and the complete unofficial omission of it from the annals of the Prunell family, photos, celebrations, christenings, birthdays, and the like was hurtful back then and something that I needed to get over.

"Hi Ma. I just wanted to call and check in on you.

"Twice in one week? To what do I owe this honor?"

"Ma, please save the sarcasm. I'm trying."

"You're right, Jewel. Just tell me exactly what it is you're trying."

"To be more connected, I guess. Well, open is a better word because I've always been connected."

"Oh, I see. Well, I'm glad to hear this, baby."

"Ma, I'm going to say something that I need to say, to get it off of my chest. It's not to hurt you, and there is nothing for you to fix. It's all me, but I've got to let this go."

"I'm listening. Is this something your father needs to hear?"

"You can make that decision. I know I haven't been fair to you. I've resented you for not being there for me, the way I thought you should have been when…when everything happened…when I was raped. I couldn't touch Chase when he was born because I was scared of him, the responsibility of him all by myself, and all I knew is that his existence wasn't a good thing. He was a problem. So, I couldn't allow myself to embrace him. And, I was angry at you for not helping me to love my son. I know this is ridiculous and not on you, but I'm just telling you how I have felt, and why I've pretty much blocked you and Daddy, and any type of love from being in my life."

"I don't know what to say."

"You don't have to say anything. I just want you to know that I hope you and Daddy and I can be closer. I see how you all are with everybody else in the family and I've missed out because I've rejected the love. It has always been there. You just couldn't reach me, and now that I'm dealing with some things, I know it wasn't your fault. I can't continue to blame you."

"This is a lot. But, I'm glad we're talking."

"So am I. God has helped me when no one could. Some things happen in life that no one, not even a mother can answer."

"Jewel, I wish it was me. If I could have taken that for you, I would've taken it. That entire situation was a nightmare. To know what that man did to you. I mean he was a grown man. I'm a woman and to know what he did to my little girl. And then to see you draw back. You used to be so much more engaging. But, you've done well. It is only God that you are who you are today. I just didn't know how to help you. Nothing we did seemed to be enough. And, you know, it's funny. I knew when I carried you, you were a girl. You were the sixth one, and I felt different with you. I guess by the time women are having their sixth baby they think they got this thing in the bag already. But, with you, I kept feeling turmoil. I knew there was warfare against your life from the get-go. Not that the others aren't special, but you were different. Nothing the devil has tried against you has prospered. You may not be as close to me as the others, but I know God has you."

"Well, hopefully we will be closer, Ma."

"We will be. Your dad and I wanted to do something special this weekend for you and Chase. You were right. He is part of you and we want to try and do something."

I guess I'll have to take the "part of me" statement. Hopefully, Ma will say he's part of us one day.

"Like what?"

"It's a surprise."

"Well, whatever it is, please keep it simple and as private as possible. I'm already trying to figure out how to present him to people. This is his first visit, and he hasn't even met anyone yet. He doesn't need to be overwhelmed. I could be wrong, but he doesn't strike me as the fru-fru official grand reception type."

"I'll try my best, but I can't make any promises. We heard what you said the other night. And, we need to look past how he got here. He is your son. You've missed out on too much already. Now, I can't promise you nothing concerning his no good daddy."

"Ma, if I can let it go, you have to let it go. It's not easy, but if I looked that man in his face, and you and Daddy don't have to, you both have to let this go."

"I know, baby. I just can't stand what he did to you. It just doesn't seem fair."

"Life isn't fair, and you know what? That old man has suffered. It was written all across his face. God is in charge, and that was twenty-eight years ago. Had he gone to jail, I'm sure he would have been out by now. And, Chase is his father's son. He's been raised under his influence and teachings in the ministry, and I can tell you about the healing anointing that is on his life. I struggled to see Chase for who he was when I carried him and when he was born, and I refuse to do that to him now. Chase is not his father, and he is certainly not what his father did to me."

"Your daddy and I are shocked by the whole thing; but we are proud of you. I guess it's just time for us to finally meet our grandson. We need to try and do whatever we can for both of you. So, can you allow us to plan Saturday night?"

"So long as Chase doesn't overturn our decision. He's a grown man, and I can't impose us on him if he's not ready."

"Saturday night then, good. I'm sure he'll be fine with it."

In one ear, and out of the other. But, this is the same gumption that the very capable First Lady Caroline raised eight children with. She is ten trips, but she's the only mother I have. And, she has been a good mother. *Lord, thank you for restoring the rela-*

tionship with my parents. Everything the enemy has stolen I'm taking back with the authority you have given. Thank you for giving me back what the strike from the enemy and the pains from the days of my youth destroyed. Thank you for allowing me to see this day of victory. Please prosper all of the broken relationships. Father, let us be one and submit to you so that we can all be healed and set free.

MEET THE FAMILY
Restoration

I can't describe the feeling of seeing Chase. This makes me wonder what it's going to be like to see Jesus face to face one day. I can hardly contain myself just preparing to see Chase, so how much more for the King of kings, and Lord of lords? That, I can only imagine.

Noey, Danne, Aliyah and Chante did a conference call to huddle on who is going to the airport. Really, the call was gratuitous because I already knew who was going. Even though Aliyah's in the hospital again, she still chimes in as much as possible. And, I like to know her take on the situation because she is a mother who has a restored relationship with her children. Noey wanted to come, because she always does the grunge work and get's to ride second. She wasn't having it this time. Chante wants to come because she hates to miss anything although she really doesn't have to be a part of anything either.

Chante is one of the crew who really isn't. We are her only friends, but she really doesn't know how to be a friend to anyone. Chante doesn't ever want to put in time but is the one who shows up and wants to be the mistress of ceremonies. She is the one who'll tell you everything you did wrong, while her junk is straight jacked up. She is very cold emotionally, and we all know why. Immediately after her parents' fatal car accident in the 1980s, Chante went into foster care until she went to live with her grandmother a number of years later. So, Chante looks at the rest of us and has a "man up" attitude when one of us breaks a nail halfway down our finger or a best friend dies. On the scale of trauma and emotions, these two extremes, and anything else that can possibly happen in life, rank the same. So, it is very hard to deal with Chante because her emotions stay on "off" and she expects yours to do the same when you want to punch her in the face. Chante is the type who'll borrow your car, hit it, park it, and act like nothing happened. Or, she'll ask you to lend her money to pay her rent, go on a get-away weekend two days later and act like you are not a cultured person. And not that she'll steal a sister's man, but she is the type who has to let you know that if she wanted to, she could. She enacts this end without words by wearing butt-tight jeans with the thongs showing from the waist, shirts with her complete boob-line showing, and her French-manicured toes with no bunions or corns in some flip-flop shoes. Now tag for tag, she really can't touch us, cause I'm seven years older than Chante and can bring it tighter than she could any day. Cheezy and hoochie is just not my style and unbecoming to a so-called lady who knows Jesus. We talk about her to her face, and nothing changes. She admits she is selfish, ungiving and trifling. Yet she is who she is. Most times I don't even understand why I put up with her.

Danne didn't have to really say anything because she knows that I would not cut my foot to spite my hand. She knows she will definitely be on the trip. After all of the rigormoroll, I let the crew know that Danne and I would go and everybody else could come to the house later. I am just getting to know Chase, and since he already met Danne, I think it would be better to just stick with what we know has worked well so far. Of course, I want all of them to meet Chase. After all, my girlfriends have been my support system for most of my adult life. They were the gab gals, the ones who I confided in, and trusted. These had been proven and tried. They were solid, set in stone. We all know the good, bad and the ugly about one another. So, I realize Chase coming to visit shouldn't be just about me and him. I've kept these Negroes up for years while yearning for this day. So really, they were just as amped as I was. Chase was on his way to New York.

Waiting for the flight to land seems like a short eternity. "I don't know why I'm so nervous, Danne. It's not like we didn't already meet…just a week ago."

"Probably because it's his first time to New York and you really don't know each other well enough to be completely comfortable yet."

"True. And, probably because I'm hoping that everything goes well…that he'll have a great time, love his new family and we'll keep working toward a healthy relationship."

"There you go, Jewel. That's a done deal. Chase is stand-up. He's an Ace. He's been waiting for you just as long as you've been waiting for him."

"As usual, you do make good points…There he is, pull up!"

I jumped out of the car to embrace my son. There is nothing that can describe this feeling of fulfillment and hope.

"You can put your bags in the trunk. Is that all you carried for a weekend?"

"Yes, Momma."

"Is Evey still inside with my precious grandbaby, Ruth?"

"No, she opted not to come."

Opted not to come? What does that mean? "Is everything Okay?"

"Everything is fine. She just felt this time, it might be best for you and me to spend some time alone. She really hated to give up the prospect of you treating her to a shopping trip, but hoped that you and I could just really get to know one another. That's all."

And here my friends and family are all lined up to meet them this weekend. "Okay. So long as you being here is ok with her."

"It is ok Momma. She knows how much this means to me. And besides, she didn't want to leave Pop and all of that just yet. You know, everyone is making adjustments, and she's at home with Pop so I could be with you." I didn't really understand that, but decided not to ask for clarity. All of this was really not my business.

"Well, I'm glad to see you, and to be honest, since I thought you and Evey were coming, my friends and family planned quite a weekend for us, but all of that can change. What matters to me, is that you are here."

"Momma, I want to meet everybody. We can do whatever you want, so long as I can get about two hours of sleep before I get back home."

"Could you two get in the car? We can smooch on the way home," Danne interjected while yelling through her car window.

"Welcome to the family!"

When we pulled up to the house, I fought to hold back tears. Who would have ever believed that the baby that we gave away twenty-eight years ago would be coming to the place that I called home and calling me "Momma."

"Now, I'm warning you right now. My friends are loving and crazy; your family is crazy and loving. We've been waiting for you for a long time, so if we act crazy and loving, forgive us!"

"Bring it on, Momma."

Noey acted just like Noey. "Hey Chase. Where have you been all your life? It's about time! I'm your Aunt Noey." And she leaned over and gave him a big hug.

"Hi, I'm Chase."

"Is Chante here yet?" I asked.

"Now you know the answer to that. She'll be here probably about Monday or Tuesday." Noey explained, "Chase, that's another one of your aunts who'll be late to her own funeral because anybody who knows her will have to think about how late she always is, and the time spent thinking about that alone is going to make them roll her body in late. Everything about her is late."

"Now, that is the truth. Chante is always late, but she'll show up on the scene at some point in time," I clarified.

Rashaun surfaced from the basement. "This is Rashaun and Tysheem. They are my godsons. Rashaun and Tysheem, this is my son, Chase."

"What's up." This was Rashaun's best attempt at being cordial and socially adept.

"Hello, Rashaun is it?"

Tysheem was shockingly forward, "You can call me Ty."

"His momma and I are best friends and they spend quite a bit of time with me. But, they'll be hanging with Aunt Danne this weekend, right Rashaun?"

"Yeah, whatever." I had no choice but to ignore that response. Chase didn't need to see me go broke five minutes into his visit.

"So, let me show you the loft, and after that, Rashaun can show you all that video, Wii, PlayStation III and game room stuff we have downstairs. That's where the men tend to end up around here."

"Okay. I do enjoy the Wii, but I can play games anytime. I am here to spend time with you, so you let me know what you want to do, and that's what I'm doing."

Why haven't I met a man like my son yet? "Okay. Do you want to eat in or go out?"

"I just said I'm doing what you want to do. I just want to let Evey know I made it and settle in, and we can do what pleases you."

Again, why haven't I met a man like my son yet? "Since we're going out tomorrow night, let's all just eat in. Noey is a great cook and we'll both whip up something real quick."

I showed Chase the loft suite and then proceeded to the kitchen. Noey had already had two homemade pans of lasagna in the oven, some sautéed string beans on the stove, a fresh garden salad, and Italian bread.

"Sit down, Jewel. I've got this. Jayden is already on his way over here with the girls, and I told him to stop at Paneche's and pick up a large fresh fruit tart and some tiramisu and a key lime pie for dessert. It's not a five course meal, but hey, it'll do."

"Thanks so much, girl."

Dinner was great. The food was great, and Danne, Noey and Chase talked as if they'd known each other for fifty years. Jayden, Noey's husband, and Chase also seemed to hit it off. Jayden offered to take Chase to play indoor racquetball first thing in the morning.

"I'd love to show you how a southern man humbly puts a northern man in his place, but, I'll see what my mother is doing." Chase even knew how to engage in the machismo egotistical lingo with Southern charm.

"Who, Jewel? She can come and watch this northern man have some mercy and not totally annihilate you, so that you will play with me again. But, know this, you are going down brother. You are going down." Jayden had such confidence that he would beat Chase, that Noey and I began to spark interest.

I challenged Jayden like any proud mother would. "You want to play Chase, I'm there."

"Game on, then," Chase concurred.

"Six am. And don't be a second late for your beating, Chase," Jayden retorted.

So, we made it an early evening to rest up for the racquetball match. For the first time, Chase and I really had the opportunity to be alone. I figured it was time to get to know one another. "So, um, tell me about yourself."

"There's really not that much to me. You've seen how I live. You know, most of my life is about the ministry and Evey and Ruth. As a matter of fact, I don't think I've ever missed a Sunday outside of when Evey and I got married and went on our honeymoon. And, I did stay home for two weeks straight when Ruth was born."

"Really?"

"Yup. I pretty much don't want Pop to be burdened with carrying the ministry by himself. He counts on me the most out of all the elders, so I'm always there. I don't even think I've ever even considered doing too much of anything where it would trouble with my Sundays. And, you know Pop is getting older now, so—"

"Exactly how old is...Prophet Swanson?"

"Oh, Pop will be seventy-two in a couple of weeks."

"Seventy-two?" I repeated as I quickly did the math. *He must have been around forty-four when he raped me.*

"You didn't know how old he was, huh. What do you know about my father?"

"Nothing really. I just knew his name, he had a wife, and some children. And, of course, he was a powerful prophet. That's about all I recall."

"Do I make you uncomfortable when I talk about him? Do I make you uncomfortable?"

"Not really. I'm not at ease, but I'm not exactly uncomfortable either."

"You're not at ease with me or talking about my father?"

"I'm definitely not at ease with talking about Prophet Swanson, but I'll learn to be good with it. I can't expect to walk into your life after twenty-eight years and expect things to be different. And, to be honest with you, I really wouldn't want to try and touch what you have with him. Since you asked, I'm being honest. But I don't want anything to stand between us. We've already missed out on so much."

"I know. Pop is concerned about my relationship with him changing. He wanted me to come and be with you, but couldn't help thinking that if I find out more about you, I'll resent him."

"Well, you can let him know this isn't about him. After all we've missed out on, this is certainly not going to be about him. Sorry. I will never be happy if I know you've developed a resentment toward your father because of me. He doesn't have to worry about me messing up his relationship with you. I just met you last week." I felt my blood pressure rising. "And, I don't even know him, for goodness sake." The reality finally hit me. I actually have a son with Prophet Swanson.

"I don't mean to upset you, sorry."

"I'm good. I really am. Just take me in stages and we'll never go wrong. I mean, think about how ridiculous all this is. How can I possibly threaten a twenty-eight year relationship? I may take a few minutes to get adjusted, and may never be fully comfortable with your dad, but I don't want to interfere with anything about the two of you. I'm the one who needs to be jockeying for position, if anyone. Since they took you away from me when you weren't even six weeks, I haven't gotten a piece of information, voluntarily from anyone about where you were and he's had the knowledge and ability to reach out to you like it's nothing. If anyone should be tripping, it should be me. But, I'm trying not to harbor any ill will, nor do I want to compete with someone whom I can't compete with if I tried."

"Who took me away from you? I always thought you didn't want me, because of the…story. I knew you loved me, but was told you couldn't raise me."

"I couldn't raise you by myself. I knew that the moment I felt you kick. I was only twelve. I hoped that someone would step in and help us to bond, not simply take you."

"Who took me, or gave me away?"

"It's funny, I can't truthfully answer that question. I don't know. I just know when you were only a few weeks old, you were gone and after my six-week check-up, I was on my way back home. No one asked me any questions. They just took you to have a better life and I was supposed to get back to a normal one."

"Wow. So where did this 'you couldn't take care of me' come from?"

"Chase, think back to when you were twelve. I was twelve and everything I had known about life changed just like that. I just didn't know how to cope. Looking at you made me scared.

Overwhelmed is more accurate. You were for real, not a doll or something that would go away. I didn't have confidence in myself to do it on my own, and I presumed, which may have been wrong, that no one else wanted to help because of how things went down."

"What do you mean by how things went down?"

"Chase, there are some things that a child should never hear his momma say. I can't really go there. Just imagine what my family must have felt like knowing that I was in the predicament your father put me in. It wasn't a pretty situation."

"So I made you uncomfortable."

"That is putting it mildly. It wasn't the essence of you that was the problem. Something in me loved you despite the fact that just about everything about your coming and arrival should have said otherwise. I've always loved you, but it was difficult. I had hoped that my aunt or grandmother or somebody would've taken you until I was about sixteen or seventeen and got out of school. But, of course, things ended up quite differently."

"What about your parents. They didn't want me?"

"I can't say that. You might be surprised, or maybe not, to know that before I found you, I can't recall ten minutes of conversation with your grandparents about you since the day…well, since you came to be. The whole situation is something we just didn't talk about. If you want to know the truth, I went through the entire pregnancy without any talk about it, about you, about anything. At least, I don't remember anything at all about it. It was just like I needed to wait things out until you came."

"Until I came and then what?"

"I believe they wanted to do what they felt was best for me, and like most parents, thought I probably wouldn't want to raise a child I didn't…ask for, or reminded me of what happened. So, I can't say their decision was based upon not wanting you either. But I can say that not one day since the day you were born, as a matter of fact, since the day I knew you were coming, that you haven't been the greatest concern of my heart. You changed my life and if you can imagine what having Ruth has done to you and Evey, you can know what having you did for me. The inherent bond has always been there; we just weren't able to cultivate it. I'm just so grateful to God for the opportunity we have now. God didn't author the situation that got you here, but you are here, and besides Jesus, you are the best thing that has ever happened to me. Just watching you stand in my house—your house—is a miracle."

"My house? This is a house, so don't play." We had a brief moment of laughter.

"So, you never had any other children."

"Not yet. Maybe that may change one day. And it'll probably have to be real soon."

"This is amazing, Momma. I've always imagined that you loved me but that you probably had a whole bunch of other kids, moved on with your life, and maybe one day I'd meet somebody in our family. I dreamed one day I'd run into a brother or sister and maybe even find you. Wow. This is 'the more than that' only God can give."

"That's funny you've imagined me with a bunch of kids, I'm the only one that doesn't have any."

"You don't have any? What am I?"

"I'm sorry Chase, I didn't mean it like that. Really, I've been living as if I didn't have a child, at least to those on the outside looking in. And, to the family for that matter. But, I've always remembered you. Every single day. I thought you were adopted and…well, it really doesn't matter, because you are here. Can we just work with the time we do have? One thing I know about God. He knows all things. Solomon came from the wife that David really should have never had. David repented, and through Solomon, Joseph came to be the father of our Savior. Rahab the harlot was also in the lineup. So was Jacob, the trickster turned man of God. These are the truths that helped me to fight and believe that one day I'd find you, and you would be a good Godly man. It's not about how you got here, the fact is you did."

"I'm sorry you had to go through the pain you did for me to be alive. You may not have been around, but I'm grateful that you and your parents didn't stop me from having life."

"That was never an option. I can't stand here and lie to you. There were times when I wished I would have miscarried, so that the pain would go away and the torment would have been over. But once you started growing and moving, that was over. I was scared and almost out of my mind, but knew better than to touch God by touching you."

"So how did you make it?"

"God, Chase. God. There is no question about it. When I couldn't talk to anyone, I talked to God. I listened to music. There were days I couldn't get up out of my bed, and a song would do it. Then there were all my days of Sunday school, and all that I had known about God through the Word. Just feasting on the Word of God. Praying and crying out to God to keep me, and to heal me. No one can get His glory on this. Only God kept my mind. My Aunt Beefi took good care of me. So, don't think for a moment I was out there. I was in the fiery furnace, but did not get destroyed. I saw the flames. I felt the intensity of the heat, but I was insulated from it. I saw the darkness. I knew the doors were sealed to bind me. But, I saw the light. The keeper of my soul, kept my soul. Chase, no one could reach me but God. I was so lost, that only He could do it. And, He took me, just as I was, and kept me. So know that your momma does know Him. Chase, I know Him and He is my everything."

"I know the Keeper Momma. He's the Comforter. He spoke to me immediately when I found out the truth about you. He let me know that I could trust Pop. I thought for years, that you were in a home or in jail. I knew you loved me but couldn't take care of me. So, why else wouldn't you be there unless you were locked up or on your back somewhere? So, I asked Aunt Catherine to take me to visit you, and she said that wouldn't be possible. She knew exactly where you probably were but called Pop to come and explain the rest."

"And what did he say?" This was the million-dollar question.

"He started off by saying that all the years of planning what to say still didn't prepare him for having to say what he was about to say. That he loved me, and nothing would ever change that. And, that he prayed that I would still love and respect him. He reminded me of how he often referred to the dark days of the ministry and how God had brought us through. Well, he had fallen in ministry when he conducted a crusade. He was at the home of a friend and had been away from home for at least a month or so. He had been watching pornography for years, and had the taste for younger petite women. One night after service, he says something came over him, and before he knew it, he had his way with one of his friend's daughters. He understood what it means not to be at ease in Zion. There was such a great move of God that night, someone who came out from a hospice on a stretcher ran around praising God. He had been used to seeing the miraculous, and didn't think that he needed to be delivered himself. God was using him, so everything was good. But, he didn't know what came over him. There was such great lust and you were the youngest and probably the weakest. He took what he needed and the next thing he knew, he realized what he had done. He had to come home and faced Ms. Edie, the general board of Bishops and almost lost the church. The entire family was humiliated, and most people left the church, especially when they found out it was a young girl he fooled with. Then a few months later, he got a call to come and pick up his son. He didn't think it would be fair to ask Ms. Edie to have to raise another woman's child, although she was willing, and the new protocol he followed required him to have personal accountability. I don't think Pop has been on the road since then. And, he pretty much tells all the ministers to travel with their spouses, if possible, and not to commingle with people outside of the purpose of ministry, to fellowship and go back to the hotel rooms, alone."

Chase, let me make something clear to you. Your father did take my innocence. But it wasn't freely given. He forced me to have sex with him. It was not just him having his way. These words ran through my mind. I wanted him to know that this was a rape. But, Prophet Swanson already repented, and it was under the blood. And, knowing this fact did not help Chase. It only served my own interest in everyone knowing I wasn't responsible. Humility said to shut my mouth and leave that alone.

"Did he say anything else about me?"

"Not really. I can only recall him saying that you were a young girl."

"Oh."

"So, he let me know why I stayed with Aunt Catherine, and because of the fact that his relations with you weren't appropriate, he thought it would be best to leave you alone. Your people gave me to him and Aunt Catherine, and he promised he would do right by me, and he would keep his promise. And, if you wanted to, you would reach out to me."

Wow. He sounded like an honorable hero martyred for his criminality.

"Would you like to go to the lake or something? I need a change of scenery. Some fresh air or something." I often drove to the lake by my home to sit there for hours and look at the water. I didn't have to hear those words to know that I was absolutely nothing to Chase's father, but hearing it was devastating. My only sexual contact with a man was really what it was: violent, demeaning, and absolutely meaningless. And, I guess he did do a good thing. He really didn't have to take Chase. He could have given him up.

"It's getting late and you need to be up on your game to beat Jayden. He's good at racquetball. And, you have a large family here too, you know. I had to keep them away tonight, or else fifty people would've been at the airport, and that's just the immediate family."

"Momma, I know this is hard for you. But now it is going to be good."

"I believe that, Chase. There's just one more thing I'd like to know. Who named you?"

"Pop. I don't know who named me Brandon. That's the name Pop said I came with. He re-named me and added Chase, hoping that I would Chase after God, take up my cross and follow Him. Wherever He leads me, I'd follow."

"Phenomenal. Now I get it. I couldn't figure out what inspired your name."

"Can you let me know what your expectations are?" Chase inquired.

"For us to get to know one another. And, for us to be as close as possible. And, you know, when Mike told me he found you, I realized that you're not in need of a mother. You're a grown man with others who have 'mothered' you. So, it's probably safe to say I'm too late for that. And besides, your wife and I are what, somewhere around seven years apart? It would be kind of crazy for me to think I be a mother to you at this point. I hope that you and I can respect one another and be friends."

"That sounds good and I'd like to work toward that too. But remember, Momma, some grown men all over the world still have mothers. For what it is worth, you are mine."

Wow. Tonight's conversation was something to think about. Men Chase's age and even younger have tried to woo me. And for Chante, she'd be all over someone like Chase. Life is funny. Normally, I would never look at a man a couple of years shy of thirty and think that he could view me as a mother figure. Maybe a big sister, but a mother? With the dating trends of women our age because of Black man shortages, someone Chase's age is a viable catch. I'll have to wrap my mind around the reality that had things been different, I would have been one of the primary persons who influenced Chase in life. Twenty-eight years of would-haves, could-haves sure do play out differently in reality. Clearly, Chase was looking for us to have a substantial relationship. "Momma" was not just a salve.

RESTITUTION
Healing All Around

Chase soon found out that people in their forties can stand up to a trim and fit young man any day. Chase got a taste of Jayden's stamina on the racquetball court. Jayden played like two hours were two minutes and he was just getting warmed up. Chase bowed out like a dignitary after Jayden's bragadocious sportsmanship reached unbearability. My innate loyalty to Chase had me acting quite unseemly for the reserved Jewel, screaming and hollering although it was clear Jayden would cream Chase after the first few plays.

Chase and I decided to rest at the house until the mini-grand dinner party Lady Caroline was planning. I normally don't do too much phone time with any of my siblings, but today would be an exception. I wanted them all to hear it from my own mouth that Chase was in town and to let them know how important he is to me. If I reached every single one of them, and spent ten minutes on the phone with each one, I'd have over one hour of talking to do. And, there was no way any single one of them would let me off the hook in ten minutes after almost three decades of dealing with Chase's existence through tacit means.

I'd start with Harris, Ford, Honor, and Justice. My brothers were always easier. For some reason, I never care to discuss anything at all with my sisters beyond our parents and their children. Our lives have been so different. And, I've been comfortable with this especially since the day my sister Diamond bruised my heart. I've learned to stay out of the line of fire.

When my niece Carolina was a baby girl, Grandma Caroline and I took care of her while my sister and her husband worked.

Although I was in high school, I ran home as soon as possible because I couldn't help but love my sister's new baby. She was so pure and had eyes of hope of what she may find in the big world in which she found herself.

One day when Diamond picked up Carolina, Diamond fussed because I hadn't given Carolina the baby food she packed. Little did Diamond know that Ma had been feeding Carolina fresh ground veggies. I explained to my sister that Ma raised all of us and we turned out all right, and besides a pediatrician said don't fuss if babies don't stick to a regimented diet and schedule. Before I could finish explaining, Diamond said, "God knows exactly who to give children to, Jewel." She said so much more, but I couldn't recall it, because I didn't hear it. A dagger went straight through my heart.

I knew then, that Diamond, along with my other sisters, really just didn't understand who I was, where I was, and what I had been through. I acted as if nothing happened. And, so did my mother and everybody else in the room. I couldn't believe she would go there. Over the years, I'd come to learn that none of them thought they were going "there." "There" didn't exist to them. It was just a destination in my own inner sanctum, kept behind some very concrete emotional walls. I couldn't relate to the joys and pains of motherhood or marriage. So as the complete women carpool crew grew closer, I remained in the periphery. My greatest value checked in when they needed a check, check-up or a weekend sitter.

"Morning Harris. Are we going to catch up later this evening?"

"Now, you know I am. Sabrina and all the kids will be there. You know nobody is going to miss tonight. At least miss it and survive missing it. Do you need me to do anything?"

"No, not really. I just wanted to let you know for myself that I found my son, and we are both very happy."

"I can't believe it girl. The only thing missing is cameras for reality TV. I can show up with foil over half my teeth to make it look like a real grill. We want Chase to feel right at home." Harris can make an assassination of a national hero look funny with his sense of humor. He got clobbered with the funny bone and never knows when to stop.

"He'll feel at home if you just be yourself. So how about you be you and that should suffice. Wait a minute, that goes for everybody else but you. You need to be on your best behavior. No, on my best behavior. I'm hoping that you all will be happy about it as well."

"Well, that goes without saying Jewel. You know we're going to do him right."

I hope so.

"You do know that, don't you?"

"I hope so. Forgive me if I'm a little nervous. It's hard for me to imagine everyone just being so elated about a family member that disappeared and no one talked about for almost thirty years."

"It's really not that hard. If that's what you're calling for, get some rest girl. We've got this. You're right, we haven't talked and all of that. But you didn't talk to us either. I didn't want to bring up anything that you might have been trying to forget."

"I did talk, but to Ma and Daddy, and after getting shut down a couple of times, left it alone. But, that is neither here nor there. I feel much better after talking to you. If you say you got me, then I know it's going to be okay for us."

"Jewel, you don't have to worry. God got this, and so do we. You know we all got together on this already anyway. You know how Ma is. Now get off my phone and I'll see you later."

"All right. Love you."

"As a matter of fact, what is my nephew doing now?"

"Nothing, he just finished playing racquetball with Jayden."

"Okay, I'm not even going to go there with you. How you got my nephew all up with your friends before you brought him to the family? How does that happen, Jewel?"

"It wasn't done to put you off, or anything like that. It's just that—"

"Can we swing by and pick him up? Ford and Justice are on their way over now to watch the game."

"I'll see if he wants us to do that, hold on."

"Jewel, I didn't invite you, boo. We gonna watch the game and you know good and well that's not you, so find out if he wants to watch the game."

I could be the President of the United States of America, and my brothers will still think they can tell me what to do. Chase, of course, went to watch the game. I knew he was in good hands. Anyway, he is a grown man and can handle himself.

Since Harris apprised me of the Prunell pipeline in operation with Caroline at the helm, the only thing left for me to do was to relax and get ready for this evening. Maybe Noey and I can mix things up tonight. I decided to hit Noey's closet. She is always crying broke but stays with the latest gear. We tried on about fifteen outfits, and nothing seemed to do it. Tonight, I'll trust Noey and go out on a limb with what she thinks looks good on me. I've been so used to covering up everything all the time, I almost felt like a fish out of water with the knee-length knitted black dress we selected. It hugged the hips and thighs a bit too much for my taste, but I decided to be a bit daring tonight.

Like Noey said, "You don't always have to look like Mother Theresa or the Bishop's wife. You're single."

"But I'm not trying to have that look tonight. How am I going to look like I'm sizzling hot at forty and oh, uh, by the way, please meet my twenty-eight year old son?"

"Jewel, are you determined to punish yourself forever? Why can't you be comfortable showing some of what you've got? Look at me. How you think Jayden got locked in? And, you know I didn't give it up. But, he noticed some of what he had to look forward to, and can't stay out of, let the truth be told."

"I just don't want to have to show my stuff to attract somebody. I want somebody who is not primarily interested in a cute face, big butt and hips. I want somebody who is concerned about the real me."

"Ok, stay in la la land if you want to. You know I love you enough to come visit you every now and again. But the reality is, clown, men are attracted to women. They have to like what they see. And, I'm not saying to flaunt what you've got, just accentuate it, and don't cover every inch of it up. Jesus!"

"You sound just like Xavier. He used to harass me with the same junk. Whatever happened to modesty? Whatever happened to men valuing that? Unless a brother is legally blind, if he sees me, he can see the back, the legs, the hips and everything else. I shouldn't have to parade it. I think I look good."

"I'm not saying you don't look good. You are banging. But you can afford to change the image a bit. It's too…too…boardroom, church hostess, he-ka-na-shunda, okay? All I'm saying is lighten up a bit."

"I'm trying. I'm wearing that tight black dress aren't I?"

"Fitted, not tight. It's all in a word babe, all in a word. Praise Jesus for everything. But this is not a he-comin-ona-hunda moment. We are going to feast, fellowship and celebrate just like God intended. And you need to look good."

"Fine. Nobody but my family is going to be there anyway, so it really doesn't make a difference."

"You never know, always be prepared. Let me talk the language you understand, 'be ye also ready.'"

Noey does do practicality well. She managed to get a great husband who worships the ground she walks on. Literally. Jayden visited Noey every single day when she carried their firstborn, Lissa. Noey was on bed rest in a hospital about one hour away from Jayden's job. Nothing stopped him from leaving his job every day and going to bring his wife dinner. Jayden paid Noey's hairdresser to do her hair in the hospital, on bed rest. For what?

I don't know. I guess so Noey could continue to look fierce for her visitors. And if that's not enough, Jayden painted his wife's toenails—yes he did. He made sure that she felt as good as possible while she lay on her back for eight months to carry Lissa. So Noey must have done something right to remain a virgin and still snag a winner like Jayden. The man has A-1 credit and has been working at the same hospital for nine years as a physician's assistant. Chante, Aliyah, Danne and I all told Jayden, it is because of him that we still have hope that we could one day be happy with a brother. He puts up with all of Noey's craziness, and her putting up with all of her girlfriends' craziness. Jayden has found himself, many a nights, driving in the middle of the night to pick up Rashaun or even to meet me at the side of the road until the AAA truck arrived. If Noey got a winner, then God will bless me with one too. I won't compromise. I can't compromise. And go figure. The man doesn't run around the church or ever grab a microphone. He comes and goes but lives the life.

I had to find out what Chase thought of my brothers. "So how was the game?"

"You know I didn't go over there to see the game. I couldn't care less which team won. I did have a fantastic time though. My uncles are cool. You didn't tell me all my uncles are in ministry. We are definitely going to be doing some things together."

"Every single one of your aunts and uncles is in ministry in some way or the other. They all sing, every single one of them. Even your granddaddy sings. And, I guess Ma can hold a note too. All the boys preach, and so does Diamond, when Daddy puts her up. But the baddest one, if you ask me, is your aunt, Precious. When Daddy made her the Head Musical Director, I thought the Prunell brothers would next to faint. Girlfriend plays that organ and sings her neck off."

"And what do you do?" Chase asked. All of a sudden, I felt like I wasn't just talking to my newfound son, but the church Elder.

"Go to church," I responded.

"How is it that all of them have all these talents, and you mean to tell me my momma is just a bench warmer?"

"Not at all. I'm not a bench warmer. I'm a faithful parishioner. I can still sing, I just don't do the solo or choir thing. I stopped that a long time ago. I sing every week from the pews. Everybody can't be on the microphone and God loves to hear me sing. The audience that matters is always listening."

"And why would you do that if you are a leader?"

"After I had you, I had to take a break, and catch up on schoolwork, and never went back. I just wasn't interested anymore. Everybody has a good job or career, but I am a doctor. I spent years in college, med school, then did my residency, and then worked for a few years on staff at Cornell Med until I started my own practice. There aren't enough hours in the day for me to do all that and still be as involved in church. Besides, with all of us, and all the other people in the church with gifts and talents, mine hasn't been missed at all. There are hundreds of non-Prunells sitting in the church for years that God is using too."

"We don't render gifts solely because they are needed, and everybody should get a fair shake. We need to render our gifts for our own survival and His pleasure. We've been made to bless the Body. This is who we've been made to be."

"Trust me, Chase. I may not pick up the mic, or play the organ, or direct the choir, or preach a message. But, I preach every day with the choices and decisions I make to let other people see Jesus in me. I am preaching with my life. As a matter of fact, I want to stop by and see my girl in the hospital before we go to meet the family tonight. I've been rendering my gifts, talents, time, money and if she could use it, my own blood for my girl and her boys for years. She's not the first, and they probably won't be the last. What God has blessed me with, He can trust me to give any to all of it freely to anybody who needs it so that they can see Christ. So, everybody plays their part in the body. I play mine too."

"I hear you, Momma. But all of that still does not account for why you shut down using your gifts and talents in the church."

"I've never gone back in that direction. I can't explain it. It is what it is. And, Aliyah is saved and part of the church, the body of Christ."

"All right, Momma."

I guess I never really did contemplate how long it's been since I've been involved in the organized fellowship. After I left to go down south to have Chase, I never went back to the usher board or sung in any of the choirs. Between trying to catch up and get skipped back to the right grade and staying out of church social settings, I just did Friday night and Sunday morning good church member services. Although I've always loved and supported Restoration Tabernacle, I've never really gotten back into the thick of things since the church has grown so much.

Once I put on that black dress with the makeup and hot-to-death shoes, I almost felt like someone else. I always feel comfortable about how I look. Appearance has a lot to do with how many people will accept and treat you. It's pretty safe to say I've never wanted to be viewed for my assets because I didn't want, or know what to do with attention to them.

There aren't that many, but enough memories of boys and men trying. Trying to be nice. Trying to relate. Trying to enjoy my company. But I was always waiting to see how long they would stay in that mode before they tried for more. And, I tried to be accommodating to the more. I wanted to be normal and want to kiss, or think a boy putting his hand on my inner thighs meant he really cared. But, those caresses didn't last for long. They were repulsive, and made me cringe. The only man I've ever desired or wanted was Xavier. We loved each other and he had too much respect for me to dishonor me and misuse the temple. Xavier is the only man whose touch I craved. To hold his hand made me feel like Willy Wonka in the chocolate factory. I could be me and loved the Xavier he allowed me to know. But the clown had no problems being with other women and playing games about it. That Xavier Johnson would have had me on Jerry Springer in a cameo from a federal prison in a neon orange jumpsuit for fixing him real good, if I had let him.

We arrived at the hospital with only a few moments to spare. If Aliyah kept us there all night, we'd be in trouble with Caroline, who is a stickler for being prompt. I certainly could never mention that we were late for such an auspicious gathering because I had Chase on hospital duty with Aliyah. After taking Aliyah down the road of reason, she agreed to meet Chase while she was in the ICU. She doesn't permit visitors when she's really weak, because Aliyah is always checking people's motives. And when she is in and out of it, she doesn't want the kind of "concerned" visitors who'll take her business all over America. I didn't want her to miss the moment.

"Aliyah, this is my son, Chase."

"Hi, it's a pleasure to meet you."

"From what I understand, the honor is all mine. I hear you have quite a testimony. You're going down in the faith hall of fame too."

"Yes, I am. I'm already there with them, cause the Word is in me. Little did Abraham, Sarah, Moses, and Joseph know that when they were going through what they were going through back in their day, they would be living today through the Word, living in me."

"So how are you feeling?"

I could tell Aliyah was a bit uncomfortable. She's full of pride, so meeting Chase for the first time while she was so vulnerable had to be tough for her. And, she hated to know that the girls would be dressing up and going out and she wasn't able to be with us.

"I'm fine. The Lord is doing it."

"For real, mam. How do you feel?"

"I am weak, and they said my kidneys need to open up. If they would, I'd be able to go home."

Aliyah is going to be in need of a transplant if she doesn't get a miracle.

"So do you want to go home?"

"Of course I want to go home. I want to go with y'all tonight."

"Well then, get ready to go home. Can I pray with you?"

"Go ahead. I feel the anointing of God."

Chase laid hands on Aliyah's torso. "Father, in Jesus' name, open up these kidneys and let them work as you have made them to. I command these kidneys to work now. Let the yolk destroying anointing of God destroy every infirmity and sickness in this body. Go, now, in Jesus' name. By His stripes, we are healed. Be made whole, through faith in His name. Amen."

"Hallelujah, Glory to God. You are my healer. *You* are my healer. You are *my* healer. Thank you Lord for healing me. Thank you Lord, for doing it again. Again and again. Again and again. Lord, I count it all joy. All joy. All joy. If I suffer with you, I'll reign with you. All joy. All joy, Lord. Do it again, Lord."

I leaned over and kissed my friend who I knew would be praising God all night. Healing was all around everyone who needed it. We had to go and didn't want to make an entrance.

THE CELEBRATION
Twenty Eight Birthday Cakes

"You trying to be somebody else, Jewel? Do I see thighs in that short dress? Jesus must really be coming soon." If Diamond wasn't my sister, I'd think she was a hater.

"And, you would have to say that in front of my son, wouldn't you. Chase this is your aunt, my older sister, Diamond."

As soon as the regal evening began, it was over for me just about for the entire evening. The entire family ate Chase up like he was Michael Jackson two weeks after the Thriller video debuted. He was giving my brothers the pound and the Black man chest half hug greeting. Chase is considerably tall, so that became his calling card all night. "You are tall just like the rest of us Prunells." The family hugged him, and he hugged them. Chase had cousins hanging off his neck, nephews sitting on his lap, and hugs from everybody.

My mom shocked me the most. She's short and petite. Chase lifted his short and petite grandmother off the ground like she raised him and he just got off a navy ship. "You're the only grandmother I've ever had, Mrs. Prunell."

"I've always wanted to meet you. It's such a blessing to see you." She cried and told him how much she loved him. "You were the first grandbaby. Those times were hard, but I'm sure glad that we all made it here today. Come here and give me another kiss." My spiffy mother was tiny in relation to Chase's height and stature, but she hugged her first grandson.

Then Daddy blessed him. All of my brothers and Daddy laid hands on Chase and blessed him.

Then came the twenty-eight cakes. My mother had twenty-eight birthday cakes for Chase. Since it is the thought that counts, the twenty-eight cakes said what words couldn't say. This is when I couldn't take anymore. Seeing all of those cakes–cake after cake–really demonstrated how long the twenty-eight years have been. There wasn't a dry eye in the place. While each cake came out in the arms of a family member, healing was in the wind. The air smelled fragrant and the exotic floral arrangements in tall tattered glass vases bloomed in the perfect landscape of what was happening at that very moment. Peace that surpasses all understanding was heavily tangible. Chase was able to eat a birthday cake with his family, the Prunells. And we would have photographs to capture the passing moment.

And, what would a Prunell family night be without singing. Song after song, I sat and watched. They did a piece of singing. My family kills it when they are playing around. Kamoi, the only friend I have outside of the syndicate, showed up and sang her neck off too. She is one of the leading gospel artists who blew up overnight. Who would have ever thought that we'd be singing songs of Zion and Chase would be in the midst.

I spent most of the night with the girls. We kept laughing and talking and snapping on each other. Even Helen, the trusty office manager, showed up. She has the 411 on everything. I didn't even know she knew about Chase's celebration. This would definitely be the talk of the practice because the EF Hutton of the office would certainly take back every detail to the audience that listens to Helen.

Chante showed up late, but she did show up.

"Chase, I'd like you to meet—"

"And this must be an Aunt, cause you look just like my momma."

"Actually, she isn't blood related, and everybody says we look just alike. This is my friend Chante."

"She's not kin? She looks like you more than the others I met so far."

"That's what everybody says. But we are just friends."

"Hello, handsome. Nice to meet you."

I had to bust Chante out. How dare she try to be smooth with my son, who is married. Birds of a feather flock together. Chase doesn't need to think I'm shady because Chante is so flighty.

"I didn't mean nothing by it, girl. But the Negro is fine."

"Fine is fine. But for you or anyone else, that's inappropriate. He's married, and you don't need to be that aggressive, regardless. You are so trifling sometimes, and it ain't cute. Anyway, where have you been? Why couldn't you be on time, Chante?"

"I got caught up. For real. I'm sorry."

Everything was blissful. And then came the shocker of the evening for me. Xavier Johnson walked in. Who gave him the low down? How in God's name does Xavier even know what is going on tonight? I was not ready to see Xavier when I was just getting comfortable with Chase. Thank God I'm banging tonight. The brother needs to see what he messed up with.

I tried my best not to make Xavier feel too at home with me. "Hi Mr. Man. How are you?"

"Not as fine as you are. You know I love you, right?"

"Save it for the Bishop. I'm sure he'd love to see you."

"I came to see you, and your son. Bishop told me what was going on, so I thought I'd stop by. I knew I wasn't going to interrupt your flow with anyone else cause we all know you love me. You just need to stop playing and let me love you."

"I have no problem letting you love me, or loving you. It's the others you have no problem loving that's the problem. And we are both too old for Mickey Mouse and kindergarten."

"Come here." His voice made me melt, and I hated being subjected to his swagger. This man knew exactly how to work me. And, I hated to let the girls see me Xavier-struck.

"I don't care what you say or do, I love you. And, I'm done with playing games. You are it for me. The buck stops here."

"Talk is cheap."

"I know. That's why all I'm asking you to do is give me a chance. I know I've messed up, but give me a chance to show you. Fifty years from now, you'll see that you made a good choice. No man is going to ever love you like I do. It's impossible. Somebody else may make you happy, but there is no one else who loves you like I do. Jesus gave me the up and up on that."

"How about you meet my son. Funny how you're going to meet mine before I meet yours. But let me not go there, cause this is not a time for fighting."

The girls were gabbing and I knew it. Chante was the ringleader this time, "You better leave him alone. I'm telling you, my mother had a weakness for my father and look what it got her. A man is going to say whatever he needs to get you got. So don't go for it."

I responded with confidence, "Don't worry about us. There is no us. Yeah, I'm still feeling him, but my head is in charge, not my heart. I refuse to be played by him another second."

We all stayed out so late. If Chase wasn't just here for a day, I'd skip church tomorrow. But after meeting everybody, we really needed to go so he could visit what used to be a family church. The ministry is so large now, it really can't be considered that anymore. Unlike many of Dad's colleagues, Daddy is preparing non-Prunell leaders to take the ministry should anything ever happen to him. Although all of us can just about teach or preach, none of us has the call to pastor. And, Daddy is careful to build God's house, and not a family dynasty in the name of God. And if we love God and don't want to see the work our daddy labored fall to the ground, we'll support whoever runs with the vision.

Without a vision, a people perish. Not without a visionary. God can raise up anyone to see His vision.

"Good night Daddy. See you in a few hours."

"Have my grandson in church on time please."

Daddy knows I'm always late. And he never chides me for it. "I will. He's normally at his home church early, so I might even be early tomorrow."

"And then we'll know the rapture is getting ready to take place. I hope you had a good evening."

"I did, daddy. Thank you."

"No, thank you. I really didn't see it until tonight. But you've waited twenty-eight years. You never forgot. You've been strong. Stronger than I ever knew."

"Thanks, Daddy."

"Now, you better let somebody else be strong for you and put your guard down. That boy loves you, you know."

"Who, Xavier?"

"Who else? I don't see anyone else knocking down your door to marry you."

"He's not trying to marry me. We're not even together. We haven't spoken in God knows how long before tonight. That doesn't even make sense."

"You may not have spoken, but he's never stopped calling and asking about you. That boy loves you and you better learn how to love those who love you. You're going to have ups and downs with anybody. But when it's real love, you know how to forgive, and do things differently. The boy was young, made some foolish mistakes, was full of pride, but I think he's ready now. But, you know what makes you happy. The choice is yours."

That was an earful.

"What about him cheating and lying? What about his character? I got to live with all of him. And I'm not living with someone who is not trustworthy."

"Watch your mouth, Jewel. You never know what a man has been through. And just like you're coming into your own a little late in life, he is coming into his own. Before I married your mother, there were some things she didn't know about, or knew about and never said a thing about. But, since I've been with your mother, I've only been with your mother. Boys do grow up and become men. Now, Xavier is going to make some woman a good husband. The choice is yours."

And all of my friends said to run and never look back. I really had some decisions to make. But Chase in the here and now was a priority. Finally, the Prunell family opened up to receive my son. A complete Prunell experience would require going to church.

Chase and I made it to church on time. Danne cut church today because she wanted to spend some time with just her and the boys. I normally sit in the back, or somewhere in the middle of the congregation. But not today. My brothers wanted Chase to sit in with the band, and do that front ministry. Most PKs are staple front rowers unless they are working during the services. Today, I would sit up front with Chase, just because he was there.

How could I have not prepared for what my daddy did during the service? How, after all my life of knowing him, did I not think that the Bishop was going to put the business out there from the pulpit.

"Praise the Lord, everybody. Everybody ought to praise the Lord. Aaahhh. We've got so much to praise God for this morning. How many of you know that we serve a God of restoration. Today, my heart is glad. I know I've got somebody who knows what I'm talking about, when you've seen days that you never thought you'd see. You thought you drank yourself out of a good marriage, but God! You thought you were too old to see that thing turn around, but—"

"God!" The call and response pattern was so innate, that the audience knew exactly what to say.

"Well, today it's personal and I want to see how many of you know how to rejoice with them that rejoice. If you've been waiting on God to bring that son home, set that daughter free, whatever it is you've been believing God for, if I were you, I'd be acting just like it already happened. I'm not gonna wait to praise Him! I'll praise Him like—"

And a shout fest that Aliyah would kill for took place. This is the atmosphere that she thrives in. If I wasn't up front, I would have called her on the cell so she could just hear the service.

"Just wait a minute. I want y'all to help me praise God for my grandson this morning. Almost twenty-nine years ago, we parted with my eldest grandson and now he's returned home. Why don't you help me praise him!"

Oh Shoot. Jesus, please don't let him go any further. I didn't realize how embarrassed I have been about having Chase so young until my daddy did what he has been doing since we were little: publish our business as his from the pulpit. The life of a PK. It's not that I cared that people would know. There would just be so many obvious questions like how in God's name can I have such a grown son? And, I refuse to present Chase to people through an explanation, especially one that he is a rape child, that would disparage his father who God has restored and is still in ministry today. Then, on the other hand, I don't want to have to be the one who put my parents through hell by having a baby in my adolescence. Please give me wisdom because these church folks are not going to let us get out of the door if Daddy doesn't shut up. What they know and think doesn't matter. Feeding into this foolishness is what kept me in mental bondage for so long anyway.

"Before we move on, I already know you all may have to double-check my insurance policy cause Jewel is going to try and get the Bishop. I need those of you who love your pastor to look at Jewel and stretch forth your hands and say, 'Jewel, leave the Bishop alone.' But, I know there is no other way to get her to come and sing for us this morning. Is it all right if I just have my daughter come and sing for a few moments? Come on Jewel and sing for Jesus."

No he didn't. No he didn't put me on the spot. This is exactly why I'm always late and sit in the back. And people actually wish they were PKs. They must not have a clue. If I sit and don't move, I'll be rebellious and a bad example to others who are called to serve. Everyone should always have a song on her heart for the Lord.

As I walked to the pulpit, the words from the old school song hit my spirit.

"As my daughter comes, many of you may not know that years ago she used to sing all the time in this church. You're about to get a treat this morning."

"Praise the Lord everybody. Key of A flat please." God please help me to keep my composure and to minister to you as this song ministers to your people. "I might as well tell it, before the Bishop does." I looked at the thousands of parishioners I had seen week to week almost all of my life who never knew the real story. There was nothing to be ashamed of, nothing to keep under the rug of life. I pronounced with dignity, "Today, I stand amazed because after many years of a silent travail, my son from my youth and I have found each other. I'm grateful to God for watching over him and protecting him and making him the man he is today. To God be all the Glory." There it is. The cat is out of the bag.

"How can I say thanks, for the things, you have done for me. Things, so underserved, yet you gave to prove your love for me. The voices of a million angels, cannot express, my gratitude, all that I am and ever hope to be, I owe it all to thee. To God be the glory..." Some things still haven't changed. My voice is straight Brooklyn church, strong vibrato, velvety and raspy. I still can't sing without going old school and weeping, especially when I sang those words from a different station in life today. Chase was sitting there before my very eyes.

None of my secular degrees, qualifications, expertise, or accomplishments mean a hill of beans when it comes to my father, brothers and their demands for my life. When the crew hears this, they're going to get me for not busting the Bishop up for calling me out like that and I'm a grown woman. I didn't mind it after all, because God moved and people were encouraged and blessed. I owed God for the things, so undeserved that He gave to me. Ultimately, that is what matters.

After church, the Rona Barretts made their way over to Chase and me. Of course, I was gracious and careful not to fuel their fire, even though most of the people were well-wishers and some provided soft rebukes. The "How come you never told me you had a child", "I've known you all these years and you ain't never mentioned no son" and "I thought we were friends" commentaries came left and right.

But the church gossip president, Mother Fitzgerald, went straight there, "What a handsome gentleman you are. I didn't catch your name son."

"Elder Chase Swanson, mam."

"Elder Swanson. Why does that name sound familiar? Is that Swanson with an 'a' or is it Swinson with an 'i'?"

Sis. Fitzgerald works diligently to make sure that when she spreads the biz, she is well informed so that she can be the authoritative voice of church gossip. This has been her unofficial occupation since I was a little girl. I wish the former Bloomingdale's buyer didn't retire almost twenty-five years ago. At least when she worked, she didn't dedicate as much time to publishing OPB (other people's business). I must admit though, she is the fiercest, fittest-dressing gossipmonger. Girlfriend brings it lovely and has enough wigs to make every outfit say all my time is spent in dressing and causing trouble.

"It's Swanson, with an 'a'."

"Now, I know that name from somewhere. Are your people from the south?"

I was trying to talk to others while overhearing every word in Chase's discourse with Sis Fitzgerald because I knew when I saw her coming, there would be some aftermath. Danne picked the wrong Sunday to be absent. She would have definitely broke this mess up.

"Yes, actually, I'm from Mississippi and been there just about all of my life."

"You don't say. Would you happen to know Prophet Delayne Swanson?"

"Yes, that's my father. Have you been to our church in Mississippi?"

"No, not quite. I just knew of his ministry years ago. So, Prophet Delayne Swanson is your daddy?"

"Yes, mam."

Why the heebie jeebies would Chase tell a church mother who his daddy is, and he knows what his daddy did to me? He is not brand new. He is a church elder. Can't he tell when he's being pumped so the gossip whore can work her works?

"Chase, I believe your uncles wanted to see us before we left; we really need to get going now. Sorry Sis Fitzgerald, we've got to go." I'm not going to let church folks steal my joy. "I'm sorry I had to break that up."

"I could feel you Momma. I know she was trying to find out who my daddy is. It was quite obvious."

"So why did you play right into her hand?" I asked with an irritated tone.

"Because the truth is the truth. At some point in time, people are going to know my last name, and someone may make the association that I am my father's child. I'm not ashamed of it. He's a good man, and he's been good to me."

Wow. Men always stick together. And, Chase really should be all right with who he is, and with his relationship with his father. The truth is just something that has been hidden for so long, that it is a reality I am not comfortable with, particularly when disclosing the whole truth would only be hurtful at this time. And, to be honest, I was still highly embarrassed about the whole situation. All anyone had to do is the math and would know that I was raped.

"Remember to tell your father that he definitely doesn't have to be concerned about your loyalties to him. He took care of you when it was embarrassing and hard, and he did what a lot of preachers won't do. He took care of his responsibility and you turned out all right. And, you're strong." Being a fierce cookie about the situation would make me feel better, but it wouldn't be the right thing to do. God can trust me to walk upright and not stay in the past. If I focused on how this affected me and insisted that a man who met me a couple of weeks ago put me first because of what happened almost three decades ago, I just might lose him. I'm not going to make him choose, or be uncomfortable with his loyalties and who he already is.

"I know this is messed up for you, Momma. If you can show me how to be more sensitive or another way, show me."

I took Chase's hand and began to rub it. His hand is so much bigger than mine. I missed the stages of growth from when I could almost fit his entire body into the palms of both of my hands. He was a real human being, with a real heart. And, his heart appeared to be good and one after God.

"One thing I've learned in my life, Chase, that isn't easy, but just may be true. Sometimes, there is no answer that is just for everyone involved. And this is one of those situations, especially when we allow our flesh to rule, or give place to the devil. Just like favor isn't fair, sometimes life itself isn't fair. What your father did to me, or the effects of it, will never be fair to me. Never. I hate that, but it is the truth. I hated your father for so long. I can honestly say, I never wanted to see him dead or anything like that. But, I wanted him to hurt like hell, so he could know what I was fighting to come out of. Do you know when I realized that hating him wasn't going to make one bit of difference in his life but was jacking mine up, that is when I began the healing process. I couldn't live in that reality anymore, because if I did, there would be losses somewhere, to what little dignity he may have left, to how you feel about yourself, to even how Ms. Edie may feel about me. So, I guess what I'm trying to say is, there is no other way. It is what it is. And with God and His peace, we all can have another reality. I can handle this. I'm a bit embarrassed by what is possibly brewing with what people will know now, but all of that stuff isn't for me to contend with. I have to live above the storm, or I'll be back into depression, and that's not about to happen. We can talk about Christ-centered living, or we can do it, and that just may not be a piece of cake. Sometimes, it's a bitter cup. I refuse to deface your father or dishonor you by trying to explain anything to a people who really don't care to know the truth anyway. What's important is that we now have the opportunity to be the family that we are supposed to be. This is where I am on the matter. And my feelings may not always be where they need to be, but they will be, because God runs this ship. Jesus is Lord."

This is the type of stuff that Noey loves but wishes we could just get a good swing on a fierce cookie to help appease the flesh. My girls love me, but know I will only go so far with defending myself or pushing the envelope.

"Since you're giving me messages to give my father, I'll give you one. No one can ever interfere with our relationship. I know God didn't do this, but I'm glad I'm here, and if anyone had to go through what you went through, you have done well. Your heart is incredible! I'm a blessed man. I thought I had it all, with Evey and Ruth, Aunt Catherine, Pop and Ms. Edie, and all my brothers and sisters. But, after this weekend, I know I've got the best of both worlds now. I didn't have a clue I had all this family and such a great human being for a mother."

If he only knew it took years for me to get here. God is healing me and he is certainly part of the process. "Chase, I want you to know how much I love you."

"I love you too, Momma. I've never been away from Evey this long and can't wait to get back home. I feel like I could stay here another week, but I've got to get back to my good thang."

"I know. I do appreciate the time we've had together. And, the family is just so in love with you."

"I can't wait to get back and let Evey know she really missed a delightful weekend."

"Please let her know that the next time she has me thinking she's coming, she needs to show up. Don't have my feelings out there. She's part of you, so she's part of me."

Chase was booked on the last flight out, and of course, Ford and Harris wanted to do the airport thing. So, I had to come to grips with the fact that Chase, who had been "my son" in my thoughts and dreams was their nephew, and had cousins and grandparents who would want to spend time with him. So my mother-son only notion only lasted for a hot minute. He was part of a bigger picture, in a bigger family.

"Ford, please stop by Momma and Daddy's because I don't want to hear it if he leaves and they don't get to say good-bye."

"When is Chase coming back?" Ford asked.

"I don't know, we haven't worked that out yet. With my schedule and his commitment to the ministry, it won't be easy to do the back and forth too often."

"I would say we could try and check him out, but I don't think that'll work out, because I promise you, if I saw his no good daddy—"

"Ford, please," I pleaded.

"For what that [N-word] did to you? I'm saved, but I ain't that saved. I'll whip his butt, repent, and then whoop later."

"Ford, I'm going to tell you like I told Momma and Daddy. If I can forgive him, everybody else needs to let it go. Do you realize that that man is the only father Chase has known? Chase is whom I'm focusing on. I'm not going to tear down the only man who he's known and apparently respects. So please don't go there with him about his people. For me, please, Ford. And, it's not good for me either. I'm fighting to be okay with where we all are today and fueling a fire that's down to burnt ashes is not it."

"Whatever, curly Sue. If I ever lay eyes on that man, it won't be a good day for Chase cause I'm gonna put my foot up his father's [a**]."

"You need to get saved all over again." This is why my mother warned me not to ever discuss the matter with my brothers. She knew they'd be in jail over this mess.

BABES AND FOOLS
Our Boys

Before I could put my hair up and relax, Danne showed up with Rashaun and Tysheem.

"So what's up? How was your day?"

"Tired. Can I go to bed now?" Tysheem is normally so vibrant and I've almost got to inject him to go to sleep.

"I ran them ragged today. What went down with you all?"

"Nothing much. You missed Ford and Harris by a few seconds. They took Chase to catch his flight."

"So he's hanging tight with the uncles."

"Yes, he is. He thoroughly enjoyed meeting everyone, and are you ready for this?"

"What?"

"Daddy called me to sing this morning! He just put me on the spot."

"And what did you sing?"

"To God Be the Glory. And you know what? It felt good. Not so much to be back doing stuff on the pulpit, but to participate again."

"So you gonna start singing again?"

"I don't think so. Not doing the solo or choir thing, I really can't commit to that. But there are so many things I can do to enhance the ministry and I'm going to bring them to Pastor Charles."

"Like what?"

"The church is growing, so it's time for us to develop emergency response protocol. We do have at least two other doctors that I know of, and a bunch of nurses and other medical personnel. So, we can develop a program, do some training, and establish the appropriate protocol and personnel."

"Not you. After singing one song, you want to be some ministry leader overnight. You are hilarious."

"Yeah. I've been thinking about it for so long, but never wanted to be bothered. I've been sitting there, probably will remain there for God knows how long, so why not just bring what God has given me to the table?"

"Then, we can institute an HIV/AIDS ministry for real. You know how many people are infected and don't have a clue? Or people who do know but are too embarrassed or scared to seek treatment? Or people who need to know the ins and outs of how to change their lifestyles to maximize their health and life span?"

"I get it Jewel. It's needed, doable, and I say, go for it."

"I'm going to speak with Elder Charles before I lose the gumption on this. Then we'll put a team together to get both ministries up and running. Among this, the boys and trying to get back and forth to visit Chase, I might need to scale back the practice a little bit."

"Can you see how well you do at managing before you actually cut back? You just might become more efficient and may have to get up earlier. That's all."

"Now, I'm not about to sacrifice my precious *zzzzz*s. That is what keeps me sane. I might have to actually use the gym and figure out that apparatus that's been sitting in there forever. But, sleep, that can't be touched."

"Anyway!" Danne interjected. "Aliyah did mention going to Chicago to me, but I think you all need to huddle on this one with the boys. Tysheem is crazy dependent on her, and he doesn't do well when she's not around. Rashaun is betwixt and between. He needs stability and assurance. So, you need to insert some professional counseling for the boys. And, Aliyah needs somebody to bust her up. Unless you two know something I don't know, she needs to make plans that include her boys, long term.

They can't keep packing suitcases and coming over here for a week, two months, four days, and all that. Either she's gonna keep them and get some care for her and them, or you need to keep them."

"I've pretty much already communicated this to her already. Aliyah doesn't see the virtue in counseling, she can hardly appreciate the need for them to do homework, or take books to school. She's doing her best, and she may seem to be selfish, and inconsiderate, but from her point of view, she is so consumed with being as sick as she is, as long as she has been and wants to fight the good fight of faith. So, much of what we need is cursory to her. In her mind, if we could just walk one mile in her shoes, we'd shut up."

"But I'm not shutting up. Rashaun is clowning because he doesn't have any tools to cope. This isn't just a matter of shut up and sit down, or cast the devil out. These boys need help."

"And you and I know that, so we can both make sure it happens for them. I got the funds, and if you can just commit to helping me as much as you can with some time, then we can help her do what she can with them."

"Now, don't think I forgot to get up in your business with Xavier. What's the deal with him now?" Danne caught me off-guard.

"Nothing. We just talked."

"And?"

"And, he's talking a bunch of good stuff, but we shall see."

"Oh, we're gonna see? So that means you're open?"

"It means I'm not closed. I'm really seeking God and that's he long and the short of it. Only God knows what lies ahead. He could really have changed, grown up a bit and he is the only man I've ever loved. On the other hand, he could still be a slickster, and we both know we don't have to look far to find him some good company."

"Ok, just be careful. Slicksters do genuinely love too, but if their character isn't there, it just isn't there. It's not about how you both feel about each other, it's what he will do that matters. Is the man who will do right by Jewel, instead of jerking you, trying to save his own face? That's the question. Can you see him as a covering who will protect you, provide for you, and love you as he loves himself? Is he the one who will push you around in a wheelchair, roll you over and wash you himself if he had to? Until he can love himself enough to love you or anybody else right, don't even think about it. Be careful."

I appreciated words of wisdom. "I will. Anyway, I've got so much more to manage now, so I can't even keep standing here talking to you. I need to at least check in with the boys and get them ready for school tomorrow."

Of course, a phone call from Aliyah changed the scheduled program. "Jewel, Chase is anointed. Do you know my kidneys started to work that night when you left? All day yesterday I was using the bathroom. I had to tell them to bring a urinal by the bed I was going so much. If everything else tests ok, they're going to let me out by tomorrow. God is good!"

"Ok, so you and I need to talk to the boys before you leave, then. We'll be by later tonight."

Rashaun, Tysheem and I had the best intentions, but didn't wake up until the next morning. Aliyah would certainly be perturbed, but had to wait.

The Sunlight entered the room and I couldn't wait to get up. Mornings were no longer a drawn-out battle between the uncertainty of what lies ahead and wanting to freeze time. Mornings were the beginning of another day to embrace, a new day to make things happen. Speaking with Chase had become a priority.

"Words cannot express how I feel this morning, Momma. To meet my cousins, my uncles, and my grandmother and grandfather. You just don't know what this weekend did for me. I have an entire family that I never knew about. And we all love ministry. I mean this is so amazing."

"I'm glad you're happy. So when can you come back to visit?"

"We'll have to work that out. During the week is better for me, and so far as I can tell, it doesn't work for you as well as the weekends. You can always come here, and we'll get up there as much as we can. I'd love for you all to come down here."

"Chase, that may take some time. I can come and bring my godsons from time to time, but the rest of the family may need some time. You are always welcome here."

His tone changed. Maybe he never thought about the fact that my family did send him to his father and never followed up because they did not want any communication with the man who raped me. "It would be nice if this could be one big happy family, and I have to be careful what we speak. Anything can happen. Right now, that's not about to happen, at least without some of your uncles going to jail behind it."

"I hear you. And, I'm cool with that. That's understandable. So, let me know whenever you want to come down. It'll be a while before I can leave the church on a Sunday. Or, I'll come up on a Thursday and leave on Saturday night. Anyway, we'll work it out."

He would probably never know that hell began on earth when his father left my room that night. I was never able to sleep soundly in my parents' home again. Even in my own home, every sound that is made has the potential to pull me out of a deep sleep. After years of functional insomnia, ridiculous fear, and an aversion to greasy preachers, I had to forgive. But, forgiveness did not put me in a place where I was ready to fully embrace Prophet Swanson. I am certainly not ready to run into him almost every other weekend or so. After all, I spent so many years wanting him to feel the pain I felt. I just wanted him to know how much I struggled, as if that would have actually made a difference. The family was definitely not ready. But Helen was surely ready to remain engulfed in OPB.

"Helen, I'm going to have to run across town to an appointment this afternoon. And for the next few weeks or so, let's book appointments that will have me out by no later than seven pm. I've really got to get home by eight o'clock at the absolute latest."

"Ok, boss. When are you going to switch over to friend and tell me about this son of yours?"

"I didn't know I had a friend hat with you, Helen. You pull that office manager hat so much, the friend hat is dusty."

"Listen Dr. Prunell, I've been good waiting for you to tell me. Don't let me have to dig."

Helen couldn't be funnier with more gall if she were made from a gutsiest woman alive kit. She had no shame in her game. "Helen, the truth is my son came up for the weekend. I visited him, and we are getting to know one another. He is the long lost love of my life. He has a beautiful family and this is going to be a great journey. That's it, kaputz, and mind yours."

"Dr. Prunell, don't make me have to talk about you behind your back. This abrupt stuff doesn't work for the real you. How can you know how nosey I am, and never let me know you have a child?"

"You don't know as much as you think you may know about me, Helen. We're good, you know the basics, and that's enough. What I do need you to do is find me a good sports program or boys' mentoring program around my house, for Aliyah's boys."

"Done deal."

"Also, put a call into my attorney. I need to hear from her asap. Like yesterday."

All of the head knowledge and years of practicing medicine have not been able to quench the disdain I have for an annual visits to the gynecologist. Any type of inquisition into my private parts and reproductive organs take a hit on me. If I were a drinker, I'd be drunk every time. It's almost humiliating, because I have to go through a few moments of breathing and coaching myself to relax so I don't tense up and have to put my doctor through the ringer. Pap smears can save a life, so I do what is necessary to stay on top of my health. A normal exam would take me back to the many times a doctor's hand went to examine the uterus while pregnant with Chase, which was in the same part of the ballpark where Prophet Swanson protruded past every natural resistor to pound my feeble young flesh. Menstrual cycles are a trigger as well. Every time I see the blood, I think of the trace of blood that night, or the blood that I saw for weeks after Chase was born. If there wasn't an occasional flicker of hope that one day I might get married and have another baby, I would have been fixed a long time ago. I'm much better at this stuff now. I don't get up with tears anymore. And, by the time my doctor is ready to examine me, I'm usually good to go.

All throughout college, my girlfriends suggested that I simply start screwing boys left and right. If I got a good piece, I'd overcome all of this traumatic nonsense. According to them, I had a horrible introduction to the world of Black men and their greatest asset. I needed one grandiose experience to register and replace the incident that governed the activities and trauma that seemed to dictate my decisions with men. So, I agreed to try it. Anything would be better than where I was. Butt-naked and all, I just couldn't. I looked at the poor jock, who just about every woman on campus wanted, who de-valued himself to the point that he would jump in the bed with me, and he didn't even know me. As much as I wanted to try anything that might have helped me to escape the walls and see what everyone else raved about, I just couldn't bring myself to do it. I didn't want to complicate matters by indulging into the world of frivolous sex. Someday, I would be healed and preserve my body and the ultimate expression of my love for my husband. I'll never know if their theory had any merit. I had to trust God and believe that His way is the right way. If I receive double for my shame, I know one day the triggers will have dissipated.

Like I needed to close out a day with the gynecologist with any more drama, Rashaun cursed Aliyah all the way out in the hospital. I mean a thorough cussing.

"I'm warning you Rashaun, you're going to visit those words coming out of your mouth again, and they're going to whip your behind. You have no choice. You've got to honor your mother if you want your days to be long and to see God's prosperity. I know you didn't ask for any of this, but you've got to find another way to manage your emotions, or you're going to mess yourself up. I'm telling you."

The boy shut down, and said he didn't care. Tysheem just cried, and of course, doesn't want her to leave. He tries his best to defend Aliyah and fights with Rashaun, who has no mercy on him, whatsoever. Nonetheless, I did what I have always done, assured Aliyah that everything will work out and be all right. Aliyah would come home with me until her flight left, and my attorney would prepare papers to make me their legal guardian, and in the event of my inability, Danne would take care of the boys. Rashaun wasn't happy about that. He wanted to go back to Chicago with his relatives he had not seen since he was much younger. Or, he'd rather be with Danne. We could see that this part of the journey was going to have challenges.

As I sent the boys down to the car, Aliyah let it all hang loose.

"He can't stand you, you know."

"What have I ever done to him but be there for him to act like this?"

"First off, he knows how much you mean to me, and he thinks you influence me too much. He's just trying to control me. I'm not sure if he's talking to BJ. I told him to stop taking his collect calls. And, you make him have to go to school, and be responsible. He hates authority, and that's what you represent to him. Besides me, you can see him coming before he gets started. He can't get over with you. If I was on my P's and Q's, I'd be getting more of it from him to. But don't let him stop you. I chose you to be my friend for a reason. You have everything I wish I had and never did. You're smart, a natural beauty, nice to people, would help a rat, and love God. Dang. How many African American females do you know who have their own practice on the upper east side of New York City? Especially at your age. Jewel, I know you had something in you that you would fight till the end to do whatever it is you believe is right in God. I've never seen anyone with your discipline and I didn't have that. That's exactly what they need. So don't back down. Whatever you do, don't back down. And, thanks. I know I don't say it often, but I thank God for you all the time. You, Danne, Noey, Laurel, and even Chante. All of y'all, God had to give y'all to me. This is a God thing. And people don't understand it, but God has everything just the way it needs to be."

"You have no idea how much I glean from you Aliyah. You're so practical, duh, have such a gift of faith that it can only be God. And you are so daring. Who would ever believe that you've come from where you came from to where you are today? I admire your courage to go after more because you know you can have more. Okay, so the attorney is coming by tomorrow night for us to fix up the paperwork. What I need to know from you is how long do you plan on being in Chicago? I can't work with a whenever. We've got to give the boys some frame of reference, and if it's going to be for some time, then I'm going to put them into counseling."

"Then put them into counseling. I know you don't want to hear this, or agree with me. But I'm coming off of everything. Completely. And I'm not going into another hospital. I'm tired. I've seen God heal me from cancer in the throat, from boils all over my body, two mini-strokes, colitis, kidney failure, congenital heart disease and Jewel, I'm tired of suffering. Either God is going to do this all the way, like a miracle from Him and Him alone, or I'm going to be with Him. If that is the healing He has for me, then I'll take that. There is no more sickness in death. And, I'm not afraid of death. I don't want to die, but I'm not going to live like this. So, I'm going to talk with Rashaun and Tysheem when I get out of here, and let them know if they never see me again, God has let me do whatever needs to be done so that they would be in the right hands. I've spoken with Bishop Deuce and he told me 'daughter, you've fought a good fight. Don't fear. God is Jehovah-Rapha.' So, I'm going to lay on the altar at Apostle Merriweather's church until I get up healed, or die. One way or the other, all is well."

"Aliyah, all you have to do is stay on the meds and take them properly. You have never done that. Healing comes in many different forms. God made doctors and gave us and scientists the wisdom to take things out of the earth to bring healing to our bodies. Most of my patients live with AIDS when they change their lifestyle and take medication diligently. You wake up and eat a Snickers bar, and drink Coke and eat chips for lunch. With all of that sugar and crap you put in your body when it is fighting for nutrients to help you be healthy, you want to put God in a box?"

"Call it what you will, Jewel. I believe God. Even if He doesn't heal me, He knows my desires and my requests. I am not going to live popping pills and you know how sick that medication makes me feel. I can't keep doing it. I just can't."

"Ok honey. Okay." Talking to Aliyah from a voice of reason is pointless. She believes what she believes, and that's that. I learned this early in our relationship.

When Aliyah first moved to New York, she rented a studio in Harlem. She was brand new to the area, Bishop Deuce's ministry and paying bills. Aliyah and I had just met, and she asked me to stop by to meet her son, Rashaun and have dinner. I would never forget this visit. Aliyah was so grateful for her pad, and walking into it made me see the variance between the worlds each of us lived in. There were hardly any lights. A more accurate description would be to say it was completely dim. When I asked to use the bathroom, I decided to flush and pretend I tinkled. There was mildew and mold all over the tiles on the walls, and in the crevices on the floor. In the living room mice ran past the wall with her 1972 console television on it, as if it were the Indy Mice 500. Those rodents acted like Aliyah and Rashaun were visiting them and had no fear of being seen, and Aliyah made no attempt to kill them. I could not believe the obliviousness to these creatures running around, could hardly keep myself from cringing and wanted to leave. But, to Aliyah, this was a place of peace, a roof over her head, with sufficient heat. That tiny place was a far cry from living in crack houses, abandoned cars, or sleeping at the side of a building in Chicago.

Obviously, I became concerned about eating anything prepared in the apartment, but did not want to offend my "new" friend. I knew Jesus loved me when Aliyah burned spaghetti and we couldn't eat the dinner she very much intended to serve from the first home she ever had, and from her heart. We ordered Chinese and God knows, I was eternally grateful.

While we were chatting and getting to know one another a bit better, a bill collector kept calling Aliyah about her past due cable bill. Aliyah politely asked me to excuse her for a minute, "Look, I told you to stop calling me, I don't have no debts with anybody. The man of God told me I was debt free. Now, do whatever you have to do to get that straight over on your side, cause I'm not paying no bills to anybody; they've been wiped out."

I, being Jewel, could not help myself and asked Aliyah when she hung up, what was that all about. She blissfully explained that these people from the cable company kept calling her and sending her letters that she owed them a few hundred bucks for the cable bill. She said, "The devil is a liar. Bishop told us that God was canceling debt and He was getting into the computer systems and wiping out debts. So those people better stop calling me."

At that very instance, I knew Aliyah believed everything Bishop Deuce said, just as she did Apostle Merriweather. And in listening to them, and even misapplying the principles of God, she expected God to move on her behalf. To clarify what Deuce must have meant, or failed to relay through proper teaching, would mean to undermine her confidence in her bishop, or what she thought she heard from her bishop. And knowing Bishop Deuce, it wasn't Aliyah's hearing that was the problem. He's a cliché preacher who loves hype and getting people to give their last penny, by faith, in the name of God, for him to squander it and mismanage the church properties and finances, all because of his great call and anointing. He couldn't care less if babes in Christ took his words literally without any type of accountability to bring balance to the revelation gifts with proper teaching. As long as the people always got caught up in the "anointing," he would do as he trained all of his ministers to do: get them to give in the height of the move of God. He had to keep the money coming in, so he could continue to help his family and stay greased up in his Chicago pimp-style, custom-made, bright neon suits with authentic gator shoes to match.

Everything in me wanted to tackle the foolishness of not paying the cable bill. She used the service, so she had an obligation to pay it. Stewardship, her witness among the world, all of these things ran across my mind, but was too much for her to handle, when she was in the midst of a hype ministry. So, I offered to pay the bill. Aliyah flatly refused. She would not dare insult God, by working against what He already said. She was debt free, and would never pay any cable bill. God wiped her slate clean, and that was that.

A few weeks later, Aliyah ran into my office. I was shocked to see her there, I hadn't even realized that she knew where it was.

"I know you're busy, and I'm not staying long. I just stopped by to show you the proof that God wiped out the debt like he said he would. Look at this letter."

I read a letter from the cable provider stating that after many attempts to collect the debt, they decided to waive the balance and her bill balance was $0.00. She told me repeatedly, "I told you God would do it. He went in them computers like I kept telling them He was going to do."

I smiled and rejoiced with her. I didn't bother to tell her that the bill collectors keep notes and probably decided to wipe out her bill because they thought she was incompetent. Or, that someone from the church got her account and decided to help her out. Either way, Aliyah got the results she expected, even by exercising foolish faith. God knew what Aliyah knew, and met her right where she was. She would grow over the years in Him, from faith to faith.

So, Danne, Noey, Laurel and I agreed to go on a fast and pray concerning this entire situation. Although I was completely comfortable with keeping Aliyah's boys, we all wanted her to live and be around for them, and for us. She was part of us. The crazoid of Faith.

Laurel is cool with all of us, but tends to keep to herself. This member of the crew is the e-mail or voicemail buddy who we see on television from time to time. Laurel is a world-class singer and travels all over the world as a vocal director doing tours of popular plays or singing background for the cream de la cream of fru-fru entertainment. She is a regular for Andre Rieu and other opera and classical singers. When she is tired of traveling, she takes a respite and may pinch-hit in the studio as a vocal coach for popular singers. Laurel is hardly around, and when she is, she tends to want to rest from living in hotels, arenas, and airports. But, when the kid shows up, it is up and poppin. Laurel does not forget anything. She is a human sponge that remembers every detail of everything. She has a captivating personality that always makes her the center of attention whenever we are together.

"Now, you know we're not about to convince Aliyah that she is crazy, you do know that," Laurel contributed.

"So we just let her be crazy, and have to take care of her children?" Noey wasn't feeling legitimizing any more of Aliyah's ridiculous ways.

"No, we've got to get the wisdom of the matter from wisdom. The girl needs to do what she needs to do, but if she isn't convinced of that, or committed to that, she is the one who is going to be out of here." Again, Danne provided the bottom line.

"So, let's all agree to pray and fast concerning this situation. Let's believe God that He will direct her paths, so that His will be done." I thought the best thing to do was to give the situation to God. We really didn't have any way to make Aliyah comprehend what was so plausible to most other people.

"You can fast, but I'm going to eat." And Laurel meant every bit of what she said. "I'm not fasting over no foolishness. Remember when Bishop Douche, oops, did I say Douche? Yes, I did. Remember when the Bishop told the church to go home and pack up if you want to move. You can't have faith without works, so if you believe it's time to move, pack up and wait for the moving truck? And do you all remember how Aliyah packed up a bunch of suitcases and boxes and called me, Danne, Belle, and Geneva to come with our cars because she was moving? And when we all lined up to pick up her stuff, she had no new address to move to? And, then she said go to mid-day service because there would be a Word there for the new address? And we all drove from Harlem to Queens with our cars packed up with all of her stuff in them, and then she came running outside with keys."

"I remember that good story. That's when I knew Aliyah had favor with God because she was so crazy and that's when some sister in the church had just gotten married to a brother in the church and they had just gotten back from their honeymoon.

And the sister got up to testify that she had an apartment fully furnished in Kew Gardens and no one to live in it, and didn't want to rent it, because she owned it and never wanted to give up such a good location. And Aliyah ran over to her and told the lady her stuff was outside and she must be the one God wanted to keep her apartment for her." I remembered that miracle as if it were yesterday.

"And the lady didn't know Aliyah from a cup of milk but gave her the keys to her apartment. I remember when she called me crying, saying she didn't even have to buy a broom or toilet paper. The lady had everything she could possibly need stocked up in the apartment. Yup, girlfriend is radical, don't make sense at all at times, but winds up walking into stuff we have to work for and do the right way." Noey couldn't understand how Aliyah was so crazy and got away with nonsense all the time.

"That's precisely why I'm eating and ain't studying Aliyah. She's going to be with Jesus, one way or the other, healed and shouting full time or her body in a coffin, resting until He comes for the righteous dead, or with Jesus in paradise, whatever y'all believe. So either way, God got her back, and I'm not going to deny myself because He works it out every time. So I'm gonna eat cause I don't get to Bacci's that often."

So the focus shifted back to Aliyah's boys. Rashaun and Tysheem are settling in pretty well, considering the circumstances. Rashaun and Tysheem both go to a community youth program after school each day. Tysheem is doing a sports track, and Rashaun is doing a community service track. Rashaun is going to have to work and do outreach to help others. They are both adjusting well and talk to Aliyah just about every day.

Xavier has used the boys as a segway for calling me five times a day. I let him hit the voicemail most of the time, for GP (general principle). He must understand that a brother cannot play a sister and then think he has it like that. He must prove himself and work hard or else he can keep it moving.

"How are the little fellas liking the programs I recommended for them?" Xavier just wanted to have some dialogue because he already knew the answers.

"They seem to be alright with it, so far. They haven't complained, and Tysheem doesn't want to miss one swimming class."

"I speak to their instructors regularly and they are both doing well. So it looks like a good fit for them. Rashaun helps to deliver food to a convalescent home and he also goes to a large group home for boys. He is seeing how most kids in NYC whose parents have died from AIDS, or are strung out, have to live when no auntie or grandpa takes them in. He's seeing that he may not have the best thing with his mother, but he has it made compared to other kids in the same shoes he is in." Even though Xavier used the boys to get to me, he did genuinely care. He has a passion for young people, especially those who need intervention.

The truth is, I was glad to have Xavier assist with the boys. Although I had a son, I didn't have any practical experience in knowing how to reach boys. The influence of a strong man was not only needed, but critical.

"That's good to know. I ask him about what he does, and he says, 'work'. Homeboy is a trip, but I love him so much. He's really pulling through this, and he'll be a better man than most."

"Speaking of pulling through, when are you gonna get over what happened between us? I gave you enough time to have your temper tantrum and it's time for us to move on."

Xavier was a master at turning things. He cheated and then processed our entire stalemate situation as me having a temper tantrum. "See, I can't stand that arrogance I hear. How about some humility? How about you understand my decision to walk away from you because any self-respecting woman wouldn't put up with what you put me through? Preacher, you don't get to cheat and think it's nothing. And if you can't see that, then there's no use trying, because you'll see no harm and do it again."

"You know I know I did you dirty. I'm sorry. I've already apologized over and over again and can't change that. What do you want me to do? I know you love me, and I love you. I can't undo my son."

"Xavier, Jr. is not responsible for what you did, he really has nothing to do with this," I interjected.

"As I was saying, I can't undo Xavier and I'm not going to keep apologizing for him."

"You just don't get it. You can't apologize for him. Nobody asked you to. It's what you did to get him that's the problem. Why would I want to marry you when you are not only capable of all of this, but won't even tell the whole truth about it? This doesn't add up to trustworthy to me. And I am supposed to say 'yes' to a man who has this track record and trust that he'll do right by me for the rest of our lives?"

"Look, Jewel, unless you can forgive me for real, we can't have a viable future together. I know I've done too much to you, but I've been taking care of Xavier and living right. None of the other women I've been with have connected with me the way you have. I've never been able to talk and share the real me with them the way I can with you. You are the only one I can be transparent with, and cry to."

"Have connected with you. So none of this has anything to do with Jewel. Not who I am as an individual, and my worth as a woman. It is all about who I am to you, how I make you feel, and what I do for you. Helpmates have identities, Xavier. I matter. I matter to God beyond my ability to help you. I matter to me. And my worth isn't just in how I am able to make you feel. Until you can value me for me, you can forget it. This is what makes women marry men they love and they still have miserable lives. I am not an Edith Bunker. You need to find someone else whose worth is revolving on an axle that revolves around the planet of Xavier, Archie. Only when you see my worth, will you value me enough to cherish me, guard me, care for me, and provide for me. Then, I will want to be Jane to swing on a vine from tree to tree following your lead in this jungle of a world, Tarzan. Then and only then will it be about you, because then I'll know that I am part of you and you will make life decisions that are best for me and you. So, first you've got to see your own worth or you'll never be able to see mine. Then I won't have a problem trusting and submitting to you as my husband and covering. Until I am convinced that you are conscious of this, and committed to doing right by us because you consider my well-being just as yours, and not just what works for you and how I fit into that, you can go find someone else. I'm not interested. You ever heard of the expression, 'I can do bad by myself?' We'll I'm not doing bad by myself. So why? Why would I go from good to ring around the rosey where will I end up in this equation with you?"

"You sure do know how to tear a brother up."

"I'm not tearing you up. I am communicating with you and the chips must land where they land. If the shoe fits, wear it. I'm seeing God do things in me, because there are things that I don't want you or any other man to have to pay for because of what I've been through. But, I am not yard sale material. Marriage is forever, and I'm not signing on the dotted line until I am confident that I have been found as a Good thing. I love you, and you already know that. But love isn't the only essential to a successful marriage. I'd rather be single than be miserable until Jesus comes again or one of us dies."

"So you think we'd be miserable?"

"Not if we both do some soul-searching. If you heard what I said and make some adjustments, then fine. I'm not your momma or your pastor, so the rest, is not really for me to say. But when it comes to how you have treated me as a woman, there it is. These are real issues that need to be addressed."

I used to think Xavier was the only man I could ever love. After all, he had been the only one who miraculously got past the thick walls. Xavier and I are so compatible. We have the same love for people and ministry. We are both sticklers for the sanctity and supremacy of the Word of God and very much against the present day arrogance, prostitution, and manipulation of the masses by false teachers and pulpit pimps. We both come from large families and are PKs. Our personalities also click. I have fallen asleep many nights just wanting to know the thoughts of Xavier Johnson, to wake up and hear him snoring on the telephone line. And, he is the only man with whom I've had a chemical attraction and to whom I could actually see myself wanting to give children. I appreciate his style, although he struggles with mine. As a wise church mother once told me, "You represent Jesus. Don't cater to a whore. A whore has a whore's taste." And, this is the only main objectionable issue with Xavier. He has what he and a litany of whoring preachers describe as a "flesh" problem. The personality traits that come along with catering to perverse sexual flesh issues: lust, lying, infidelity, fornication, pornography, adultery, sodomy, homosexuality, effeminate predilection, rape, and manipulation is enough to cause me to run as fast as I can from Xavier. Not because he can't change, and God can't deliver him. But because he is too well ingrained into the lifestyle, and buys the defeatism that comes with not knowing whom we've been made to be when we are born again. This born again but live just like the sinner who does not know God stuff won't fly over here. I refuse to sit in the front row of a church, help prepare sermon notes, wash his clothes, cook his meals, rub his aches and pains, honor him, defend him, love him, be his wife and the mother of his children, more than help secure our financial future and wonder if the new babies in the church have his DNA, and find out, through disease or through a law suit, that one or a number of them do have his DNA. Nowadays, sorry doesn't cut it, especially when the penalty is AIDS. I won't treat AIDS patients and become one because I loved a man who won't sever himself from the company of defiled men with a reprobate false gospel mentality and existence.

I often think of the alternative: How I will feel having to see him with someone else, as if I don't already know the feeling because some woman or fling popped up every other minute when we were dating. God can deliver. I've prayed for him, for me, for us. I've tried to understand, to be more temperate, to be quiet and to wait. Yet, the most important thing is He, who knows where I've been and what I need, will send the right man who will be a blessing and not add sorrow to my life. I must believe that as my heart heals, I, in turn, will love freely, without the penalty of my own life because of the man's weak character and lack of regard for God, and the sanctity of the institution of marriage. I'd already seen too many dark days and cannot live under the bondage of a loving husband and his doc cohorts who justify cheating.

FRIENDLY FIRE
Texan Flames

"Rashaun, how about you, Tysheem and I go away for a weekend to Texas. This might seem like a huge leap for you, but there are Black cowboys, and there's a rodeo going on that I thought we could check out."

"You buggin. Black cowboys?"

"Definitely. There's a local chapter here in Brooklyn, and I noticed they even ride their horses off the parkway on my way home from work. And, there's even a place where I can take you all to get some horseback riding lessons, if you want. At least do what I've been telling you since I've known you, hon. Don't be afraid to try things that are new to you just because you're not familiar with them. Remember you didn't think you'd like alfredo sauce? Pesto sauce? Paella? Lamb chops? Going to get a massage? Playing polo? And you tried all of that stuff and now you love all of that, right?"

"Yeah, I see your point. You right. So when we going?"

Convincing Rashaun wasn't as difficult as I anticipated. "We are going next weekend, if that's what you want to do."

"I'm good with that. Is Xavier coming? He's cool."

"No."

"Why not? He's cool and you ain't getting any younger. You need to get with him."

"He's been working on you too, huh?"

"Nope. It's just that you got it going on, and you by yourself. You need to get with him and we like him."

"Huh. Well, first of all, Aunt Jewel is single, and he doesn't need to be cramping my style when I'm going to a rodeo with black cowboys. Second, it's not really appropriate for us to be traveling together when we do have feelings for each other. He would have to meet us there and do his own thing. Give the devil no place. Besides, I haven't told him a thing about it. This trip is just for us, okay?"

"All right. If that's the way you want to play it, it's on you."

And that's the way I wanted to play it. If I could change Xavier, I would. But I can't. As I had been often reminded in listening to the messages of my favorite televangelist, Jocelyn Breyers, what if he never changes? Then I must change. And I'm not willing to ever change to accommodate a cheater. So, at least on this rodeo trip I'll get to see some brothers who own horses and can rope cattle, and the boys will get to see some brothers who own horses and rope cattle. We can all be inspired for completely different reasons.

I needed a time to bond with the boys and have a change of scenery to put the HIV/AIDS initiative together. Pastor Charles loved the AIDS/HIV ministry idea, and asked for a complete list of initiatives, tentative calendar of events, personnel, and resources needed, should Restoration Temple launch this new ministry.

Until things were absolutely clear with Aliyah, my primary obligation was to the boys and their welfare. They needed to see a better, brighter, broader, different view that living a Christ-centered life has to offer in not only accomplishments, but complete fulfillment.

Danne didn't fall for the change of scenery excuse. "So you are going to this rodeo to hook up with Black cowboys. You know how many other women are going to be there looking for a catch?"

"Not so. I'm going to take the boys to see the vast expanse of what men like them do. Everyone isn't shooting hoops, or aiming for football. There are Black men playing golf, hockey, and anything else they desire to do. And, while I'm there, I'm going to get around the exact type of Black man I'd love to get to know better. You know I don't do the hook up thing."

"Cut it out. We know you don't do the sex thing, but how about I go with the boys and you go visit Chase, or work out your program at the church? How about that? How about I make the entire trip on me? There's an offer you can't refuse." Danne was determined to make me admit something that just wasn't there.

"How about I want to go? So sit down somewhere."

"Uh huh. Case in point. You want to go. Shady. I don't see why you just don't do more of your medical association conventions."

"Because, I'm not trying to compliment a man whose work is just as or more demanding than mine, and who wants me to simply fit into his world. And, that is not all doctors, but they have the same pickings as NBA and NFL players, women who constructively hunt for a cha ching bling husband who can finance the snot out of their nostrils. And, I don't necessarily want someone who is out there like that."

"You have a rationale for every reason for everything and every situation. When are you going to learn to just live and do it. You preclude success by knowing so much about this type and that type. Now, you are getting on a plane to go be seen by some Black cowboys. Whatever your strategy is, hope you have some success."

"First you all say I don't get out of my normal routine enough. Now I'm going with the boys to a rodeo and that's still an issue."

Danne decided to give up and end the conversation. "Have a great trip. Call me when you get back."

In preparing to see some fine Black cowboys, I don't know what made me think that Rashaun and Tysheem wouldn't fight me in trying to switch up their jiggy attire to some hip cowboy gear? They were not trying to trade in their Timberlands for some cowboy boots, jeans half-way to the floor for a fitted pair, or hoodies for a clean country-western shirt. They liked the bling

bling belts though. So, we compromised and they agreed to at least do the boots and on one day, wear a cowboy shirt.

At the airport security checkpoint, Rashaun was selected for a full search. He carried on and on about being discriminated against because he was Black.

"Rashaun, close your mouth right now! Do you want to be pulled from this flight, banned from flying from this airport and put on a federal list where you will always be under suspicion?"

"No. You ain't a Black man so you don't know what we go through. Why am I the only Black man being searched?"

"Listen, if you're going to be rolling with me, you're going to have to put down some of that crazy thinking. Now, if you want to come up here one day when you're free and see if they only stop and check Black men, fine. But they check anybody and everybody."

"There you go."

"Look, racism exists, but so does paranoia. If you think anything anyone does to exercise some accountability or authority over you is because you are Black, you're going to have a difficult time in life."

"Whatever. That's why so many of us are in jail and on the streets."

"That's a bunch of bull. So many of our Black men are in jail because they did stupid stuff. Most of them made bad decisions. And then, their Blackness became relevant, not their own actions. Cut it out. Too many Black men defy authority, so instead of just going through the checkpoint, you have to cut the fool. Do you think it matters to a Black mother whose son was stabbed to death, that a Black man did it, instead of someone else? Black men have a host of issues and reasons why they trip, but they do trip. And that's why I love you the way I do. Because regardless of what you've been through in life, there will be no excuse. God has given you a way of escape. And the first step for you to be successful in life is to get out of that "the man" mentality. Authority is not your enemy. Checkpoints are to protect us all from terrorists. Most of the men in jail are people who defied rules, order, and authority at some point in time. Every human being must be subject to some sort of authority. I'm a grown woman, and make more money than my own father, but guess what? I still listen to what he says. When I get married, guess what? I'll have to listen to my husband. As a doctor, I have to obey and comply with state requirements to be licensed. People and their personal biases may affect you and other Black men, and that will probably never change. But what are you going to do about that? Cut the fool every time? Don't you ever act up like that again. Get on the plane like everyone else and close your mouth. Acting up is not cute at all and does not make you a man."

These boys not only make a sister have to get up so much earlier to get them situated for the day, but to really pray for us as a unit. Sometimes I want to jack Rashaun up, but realize that it will only be a temporary response to frustration. This boy received most of what he battles with honestly—he was born into the craziness.

I remember Aliyah telling the crew one night as we dined at one of our favorite gathering places that she wouldn't try a chicken with a peanut sauce. She had a particular aversion to peanut butter. Of course, with Aliyah, there's never a normal explanation so we all awaited the rationale for peanut butter rejection. And, after hearing it, we completely understood. Aliyah recalled crawling around as a baby, eating what she thought was peanut butter, when she found it splattered here and there around her grandmama's apartment. Later on, she would come to know the difference between real peanut butter, and the feces she consumed from a pet dog. Aliyah's grandmother's apartment was that nasty, unkept and unsupervised, that a baby could crawl around and eat dog mess. This is the environment where Rashaun spent a substantial part of the beginning of his life, and he was now getting to the point where he comprehended that he had to be raised, not just minimally nurtured.

"Let's unpack and hit the road then. While we're down here we need to hit up the best country restaurants, and oh, drive around and see some real ranches," I stated.

"So long as we get to see the cattle roping and oh yeah, that bull riding thing is most def," said Rashaun.

It's amazing how much the boys have different preferences. And, I am so used to just me and the girlfriends and what interests us. I don't mind compromising, because the boys are making me go beyond Jewel. And, I can't help but wonder how much I would have already been accustomed to loving what young boys love had I raised Chase and had to provide a well-rounded environment for him.

Just as I thought of Chase, which was more than ever, nowadays, I noticed a number of frequent missed calls from him.

"Chase, I didn't bother to check the messages. I saw that you called and I'm sorry I missed them." I never wanted my son to think he had to go through red tape to reach his mother.

Ignoring my reason for missing him, Chase blurted out, "Pop had a heart attack. And, he's in CCU. The doctors don't think he'll make it."

I was on the bridge with this one. I was a bit bewildered with the thought, *What in the world makes Chase think this is something I need to be trying to process?* It only took a few moments to put myself in his shoes. The only parent he had known for most of his life was in danger. I needed to have compassion on many levels. Swanson did repent and asked for forgiveness.

"Chase, I'm sorry to hear this. What can I do? The boys and I are in Texas for the next two days."

"We're all praying. They want to put us out of here, there's so many of us. You know, between the family and the church family. And, all his pastor friends."

"I'm sure. I understand." Swanson did have a healthy following of people who respected him, and loved him. When pastors are down, the people who appreciate real shepherds feel the agonies of their leaders. But for Chase, Swanson wasn't just his pastor and colleague in ministry. Swanson was his father.

"I can't stand seeing him like this. I've never seen Pop weak like this before. He's used to being on top of everything. To see him lying there with all them wires on his chest and arms and all over the place, is too much."

The doctor in me chimed in, "Don't worry about all of that. I'm sure they're keeping him sedated so that he can begin to recover and put absolutely no stress on his heart. So what exactly are the doctors saying?"

"Well, I'm not exactly sure. My brother Corey has been dealing with the doctors. As a matter of fact, why don't you talk to him?"

The thoughts preceded the mustering of compassion. What the hell is wrong with Chase? I'm not trying to get all involved in his family drama. I know I'm supposed to care. This could be my own father. But, if I get involved, maybe I will really end up caring. I'm not supposed to be this involved in any type of care for a man who raped me, forgiveness or not. But obviously, Chase wanted me to help.

"Wait a minute Chase. When did all of this happen?"

"Last night. Well, early this morning, around three am."

"Ok. Actually, if you want me to. I'd rather speak with his attending, cardiologist and any other doctors. Depending on how bad the heart attack was, he could have multi-system failure, and have different specialists involved. Go to the nurse's station and ask to have the doctor paged, and put my cell as the return contact number. Tell them a family physician is calling to connect. It may take a while, because they may have other patients, but when I hear something, I'll call you back and let you know what is going on medically."

This is that savior complex Danne always beefs at me about. I can't believe I'm getting involved in this crisis when I'm supposed to be enjoying the dry Texas breeze. Yet, I needed to do as much as I could for my son.

"Did he ever have a heart attack or stroke before?"

"Not that I know of. He has high blood pressure though."

"Ok. Chase, just keep praying. Believe me, prayer makes the difference. We can do all we can do, and many doctors think it is them. But, we are not God. We can do all we know how to do, and that may not be enough. But, when God says otherwise, that's when real miracles take place. So don't get weak in believing. Trust God."

"We have no other choice, Momma."

Hearing that Prophet Swanson is in CCU did not make me feel good. That pit in the stomach feeling was clear as day. My baby had to grow up without me, and now, as soon as we are developing a relationship, Prophet Swanson is direly ill. *God, please touch Mr. Swanson's body. Allow him to know you as Jehovah Rapha, and let your healing virtue flow from the crown of his head, to the soles of his feet, right now, in Jesus' name. By your stripes, Swanson has been healed and made whole. Lord, please, not now. Guide us, Holy Spirit, and let us walk in your perfect will concerning this situation. Lord, let your will be done.*

I had to hit Danne up with the latest.

Danne gave the predictable response, "Jewel, take those boys out and have a good time. I hate to sound crass, but if the man is dying, he's going to die anyway, and Rashaun and Tysheem don't have anything to do with that. They don't need to be disappointed."

"I'm not going to amend their schedule for this. I'm just expressing."

"Ok, just making sure. Express then."

I didn't want to belabor the issue with Danne. She and the rest of the syndicate kept harassing me for feeling like I had to accept everything about Chase, including his father. I understood their reasoning but wanted to really walk in forgiveness. That would require not just letting go of the past and all of the issues that came along with the rape, but since Swanson had actually changed and was no longer a threat to me, trying to treat him like I would any other human being.

So before we got started, I switched gears. "Forget it. Have you heard from Aliyah?"

"Yeah. She said they want to take her to the hospital. She's having hot and cold sweats, changing clothes about three times in one night. She said the boils are back, and she has a huge one in her inner thigh, and she is losing her voice again because she has the white fungal yeast growth all throughout her mouth and down her esophagus."

"Can I ask you a question?"

"You just did."

"Why the hell is she calling you with all of this and I'm the one with her kids and by the way, the doctor in this picture?"

"How about you just answered your own question. She needs to do what she feels she needs to do, and doesn't need a doctor. She needs someone who will just listen. And, she knows you're not just going to do that. Besides, she knows her kids are good with us."

"What about her kids hearing her own voice and knowing for themselves what she is saying? This isn't that difficult. It doesn't take a rocket scientist to know that a mother in her condition should be calling her children, or at least answering our phone calls."

"That's in ideal land. But Aliyah doesn't and has never existed there, okay? At least she is in touch. So we take what we can get."

"Rashaun is at the point where he doesn't even want to talk to her anyway. He is emotionally blocking already. And Tysheem craves to hear her voice. He is so clingy and Rashaun could go the distance without any type of affection. They are so different.

Anyway, let me hit you up later; this must be one of the doctors calling on the other line."

After speaking with the attending, I decided to call Chase back after the boys got involved with at least one activity for the day. The conversation would be a minute, and they had already been uncharacteristically patient.

To our advantage, there were two open appointments for horseback riding lessons. I had one hour and a half to handle business. Chase was at the top of the list.

"Chase, I spoke with Prophet..uh..your father's doctor. Based upon what he told me is going on with him, they are not trying to do anything right now, other than keep him knocked out so that he can begin to recover. He has had multi-system failures, so in a nutshell, his heart, kidneys, and lungs all need TLC. Real TLC. They are having difficulty regulating his blood pressure and getting that under control. So based upon our conversation, they're going to change the blood pressure medication to see if that makes a difference. Things can go either way right now. So, you all need to be resting as much as possible, because you'll be more effective to be there for him when he does wake up."

"Ok. So what do you think?"

"It's all in God's hands right now. I can't say one way or the other." It would be irresponsible for me to provide false hope. It was solely a matter of trusting God.

"Could you please let everybody know. We need as many people praying as possible."

There's no need to wonder how Daddy will react. Daddy is always one who doesn't get involved in emotional turmoil. He'll wait until the cool of the day to know how to handle a matter. Even though he hadn't spoken to Swanson in years, he loved him enough to let him walk outside of his home alive, after raping his youngest daughter, so surely, he would have compassion now.

"Daddy, I'm in Texas for a few days. But, Chase called me earlier to let me know that Prophet Swanson had a heart attack."

"Oh really. How is he?"

"He's on the line. It's too early to tell. He is in CCU, which is normal for someone who had a heart attack of that magnitude." I didn't want to violate Swanson's rights and broadcast his business, cause I know when Daddy hangs up, he'll tell the boys.

"So the reason I'm getting this call is because?"

"Chase asked me to let you know, because he is soliciting the prayers of the saints. That's why, Bishop in the Lord's church."

"Don't go there with me, young lady. Watch it. I'm just asking to know what you all expected me to do."

"You're right. I'm sorry, Daddy."

"Are you okay?"

"I'm fine. I'm really concerned about Chase. I still have you and Mama, so I can't imagine what they feel like. It's no joke to watch parents suffer."

"Ok. Well, I'll call my son in a little bit. First, I'm going to go to God."

"Which one? Please don't call Ford yet cause he—"

"I'm talking about Chase." Time almost froze. Daddy called Chase his son. "I'm going to call him but I need to know what the Lord is saying first." Somehow, I felt at peace.

The boys and I managed to enjoy our cowboy experience. Tysheem may have enjoyed it a bit too much. Now, he wants a horse. They learned quite a bit about driving a herd, and watched a few competitions. I did get to meet and exchange information with a 36-year-old Caucasian ranch owner. He bragged of putting out some of the best cows that yield the highest grade in beef, and is a fourth-generation farmer. Harlan Jimmy Pickett was quite a gentleman.

"Can you make a few moments for me before you leave?" Harlan asked with stolen glances while tending to one of his prize horses.

"To do what, exactly Mr. Harlan?" I didn't even know this man. "Just let me show you around the ranch," Harlan continued. "Or, join me for a good ole Texas barbecue. Please allow me to show you proper Texan hospitality like no other. I promise, you won't regret it." Clearly, Mr. Pickett had some cowboy swagger and wasn't about to give up.

I had to admit, I was curious and interested. However, I also battled with the automatic distrust I've had toward men. There would have to be some precautions. "Ok. Can we opt for the barbecue?" I asked. At least that would be in public.

"Barbecue it is. In these parts, it's really easy to make a fine woman happy." If Harlan only knew what that open flirting was going to cost me with the boys, he might have refrained.

Rashaun rode me about flirting with a white man all the way back to our lodge. He didn't waste one second.

"How you gonna play a brother for a dude? What's up with that?"

"I'm not playing a brother. I'm just seeing what's going on with the dude, and guess what, the brother doesn't have me locked down. I'm a single woman. And if a good man finds me who is Caucasian, yippee!"

"I can't believe this [sh**]." My openness to Harlan seemed to be an affront to Rashaun and all Black men. But that still didn't give Rashaun the right to curse.

"Say it, and I promise you, I'll pull this car over and jack you up. You are going to learn to stop cussing," I threatened.

All of my antics never move Rashaun. He simply cracked up laughing. "It's cool. I'm just not living with whitey. I can tell you that right now."

"How do we get from meeting a man to living with him? Please, it's not that serious."

But, I did hear what Rashaun said. He has processed the reality that he and Tysheem just may end up with me for good.

"And, I need you not to be racist. There's nothing wrong with being proud of who you are, but don't go there with that whitey stuff. You wouldn't want any white people calling you a [N-word]."

Anyway, the knuckleheads behaved at the barbecue. Words cannot express the fulfillment of smelling and savoring the delicious fresh barbecue sauce, pan-seared blackened catfish over a fireside stove, fried corn puffs, potato salad, a spinach and beets salad, and beef, beef, beef. Mr. Harlan Jimmy Pickett out-did himself. And, he managed to make me and the boys feel at home. We were the only African Americans present.

After a wonderful evening in the beautiful Texan night air, Harlan asked, "Do you mind if I see to it that you make it back to your room?"

"I'll be fine. The boys are with me. We've got OnStar in the rental, and I've got a GPS." An alarm went off. Why does he need to know where I'm staying? He could be genuinely hospitable, but I can't pretend as if I haven't lived most of my life with ingrained paranoia when it comes to situations like this.

"Well, please call me when you've made it back. This is just how a gentleman treats a lady. Do you mind if I call you later this evening?"

"Not at all. I do have some things I need to tend to, but a few minutes won't hurt."

Harlan was a fine man. He had that Edward Scissorhands haircut thing going on, which was quite progressive for the cowboy look. His nails were well manicured, his six-pack was talking. Scratch that. It was screaming. His teeth were white, and his skin was quite clear. The rich blue denim skinny jeans fit as if they were custom made, and taught to glide against his athletic body. He definitely had the look.

Harlan Jimmy Pickett and I talked for almost three hours. I learned about his passion and great family tradition and business. I also discovered how blissfully ignorant I was about progressive and advanced farming techniques and would never underestimate a farmer again. Clearly, Harlan is quite wealthy and also has a PhD in agriculture from an Ivy League university. He's never married, had any children, and was quite frank in disclosing that he definitely never dated or thought of dating a Black woman. He just saw me and thought how attractive I was. He loved the fact that I didn't flaunt it, and in his words, "just owned it." Harlan just may be the man I've been waiting for all of my life. If I were a gold-digging woman, or one looking for a sugar daddy, then I would have been impressed by the family crest that he had around his neck on a gold pendant that denoted generational mullah.

The flight home was without incident. Rashaun and Tysheem were quite comfortable, and acted like they knew how to do this. What I wasn't ready for was what took place when we landed. Mr. Xavier Johnson was at the gate with about two dozen yellow roses in his hand. Brother man was trying, but a little too late, especially after meeting someone who I never ever thought would tickle my fancy, Mr. Harlan Jimmy Pickett. But common sense and good manners dictated that I should at least act grateful and not hurt his feelings. Xavier didn't have to be thoughtful.

"Hi. What a pleasant surprise. How'd you know when we were getting in?"

"I have my resources. Anyway, not to be rude, but I didn't come here for you. So please step aside and let me welcome my two friends home."

And there it was. Xavier gave Rashaun and Tysheem friendship roses, and put their luggage on a cart. No he didn't.

"As a courtesy, would you like me to get yours?" Xavier asked smugly.

I could see that Xavier was enjoying his little plan to make a statement, without making one at all. What Xavier would soon learn, if he hadn't already, is that I'll always have an answer for the trickiest situations.

"I'd like you to be the gentleman that you say you are. So I believe I don't even have to answer what you really shouldn't have even asked," I offered as I released the handles to my luggage and walked away. Jewel girl sniffed the boys' roses and told them how fortunate they were. Homeboy never met me at the airport at all, nor brought flowers. Since Xavier wanted to take me there, I thought I'd mess with him in the process.

"I didn't want you to have to take a car home, and I wanted to check up on the boys," Xavier explained.

While there may have been an iota of truth to why Xavier was waiting for us, we both knew he was trying to get up on his game. So, I worked with what he said the program was. "Thanks. Check up. The boys are right here."

Meanwhile, I chose to seem over-saturated with anything other than Xavier Johnson. Harlan Pickett had impeccable timing to help a sister throw a brother. The cowboy had swagger in his text messaging, "Hope u landed n r STR8. .02. When u get tired of commercial, LMK. U'll B on PVT, Harlan style. BBN" The automatic smile was unintentional and telling. I could get used to this kind of attention.

"What you smiling like that for?" Xavier wanted to know.

"Because life is good, man of God."

Enough said.

LOVE PUT TO THE TEST
Motherhood For Real

Before Rashaun could hit the game room or Tysheem could boot up his laptop, Chase was hitting up the cell again and again. I had a newfound respect for mothers all over the world, especially those who raise children by themselves. Without any time to grow into managing three very different relationships with each of them, I could appreciate the more of them, less of me life that every caring mother must live.

"Chase I got your message, what's going on."

"Pop is in and out of it. They keep putting him back to sleep."

"Ok. You said it was urgent. Has anything changed since we last spoke?"

"When he first came out of it, Ms. Edie was with him, and she said he cried, said he was tired and wanted to see you."

There are some moments in life where a human being has to verify that her existence is authentic in this present world. So, I pinched myself to make sure Jewel was really Jewel. I must not have comprehended what I thought I heard.

"Say that again. I think I didn't hear you correctly, Chase."

"Yes you did. Pop said he wanted to see you."

I would have flunked Are You Smarter Than A Fifth Grader for the ability to retain and regurgitate basic information. Again, I asked, "Wanted to see me? Are you all certain?"

"Yeah. Ms. Edie said she was stunned. He said he wants to see you, and if anything happens to him, we better do like he always said, put me as the pastor and everyone continue to support the ministry. So, I know it's a lot to ask. Can you get down here as soon as possible? The way he was talking, he may not be around for much longer."

"Okay. Give me a few minutes to work some things out, and I'll see if this is something I should do."

We just landed, and I had high hopes of beginning counseling with the boys within the next couple of days. This was a strong "what the" moment.

When I was much younger, I came home saying, "What the [F-word]," over and over again. None of Caroline's children dared to curse and think they'd survive without a chopped off tongue. So, as the story goes, my mother whupped me silly and told me not to curse. I didn't quite get what was wrong with cursing, although according to them, I used the "what the [F-word]" phraseology in response to perfect cursing situations. So, I knew a strong curse word, and when to use it appropriately. The F-word was a bad word, and Jewel was not to use it again. So, the literalist in me took the butt whipping and learned the lesson. I graduated to expressing my disdain with them by screaming, "What the!" instead of "What the [F-word]!" I did not say the curse word, so I had complied with Caroline's instructions. Yet, the import was the same. Everybody knew I wanted to curse, but just didn't. That's when the Bishop and Caroline knew they had a real challenge on their hands. Again, this was one of those moments. I decided to call Bishop Prunell.

"Jewel, I think you have to consider living for the rest of your life without knowing what the man wants to say to you. He's getting ready to go home to be with the Lord now."

"You think so?" I asked the Bishop who happened to be my daddy.

"Yes." Years of witnessing Bishop Prunell's accuracy and compassion let me know at that very instant, Chase's life was about to change forever. And, how I conducted myself would affect Chase's life.

"Do I have an obligation to go?" I asked, really wanting to hear from my daddy.

"Of course not. You decide, and know you will live with your decision. Just remember it's not only about you anymore. Weigh all the factors."

There wasn't a decision to be made, then. "There really is no question for me. I know it is important to Chase, and he is what I'm concerned about. And, if there is anything that Swanson needs to let go of, I don't want to be a hindrance in any way."

"And that's a good decision. We have to love our enemies. Not so that we can see them receive God's judgment, but love when you know you don't deserve it, will break the wickedest of men. Love is powerful. That is what God's grace is all about. And you are passing the test. We don't deserve God's love, but, God!"

"But God, Daddy. But for God's love, I would have never made it. And, really, he's not even an enemy."

Xavier volunteered to be the hero and keep the boys. "You know they are too much for your daddy and em, and you don't need to wear Danne out, cause she's in for the long haul," Xavier noted as he planned to stay with the boys.

"She's in for the long haul, and they are family to us, so wearing out isn't an issue. Anyway, thanks. I hope to be back within a day or two, or else some of my patients are going to tell me off. And the boys seem to like you a lot."

Xavier never misses an opportunity. "Stop trying to be so hard, Jewel. You do too, and we both know it."

"Don't push it brother." There was a time when I would have melted over Xavier's attention. He just had to throw a son and other women in the mix to kill all of that. Men have a difficult time understanding that all of their efforts don't mean a hill of beans once they have broken trust and cross the bounds of respect and decency. This is especially true for Xavier. He's the type that if I ever thought of playing him, I'd be so finished that he would have a genuine struggle remembering my name. He would never tolerate me if I did to him, what he did to me.

Danne, Noey, Laurel and I did the conference call thing. "Y'all won't believe I'm on my way back to the airport. Chase's father had a heart attack, and they're concerned about him surviving it."

"So why are you going down there? There goes Jesus's baby sister again, always doing the right thing," Noey chimed in, probably with a head full of pink hair rollers.

"Let's wait to hear the explanation for this one, Noey," Danne challenged. I knew she was about to hit me for doing so much more than I was obligated to do, once again to my own discomfort and detriment. "And, this better be good."

So, I felt a bit defensive. "It's really simple. Chase said he asked for me, and even if he didn't, my son's only parent he has ever known up until a couple of weeks ago may be dying. If he asked me to be there, what am I to do? I can at least be there for him."

"You know I'm with you, Jewel. Folks can jack us up, all in the name of Jesus between the 'hecananananashas,' but we still have to do what is right. And if it were my son, I'd be there." Laurel said. She definitely would be, because she is a do-gooder all the way. "But, when nobody's looking, punch him right in that good old chest and tell him that was for what you did to me, and then tell the people you have Turrets Syndrome. I'd at least have to do that and answer to God later."

We all burst out laughing even though that was a sick joke. Laurel is going to find a way to make any situation funny.

"Well, please keep them in prayer. All I keep thinking is it could be my mother or father. I've seen death so many times, but when it's close to home, that's another story.

"Did you meet any Black cowboys?" Danne didn't want to hear the melodrama and her nosy quota for the day had not yet been filled.

I shared all of the intriguing details about Harlan Jimmy Pickett with the girls. Although I've never had any issues with men of other races or nationalities, I never even thought of any significant involvement with one either. My role models were my father and my brothers and the natural affinity I had toward men—albeit very minimal—were for men who looked and believed like them. No one in the crew is a Black nationalist or pro-Black. We are all comfortably Black. So everybody was cool with the concept that Jewel just might end up with a wealthy Caucasian cowboy, or at least have a time with a man who would show me that there is so much more to a good relationship than trying to compromise with a cheating man.

"You all are the ones who keep giving Xavier dap with me that he doesn't have any more. I'm not there anymore with him like that." I told the girls this with the deepest conviction.

Laurel giggled as I rehearsed the reason. Then she let me have it. "Yeah, right. Let that brother stink from a hard workout and come with his swagger in your face and watch them dimples let him in. The brother only keeps coming because he knows when he gives off the scent, you get drunk in it. Men don't like rejection at all. And he knows your words are just words, not real rejection. You are rehearsing a 'you better respect me' script to him and he is loving this. He knows he got it like that, baby and all."

They had a point. But Harlan had my attention in a way that no man did for quite some time. I was willing to see what the end was going to be with someone who I would have never even dreamed could be the one.

Nonetheless, Chase needed his first and new mother. When I saw Evey's face, I realized that truly, God can restore everything the cankerworm, palmerworm and the locust have stolen. My daughter-in-law was waiting for me as if I had known them for a lifetime. During what had to be one of the most challenging times in their lives—when the patriarch of the family and their loved spiritual leader was in the balance—the door was open for me to be a part. Suddenly, I began to see this trip as something so much greater than "me" having to have another encounter with the perpetrator of a crime against me and the ensuing years of struggle, hurt, and longing.

"Hi, Dr. Prunell. Can I get you anything before we head to the hospital?"

"No. I am perfectly fine. Where is Chase?"

"At the hospital, mam."

"Evey, please call me Jewel. I know that technically, I'm your mother-in-law, but girlfriend we could be homegirls. It may be a bit awkward because of the age thing, but you calling me 'mam' makes me feel a bit old."

"It's a southern thing, that's all. But, I'll call you Jewel, mam."

"And, I want you to hear it directly from my mouth to your ears, I miss you and that pretty little missy."

"You should know there's another on the way," Evey disclosed half-happily and half-mourning.

"Wow! Congratulations."

"We are happy. But everything with Pop makes it, you know, a bit hard. He may not be here to see him born, and to bless him," Evey cited as she choked up.

"I'm sorry, I don't mean to be insensitive."

"No, you're not at all."

There wasn't too much more that Evey and I said to each other on the way to the hospital. She was definitely preoccupied with the heaviness of the situation. From Evey's perspective, she was one of the fortunate ones: a young girl who was blessed to marry into the man of God's family, and marry a great Man of God. So, Prophet Swanson wasn't just her father-in-law, he was her pastor since she was a young girl.

Lord, please prepare my heart for what is to come. Allow my words to be seasoned words of purpose, healing and encouragement. Help me to see beyond me, and beyond the moment. Let my words and actions speak life to everyone involved. Let me be a blessing, as your people go through this time.

As I walked down the long corridor, the steps I took seemed surreal. Why am I here? Who else, in their right mind, would be doing this? Are you really going to go through with this? I saw Ms. Edie and her eyes looked bloodshot. She glared at me, and didn't budge or motion to say hello. What, in God's name, should I be saying to this woman? The man isn't gone yet, and as a doctor and a child of God, I'll never mourn the living as if he is already dead. I leaned over to try to embrace Ms. Edie. However, she was tense and didn't attempt to be receptive. She had to be in a place that no loving wife ever wants to be in. I couldn't personalize her reaction. The reality is, I'm not family to this woman, and probably the last person on earth she wanted to see at this time.

Evey noticed the interaction and assured me, "Hold on, Ms. Jewel, I'll go get Chase, I'm sure he's in with Pop."

I just stood there, watching family and church folk talking, weeping, praying, and some just sitting around, being there. Outside of Evey and Chase, I had no connection. At that very moment, I wished I had a spouse or friend whom I could lean on. Chase arrived at the right time.

"Momma, thanks for coming. Pop wants to see you. The nurse wanted to give him some pain medications, but he knew you were on the way and didn't want to go back to sleep yet. He's waiting for you."

I was ready to get it over with, and "be out." When we walked in the room, Ms. Edie's sons gave me the same non-speaking "look at this woman" greeting.

"Pop, Jewel Prunell is here."

"I had a heart attack son. I can still see." Prophet Delayne Swanson's voice was so hollow.

"Hello Prophet Swanson. I came as soon as Chase told me you wanted to see me."

"Thanks. I'm going to ask the rest of you to leave us alone."

If eyes were daggers, I would have been dead. Chase's brothers looked like mine would look, if they saw Swanson. I didn't know how we got from love and forgiveness on my last visit to this.

"Dr. Prunell," and there was a pause and gasping for breath, "I'm so glad you made it."

"It was a tight turn-a-round, but given the circumstances, I wanted to be here."

"Hear me. I'm so glad you made it. I'm glad you did. Tamar didn't make it. Uriah went on to be with the Lord at the hand of David's wickedness to cover himself. A whole lot of people don't make it. But you did. And, I'm sorry for taking advantage of you. Had it not been for the mercy of God, I would have had a very different life. Probably would have spent most of it in jail. Sometimes we never think of the people we've harmed along the way. I'm glad God gave me a chance to get things right before it was too late."

"Yes, sir." I really just needed to keep quiet and listen.

"I know my end has come," Swanson admitted as tears streamed down his face. "And, my work is done. I couldn't care less about my name. I know it is good in heaven."

"And from all those people in the hallways, it's good here too. I'm sure many people have found you to be a great father." I wanted to be encouraging.

"You and I have never talked as two parents. But, we are two parents. So, from one parent to the other, I need to let you know my heart." For years I have listened to patients with stressed breathing, struggle to talk. That time, I didn't want to miss one word. Jewel Prunell never thought that she and Delayne Swanson would ever have to talk about their son, Brandon Chase. So I continued to listen as Swanson spoke. "God trusted me with Chase and He has everything planned out. I know the church is in good hands. He is not the most gifted one, but he has the heart that God can trust. So, Chase will pastor, and there are other great leaders to help the people. I've given them everything

I've got. And I hope his brothers and sisters will be as they have always been with him. They'll love him just the same and serve him like they served the God in me." Somehow, I felt as if I really needed to digest every word because this man did have the keys to Chase's life. As a Godly leader, he did know how to reach our son in ways that I never wanted to realize. "My wife loves him. She loves him dearly. I can't imagine how hard it has been for her to love him. That's how much she loved me. She took to him at best as she could. But the truth is, she has never treated him like the rest of ours. She would only let him get so close, and watched every move I made with him and compared it to the others. I know Chase felt that, but no one would ever know it. That one looks at the bright side and never complains. Never. And, she'd probably take me out of here if she knew I was telling you this. So, it's not an accident that you found him when you did. He's going to need you and your family now. I've been the best father to all my sons and daughters, even my spiritual children. I made some mistakes along the way, but I've given them everything I got. And, when I'm gone, don't let anything stand in your way from being a mother to him. He's going to need his mother."

Prophet Swanson was obviously in incredible pain.

"Do you need pain meds? Cause it'll take a few minutes for them to kick in."

"Yeah, I think I'm going to need them now."

As overwhelmed as I was, I slipped my head out the door and asked Chase to see to the nurse for pain medications. Being in MD mode helped me to hold back the tears.

I assured Prophet Delayne Swanson, "I heard what you said; you just need to be as comfortable as possible."

"What's going to make me comfortable is going to see Jesus. I'm at peace with God, and with all men."

"Yes, you are. We are at peace. And, you have been a great father to Chase. Look at how much of a man and kind-spirited person he is. Growing up, I was so concerned about who was keeping him, and taking care of him, and seeing him now, I know that those years of worry were wasted. God really gives children to us and trusts us to give them back to him." Those words caused my stomach to flutter. "And, we know that Chase didn't come through ideal circumstances, but I'm glad if anything had to come of it, that our son is who he is. You raised him well." And those words hurt, but were the truth. It wasn't fair, but it was the truth.

Even at his last hour, Prophet Swanson preached. "Only in the Kingdom can we ever see a day like this. Jesus' kingdom is not like this world. When you and I can be at peace with one another, the world would call us crazy."

"And, I'm glad to be part of the Kingdom of God. Who wants to go to hell, or live in hell on earth, fighting to hold onto unforgiveness and bitterness? Prophet, meeting you has freed me from so much. I thought I knew the Lord. But to know the Savior whose blood covered the offended so that we could be healed, and the offender, so that we can be free is to know Him on another level."

"You preaching little lady. But, let's get somebody back in here. I know my wife. And she's been through enough so I don't want her wondering what we're doing in here for too long. Just remember, God knows I've poured out all I can into Chase, and I guess it's your turn now. You have wisdom beyond your years. Whatever he needs from a parent will come from you. And please tell your parents—"

"Let me call them, and you tell them yourself." My daddy doesn't like being put on the spot, but he may never have the chance to speak to Prophet Swanson again. And, my daddy needed to let some things go. They spoke for a few minutes, and I left the room.

"Thank you." I touched him on the hand, and left Prophet Swanson's room. The entire interface was heavy. He basically handed the baton to me to be there for our son. God would have to truly guide me, because Chase and I didn't grow up together, and we're only twelve years apart in age.

As I walked out, Ms. Edie came up to me. "What did he have to tell you? What was it?"

"Ms. Edie please calm down."

"Don't tell me to calm down. What did you two have to discuss?"

"You two? Nothing. He just apologized again and wanted to let me know that he is dying and he hopes Chase and I can have the type of relationship where Chase can come to me, if he needs to. That's all." I had enough wisdom not to go into too much with her, because she would have been insulted.

Ms. Edie wasn't going for the oke doke. "That's all? Why would that need to be private and take all this time? And why would Chase need you now? Huh?"

"All what time? I asked for pain meds for him, and we had a few awkward moments of small talk. I don't even know your husband. Why am I being interrogated, Ms. Edie? I can't believe this. Why do I have to defend myself to you or to anybody for that matter? I didn't ask to be here. I didn't ask for any of this, ever."

I walked off to find my son. "Chase, please, let me get my bags out of the car. I'm going back to the airport."

"Tonight? It's too late. Please, what is going on?"

"Nothing. I don't do drama. And, I'm not going to go off on Ms. Edie I know she's hurting, and I'm not going to be mistreated, either. So the best thing is for me to go. You be with your family, and you can call me anytime." I said this, all within hearing distance from Ms. Edie I noticed Evey comforting her, and torn between whether she should try to even play herself and reach out to me.

"Hold on a minute. Please," Chase pleaded.

"Chase, look at me. I know we are getting to know one another. So let me help you. This is not a time for nonsense or drama.

When people are hurt, they sometimes hurt others. I'm not going to let Ms. Edie play me, nor am I going to play her. And all of you need to be there for each other and don't add a lick of stress to your father right now. It's really about him. Don't give any attention to this. Please. And remember, folks are going to be watching your loyalties right now. So don't play yourself with them for me. Your brothers and sisters are going to scrutinize what you did when their mama, the woman who halfway raised you, and I had a few sour words. I'm too tired anyway. Just ask Evey to give me the keys to the car and I'll get my bags over to a hotel myself. I'll text you with the information to where I am staying."

"No. I'm going to have someone take you to a hotel, unless you want to go to Aunt Catherine's."

"Is your family going to be piling up there?"

"Probably."

"Hotel, then."

"Aunt Catherine will not care. Trust me. She will handle up on anyone who tries anything with you. She protected you before she ever met you."

"Chase, I'll trust your judgment. I'm tired, and just need to get away from here for a few. I'm sorry. I probably should've just let her vent and not have responded the way I did."

"Momma, I'll get to the bottom of this. One thing they gonna have to learn is you are part of my family, so whatever that means to this family, they are gonna have to get used to it. I'm gonna call Aunt Catherine. She'll fix you up real good. Thanks for coming. Now, Pop can be relieved with whatever it is he was carrying."

I hugged my son. "I'll wait right here."

I walked over to Ms. Edie and the ensuing audience of her supporters. "Ms. Edie I'm sorry I spoke to you the way I did. I didn't come to cause any harm. I'm leaving first thing in the morning."

First Lady Edith Swanson uttered "Grace and Peace," without breaking her blank empty stare. Did she just go churchy on me? Yes, that's exactly what Ms. Edie did. Her husband was dying and she had no ability to curtail her emotions toward the girl he wanted to mysteriously see on his deathbed. Prophet Swanson wasn't stiff yet, and already, Ms. Edie had me on ice.

Evey came to drop me at Aunt Catherine's. She and I struggled to maintain a conversation. I just took the ride with tears streaming down my face, wondering if there would ever be a day when I could be in relationship with my son, without there being some craziness and adversity. I had to remind myself: The glass is full.

When I arrived at Aunt Catherine's I couldn't hit the pillow fast enough to escape and delay processing the long day.

I woke up the next morning to good old country cooking. I could smell thick fresh bacon and hear it crackling.

"Good morning, Ms. Catherine."

"Morning, Precious. I know it's early, but I wanted to get on over there to see my brother before all them lunatics start coming to see the mand of God. Glad to have you back, be it under these conditions. But, I'm glad you're here. This means a lot to us, you know."

"Morning to you. I'm gonna have to head home today. I just came to speak with Prophet Swanson and I've got so much on my plate at home. But thanks for everything."

"I understand, and wouldn't want to be here an extra second either if I were you. But I ain't you. I'd look these nincompoops right in their faces and tell them to 'sit down rascals and take a minute.' Sometimes you've got to help folks out. And, as for my sister-in-law, don't study her. She may try to clown, but God'll whip her back into shape. She only gets so far and then she's got to turn around. She can be a bit much, but she do love the Lord. So He deals with her. And, God knows, I'm anointed to help her out. So if you ever need some of this anointing, just let me know."

"I need some of it right now. No, I'm only kidding. As soon as my assistant books my return flight, I'm out of here."

"Can you book it for tonight? How often will you get to come down here? Let me at least fix some lunch, or you can treat us to lunch downtown."

"All right, Ms. Catherine. I'm going to go back to bed until you get back and you're ready for lunch."

Lunch never happened. I waited for hours, and couldn't reach a soul. Somehow, common sense kicked in and just as I thought, Prophet Swanson passed away. I rested in the garden, and wouldn't dare update anyone about what was going on. The Prunells, especially Ford and Justice, would turn this entire town upside down if they knew Ms. Edie slammed me in the hospital in front of her family and church folks. The girls would tell me that's exactly what I get for even being involved. Noey would contribute, you're always trying to do the right thing, and Danne would just listen. Laurel would be on the next flight down here to snatch up Ms. Edie's wig, hell to the naw style, and ask the rest of her clan if they want some too, sprinkled with some Brooklyn in it. I would have to be completely on the other side of this if and when I ever said a word about it to anyone. I didn't want to be rude and just break out.

Before long, Ms. Catherine, Chase, Evey and Ruth all came back to the house together.

"The old man left us. Yes, he did. And I'm gonna miss the old bat."

Chase just sat down looking as if the world crashed around him. Evey didn't even sit down.

"I'm so sorry." I didn't know what else to say.

I reached for little Ruth, and Evey held her even tighter.

"Ms. Catherine, I hate to be rude, but I've got to make my flight. I'm gonna take a car to the airport, and be out of your way."

"Out of the way? Pop just died and you're talking about being in the way? Momma, can you just relax for a few days? I'm gonna need you right now," Chase spoke as he loosened his tie and wrapped both of his hands around his head.

"I'll see what I can do. I have the two boys at home you know. I'll have to check on them first and see." I corrected myself before I even finished. "As a matter of fact, Chase, it's not a problem. I'll be here for you. Whatever you need me to do, I'm here for you, Chase." As I spoke, I heard how ridiculous I sounded telling my son that two other children's needs were more important than his on the day his father died.

Evey kindly suggested to Chase, "Sugar, maybe we should let her get back to the boys. We understand Ms. Jewel didn't plan on being here and we do have plenty to take care of. Ms. Edie and the rest of us have everything under control."

I listened and recognized that if there was a divide, Evey demonstrated where she stands. Maybe, she was trying to keep the peace. But the question remained, "What have I done?"

Clearly, Chase was on edge. He checked Evey right in front of my face. "Evey, I'm not gonna have you insult my momma, now. And I already told you not to get involved in that mess. Ms. Edie and them is wrong, and they gonna have to answer to God. You better learn how to stay out of all that messy women stuff. Pop wouldn't want any of this right here. None of it!"

Even though no one should ever interrupt a husband and a wife, I took the opportune moment to jump in. "Can somebody tell me what is going on? If I said something, or did something out of the way, can somebody please tell me?"

Ms. Catherine dared to answer. "You haven't done a thing. Ms. Edie and her church hens are just starting to mess up again. They are cantankerous and love confusion. So, it's really nothing to talk about."

But Evey didn't like Ms. Catherine's response. She stood up for her mother-in-law and asked me, "We want to know what you doing here. How come if everything was the way your folks said it was between you and Pop, why are you hanging around? Why he asked to see you then? What business did you have to discuss with him, after Ms. Edie took care of my husband his whole life."

I couldn't believe what I was hearing. "Are you suggesting something else, Evey? Are you out of your mind? I'm not going to go through no crazy stuff with anybody and you're right Chase, this is a bunch of mess. You called me and asked me to come. What is wrong with these people?" I was almost out of control and crying. My vision was blurred and I could hardly see. I was on the bridge and about to have a crash in the middle of it. I knew the tone and words weren't appropriate at all. Jewel was just tired.

"This is the kind of stuff that makes people leave the church and never want to come back again. I'm not 'hanging around' Evey. I came because I was asked to be here. And what did you mean by if things were like my folks said? Do you want me to stand up on a rooftop and deface the memory of your father and pastor and let the world know that he did rape me? Have you ever had a pillow thrown over your face and a man stick what felt like a block of chopped wood up your stuff? And you're asking me about business with him? Are you out of your mind? The only business I had with Swanson was to let all of that go, and try to have a relationship with Chase. Anything else, Evey?"

Ms. Catherine jumped in right on time. "Well, I have something to say. Ms. Edie didn't raise Chase his whole life, Evey. She's just being a bit dramatic now. He didn't even move in with them till he was fifteen. Everybody knows Chase spent most of his days right here with me or in my hands or on my lap as a baby. And, none of us was his momma. We all love him, and if you ask me, nobody could love him more than me. But nothing in this world is like a mother's love."

I was still on the bridge. My uncensored thoughts ran out the gate of my mouth while I was already in "going off" flesh mode. "I can't believe that you would even entertain such nonsense."

"So why didn't your people report him then. They just sent Chase down here and now you two had to have a private conversation," Evey continued with the absurd theory Ms. Edie and her crew must have been working with.

All of the nicey Jewel was gone. I knew I should have just got up, packed my things and left because people don't like the real me when I'm pushed to the edge and fight. But I didn't. I let Evey have it. "So you bird brains ignore a lifetime of evidence because of one conversation that Ms. Edie couldn't be part of, and turn this whole situation out. This is deep. So what is the story you are working with, then, Evey? I can't phantom what kind of nonsense must be running through your mind. What is it that you are getting at? How did the twelve-year-old end up pregnant by the great man of God? You people are unbelievable."

Evey calmed down. "Nothing. It don't matter no way."

But, I was already provoked and fried. "Chase, Ms. Catherine, I'm just going to say one thing, and then I'm going to a hotel. For the record, there was never any fishy, unethical, or shady behavior on my part. I was twelve years old, and I'm not sure how seductive a twelve year old can be to cause a grown man with a church, wife and family to fall anyway. I don't know where this is coming from. I just wanted to be a part of Chase's life, and I'm not about to parade the truth of how I was robbed of twenty-eight years of his life to everyone in order to make people understand that I was not a young hoochie showing up to soothe the old man on his deathbed. I can't believe one conversation yielded this. The Holy Spirit may not show you who I am, but if you bothered to consult Him, he would let you know who I am not."

"Momma, please calm down. And you don't have to go to no hotel."

"I know I don't have to. But, no one is coming up in a room I pay for talking trash to my face either. Did you hear what your wife just insinuated? I should have stayed home."

And Evey agreed. "I'll be happy to take you back to the airport as soon as you're ready, Ms. Jewel. Ms. Edie shouldn't have to be going through this right now."

"Evey, I know you're loyal to Ms. Edie. You don't really know me from Adam. But if all of you would go to God, you would see how wrong you are. This is beyond insulting."

"I'm not trying to disrespect you, mam. It just doesn't make sense and my concern is my mother-in-law."

Chase interjected, "Evey, baby, I asked you to stay out of this. You're crossing the line."

"Ms. Jewel, I apologize. Ms. Edie is hurt and she is my mother-in-law and I've got her back. That's all."

I felt like I was fighting a losing battle. Evey wouldn't dare question her mother-in-law and First Lady who she has loved and trusted since her youth. I walked into a landmine and didn't even know that there was a war going on.

Even though the glass was half full, and I knew the power of God kept me to even be in a place where Chase would fight for me to be in his life, I felt defeated. "Evey, I hope you can say that about me and mean that one day. I haven't done a thing to Ms. Edie. If trying to be a part of Chase's life is the problem, then you're right, there will be a problem. I'm not going anywhere. I'm here to stay. And, I'm not going to keep going round and round in circles with anybody who doesn't want to be bothered. We shouldn't even be here when your father-in-law just died. So, Evey, it's up to you. Either way, I'll survive. I survived when that pillow was on my face, and have done pretty well up until now."

Despite Ms. Catherine and Chase's protests, I went to a hotel. Enough was enough. I found out firsthand what it meant to live through added insult to injury, and I refused to go down as a thorn in the flesh of Chase when his father died. Every single one of my sisters-in-law would be just as fierce if my mother ever tripped on anybody about my father. So, it is now evident that the church family never got the full story about the fact that

Prophet Swanson raped me. And, at this point, I dare not get in trouble with God by fighting to preserve my own dignity and reputation at the expense of grave digging. Chase had enough to deal with already.

Not that Harlan needed much help, but in the face of the drama, Mr. Texas looked better than ever. He wasn't related to any of the sordid past and was a refreshing new person. I decided to reach out to him. "Harlan, I'm sorry I couldn't get back to you earlier. I had to take an unexpected trip but I'm trying to unwind now. How are you?"

"Anxious to fly and meet you just to take you to dinner. Where are you?"

"In Mississippi. And, it's too late for all that. They don't have a night life in these parts."

Harlan would give Noel Jones a run for his money with knowing how to romance a sister. "They don't need one. If you have an address, I've got a gourmet meal ready for you."

"Harlan, you could almost make a sister fall for all of this."

"You don't have to fall, sister. Just walk in it. It's genuine, good and if you want it, it's yours."

"How about breakfast tomorrow morning instead? I'd feel better about that."

"I have a few meetings in the morning, but by the time I get to you, it'd be dinner time. How about dinner tomorrow?"

"Fine."

Meanwhile, Xavier offered to join me in Mississippi. When I called to check on the boys, he refused to let me speak with them. Knowing me the way he does, he could hear that something just wasn't right. He insisted that he leave the boys with Noey or Danne.

I quickly killed those options. "No, they don't need to be around Noey's girls like that. And, Danne is better on weekends. If you need me to come home, I will."

"No, I'm good. They have been hanging tight with me. And we're playing Play Station III right now. So we are just chillin. You sure you don't need me to be there with you?"

I knew Xavier loved me. If I would have let him, he really would have come to Mississippi. The last thing anyone needed was for a country boy like Xavier to confront the foolishness Chase's family was dishing out. Nobody would have thought of Jesus until the dust cleared.

"No, really, I'm fine. I'll be home in a day or so."

Besides, Harlan and I had plans. On the mental scales there was a great imbalance. Dinner with a man who parks a private plane outweighed a man who's chillin playing Play Station. There was no comparison.

I felt so bad about the entire blow-up with Evey. I called Chase to apologize.

"Momma, I'm really sorry about what happened tonight. You know how church people are. And I'm surprised at Evey, she normally is much better than that." He sounded as if he couldn't take one more thing.

"Chase, I do know how church people are, and at some point in time, they have to stop. They are wrong to put me out there like that, but it is all good. I was offended, but I've calmed down. I've been in church all my life so I really should have been prepared. This stuff really isn't important. Do you need me to do anything to help? Anything at all?"

"No, just knowing that you are here is enough. The elders are taking care of the service, Ms. Edie and my sisters and em is handling the arrangements. We'll probably do everything next weekend on Friday and Saturday."

"Do you want to meet early tomorrow?"

"Yes. I'll pick you up for breakfast, and we can talk then."

At breakfast, neither Chase nor I consumed food. Sitting with Chase and looking at his countenance spoke of the depth of love he had for his father. This encounter helped to highlight the humanity of the very ones that the devil uses to destroy the lives of others. They have families that genuinely love them, whether they know of their wrong or not. I could never watch the news again and tell a wailing mother to shut up, her son did it. The man whom I spent years wanting to hurt, was a pillar in the community he belonged to. Despite the knowledge of what he had done, his family still survived, loved one another, and did the work of the Kingdom. The prospect of living life without his buddy gripped Chase's heart. The weight of carrying the ministry seemed like huge shoes to fill.

"Listen Chase, do you believe your father was a man of wisdom?"

"Yes. I can't believe he's gone. Pop is never coming back."

"Do you believe he heard from God?"

"Of course."

"He set things in order before he had the heart attack, didn't he?"

"Yes, he did. One thing about Pop. He is always gonna have the business straight."

"And then when he realized that he was going on to be with the Lord, didn't he reaffirm to everyone what he believed was right and good with God?

"Yes."

"So then, the man knew what he was doing. I believe he honored the Lord, and the Lord honors the decisions His leaders make according to His will. So, God knows exactly what's in you, what you can handle, and although you probably never wanted to see this day, our Father knew this day would be here. And, you are ready for it. Trust Him, and lean on Him. If there's anything I can show you, it is how to just take it day by day. Each day you will learn how to get through this. You will always miss your father, but you will learn how to live with him in the arms of God."

"I don't want to learn to live without him. We have to learn to move on."

Chase had to meet his siblings at the funeral home. I opted to wait in the car.

"Please don't be like that, Momma. Come inside and we'll just be a few minutes. I promise I won't make you wait long."

"Chase, the wisdom of the matter is to let your family handle this without me being around. This is a hard time for everybody and emotions are flying left and right, and I don't want to get killed in the crossfire."

"I understand what you're saying, but you're my momma and they're gonna have to get over it. Come on."

I recognized a few of Chase's sisters and brothers and offered a light smile. One of his sisters, Ceda, pulled a stunt for which my sister Diamond would have won a street-level Oscar.

"Can I offer you a ride to the bus station or the airport? This is my father's funeral."

"Miss, I don't know who you think you're talking to. But let me let you know right now, you don't have the power to shift me. So please, be respectful, or excuse yourself."

"Who do you think you are?" Ceda smugly inquired.

"I hope you won't take this as an offense, but surely you can understand why I'm about to walk away from you. If there's anything you'd like to speak with me about, when you can have some manners, we'll talk. When my son comes out, please let him know I'm outside waiting for him."

Candace jumped right in. "Your son? Please lady. How do you just meet somebody and then call him your son. 'Hi, I'm your momma Mr. Grown man. Who raised you all of your life?' You may be his birth mother, but my daddy and momma raised him!"

"Is that what this is about? Because if it is, you don't have anything to worry about. I know I didn't raise him. Nobody, and I mean no one, knows that more than I do. I did not raise my son. Excuse me. Let me get it right. I didn't raise Chase. Is that going to make you feel better? I'm not trying to take anything away from your mother or Ms. Catherine. Everybody who raised him helped to make him who he is, and guess what? If he didn't come from my womb, we wouldn't be having this conversation. So whatever part I did or did not play in Chase's life, please know that you can tell your mother, your brothers and sisters, and everyone else who wants to know, that I agree. All I did was give birth to him. That's when the real hell began. You all don't have a clue."

Then I walked away, disappointed in myself for even giving the Swansons that much information. The fresh daggers in my heart made me want to high tail it back to New York. But all my days of hoping for this one, where Chase needed me, would not be jeopardized because of an argument. I high-tailed it back inside to wait for Chase.

"What happened?" Chase asked.

I was determined to just let it go. "Nothing. How's everything going?"

"Don't try to gloss over it. Tell me what happened. Look at your face," Chase insisted.

"Chase, I'm not going to say anything. I handled it as best I could. I would like you to realize that it is clear that we are going to have to protect our relationship. I didn't think it through beforehand, but it is obvious that our relationship is difficult for Ms. Edie and the rest of your family. And, to be honest, I can see that. Everything happening this way is just making it so much more exaggerated. So, I will be here for you, but I'm asking you to consider how they are looking at this. They may need to accept this in doses, or stages. This is really ugly, and it doesn't need to be this way. God is not pleased with all of this."

"So what are you saying?"

"I'm saying that if you love Ms. Edie at all, embrace her, let her know that things aren't going to change between you two because I'm around and your father is gone. You're still one of the boys. I can't think of five women I know, who would have stayed with your father, and took care of you, as much as she did. Her irrational behavior right now is rooted in that. And your brothers and sisters are going to make sure that her sacrifice wasn't for nothing."

"It wasn't. This is way out of proportion, ridiculous!"

"And you're a man. She's a woman and we do act crazy when we're threatened. And, she wouldn't feel threatened unless she really loved you. A mother is made to love her own. C'mon Bible teacher, you know how we do when we have to love and raise someone else's. She needs reinforcement right now, and for her to see you stand as one with them will help her relax and calm down. God will give us the wisdom of how to move beyond this. I'm secure that we can move past this. But, Edie and all are tied up in this and her husband just died. So, I'm going home."

My tall, strong and handsome son hugged me. The baby whom I once feared holding, was holding me.

The two women before Solomon each claiming to be the mother of the son Sunday school lesson, came to heart. I could sacrifice my right to be his mother for the other woman, so that Chase wouldn't have to be divided and die on the inside. Just to be part of his life, to have his ear, and to have his love was enough. And, he loves big enough to go around. Thank God for temperance cause every other part of me wanted to scrap and punch Ceda and Candace in their faces or at least call in Laurel for a good cussing.

Before leaving Mississippi, I wrote Ms. Edie a brief note and asked the maître d' to have it delivered, along with a huge bouquet of bereavement flowers to both her, and Ms. Catherine.

"Dear Mrs. Edith Swanson, Please accept my condolences on the loss of Prophet Swanson. Ms. Edie, I came at the request of Prophet Swanson to talk about Chase, not to embarrass the family. I truly came in peace. I cannot thank you enough for what both you and Ms. Catherine gave him and have been to him, as the two women who raised and nurtured Chase. You have been incredible, to survive all that you have as a wife who chose to be a mother, to "our" son, Chase. God knew you and I could both handle the assignment of being chosen to choose to love in the hardest circumstances, when others would walk away. I trust that one day, you will be able to see me simply as a woman, just like you—a living testimony who survived."

A SWEET REPRIEVE
See the Love

Harlan did everything he possibly could to sweep me off of my feet. The Bachelor has nothing on this fine specimen of God's choicest man. I dared not disclose any of this drama to a man I hardly knew, more or less one who may see me as too much baggage while I'm still on display in the window. There wouldn't be much difficulty living a life where la la land dreams are an everyday reality. Harlan has dignity and an assurance of who he is, and that makes him quite attractive. Although he tried to persuade me to fly back to New York with him, I gently told him, not yet. After a few grueling days with Chase's volatile family, Harlan looked better and better. His interests and conversations were light-years away from Wii, X-Box and Play Station.

I couldn't wait to smell the New York air. After leaving the Swansons, the cold mean looks from New Yorkers seemed endearing. I love New York, and my homegirls who wanted every detail of the trip. Once I gave them a blanket answer revealing nothing, they all knew something was up. If all was well, I'd be blabbing all the information. When Jewel got quiet, it was because she was going through something she just didn't want to share.

"Let me know if I got to go down there and turn that funeral out," Danne offered.

Men, diamonds, money, home ownership, multiple vehicles, trips, portfolios and all will never change the core of our friendship. Danne, Laurel, Noey and I will all clown in a minute for one another. And sometimes, that is not good.

"It's not that type of situation, girlie. All is well." I had to say what I chose to believe. Everything would work itself out. The glass was full.

And, if I thought I couldn't put one over on the girls, when I got home and saw Xavier, trying to conceal the hurt was more difficult.

"What's wrong with you?" Xavier was digging.

"Nothing. Everything is fine. How are the boys? Did they behave?" I tried to blow it off and deflect.

"Of course they behaved. They didn't have a choice. But don't try to divert, Jewel. I know you. You are carrying something. Stop trying to punish me and let me be here for you. What happened?"

"I just came from watching my son have to deal with losing his father and that wasn't easy for him, for me to watch him, or to deal with the situation. I'm human, and it wore me out just a little bit. But, everything is fine."

"No it's not. I know you and something affected you. But, if you choose not to share with me, what else can I do? Remember, I'm here for you. And, I love you. I wish you could see that."

There was a time when words like that from Xavier would have made me melt. But the expanse of his betrayal was not incidental, but deliberate repeated efforts to publicly disassociate himself from me after he made a child with another woman.

"Please, Xavier. Let's just stay friends and stop that love stuff. Anyway, this isn't about love. It's about leaving the stuff in Mississippi where it belongs."

"You're not available for love, Jewel."

"To the contrary, I am. I'm not available for hogwash, lying, cheating and all that drama. I've been hurt and am not going to sign up for life-long hurt when you've already given me a good indication of what I can expect from you."

"Wow. That hurts. How long am I going to have to pay for the mistakes I've made in the past? You can forgive everyone else, but what about me? Don't you believe I have changed? That God can truly change a person? Look at me, I'm here now. Whatever you need, whenever you need it, I'm here for you. Tell me, Jewel, what more do you want me to do?"

"Recognize that if we ever had a future, you completely complicated that by having a baby with another woman. For me to be with you means I have to deal with baby mama drama. It's not like I met you with a child. Now, our relationship will have to handle the sensitivities of your son, and his loyalties to his own mother, his needs, and what happens when they conflict with mine. I've waited all my life for a good husband, and do not have to settle for a man who cheated and asks me to live with three grown adults making decisions that will affect our day to day life, instead of just the two of us."

"Jewel, people do it every day. It's not a piece of cake, but this is reality for so many people and when you love somebody, you make it work. We can do this. You take Rashaun and Tysheem and can't think of loving my son? What about Chase, and the women who raised him?"

"Don't go there. This is not about me not being capable of loving Xavier, Jr. That's out of bounds, baby. It's not even comparable."

"Is it? Think about it. His father brought home a child from a crime he committed and his wife forgave him, and had a hand in raising him. I know your heart is big enough for this. You haven't even seen Xavier, Jr. yet."

"And whose fault is that? Should I call his mama and ask if I can see your son saying I'm the woman he was with when the two of you laid up with each other? Or should I brace myself for looking at a child that probably looks and acts just like you and see that you robbed the so-called woman you love from giving you your first child, your first son."

"Jewel, please forgive me. Can we get past this? Do you think we can ever get past this? That's the question I am going to leave you with. Yes, I have a son, and I'm not going to keep apologizing for his existence. He is here, he is my responsibility, and I love him. Of all people, you should understand how I feel about him."

"I do. And I wouldn't want you to feel any other way. I wouldn't respect you at all if you didn't love Xavier, Jr. A wife should be first in a man's life. And, Xavier, if I'm going to be a wife and a helpmate, I'm going to be first. That's not negotiable."

"So can we move past this?"

"I thought we already did. It is what it is and like I said, I'm going to be first in a Christ-centered marriage."

"Well I hope that that marriage is with me. I'm not going to expect an answer right away. But Jewel, we are a fit. You are the one for me, and it took me a while to see that. And missing you and living without you in my life helped me to see that I'm like a fish out of water without you. I need you and want to be there to love you for life. We've both made some mistakes and proven that we are still deeply concerned for each other. Wherever the waters take me, Jewel, let's ride the waves together. Will you be my wife?"

I can't believe this Black man asked me to marry him at that time. As much as I love Xavier, I would not dishonor him by making a move that was disingenuous and do it with a heart that is not pure toward him.

"Xavier, please. It's not fair to put me on the spot like this."

"Jewel, don't answer me now. Shhh. Don't say another word. Just think about it, and let the Lord deal with you. You're my best friend and I don't want to live one day in this life without you. All I'm asking is for you to give it some thought, and when you know that you have truly searched your heart, then whatever you say, is what we'll do."

Then the man kissed me on my forehead. He was close enough for me to smell him, and I hated the vulnerability I felt with him.

"We know what real love is. Ours has been tried, and once you stop suppressing what you feel for me, and stop fighting the love that exists between us, we'll both be very happy. And maybe then you'll allow me to put this on your finger."

Homeboy whipped out a 2.5 karat, IF rated, princess cut, diamond ring in a platinum setting. This was a steep purchase for Xavier, and clearly he meant business.

"I'll think about it. But to be fair to you, you should know that I am not inclined to make any decisions soon. Right now, too much is happening and I'm enjoying the changes."

"Does that include Mr. Texas?" Xavier is a hot mess. I bet he's peeping at me through the boys. "You should know that I didn't have to even pry. The boys want me to get with you. They seem to like me."

"You never fail to surprise me Xavier. One thing is for sure. Life with you will always have some sort of twists or turns, be they good or bad."

"Babe, I need you to forget the past. I know what I want now, and you are precisely what I need. I know you love me, and I love the real you, the one that punched my lights out when we were younger, and the one that everybody thinks is so together and strong, yet is just as sensitive as the best of us. I'm never going to stop loving you. You caught my heart and it's too late for anyone else for me. I may not have millions of dollars, but what I have, is yours. And, you, me, and all of our children will make it."

"Xavier, I've never stopped loving you. Love has never been a question for us. Trust, fidelity and the same expectation of honor is where we fall off. You keep saying to forget the past. The past is what points to exactly what I can anticipate if we do get married. What if you have not changed? Then what? I'm stuck? No, I'll be taking my time on this. It would be easy if I didn't care, but I do love you. And why now? Is this engagement because of Mr. Texas, or what?"

"I'm not thinking about no other dudes, babe. I'm not pressed because I know you are my wife. I messed up, so I'm willing to wait. We need to get married because if we are going to have babies, now is the time. And, if Rashaun and Tysheem are going to be with us permanently, we need to get and keep a routine. They need consistency. But most importantly, I'm a man and want to be able to slap that bootay without repercussions. We need to make it legal and right before God."

The smirk on Xavier's face said so much more than his words. Meanwhile, I heard my father's words, "Love them that love you." Xavier had it all worked out in his mind. He's very persistent and I needed to trust him for "us" to even happen.

I acquiesced just a little bit. "Just don't expect too much too soon. We'll see."

Rashaun and Tysheem weren't the slightest bit interested in the last excursion. All they wanted to know is if I got the ring, and if I would stop being ridiculous. "He's good people, you know."

"Is he paying you to say that?"

"No. He just is. He's not perfect, and no one is. But he got your back."

"He does?"

"Who else is breaking your door down to watch us and go from Long Island to Connecticut every day to work? I don't see no other brothers trying to get with you." The boys sounded like my father.

"I've never suffered from a shortage of wanting brothers, Rashaun. Xavier is just one who got through, that's all."

"What do you mean 'got through?'"

"Got through to my heart."

"He ain't always gonna hang around if you keep dissing him. So you better not play yourself."

"Alright, I'll take your counsel under advisement. Meanwhile, how have you all been doing?"

The boys decided they don't like Xavier's cooking, and wish I would cook more often. With all of the impromptu trips, meetings, and responsibilities, these young men want me in the kitchen. I pledged to try and cook once during the week, and if we are home, once on the weekends. They both want to switch to local schools, because Rashaun is preparing to be recruited for college for swimming. All of these plans—including Rashaun's mention of college—took place from spending a few days with Xavier. He had a good relationship with the boys.

Harlan Pickett, however, had my attention. The debonair Texan flew into New York to take me to dinner. Who would think that a cowboy could surprise a native New Yorker? Harlan took me to a wonderful bistro that I never visited. Dinner was fabulous and perfected when I spotted the blue bags and boxes, and knew that he stopped by one of my favorite stores, Tiffany's. First, Harlan presented a classic Atlas Dome Quartz Resonator Watch, which was a nice addition to the watches I had accumulated over the years. He took the liberty to slip the 18K Atlas open bangle bracelet onto my wrist. "Jewel, I was taught you buy a woman what you think she would appreciate. So how did I do?"

"You did wonderful. I'm almost speechless. I've never had a man fly into town on his private jet and shower me with lavish gifts." The BAP in me sized up the Tiffany's tab to be about $8,000.

"But I'm the type of man who believes in the overflow. I also want you to have what I think you should have. This gift is symbolic." Finally, Harlan presented his choicest gift: A necklace with a Fleur De Lis Key Diamond Pendant. "You should know that there is something about you that makes you the perfect woman to have the key to my heart."

"Are you trying to buy my adoration, cause if you are, it won't work." Although I loved every single gift, I could buy all of those things— which are meaningless in the total scheme of life—myself.

"Absolutely not. A man has a right to embellish perfection."

Although those gifts were probably kibbles and bits to a man like Harlan, I didn't want to accept them without a clear understanding of where we stood. "Harlan, right now, just for now, what are your intentions?"

"To move you to my ranch, or to take care of you if you choose to stay in New York. For us to learn what makes each other thrive, and what inspires each other. To one day watch you look at me and know that your eyes are eyes of devotion and hope that whatever happens, we'll always have each other."

I wasn't ready for all of that. "Wow. That's a bit much considering we just met one another."

"Have you ever heard of love at first sight? You've got something about you that makes me love you. It doesn't make sense at all. Sometimes life doesn't make sense at all."

"Harlan, do you have any idea what my life is like? I hardly know anything about you. What would we be getting into if we were to throw all reason out the window, and jump into a relationship right now? You don't know what you'd be biting off if we got together. There's so much more than meets the eye."

"So tell me Jewel. What should I know about that would make me run from you."

"Hopefully nothing. But, realistically, there are some things that need to be worked out in any relationship. Like for instance, I just found out that my son is alive and well. I had him when I was quite young, and we just met a few months ago."

"Okay, so you have a son."

"Yes, and a daughter-in-law and granddaughter."

"A granddaughter? Didn't you tell me you were 40?"

"I am. But like I said, I had my son when I was much younger and he is a grown man. We are getting to know one another, but we are bonding and our journey has definitely been challenging and great at the same time. He's special and finding him is an answer to prayer."

"What else?"

"I'll probably be adopting two boys, one teenager, and one adolescent. My girlfriend is quite ill, and I'm their legal guardian.

They are a handful, have been through a lot in life, and more likely than not, wherever I go in life, they'll be right along with me."

"Okay, so now we have, in sorts, three sons."

"Yes. And, my father is a bishop in the Lord's church. So, I have a very strict background and upbringing. And, I tend to be inflexible when it comes to having a lifestyle other than one that pleases God. In other words, I'm what most people would consider a holy roller."

"I can live with that. I need somebody who can make me a better person. I've grown up Christian, and believe in Jesus too. I just don't really go to church and all of that kind of stuff."

"So, do you want children?" I didn't even know why I asked Harlan if he wanted children because I wasn't ready to make an exclusive commitment to the man.

"Of course I do. You are in great physical shape, so unless there's some other problems, you're still young enough to have a few babies."

"You do know that I have a medical practice. And at my age, I can't foresee a few other babies. And all of this is way too premature anyway. We hardly know each other."

"Jewel, I'm healthy, wealthy and just looking for a fabulous woman like you, who is smart, aggressive, not a snob, intellectually stimulating, physically fit, and God knows you are gorgeous. So please forgive me, I'm going to try to get to know you because I like what I see."

"As much as I love jewelry Harlan, I don't think it's a good idea to take all of this," I stated knowing that Lady Prunell would have a fit if she knew I took this from a man I barely knew.

"Well, I'm certainly not returning anything. So it's either yours or the waitress's. You decide."

I chuckled. "Well then, you leave me no options but to make a space for this fabulous bangle in my jewelry chest. Thank you."

"You're welcome. I hope you learn how to open up and receive. It's just as bad to not be able to receive than it is to give. Don't interfere with the sowing and reaping process. You deserve to be spoiled."

Until Harlan said those words, I never really thought about the fact that God had blessed me to be able to give so much to others and to acquire whatever I needed and even think I want. Outside of the syndicate, I wasn't used to receiving from others.

Harlan was a sweet reprieve to the heaviness and drama. He was fresh, new and had no other agenda than to see about Jewel. Of course, he was so good, that he seemed too good to be true. The glass is full and I made a decision to believe the best until I had to accept otherwise.

THROWN IN THE WATER
Now Sink or Swim

"Chase, how are you holding up?" I wanted to gauge where Chase was in dealing with the unanticipated death of his father.

I didn't know what to say. As the reality of Swanson's death hit Chase, he found himself in a place that he had not known before. No words could comfort him. Only God could help him to cope. What I heard in Chase by listening to what he could not audibly say, made me want to comfort him as much as possible. Even though Chase and I really didn't know that much about one another, we were immersed into "being there" for one another fairly early into our bonding phase.

Chase earnestly admitted, "Okay. I didn't want to have to pull on you, but somehow I need you. I know it's a lot to ask you to come back. Maybe you being here will help me to face this better."

Although I was confident that nothing could help Chase face burying his-what I would have to accept-hero, I needed to give him whatever it was that he thought I should give.

"Let me make arrangements and I'll let you know as soon as I get there. Okay?"

I promised myself I wouldn't get involved any further. But, my son needed me. The pain of losing the only parent he has had a life-long relationship with must have been unbearable. I could not imagine living without my mother or father. At the same time, I had to face the feeling of knowing that someone who I spent most of my life wanting to hurt, was now gone. In the oddest way, I regretted wanting a man, who had been compartmentalized as "the rapist" in my mind, to suffer. The last chapter in his life was written, in his earthly existence, and the closing of the book was so hurtful and devastating for the people he loved. And, all of this meant hell for me with his family, because now was the time to develop a relationship with the fruit of my womb.

While Chase pulled on me, I needed to pull on my dad. He was the one who would be spiritual in all things and I needed to do what was right.

"Daddy, Chase is in a place right now that I don't ever want to be in. He is hurting, and I really don't know how to help other than to be there for him."

"That's all you can do. God has him, and he'll be fine. How about you? How are you handling all of this?" Bishop Prunell, as usual, wanted the 411 on Jewel.

"I'm good, Daddy." Sometimes things happen all around us to let us know that what we have to deal with is really not even a problem or an issue. Chase's world turning upside down helped me to see that really, I was truly blessed.

"Are you sure? It had to be a lot seeing him before he passed and being around the family."

"It was, but it was nothing compared to what I lived through without knowing where Chase was and how he was living. I'd rather be right where we are than where we used to be. This isn't an easy place, but it is a good place."

"I'm not asking you to compare, Jewel. I just want you to be all right in all of this. I'm concerned about you, that's all. It was a bit much for me to just hear Swanson over the phone. So, I know it has to be a bit much for you to be in the thick of things."

"Thanks, Daddy. I appreciate your concern. I know you all love me. I'm really not comparing, per se. I'm just letting you know that based upon what I have lived through, this is really not as difficult to endure. In the meantime, can we just focus on Chase? He is the only reason I am going back down there, because God knows I can live without ever seeing those people again."

"That's what we tried to protect you from. But you were too young to understand that."

"I understand now, Daddy. But all of that came at the expense of what mattered most, a relationship with my son. Whether or not we comprehend this, I was made to know how to nurture Chase. Can you imagine your life without one of us, Daddy? If you saw Mama birth us, and then met us twenty-eight years later? In the total scheme of things, the rape devastated me. But what kept me heavy and mourning was the void that came from a missing child. So, maybe I'm not making objective decisions with Chase right now. I can't."

"I'm so proud of you, Jewel. I watch you now and you've done a wonderful job finding my grandson, and just doing the right thing. Do you want me to send someone to go with you?"

"No, I'm good. You know I'm not into that church adjutant stuff. I'll handle my business myself. But thanks for offering."

"What about one of your brothers? I'd feel better if someone went with you. How about Xavier?"

"Absolutely not. Your sons will cut the fool the way those folks have been acting, and so would Xavier. None of them are blood washed enough to refrain from punching some of those clowns in the face. I'll be fine, Daddy. Don't worry."

Just when I thought I was afloat and ready to ride the storm with Chase in Mississippi, Aliyah turned for the worse.

"What's going on girl?" It had been quite some time since I really spoke with Danne.

"Aliyah is back in the hospital again. She said she doesn't even want to speak with the boys; she don't want any of us to see her. I'm like, what's going on? That is not like her at all."

"Did she say she doesn't want to speak to any of us? Not even Tysheem? You know he is her heart."

"She said she wrote BJ a long letter, and she won't be speaking with him for a while. Apparently she had an encounter with God while she was on the floor in prayer for days at the church. She told me, "Danne, I saw God. I saw Him."

I began to cry uncontrollably. The MD in me and the spirit-filled believer in me knew exactly what was happening. Aliyah was getting ready to die. She was making emotional withdrawals from all those who mattered to her, and her gaze was fixed toward the God of her salvation, the God that she saw. How do you let someone go whom you love and cannot imagine living without? This is a question Chase would have to answer and the rest of the syndicate would too, if Aliyah did not get better.

After trying to control my emotions, I asked, "Did she say what the doctors were saying this time?"

"No, she just told me to tell you to call and find out what was going on. She was tired, and couldn't walk, and didn't want to keep talking." I could hear Danne sniffling as well. The entire gab gal crew had been strong walking through every phase of Aliyah's battle with AIDS. We all knew something had to happen, one way or the other pretty soon.

"Danne, what about the boys? She has to speak with them. I can't handle all of this at one time. I have to go and be with Chase right now. This is overwhelming."

"I know," Danne concurred. "Can you imagine us without Aliyah? She is so crazy but she is part of us."

Aliyah would only pull away from us because she was processing her own end. She was so courageous and had to see victory in everything. She had to be seeing the triumphant Jesus in this or it wouldn't be well with her soul.

"What is she talking about, what is she saying?"

"She is talking like she is tired. She said she doesn't want to be bothered with you because you are going to push her and she just wants to go." Those were the words that sealed it. If Aliyah wanted to go, she wouldn't be around much longer. We couldn't be selfish because we didn't want to let her go, when for her to continue living as she had been for so long, she would only be continually frustrated and in pain. The plausible life she could have known wasn't relevant when the reality was Aliyah approached life the way she knew how to, and the best way she could.

I didn't want to leave the boys again. If Aliyah was at her end, I wanted to be with them. But, Danne wasn't going for that. The boys didn't need to be caught up in one home-going scene and miss any more school when they might have to take some time off if their mother passed. So, Xavier was on duty again. The only catch was that he was on vacation and had his son for the week.

"Oh, you have the baby this week? I'm sorry for asking, I didn't know."

"I don't just have the baby, Jewel. I have my son, Xavier, Jr. And it's okay to ask. I'll do it. I'll just be bringing him with me. You're going to have to meet him at some point in time anyway."

"You have everything figured out, don't you?"

"No, actually I don't. I just have us figured out and this is really a good thing. You're going to love little Xavier."

"I'm getting ready to leave soon, so I'll meet him when I get back."

"Jewel, all I'm asking you to do is meet my son. This is not the best circumstance, but when would it be? He's not responsible for being here. I am. He's just an innocent baby."

"I know, Xavier. I know about sons caught up in the crossfire. I'll be waiting. Thanks for being there for me. For us."

I fell asleep waiting for Xavier to arrive with his son. I never imagined I'd be waiting to see the man I love and wish I could trust walk in with his baby from another woman, so that he can watch the children of one of my best friends who is dying from AIDS, so that I can go to be with my only son who I barely know, while he mourns the loss of his father, the man who raped me during my childhood. Only God could help me keep it all together.

As much as I loved Xavier, I could not bring myself to be excited about opening my heart to his baby with another woman. At that very moment, I wondered how Ms. Edie must have felt, knowing that she had an "outside" addition to her family living down the street through the unconscionable act of her husband. What she endured must have been heart wrenching. Ms. Edie had so much more invested in her relationship with Prophet Swanson when Chase came on the scene. They were a married couple and already had a number of children together. What I felt was incomprehensible and too much to bear. And, Xavier and I hadn't ever been together, and were not married. Betrayal, deceit, and deception hurts whatever the layers and boundaries. Xavier is the only man I've ever been in love with for real. No wonder Ms. Edie is tripping right now. She opened her heart and eventually her home to my son, who became one of her "sons," and tried her best, albeit inequitably—to love him. She had to watch the very child who came from her husband's weakness be the seed of favor and the one that God would raise up to be the closest one to fulfill the like-passioned calling to pastor. Ms. Edie can't see past what has become known as her family—all for the love of her husband and possibly for the sake of the ministry—to see that I never was, and am not, a threat to her station as the wife and mother. I am an unwilling participant merged by love and a Christ-centered life that requires forgiveness. Ms. Fiercy and her protective children love their son and brother like he is one of the gang, because he is one of them. He didn't ask for his life or upbringing, and the baby who I once cradled in my mind as a lost Prunell, has a strong identity as a stalwart Swanson. Xavier Jr. didn't ask to be born into a triangle, or quadrangle either. Although I did not have to choose to be a part of Xavier's life, I did have to be careful to treat Xavier Jr. for who he is, irrespective of how and where he came from. In whatever relationship Xavier and I developed, I had to be mindful that Xavier Jr.'s mama is his mama and never speak words or commit actions that would undermine her as a mother to her own child. Ms. Catherine's true nobility in raising Chase to love and regard me, helped Chase to love me instantaneously.

I was sleeping hard because when I woke up, Xavier was kissing me on my forehead.

"Hey, what time is it? How long have you been here?" I asked.

"For a few minutes, brown sugar," he responded as he planted another wet one with his juicy lips on my cheek.

"Watch it buddy, don't play yourself. Don't get carried away. I didn't even hear the bell. The boys didn't go to sleep yet?"

"They didn't open the door; I let myself in."

"How'd you get a key?"

"I'm not stupid Jewel. I made one when you left keys last time, just in case of an emergency, or when I need to sneak up on you. But, I'll call first."

Note to self: Have locks changed.

Xavier was going out of his way to help me, so I needed to stop tripping.

"So you gonna sit here all night or you ready to meet my little man?"

"Where is he?"

"He slept all the way over here, so I didn't wake him. He's upstairs sleeping in the great room."

I had to be as ready as I ever would be to meet a baby boy, Xavier's first baby, that he made lying with another woman while he professed to love me. If I wasn't learning that life isn't about me, I don't know what the lesson is. What should have been my great privilege to give the man whom I loved, was snatched from under my feet through infidelity. This just may be a blaring sign for me to know that this relationship was not for me.

When I saw Xavier Jr. I wanted to punch his daddy in the face. The sucker punch kind of beat down, South Bronx style. All of what we had talked about, envisioned and discussed was resting right before my very eyes. Xavier Jr. was a handsome little boy, looking like his daddy dropped DNA and Xavier Jr. showed up. Although the baby was fairer than his daddy, if all goes well, he will be fine as all get-up, like his father. I admired his hair and features. He was going to be a great human being, like so many others who defied and overcame their past.

"He's beautiful. He looks just like you."

"Yes, he does. That's my man right there."

Who could fault him for loving and being proud of his son? Certainly, not I. He would be a monster if he wasn't a doting father. And then Xavier did what most men who reside in Ditzville may think is appropriate. Xavier tried to put his hands around my waist and act as if this were a moment in which we were looking at our sleeping son whom we created in expressing our love and passion for one another.

"Wrong move, Xavier. I don't want to hurt you, but I need you not to think it's good to touch me now. Please, don't."

What makes a man think you + him + her + (him & her baby) = smiley face + (you & him)? I had to move past the fact that the same hands did a whole lot of touching with Xavier Jr.'s mother and all of his other flings, who all meant enough to fool around with, but nothing when it was convenient for him to relegate them to mere friends when I was about to act like I never knew Jesus, decency, or self-respect. While Xavier had my confidence and trust, he clowned and I didn't want the touch from hands that devalue a real touch. All I could think of was the frequent, diversified, cheesy and degrading touches and fake embraces Xavier had with other women. I hated to go there, but how could I ever trust him again? I could tell that Xavier was a bit hurt and set back. With as much of a sensitive tone as I could muster, I asked Xavier to give me a minute. When I uttered this request, the tears began to roll down my face. I didn't want him to see how much this still affected me. I didn't want him to feel badly about it, but couldn't make myself act as if this was as simple as bringing home a cheeseburger instead of a hamburger from the local drive-thru.

"Sugar, stop crying. I can't stand to see you crying."

"I'm good, Xavier. I'm tired of crying, too. One day, someone is going to love me for me, value me enough to find me as a good thing, honor me enough not to violate me, and allow me to give them some babies in love. Don't you think I deserve that?"

"I know you do. And, I believe you're going to have what you deserve. I am that man, Jewel. Xavier Jr. doesn't stop that at all."

"How do I know that if we get married, I can trust you? You didn't come into this blindly. Xavier, you of all people know my past and it's not your fault, but I do have trust issues. I let you in and this is what you do to me? Am I going to be sitting in church kissing the babies and find out that these are the pastor's babies when lawsuits hit the media, or people ring the door bell in the middle of the night? C'mon!"

"Jewel, all I'm asking you to do is to forgive me. I know it's not fair, but the only way we can move on is if you accept my son. He's my responsibility and I've got to take care of him. We can move past this. I'm telling you right here, and right now, I'm the man that is going to honor you. Just don't push me away."

"Regardless of what happens to us, he is handsome. He is a blessing. If you feel anything for him like I feel for Chase, you'll know that when all else seems to fail, children can motivate you to keep trying and not to give up. Their love is so pure. And because of our craziness and bias, they have to endure so much hardship they didn't bargain for, and certainly don't deserve. I can tell you this, Xavier, with everything that is in me, I pray to God that he never suffers a day in his life because of your deception, Negro. I'm going to love him the way I hoped and prayed my son was treated and the way God made sure he was loved. The jury is still out on what I can say about you, though."

"Well, a brother is going to keep praying. And, I won't get tired of showing you, because that's something I've got to do for the rest of our lives if I'm going to be your covering. One thing, Jewel, is that we are going to be very happy. Once we get over this, we are going to be happy."

All of a sudden, I wished Harlan could wisp me away to Mississippi so I didn't have to wait overnight under the captive audience of Xavier's thick persuasive yah-yah.

"Dr. Jewel, remember I love you." I didn't know if Xavier loved me, or settled for me since no one else seemed to work out for him.

"I love you too, homeslice."

I had to inject the round-the-way lingo to let him know I wasn't feeling him. All the sugar, honey darlings weren't cutting the mustard this time.

Xavier, Jr. would be sure to win me over. I loved his daddy, so I had to love him. People do make mistakes. But people rarely change. Only God can truly change the character of a man, and heal my hurt. I had to make a decision to forgive or Xavier would continually face me and Xavier Jr. in terms of his sin. The thoughts I used to have of how much I needed to fit into his life and be a good wife for him has now been consumed with how I could ever want to be his wife. I couldn't stay there, I had to face up with the girls before I left. In a few short weeks, life's terrain has shifted so much that we hardly had the chance to catch up with each other.

"Danne and Laurel, I'm sorry for waking you up so early, but who knows what's about to happen next. So before I get caught up down south, I wanted us to have a plan of action for the boys and find out what's happening with Aliyah."

"Let's call Noey," Danne suggested.

Laurel retorted, "Today is Jayden's day off. You know she has been screwing him since last night and will be most of the day so don't wake her."

I couldn't believe Laurel had this type of information on the intricacies of Noey and Jayden's love life. "Ok. That was too much info. How do you know all of that?"

"I pays attention dearheart. She doesn't move when he's off or answer her phone and it's not because he's controlling. It's because he's good and he pays the bills," Laurel contributed as if she were on the sidewalk reporting with the break-away edge over all other reporters.

"How about it's because she loves him and he needs time with his wife and daughters when he is off. How about that?" I suggested. "Anyway, I asked Helen to find out what's up with Aliyah. I'm hoping to hear from whomever her attending is in Chicago. From what you've told me, Danne, we could be at the place where we need to be getting things squared away with her in case anything happens."

Danne always had the critical information. "I found out she has no insurance. Mother Johnson pays her rent every month, you peel off something to her monthly, I piece her with something every time I see her, and Laurel gives her a few G's a couple of times a year. We are all her life insurance, mutual funds, 401(K), casualty, liability, property, investment portfolio, and child welfare."

"And don't forget Bishop Deuce. She hits him up constantly too," Laurel interjected.

"Y'all know what? I need Aliyah to mentor me. Homegirl has more streams of income than most of us put together." I never thought of how Aliyah worked her situation, but this conversation surely put everything into perspective. We all know she always hit everyone of us up regularly, as if we owed her."

"That's the street hook and crook in her that hasn't been killed yet. Girlfriend is going to work her stuff and be dignified and right about it, collecting the same rent from five different people each month. And if she is really feeling herself, she'll throw some hecannamashas in there so she can really think this is right and good." Laurel stated.

"It's all good Laurel. We all know how she is. And when I give her what I give her, I'm giving it to her to do whatever, so she can do what she needs to do. I'm asking you all to help me tighten things up on my end with the boys. I've got to be there for Chase and we need Rashaun and Tysheem to know that they have aunties they can count on for life. It's not going to be easy for them if something happens to Aliyah."

"I'm going to go see her this weekend. I don't care what she says. And if she's down, I'll take the boys with me." Danne is the bold one who would handle up on Aliyah even though this might be the last time.

Laurel would always do her part too. "If you go, I can fly out on Sunday early morning and be back by Monday afternoon. I have a show Saturday night and can't miss Monday's rehearsal."

"Bishop Deuce wants to see the boys and take them through counseling," Danne found out.

"If Aliyah's fine with it, then I'm fine with it. If not, I'd prefer for them to go to Restoration Temple. That's where they've been going and we only have professional certified counselors. Not real good holy church folk who need a position in the church and don't know a thing about counseling." Aliyah was still alive and capable of making decisions for her sons.

"There you go, Jewel."

"For real, though, Laurel. We don't need them being damaged by the experimentation of spiritual folks with good intentions who speak in high tongues and have no practical wisdom. Sorry, but that's how I feel about it."

"In other words, you wouldn't want them around people like their mama." Laurel never lets a potential dig go. Not even at five in the morning.

"That's not what I said. First of all, Aliyah does not just live in hakinnnannnaaaa zone. She thrives there, but wisdom and practicality draws her to those who have strengths in areas where she is weak. And, she listens and applies knowledge. If she died tomorrow, she made it easy for me to adopt the boys. Her business, what she does have in place, is taken care of. And, homegirl got her GED, went to Bible School, and was taking college classes online. She is a totally different ball game. She is super-spiritual, but she does live in reality and tries to have some earthly good."

"I see your point," Laurel conceded.

Everyone knows I'll defend Aliyah. I'd do it for any one of them, for that matter. I'm often dubbed the naïve one who has to see folks proven wrong cause I just choose to go with the best outlook in people. So everything was set with immediate plans. I still prayed for a miracle. Time and time and time again, I saw families shuffled and changed forever because of AIDS. Although cancer and other diseases have been around much longer than AIDS, something about suffering with something that is mostly preventable makes it unbearable. This is the reality with much of heart disease and even some diabetes. But the stigma associated with AIDS wears people out mentally, even almost thirty years after the world first acknowledged this epidemic.

A NEW LANDSCAPE
Awkward It Is

It's amazing how life's priorities can change without a conscious reclassification. Just a few months ago, I would never just miss so many days at the office. Never. Although I still cared about the patients, especially my senior patients, somehow all of that played second fiddle to simply being there from those in my life who needed me: Chase, Rashaun, Tysheem and Aliyah. I also felt the need to make a purposed effort to work on communicating with my mother and siblings, especially my sisters. Outside of their children, I can't remember the last time I've had a meaningful conversation with any of them. The shame that I had known since that fateful night during my adolescent years placed a silent barrier between me and the rest of the women in the family. Silence and obliviousness fortified and sealed the barrier. After years of living around it, I realized that they could be instrumental in teaching me how to live and have a healthy family. While waiting for the flight, I decided to call my sister Precious.

"Hey Precious. How are you doing?"

"Okay. What's up?"

"Nothing. Just calling."

"Jewel, what's going on? You never just call."

"Neither do you, Precious. Life is a two-way street. I am just calling to see what's up. We hardly talk and really don't have a relationship outside of the children. So, I have a few minutes while I'm at the gate and decided to give you a call."

"Where you going?"

"Back to Mississippi. Chase is going through right now, so I told him I'd come be with him. I want to be there for him."

"So how is that going? I can't imagine having to deal with a situation like that."

"Like what, Precious?"

"You know what I mean, Jewel. Not in a bad way. It's just got to be awkward."

"It is, but life has been awkward. I guess you can say, awkward is not a bad thing. Sometimes if you've been dealt awkward, you become used to different. It's not pleasant, but it's necessary, so I'm okay with it."

"You are good girl. I know I wouldn't be mixed up with those people."

"Precious, I'm not mixed up with them. And, you know what I've come to understand? They are God's people just like us. It's funny. When I see how they get down, there are so many dynamics in their family that are just like ours. They are doing me in, just like any of us would do to anyone Ma had fever with."

"Why would you even go into that? You don't have to be a hero, Jewel." Precious sounded just like Danne, and all of them were beginning to wear me out. The desire to spend as much time with a long-lost child, especially when he needed his mother, wasn't heroic. It was basic DTRT (do the right thing).

"Is that how you see this, Precious? Because I don't see it like that at all."

"I'm sure you wouldn't. But it doesn't matter how I see it because I haven't walked a block more or less a mile in your shoes. So I'm sure you're dealing with it the best you can."

"I'm doing what I think any of you all would do if you wanted to try and learn who your son really is. If you were robbed of most of his life, you would want to spend time with him and be there for him. This is the most challenging thing I've ever had to do, meet a grown man and reconcile that I'm his momma and don't know him, but need to figure out how to be there for him."

"That's all he needs, Jewel, is for you to be there. You can't fix this. All you can do is listen, be there, and if he needs it, give him wisdom. Girl, if anyone will tell you the truth, parenting is hit and miss. Staying in constant prayer to God and communication with your children will pretty much fill in the gaps for the misses. Half the time they don't want to hear you and the other half, you probably don't want to hear them because of tiredness, frustration, or whatever. But we have to make the effort. Cause if the misses are too great, they will suffer, and in many respects, for the rest of their lives. Overall, all you can really do is trust God, cause we really work for Him anyway. He trusts us with His own and our kids are God's gifts. He's got the master plan and we have to give them the truth, show them the way, bust them up and put them in God's hands."

"You're such a good mother."

"Jewel, all I've done is love them to life. And I push them to be more than Paul and me. Don't be nervous. Just be you. I do know you're better than I am though. I don't think I'd be bothered."

"Even if it was Michael? You think you'd walk away?" There is no way Precious wouldn't fight for her oldest son.

"That's tough. I know doing marriage and the family the way I have is tough and Paul and I love each other. We made our babies in love and holy matrimony and there are still times when I want to run him and these kids over with a Mack truck. I'm just being honest. So I'm not even going to act like I'm ready for all of this stuff."

"How come we never talked about this before, Precious? How come you all never said anything, or told me anything about Chase, or even what happened?"

"Like what? What is there to talk about? What were we supposed to say? How did it feel to get raped?"

"No. Precious, forget I asked."

"Is there something you think we should have said, or need to know?"

"There are a lot of questions, but somehow, maybe most of them are best unanswered. I try to figure this out over and over and over and over, but the end result is the same. It happened, and it is history. There is nothing that we can do to change anything. I guess the only thing I want to know is did you all know what happened to Chase?"

"Mommy and Daddy told us that you were coming home without the baby, he would be taken care of. That's all we knew as far as I remember. At least that's what I thought."

"So you didn't know where he was?" Somehow, that's the one thing that kept bothering me. To know that the whereabouts of Chase was hidden in the Prunell silence made it all seem like it happened for nothing.

"No, we really didn't. I guess if I thought about it, I probably would have thought he'd be with his people or adopted. I don't know. We just never mentioned it, because what good would it do? Ma didn't want violence, drama and all of that stuff that would have the church people going. So, we just left it alone. And we were young too."

"I know we were young. When you left 'it' alone, you left me alone. It's done with, but I hope this family will never have another 'it.' And if we do, never leave an 'it' alone again. I just wanted to know what your understanding was, that's all."

"My understanding was that a pervert jacked you up, and you were messed up behind it. And the baby, well—"

"You know what Precious, I'm discovering every day, that there is so much more to look forward to in the future. I'm trying to reconfigure my thoughts, efforts, and energies to a happy future. And this is a struggle, because somehow, I want the past that was wrong to be right. And it never will be. Certain things I think I'm ready for, and then find out, it is best to leave the stones where they are. I don't want to be mad."

"Mad about what?" Precious asked as if she needed to check and see if she had Vaseline for the face and a bo-bo for the hair because she was getting ready to get into a street fight.

"Precious, we're talking aren't we? I'm not coming at you. I can understand that most women who are raped and get pregnant as a result of the rape, probably don't want their babies. Part of me didn't want Chase. It's hard to explain. I didn't want him, but I didn't not want him either. I thought that Ma and y'all, or someone else would've taken him for me, until I could raise him by myself."

"Wow. I never knew that."

"I had a baby and then the plan was to just pretend he never existed. Get on with life. Now, it's just a matter of picking up the pieces and doing the best I can to be there for the man whom I couldn't be there for as a child. So, that's why I'm going. As a mother, I feel the need to be there for Chase. I can't make up for the time we didn't have together. And, I'm sure not going to miss the time we have now. This stuff, Precious, turned out to be a gift. How often do people reconcile after all this time? And not only reconcile, but get along and genuinely accept each other? I've been blessed to have a relationship with my son."

"It's funny to hear you say 'my son.' For so long, you've been the only one without kids and now you have a son. I'm happy for you, Jewel. If this is what you want, I'm happy."

"Precious, this is what I've been hoping for since I came back home without him. I came back empty-handed, but my heart never understood that. It's only now that somehow, I feel complete."

"Just make sure you're not living out of guilt. You didn't have any control over that; you were a child yourself, girl. Do you realize that you were a mother at Angie's age now? Chase ended up fine. Just give him the best that you can. Everything else, just let it go."

"That's the focus, Precious. I don't know how well I'm doing at it, but that is the standard. My fight is in the letting go. When you've lived with a knife in your heart for so long, if it hasn't killed you, once it's removed, you sort of check to make sure that it really isn't there. Life seems different without the dead weight I had been carrying for so long. Time spent checking on the meaningless is meaningless, but it seems to be part of the process. This is where my struggle is, but I am conscious of it. Just keep me in prayer."

"I will. I'll also try to start calling outside of the kids. It's a shame we've wasted all of our adult life not really communicating about this. It's as if it was taboo."

"That's how it is in many families. Somehow, if we ignore it, it doesn't exist; it's not real. But thank God we've survived."

"You are so strong. I'm proud of you and don't ever forget that. I don't want to bring up such a rough time for you, but if you ever need to talk, I'm here."

"Cool. And keep our conversations between us. I don't need them going down the Prunell grapevine." If Precious was true to form, she would be dialing Diamond two seconds after she made sure the line was clear.

There were years of wearing Precious' desired hand-me-downs—the faboo handbags, shoes, and trendy hats—falling asleep in the same house, being at every family function imaginable, and dancing around what ailed me most, time and time again. And so it has been with everyone in the family. This was a time of seeing everything line up in my life. Piece by piece, things were getting "fixed" all over the place. The successful physician the world saw was finally living a life of true contentment, most of which was taking place because of effective communication at the right time. The value of a relationship shouldn't be contingent upon how much you've suffered to have or maintain it. But, suffering sure does make you appreciate it and keep you from taking loved ones for granted.

SPICE ON ICE
A Hero Rising

Chase had already checked me in when I arrived. Even under the most pressing circumstances, he remained a gentleman, through and through.

"I can't believe he's gone. Pop is gone," Chase spoke looking as if he hadn't slept in a month or blinked in days.

"I'm so sorry, Chase. I really am. I know you're hurting." I wished I could have stopped his suffering and lift him out of the pit of grief. I couldn't but knew someone who would. Prayer would be the greatest gift I could give Chase at that time.

"And it seems like the family is breaking up and Pop isn't even in the ground yet."

"When people who we love leave this earth, it hurts so much, Chase. And some people won't handle the grief well at all. So don't charge any hearts right now. People aren't thinking clearly and it's hard to manage emotions when it is someone who is a pivotal part of your life. You're going to have to give out a whole bunch of 'free' passes. Wait until the cool of the day."

"What's a free pass?" Chase inquired. This free pass thing seemed to take his mind off of Swanson's death for at least a few seconds.

"Meaning 'you don't have to pay for that.' Go ahead and act up, act out, I won't react to the wrong. I'm just gonna let you be because this isn't the real you. And if it is, enjoy the free pass because I'm not going to give you unwarranted attention." God knows that I've employed this technique most of my life in dodging insults and all sorts of near blowups being a PK (preachers kid). For the sake of peace, most times it's just better to observe, acknowledge and ignore so that people who really didn't matter would just keep it moving. Sometimes, Jewel would throw some generosity in there and even muster up a smile and act like I'm dumb instead of taking someone to heart for foolishness.

"I see. It's just that we're dealing with grown folks who love Jesus. If this were Mr. Rodgers' Neighborhood, then I'd feel like I had to manage a bunch of babies."

"Speaking of which, how is Evey doing?" I immediately thought of the new baby on the way. "This type of stress isn't good for her during the pregnancy. She has to take it easy."

"She's with Mother. Everyone is getting ready for tomorrow."

"Well, just let me know what you want me to do. I would like to just be here for you, and rather not go to the homegoing. But, if that's what you want me to do, I'll go."

Chase appeared to be a bit annoyed by my decision to stay out of the line of fire. "I thought you were coming to go to the homegoing," he stated.

"I came just to be here for you, however you need me to be." I just hoped that meant I didn't have to watch Swanson be funeralized.

"I hope you'll come to the homegoing then. You're family. Pop accepted you and that's that."

"If that's what you want, that's where I'll be, God-willing." I'd just have to be prepared to give out a bunch of free passes and keep my own mouth in check.

"Is there something I'm missing or not thinking clearly about? I feel like you want to say something more to me. Whatever it is, it's okay."

"Maybe, Chase. It's just that this is going to be one of the most difficult days in Ms. Edie's life. Will she want to see me there? And personally, you couldn't have convinced me six months ago I'd be going anywhere near your father's family, or him. There is so much to consider, and I just want you to be prayerful about it. When I go back home, you have to live with your family, the family that basically raised you. And, I'm not going to lie to you. Seeing your father has been a lot for me to handle. I'm glad we submitted to the will of God so that we could both move on. So, don't be upset or disappointed. Just consider your mothers, especially the one who was with you when I couldn't and who still has influence over the people you are called to pastor. I'm not pleased with Ms. Edie at all, but she has to be going through hell right now."

"She really loved Pop. She's a strong woman and talk about God's grace? I'm surprised to see her acting like this with you, because I've never seen this side of her. She has cut the fool from time to time, but never like this. She really is much bigger than this."

"Somehow, even though I'm on the other side of the stick, I truly believe that. Your father told me she did her best to love you, which had to be challenging at first, unless she is the real life wonder woman. You're such a sweetheart, I'm sure she couldn't help but love you."

"I'm sort of upset, but I guess you're right. Pop is gone, and because of all this nonsense, I can't even reach out to you for support in front of the family without it being a big problem. Am I wrong for wanting you to be there with me? After all, you are my momma."

"As much as this takes for me to say this to you Chase, so is Ms. Edie. All the years I hoped for you, I never once thought, 'he has another mother.' That was a selfish thought because I couldn't imagine anyone else having that type of relationship with you. It didn't make sense. How could I be longing for you because I'm your mother, but you have another real mother? But there is no way we can deny that she has been there for you as a mother figure, she and Ms. Catherine. At the very least, she's been a good step-mom. Woman to woman, she's known you longer, helped to take care of you, and acted like you were one of the bunch, correct?"

"That's pretty accurate. But she's also been the one who said I'm Pop's son, not hers."

"She hasn't been perfect, but she was there. She had or at least chose to accept the unacceptable for whatever reasons, and dealt with it. Your father did like a lot of men do. He expected his wife to live with the results of his mistakes. Not that you were a mistake. How you got here was beyond a mistake to the women involved. So even though I'm not feeling her, she is not the bad guy in this picture. Yeah, we have God and all of that. Even the sinner knows that it takes real love to do what she did. She wasn't perfect, and unless there's something I don't know about, she hasn't even been abusive. She's just been human."

"So what are you saying?"

"Ms. Edie couldn't care less what I think. Let's not make her have to see the woman with whom her husband had this other baby—who she had to accept into the family who just showed up on the scene, and is walking into your life—getting honor as if I have been there all along. She probably feels like she's been caring for you as most mothers do. It's all relative. We've got to work with a person's own perspective and experience."

"I see you."

"So just let me know what you want me to do. I won't feel offended or slighted. I understand and don't want to fight your other mother."

"Okay. But you can at least come to the house. That's it. They gonna have to get used to you."

I stayed outside on the porch for most of the homegoing repast. Only in Christ, can these things be and true healing take place. Who else in their left brain would be with a people who clearly didn't want to see your face? Some of Chase's siblings were downright rude as they didn't speak. All of my attempts to be cordial were greeted with insolence. Oh yeah, and this is what one can expect from folks wearing Jesus bags, got some love scarves, and toting Bibles. It was clear that if Jewel Prunell wasn't the enemy, at the very least, I was an undesirable eyesore. I stood on my feet for hours, with the on and off drizzling rain. Chase, the new young pastor, had quite a bit of mingling to do. The family spent much needed time eating, laughing, consoling and reflecting with each other.

Aunt Catherine moseyed on out to the porch to throw out a lifeline.

"Welcome to the Swanson family. Excuse us for our hospitality. We're not experienced at this sort of thing. The old fart was the first to go. Besides, Nana, Big Mama, cousin Klepty—we called him that short for kleptomaniac."

"Hi, Ms. Catherine," Somehow I wasn't in the joking mood and tired of trying to make sure I didn't offend anyone at the same time.

"So how are you doing? Why are you out here in the rain?"

"The house is too crowded and there's plenty of room out here."

"Why don't you come inside."

"Thanks, but I'm fine. I'm enjoying the rain, actually. If I wasn't, I'd let you know."

"Well, you know you're part of the family, whether some of us like it or not. Chase is our boy, you know. He probably is the old fool's favorite. Oops. Did I say 'fool?' You know the Good Lord tells us not to call one another fool."

"We're not supposed to."

"Looky here then, I repent. He was an old fart too. We can get away with calling him that. Nonetheless, Chase is part of us, so that makes you part of us, cause you're part of him. At least, he came from you."

"No offense, Ms. Catherine. I have family, and I don't know how we got from let's try to make it all good on my first trip down here to all of this ice now. I really got delivered from some things in the back of the church and was able to let some things go. Now, one bad thought took off running through the minds of some people because of loyalty, suspicion, or whatever it is, and

I'm getting all of this fever. I don't do this type of stuff. The only reason I'm here is because of Chase."

"Baby, now everyone that matters knows you didn't sign up to be part of this family. It came with the territory. But, you know, some of them own shotguns, uh, well, some of us know how to load a rifle, pistol, you name it, we got all firearms covered. We know how to shoot and defend ourselves cause this is the country, girl. You may have to shoot a fox trying to roll up in your room in the middle of the night or a wood rat that thinks he paid the mortgage and is trying to bring a whole family up in the house. We pretty much get rid of the pests and stick together, that's all. It's not against you as much as it is for being there for Edie, my lovely sister-in-law."

"I understand, believe me. I do. This still doesn't make it right though. Are you all really comfortable with sticking it to me because I desire to have a relationship with my only child? Does this gun-toting family think about Chase's desires? I'm not the villain here, Ms. Catherine. Actually, because of God's grace, no one is. He died for the offended and the offender. He died for the wounded and the violent. I like it when it benefits me, so I've got to like it when grace covers the one who hurt me. Isn't this the way this thing is supposed to work?"

"Hold up a minute, I've got a few dollars in a paper towel in my breast. Is that enough for an offering, cause you're preaching, preacher." Normally, that was such a good joke I would have laughed. That time, it went straight through the cracks.

"The only thing I'm guilty of is never being able to get over Chase. Even though I wasn't there for him, we lived together in my thoughts, prayers and dreams. I hoped for these times since I was a little girl. I never really thought he was with you all, and that Ms. Edie would have a hand in raising him, or, how she would feel about me trying to have a part in his life."

"You remind her of all the pain. All the dark times the ministry went through. All the lost relationships. The people who went hard on us, and wouldn't have nothing to do with us. This is the country girl. The Pastor just can't do all of that and think folks is gonna stick with him."

"So that justifies putting me on ice today. I was on ice at twelve years old but I'm not twelve anymore. I survived and after a while, I just may have to put you Swansons in your place. I'm asking God to help me cause no one is going to stand between me and my son anymore."

"Alrighty then. Uh to the nuh. Nuh to the Uh." That statement was followed with an eighties Street Beat move which almost broke me. Aunt Catherine knows how to make light of anything. She is stomp down hilarious. "I see you need a hug. It must have took a lot for you to say all of that. You needed to hear yourself say that. Let Aunt Catherine hug you."

I allowed Catherine to go through her antics, but it really wasn't funny this time. "Are you still staying outside?" the unofficial comedienne questioned.

"Ms. Catherine, I've seen about twenty-five of you all walk by and not speak. Not one of you Swanson's invited me in." I just wasn't having it this time. All of the free passes went out of the window. I was tired of the shady behavior.

But, the comedienne proffered a comeback, "Technically, you're right. I'm too tiny to count as one. I'm probably three quarters, so three quarters invited you in. Who else is getting invitations to go inside the house today, Missy? Stop the drama, we're not giving out Oscars today. Let's go inside; my corns are screaming! Do you give a discount to cut these bad boys off?"

So after hours in the rain, I went inside.

FROM THE INSIDE OUT
A Fallen Hero

The house was packed with people like sardines compressed in a sleek can. Chase and the immediate family were all in the dining room around the table with some guest clergy from out of town. The huge Victorian house had vaulted ceilings and crown moldings that would cost a fortune to re-create today. I actually loved the finished look the rooms had, with antiques that looked as if they were cherished and well preserved. The icing on the cake was the paisley ornate wallpaper that looked as if it was older than every living Swanson.

Chase spotted me. "Hi Momma. Come over here and have a seat next to me."

I motioned "no" to him with a clearly visible head nod, yet he ignored me as he directed someone to find me a chair.

"Hello everyone." I uttered these words with all eyes on me. The pressure was commensurate with presenting a controversial thesis before a college of physicians at a world symposium.

"Mama are you okay? Cause if you're not, you know I will put her out. You know I will." Ceda, Chase's sister stood at her mama's, Ms. Edie, rescue once again with rudeness par ordinaire. If looks could pierce, I would have been spliced a hundred ways. Ceda only said what others must have been thinking. My presence alongside Chase was definitely an issue.

"No. We can't be rude or inconsiderate to anyone, even on the day I bury my husband."

"Mother," Chase said as he spoke to Ms. Edie, "please let's be nice and do right now."

I could not have been more embarrassed. I leaned over and whispered to Chase, "This is too much. You have guests and I'm not comfortable. Call me later, I'm leaving."

"No. There's just some things we're all gonna have to get used to," Chase stated with clearly audible authority. "That's all. We can't force it, but I'm not gonna have you so uncomfortable that you have to leave either."

While turning to some of the guest ministers, Chase introduced me. "Elder Brinson, and Bishop Brunswick, this is my mother too, Dr. Jewel Prunell." Chase then editorialized, "These are Pop's friends who stuck with him through thick and thin. These were his real friends."

I greeted the men of God.

"And son," interjected Ms. Edie, "since they were real friends to your father, they are men you can trust for wisdom and counsel. I'm so proud of my son, all of my sons and daughters, even the spiritual children. God has truly blessed us. Everyone has come together and done exactly what they are supposed to. Poppa set everything in order, so we're all gonna be just fine. Seemed like Chase would've been the last one, but he's the one who has the shepherd's heart like Poppa. He's the one with the anointing and the call. Right baby? And God knew exactly where Chase had to be to cultivate him so he could be who he is in God. Right baby?"

What a dig and subtle blade. Ms. Edie really wasn't ready for a smackdown.

Chase maintained a professional demeanor and carried the conversation. "God knows all things Mother. I've been predestined and made by Potter. He's still making me."

Ms. Edie continued to dig. "He's the one, when Poppa used to be in his study preparing for Sunday morning messages, or for the radio broadcast, when everyone else might be out in the yard playing, or trying to break me down for some banana pudding or ice cream before supper, he's the one who would be right at Poppa's side, just sitting quiet. I never could figure out, at first, why this boy would sit with Poppa for so long on his visits instead of playing in the yard with everyone else. Cause you know, Poppa used to be kind of short with anybody who interrupted his study time. He never wanted anyone to talk or make too much noise while he was seeking God. But Chase didn't care. He would just sit there and when Poppa would look up from time to time, he'd talk to Chase. You know. Let him ask questions. Before you knew it, Chase would be on his knees praying with him. Then Poppa would give him the mike for five minutes toward the end of the service. Y'all remember Chase's first sermon?"

"Yup. Jesus wants an ass just like you," Corey volunteered.

"And my boy sure did work that sermon. I thought I was about to drop when he called us asses. You see, he had to explain about colts, donkeys and asses. He sure did clean that up and had the people jumping when he said that's what it took to get Jesus to make his triumphant entry into Jerusalem. Prophecy had already gone out and Jesus told the two disciples to go get the ass and the colt. The ass was required to fulfill the prophecy, an animal that would normally be viewed as stubborn. Oh my Lord, how old were you then, son, about ten or eleven?"

"Twelve, Mother."

While Edie went down memory lane in part to show me how much Chase was really her son because she had all of the years of experience to prove it, I listened and watched the family's reaction to really know how much she's really been a mother to him. Chase garnered everything he could from his father since he was a young boy. The man I know as my son has certainly been shaped and influenced to some degree by a woman whose current strikes demonstrated her insecurity, and a man whose actions almost caused me to lose my mind. Thank God Delayne Swanson lived to overcome the reproach of a pedophile rapist. Swanson had fallen but turned out to be a hero. Chase would have had a very different life if the man hadn't.

The guest clergy formally dismissed themselves as the hour grew late. So did a host of other visitors. Chase seemed fixed in the chair he sat in and Evey kept asking him if he wanted anything. Evey made it clear that she would not upset Ms. Edie and had minimal interaction with me. By the time we looked at the clock, it was almost midnight. Ms. Edie declared it was time for her to rest.

"Dr. Prunell, I thought you'd have enough class not to show up today, and not to sit in my home all night. But you didn't. Will you please have some mercy on all of us and let me lie down without you in my home? It's time for you to leave."

I couldn't believe this woman had the nerve to say what she had the audacity to think.

"Sure. But before I go, we should have a word in private."

"Anything you have to say to me, you can say right now. This is my family and I trust every single one of them."

"You may trust them, but what I have to say is for you, and not for them."

"It's personal?"

"Precisely. This is very personal at this point."

We both went into the kitchen. I could feel my blood pressure rising as Chase moved to come with us. I asked him to let us handle this ourselves.

Ms. Edie sniped, "Can you please hurry up, I'm exhausted."

"I wanted to ask you something. Did you enjoy a good sex life with your husband, with 'Poppa'?"

"What? How dare you! That's none of your business!"

"None of my business. Did I hear you say 'none of my business?' Oh, I guess I can really just let myself out then. This is none of my business. I'm going to ask you again. Did you lie down and enjoy your husband after he raped me when I was a little girl? Did you? Can you imagine a man doing what he did to me to one of your precious granddaughters? Huh? Where's all of your guts and mouth now? So you laid down with a man who took my innocence, almost stifled me with a pillow over my mouth while doing it, while I haven't even been able to phantom having to be in a position to give myself to any man at all. Guess what lady? I haven't had a successful relationship yet. When your husband left my room almost twenty-nine years ago, he left me with your 'boy' Chase growing inside of me. Newsflash: There was no baby shower. There was no joyous chronicling of every development in the pregnancy. There was no birth announcement. I can hardly remember what happened from day to day. Aside from some silly idiosyncrasies, the trauma from conceiving him and carrying him blocked most of my memory. Your 'son' sitting in that dining room is my only 'son' who was taken from me. I've spent his entire life waiting to find him again. So while you were going through all of those signature moments with him and Poppa, and whoever else, watching him grow, I was void wanting to watch him grow. Wanting just a few moments of what you've had with him. So, our lives have intersected Ms. Edie. But none of it, none of this, was because I chose it. And neither did you. So why are you making it hard for me? All I'm trying to do is be there for the son I lost. While you were trying to get over having to accept him, I was trying to get over losing all the time you've had with him. So, with all of your mean-spirited behavior, know that I'm not going anywhere. Chase wants to know me, and that's all that matters. You've lost a husband and he lost a father. I do not know what you're going through, but we've all been through. Will I ever be able to be here for him without it being a problem for you? I don't even know how to reach him. As you've painfully reminded me, I don't know him as well as you do. But the bond that God has given us, you and nobody is going to break or destroy."

"Are you done?"

"We've both had to deal with the pain. Can't we both share the treasure?"

"I guess you're done. I'm asking you again. Are you going to make me have to put you out, or are you leaving on your own?"

I immediately walked out to get my handbag. "Just one more thing. Don't let anyone ever tell you all that chivalry is dead. This has been quite a display of good manners and brotherly love. You all know how to treat folks. And God help those who have been touched by you Swansons."

"Momma, let me take you."

"No. Stay with your people. Remember what I told you earlier. I'm going to find my own way."

"But it's pitch black out and this is the country."

"So what. What could possibly happen? Get kidnapped? Raped? Somewhere along the line, I've developed instincts to know how to survive, right Ms. Edie? Don't worry about the wild animals either. A possum would be better company than any of you all right now."

I walked outside and down the long graveled path to the main road. There was no cell phone reception, and no way to call for a car service. I exploded, ran my mouth, made things worse while I had to find my way back to the hotel in the dark. As I tried to walk to the next house hoping to ask for help there, I couldn't tell where the next house might be. There were no street lights and absolutely no reception. After about fifteen minutes of trying to figure out what to do, without one single car coming down the main road, I decided to go back to the house.

"Can someone please call me a car or a taxi."

"Momma, just let me take you."

"Okay. Fine."

Everything I wanted to accomplish was spiraling out of control. Chase was infuriated.

"What did you say to Ms. Edie? She's is the back room crying and carrying on. She said she can't believe you asked her about her performance with Pop."

"I didn't merely ask her about her performance with Pop. To say it like that makes it seem like I was comparing her to me. It wasn't even like that. I wouldn't know how to perform if someone paid me. There was a point to the question, Chase, and Ms. Edie knows that."

"What is the point to a question like that on the day we buried my father?"

"Nothing. When I said it, I was upset. I was trying to imply that she was complicit to what had been done and she needed to get off my case, because I didn't do anything to her."

"This is not good at all. This is not the time to ask Ms. Edie anything like that about Poppa. That was just tacky. You were dead wrong. We barely put him in the ground today! Remember, they are my family, Momma. And I'm going to tell you just like I told Mother. She is my mother too and none of y'all better ask me to choose."

I felt like a two-year-old being berated by the son who I was trying so desperately to reach. "You're right. That certainly wasn't the best judgment. I owe her an apology. She provoked me and I said some things she needs to think about when she's going at me. I wasn't nice at all. I let her get the best of me. Just drop me off and I'll be out of your way. Some things in life aren't fair and nothing we can ever do will make it fair or just. Unless we all yield to Christ and walk in love, this will never work. I was out of control. I know better."

"So does she. Half of all of that talking at the table was for you. You both need to cut it out. Ms. Edie always fussed Pop out when he spent time with me alone because he hardly ever did with any of the others. Anything he did for me, she thought that he favored me because he loved me more, and it wasn't that. I used to think that Pop felt guilty that I didn't have you around and for the longest I couldn't live with them, and that's why he spoiled me. But now I know that he saw something in me, and had to give me what he had while he could. His favor was for a greater purpose than just feeling guilty or liking me the best."

"Surely everything should have worked out where we can say 'to God be the glory.' I really messed up tonight. It's about God and I've got to repent to the family. Even though I can't make them accountable for their wrong, I'm not willing to live with the way things went down tonight."

"It's okay, Momma. You'll have the opportunity to say whatever you need to, because you'll see each other again. She's going to have to get over it. You are here and I hope we have years ahead of us."

"Why do we have to see one another again?"

"Since you're here, I asked Pop's attorneys to meet up with us within the next day or two. Dad had you in the dealings. He told me when he was in the hospital."

"What?"

"Yeah. He told me when he was dying that he had changed his will a few weeks ago. He said God told him to, when he saw you."

"Oh shoot," I murmured under my breath. There were a number of possibilities, but what could Delayne Swanson have involved me in?

"Is that good or bad?"

I had to take a few seconds to think about it. Swanson hadn't been in the ground for twenty-four hours and he was still surprising Jewel. "It's neither. I'm just not looking forward to being with your family again. I know this isn't about me, but I keep getting struck in the process. Your people are not feeling me right now and I am not trying to have to go there with them."

"Momma, I'm sorry about all of this. I can't believe all of this is happening this way."

"And even Evey, she seems to be torn."

"Don't worry about Evey, or Edie for that matter. They both will come around. They don't have a choice."

I wonder what Prophet Swanson set up. God has something in store for me.

Great things were happening back to back. Sometimes life brings a series of hardships, one right after the other. For me, it was rape, pregnancy and losing my son. A storm, a tornado and a Tsunami may hit a region and there will certainly be setbacks, hardships, delays and even destruction. But after some time, as long as there is still life, things will turn around. Enduring the time that is required during the rehabilitation, the rebuilding and restoring phase is the thing that most people find to be most difficult. Many people die in the midst of the storm. Others survive the storm and die waiting to be on a sure foundation again. For those who endure and never lose hope, there is always a better day, even if it comes almost thirty years later. So much was turning around at the same time, that Harlan was getting lost in the shuffle.

THE OTHER SIDE OF THE MOUNTAIN
The Better Than Life

Harlan's prospectus was dwindling day by day. We barely had time to talk anymore, more or less spend time with each other. And, I was terribly afraid of introducing him to the real life of Jewel Prunell. Xavier had a firm grip on the real me, and still chose to love me. Harlan, on the other hand, is the dream guy. He is the one who would require more and challenge me and he is the one with whom I wanted to see all the promises of God come to pass. I opted to return Harlan's phone call.

"Hello Sir." Harlan was such a gentleman, I couldn't think of anything else to call him.

"I've been trying to reach you," Harlan uttered with a genuine Texan flair.

"Please accept my apology. I've been pulled in every direction and I'm just so tied up right now."

The modern day Boaz continued speaking, "Can I do anything to lighten your load? I desire to help Jewel."

"I wish you could."

"Anything you care to discuss?"

"Not really. How about we talk about you. What's happening with Harlan?" Life wasn't all about Jewel, so it was time to find out more about the potential suitor.

Mr. Texas apprised me of a new television program he and his brothers were going to have nationally syndicated. The program would be about advising farmers of various equipment, techniques and treatments to get the maximum yield from healthy crops. Industrial farming and cattle raising was Harlan's world and passion while it was a whole new world to me.

"So tell me, Harlan, how does faith fit into your life?"

"A better question, Ms. Prunell, would be, can faith fit into my life? And the answer would be no. Faith is boundless and limitless. Faith is how my daddy and granddaddy made it through the change in the farming industry. Faith is what gave our network the edge on organic processing and inventing the equipment to adapt to the changes we've made in the crops we grow. Faith is what gives us the keys to know how to improve on the self-irrigation systems and to know what products will work to keep destructive pests off our harvest. Farmers have a view of God that a whole lot of people take for granted. We serve the Creator who made us stewards of the earth. We get to see the goodness of the Father every time the ground breaks and springs forth fruit from the seeds we planted in one season, expecting a harvest in due season. We serve the Lord of the harvest, and He is good, good, good! Now, enough about me. How come you try to shelter yourself from me?"

"To be quite honest, I know that my life is a bit much from one on the outside looking in. You might run if you knew too much too fast. And some of this stuff is complicated, embarrassing and we don't know each other well enough to be that transparent."

"Is that so? I really can't think of any scenarios that would make me run, Jewel, unless you've misrepresented yourself."

"I haven't."

"So what is it about you that you are concerned about?"

"Nothing that I'm ready to disclose. We're just not the Waltons, that's all."

"That's a relief. Neither are we. So are you My Three Sons, Different Strokes, Good Times, The Cosby Show, or the Brady Bunch?"

"A cross among All My Children, Different Strokes, and The Cosby Show. When I grew up, we were like the Cosbys. Then

All My Children became the order of the day, and now we're in Different Strokes. I have the two boys you met when I first met you. They live with me now, and the lifestyles are totally different, but we're doing fine adjusting. They are great young men."

"So the soap opera element is—"

"Like I told you before, I had my only son when I was twelve years of age and just met him again. He was raised with his father."

"When you first mentioned your son, you said you really didn't want to talk about it. Are you ready now? That must have been difficult becoming a mother so soon."

"It was. But more than that, I was hoping to find him one day, and we did. So, that's it in a nutshell, and you're not going to get any more information out of me, so stop trying to go deeper. I hate to have to be so direct, but this is difficult for me to talk about with anyone."

Harlan kept prying with a gentle voice, "Do you think you were the first twelve-year-old to have a baby?"

"Harlan, no I don't. But, I don't want to talk about this with you. It's humiliating."

"I understand. You can't operate outside of the frame of reference you have, and your own life has taught you how to cope. But you shouldn't be humiliated at all. Something had to go very wrong for you to be able to get pregnant at twelve. When I was twelve, I don't think we even had two seconds unsupervised around any girls who weren't in the family."

"Something did happen. Back then, we weren't sitting on talk shows thinking anything near wanting to have a baby and then some host sent us off to boot camp or gave us a screaming doll or a raw egg to hold for forty-eight hours. It was unheard of. We were thinking of dancing, roller skating, hopscotch, begging Ma to get our hair braided and stuff like that. Teenage pregnancy was a big deal and adolescent pregnancy was unheard of."

"It probably happened more than you know. People still get the private solution, abortion."

"That may be true but that wasn't even an option in our home. If my parents would have let me have an abortion, that would have said to me we've been teaching one thing, hoping you'd believe one thing and govern your life as we have taught you, but when stuff happens, there's an excuse for denying what we've taught you to believe in. Back then, we believed that God knows all things and that surely means He knows more than we do. So, if He knew I'd be where I was, then He would keep me with whatever situation I found myself in. We didn't have the progressive Christianity of today where we have more Word than ever, more skills, talents and gifts than ever, yet have more excuses than ever. We knew to take directives from God, and trust Him to make it all work out. So, if I found myself pregnant, somehow, God would take care of it all. For many years, I grappled with God taking care of Chase. I didn't know for sure if my baby was okay. It took some time for me to just say, 'Lord, I have to trust that you're taking care of him'. Isn't that ostentatious? Me telling God to take care of his own child?"

"Sounds like a mother to me. It also sounds like you need some TLC."

"Thanks. I really need three weeks without a cell phone, pager and five minutes to spend thinking of absolutely nothing. I just need to veg out."

"I suppose 'veg out' means a getaway?"

"That's not a pure translation. It could mean a getaway. It more so denotes doing nothing, like a glorified couch potato. But instead of eating a bunch of junk behind a remote control, or neglecting to pay the mortgage for two months, don't be completely irresponsible because when one leaves the vegging phase, you don't want to have to add weight loss, cholesterol management, or foreclosure to the list of 'to do's.'"

"So, it's manage the essentials, ignore anything else."

"Comprendes, senor."

"Well if you can get the days, I can arrange a veg out that you'll never forget."

"I'm only talking Harlan. I've been away from the practice too much lately. So when I get through this phase of adjustments with the personal life, I really need to implement a new program at church and then once my patients know I'm still their dependable doctor, then vegging out is it."

"So how about I take a rain check and I stop by to pick that up tomorrow."

I can definitely get used to Harlan. He seems like the Boaz I've been waiting for. The man who has eyes for me, and an approach that shows me all he has is preserved for me, and he won't defile the beauty that he esteems by appeasing his own flesh. This man can capture a gaze that would last a lifetime. Who can resist a man who respects himself and you? With all of what I've lived through, the challenge is not to be skeptical and wait for a big glitch, a big "no wonder," as if there has to be something wrong. So far, Harlan is a far cry from the men who want to know how a woman can fit into their lives and only be a help to them. Harlan is a refreshing friend. He's a good reason to shop for a perfect dress.

Since Noey wasn't around, we had to do the long distance dress test. When I picked the final selections, I took pictures and sent them to her via picture mail, and would await a yea or a nay. Of course, I'd have to specify what shoes and handbags I brought with me, or purchase suitable accessories up to par. Thank God I brought a cute black Francescobiasia with me, because I'm just not willing to drop a couple of grand for another handbag for an impromptu date. I'm not willing to be a real life *Sex In the City* character with a closet full of clothes, shoes, hot dates and no real dough.

Note to Self: Make sure you spend some time in the Word. You've been neglecting your own personal devotions to the Lord. With more on your plate, you need more of Him. Don't get caught up in a rut and find yourself on empty. He doesn't deserve to be short changed. He deserves more of you and you must seek more of Him.

As I looked for the perfect dress, I couldn't help but wonder how I got from there to here. I never would have thought that I'd be waiting for the reading of Delayne Swanson's will. Years ago when I first began therapy, the psychologist asked if I ever considered suing Prophet Swanson. The thought quickly left my mind as I told the trusted doctor that I wouldn't dare take anything from him. I didn't want any connection to him, nothing to do with him, and didn't want to ever see his face again. I'd rather sweep the floor at McDonald's for the rest of my life, than to look for a dollar from him. While sending over a few prospects to Noey to no avail, I decided to have a Gazebo blend cup of coffee and ran into a number of the familiar faces. Some of the Swansons were out and about. I was in their neck of the woods, and there wasn't too much else to do in the small town. Evey decided to strike up a conversation.

"Hi, Ms. Jewel. You're still here."

I tried to respond as if nothing cross ever transpired between us. "Yes, dear. How are you? How's the new baby doing?"

"Everything is fine. I'm just taking some of the family that's here from out of town shopping. There isn't much to do here, outside of bowling, fishing, or somebody's social."

"Oh, that's nice," I offered as I continued to peruse the dinner dresses.

"So how long are you here for?"

"I'm not quite sure Evey. And if you don't mind me being frank with you, are you asking for you, or for the family?" I knew I was being defensive, but didn't feel like playing games.

"I'm just asking, Ms. Jewel."

"Would you like to do lunch? I'd love to spend some time with you and Ruth while I'm here."

"I can't, sorry. The family is going to the house. Just thought since I saw you, I'd speak. When this is all over, I'd like to come up to New York though. I've never traveled without Chase, and he's not going to leave the church for a while. So maybe we can look forward to that."

There was a light at the end of the tunnel. "Thanks so very much. You know you are always welcome. This means a lot to me. Take care." Relationships take work. And some of them are worth fighting for. Evey was in a difficult position. Just a few words let me know that she did care.

Harlan loved the Noey/Jewel ensemble. I picked a perfect Willona from *Good Times* get up. The knit multi-colored psychedelic wrap dress had a complimentary fit, one I could feel comfortable in and not self-conscious. This time, Harlan decided to book a room and stay over. Between Harlan, Xavier, Chase, Rashaun, Tysheem, and Aliyah, I no longer missed the practice, which used to be the undefeated champion and focus of my life. More important things trumped the importance of what used to be a respectable front for masking my brokenness. Aliyah, and what would transpire with her sons, was certainly one of them.

"You better hurry up and get back," Danne stated with a sense of urgency and need for sisterhood support.

"Why? What's going on?"

"They want to put Aliyah in hospice. She wants to stay in Chicago and I think she needs to come here."

"Hospice!" I really don't know why I was surprised. The inevitable was transpiring but none of us was ready for it, and never would have been.

"Yes."

"Oh my Lord! Please don't tell the boys until I get back. Oh my God. I've got to go see her."

"You need to see her, Jewel. You know how difficult she is and you are about the only one who she will listen to."

"I'll talk to her. What is she saying?"

"Nothing different. She's seen God. Made things right with everybody and wants God to heal her, even if it means resting until the resurrection of the saints who died in the Lord. She doesn't want to live like this any longer."

"But she didn't have to, Danne. She's never let the meds run full course. She eats snickers and barbecue potato chips with a coke for breakfast. Do you know how many people are living with HIV/AIDS because they accept the wisdom of God revealed to man to know how to use herbs of the ground to combat sickness and disease? There are different manifestations of healing. Why not take the medication until she knows she has received a supernatural miracle? I know a lot of doctors think we have the last word, but when it's all said and done, we know God decides who lives and who dies."

"You're singing to the choir, Jewel. What you have to realize is a person has to live with what they're working with. Aliyah isn't there. She doesn't even want to be seen going to her doctor's office, because everybody there is going to know she has AIDS. And that doesn't make sense, because if they are there knowing she has AIDS, chances are, they've got it too, cause they're seeing the same doctor. She is still dealing with the stigma thing. She does as she knows, and knows as she does."

"So stigma and foolishness are why she's on her way to hospice and willing to leave two boys without a mother? She needs a miracle." I was still hoping.

"And we need to accept whatever happens. Look, Jewel. I know how you get. You've been doing great. Don't start getting depressed and crawling up in a hole somewhere. We are not God, and everything is in His hands. He gave man free will and He is sovereign. So, really, this is between Aliyah and God. How's everything going down there anyway? You've been kind of quiet about things."

"That's because the jury is still out on the entire situation and much of what I've discovered is Chase's family's business. I really don't want to bring stuff back on this side unless it is necessary. What I can tell you is that Swanson had some doves in the hat and we're not sure what's about to be released."

"What's the code language representing, Jewel? I'm too tired to figure it out."

"I'm part of the will, girlfriend. To what capacity, I have no clue. But I certainly would have never thought I'd be here more or less waiting for the will to be read."

"Call me when you have concrete facts. As a matter of fact, call me first!" Danne exclaimed. I knew she'd put the rest of the crew down with what was going on. This was an exciting yet trying time for us.

Everything in me wanted to call Xavier and let him know everything. He is the one person whom I used tell everything and not feel ashamed, insecure or defensive. But Xavier was on a different page concerning our relationship and I didn't want to give false hope, or use him for my emotional needs. I just wanted a friend while he wanted much more. Yet, I needed to check on the boys.

"How are the boys doing?"

"I am fine thank you."

Xavier would correct me for yawning too slowly and I couldn't stand it. "Sorry. How are you doing, Xavier?"

"Loving our time together. When I tell you everything is perfect, it is. Only one thing is missing, Jewel. You."

"Thanks Buddy. Anything I need to know?"

"Nothing out of the ordinary. Rashaun wants to try to be slick and hang out, and Tysheem keeps asking when you, or Aliyah, are coming back."

"Please call me when he asks for me. I don't care what time it is. Some things are going on with Aliyah right now, and the last thing they need to feel is abandonment."

"Babe, don't take this all the way to the right, okay? They just want to know when you're coming home."

"I have to go to Chicago first, but I think I'll only be there for a few hours. If I can work it in one day, I'll be home the day after tomorrow."

Lord, I know you don't give us more than we can bear. You've kept me day by day over the years. I trust you to keep me and to help Rashaun and Tysheem and the rest of us to endure. Lord, I trust you with our lives and well-being. Keep Chase and his entire family as you comfort and strengthen them. Lord, let us all be one and see you and your purpose. Just as I was talking to God, Chase called.

"Momma, I've called a family prayer at the church tomorrow morning. We can all go over to the attorney's office afterwards, first thing."

"Chase, I'm not comfortable around your family. Outside of the business, I'd rather not."

"Can I be honest with you Momma? If I were your pastor, you know what I'd tell you? This isn't about you. It may not be comfortable. It's not comfortable for me either. And it's definitely not comfortable for Ms. Edie. So comfortable can't be the standard. We have to stick to principle and do what is right. I just need everybody to work with me and we'll all get through this. I'm sorry because I know this is a difficult situation for you. And I can see how much you love me just because you're here. Don't think I don't notice."

"All right. I'll be at the prayer. I've let this thing consume my thoughts and decisions for so long that I'm used to having to protect me. It's hard to see when I'm protecting my feelings beyond reason."

"I'm not talking intellectualism, Momma. I'm talking the will of God. Most people would say you're within reason. In fact, you shouldn't even have come this far. Most people would say you should have been walked away from all of this because you don't have to put up with another thing from us. People would say you should have never even kept me, more or less wanted to find me. So it's not even about what is intellectually just. God's justice is quite different. We've got to all put down our own feelings and rights or we'll never be one. I know Poppa did something fantastic and we'll all need to be in the right spirit to see that."

While Chase was instructing me, I was smiling at his wisdom, maturity and ability to see clearly in spite of just losing his father. "I take the rebuke Pastor. I take it. In fact, I'm proud of you."

Prayer does change things. Although I was still getting the nice-nasty treatment from the Swanson family, allowing the presence of God to completely overtake me, my insecurities and thoughts, helped me to stand. My strength was in Jesus. I am who I am, and who I am is right on time for whatever it is God wanted to do. When we arrived at the attorney's office, I sat with the budding young pastor in complete silence. I didn't waste any time with the "what if" factors. That would soon be clear as day to all of us. I thought of the miraculous power of God. A man who I spent most of my life in fear of, hoping that he suffered somewhat because of the "pain" that I gave a stable home to in my emotions and soul, willed for me to be part of whatever it is he was leaving behind.

Nothing could pay for what Swanson did to me. But it was paid for. Jesus paid for it, and all of what I knew about Christ had to be made real in all of this. Jesus paid for Swanson to be free from what almost caused me to lose my mind. Jesus paid for me to be free from the hurt, pain, scars and rejection that came from being violated and defiled. After over an hour of waiting, we were summoned to an impressive conference room.

The team of attorneys introduced themselves. A managing partner explained we were assembled for the reading of the will. But before we could proceed, Swanson wrote a letter to the family and asked that it be read. The purpose of the letter was to explain why he made the final decisions. We were told to listen attentively, no copies would be issued, and it would only be read within our hearing once. Right then and there, I knew Swanson was wiser than we all thought. A copy floating around could be on the Internet in 2.6 seconds after we left the building.

After a roll call, the reading of the letter began:

> I want you all to know that I love you. God could not have given me a better wife, family, friends, and church family. Truly, I have been blessed. Even though I've failed at times, I've tried to live a life before you that should persuade you to serve the Lord always. To God be all the glory. You all know that I've been a man who believes the Bible. I believe in moderation and have taught you all how to be prudent, wise and faithful stewards over everything God has given us. I hope that after today, you will continue in what we have known to be a lifestyle of true prosperity where we have no lack, no debt, and are able to be a blessing to those in need. I have been blessed to be able to go to rest, knowing that I have left provisions for my children, and my children's children. When Mother Aimee Nelson passed a number of years ago, she left her entire estate to me. I told none of you, because I knew that was God's provision to make the ministry and the family debt free. So know that what happens today for you is partially due to Mother Aimee's blessing to our family.
>
> To my wife Edith, I could not have had a better stronger woman by my side all of these years. Without you, I wouldn't have been able to build the ministry and help all of the people we have served. We will see our reward for the work we have done. I trust that you will never want for anything. You already have the home, the proceeds from the million-dollar insurance policy and all of our children who should

see after you. I have also left one million dollars for you. I trust that the Board of Business Elders at the church will continue to care for you with a monthly allowance. God built the house, and used our lives to do it.

To my sister Catherine, we came up in hard times. You have also stuck by my side and helped us build the church since the day we stepped out on faith. Most of all, you helped take care of all of my children since the day each one of them was born. Edith and I never had to worry about a babysitter. What you did for us with Chase, you will never know until you meet me on the other side. When I couldn't bring him home, you gave him a home. I could not have fulfilled my responsibility as his father without you. I can't repay you, but sure can try. For this, the attorneys will pay off your house and give you $500,000.00. Have a burger on me.

To my children, the only ones I've made provisions for individually are Cybil and Chase. All of the rest of you, you know Pop loves you. Every single one of you has done well, and is financially secure, or should be. Work hard, and you will see the fruits of your labor. I am confident that your mother will undergird whatever you may need her to, if that day ever comes. You have made a humble Southern man proud to see how children will be greater if a man shows them the way. I am proud of all of you. I have given each of you specific gifts of my favorite things and earthly possessions, in the will. This letter is mostly for you to understand why I had to set apart Cybil and Chase. Cybil, you are the dreamer, the creative one. You have never gone the normal route and I am proud of you for living by faith and daring to take risks to achieve what you dream of. Even when you hit the ground, you get up and keep on running. This ability to fall, pick yourself up, dust yourself off, maybe even cry a little, and keep trying is the droppings of greatness. One day, you'll hit the mark and the world better watch out when that happens. Yet, I've observed you receive the least because others don't understand your choices in life. Your momma loves you, Cybil, and hopes for your best. She just doesn't know that your best is something that she has never seen before. Momma and I have given all of the children weddings, helped purchase homes, helped furnish homes, paid for vacations, given loans, and given the grandchildren just about anything. Yet, we haven't done the same for you. I know you've felt like a failure, but you're not. You're just a leader in the making. Yet, you've still been faithful to the ministry and come to see about your momma and me whenever we needed anything. So, I've asked the attorneys to hand over a bank account I started in your name. I want to help you when you need help, not when you've become successful and it's easy for you to manage on your own. To date, there is $374,689.22 in the account and all of it is yours. Use these funds to subsidize your visions after you've paid your momma back every dime you owe her. Pay your momma back and everyone else you owe first. You know the principles. The rest is for whatever risks you need to take to see your dreams come true. Risk-takers change the world and their critics understand after a while. If you need business advice, use these same attorneys. They introduced me to the financial planner and accountant who helped me when Mother Aimee died. You are not special, Cybil, just different. And this is my last gift to you.

I can't give you any more behind your mother's back. I'm sleeping till the rapture!

Chase, my love for you cannot be put into words. God is not a respecter of persons and neither should we be. I've had to love you to make sure you followed after God and stayed within the fold. The same demons that drove me wanted to destroy you, but they won't be able to. You've been bought with a price. I believe your mother Edith will take care of you like the others. She has grown to treat you just like you were her own. I've been advised to make sure, because when people die, things change all the time. The last thing in the world I would want you to feel is why didn't I protect you, since I know that is the only way you'll get what's yours. I don't believe I had to take care of you for that reason. You are the son with the most responsibility with the ministry. I desire for you to be able to give your full dedication and focus without having to compromise your desires for your family. As I leave you the one and a half acres of property you already live on, I leave you another one and a half acres to expand if you ever want. I also leave you with a million dollars, and have asked the business elders to give you a reasonable housing allowance each month. I have witnessed your discipline since you were a young man, and, the ability to run your home without any reproach or interference to the ministry. Son, remember the devices of the enemy. He will try to trap you and cause you to fall. I believe all of what I never saw because of some decisions I made, you will be able to see happen for the Kingdom of God. I have left you in a position where you can take care and never tax or rob the House of God for your personal needs or gain. My prayer is that you will always fear God and not get caught up in celebrity and gain. As you walk by faith to see the vision God gave me, walk in the same wisdom of Solomon and see that God's House is built, and the tithes and offerings given to God remain Holy and are used for benevolence, the sanctuary and needs of the ministry to take the gospel and saving grace of Jesus Christ to the ends of the earth. Run with the vision, be progressive, but remain true to who you are. Remain broken by the Lord and humble. Others may not comprehend, but only those who help in the vineyards as true under-shepherds know the weight and sacrifice that you will have to make. One million is not enough. But it's a start. This is for you and your household. The church is in great condition. God is Good!

And finally, whatever is left of my estate, I have left in trust with the attorneys as executors for Dr. Jewel Prunell. So don't anyone try to block or stop this. It's a done deal. This allotment is not guilt money. Dr. Prunell, I have asked the funds to be released at your discretion for whatever you deem suitable. I have no right to place demands on you. But I do have a request. Please use a substantial portion of these funds to set up a program that will benefit women like you, young girls who have been raped, molested, abused, especially those with children. Had God not intervened, anything could have happened to Chase. Now, you will see what we all have seen in having him in our lives. You were a brave young girl who gave my son life. There is $1,670,000.00 in funds to begin a program that will encourage others to live and to choose life.

To all of you, you can choose to quarrel, or to live with it. The same judgment that you respected through the years is the same judgment that is operating when I know these are the final words and actions I am committing in this life, before I stand before a Holy God in judgment. With love, Prophet Delayne Swanson.

I could not move from the chair. My legs were locked. This wasn't mega money, but it was $1.67 million more than I had five minutes ago, and, a decent start-up for a charity. Would it be in Mississippi, or New York? Probably I would launch it from a local office in NY and plan a national campaign. Or, I could pay off all of my student loans, mortgage and the debt over the practice. He said do what I want. There was so much to think about.

Halt. Note to self: God gave you this as a steward. Stop thinking and consult Him. He will give you the right plan.

I was stunned. Not by the money. Not even by the last minute bequest to me. But by how much Swanson really feared the Lord. In an age where so many pastors do the bling bling and can't even afford to go six months without a check or they lose everything, Swanson lived a modest humble life. He left the ministry intact, and even had enough to leave to charity. Impressive. More and more, I've learned that Swanson was an admirable human being. Real love is to deny self-indulgence to make sure that the ones you love are secure, even when you are not around to partake of it.

"Chase, I've got to call your grandfather and tell him what just happened."

"No, let me tell him. He's going to have to be my spiritual father now. I'm going to come home with you, and be back on time for Sunday."

"Are your church people alright with this?"

"No. I didn't tell anyone yet. I'm the pastor and Pop knew what he was doing when he prepared me to be with you. He didn't have to say it, but he was steering me in the direction of my grandfather and I just didn't know it. It wasn't until they were reading the letter that it hit me. It only makes sense. I need a pastor and Bishop Prunell can give me the counsel and feed me the Word of God to make this transition and grow. He's the only father I've left, and now I know why. Just call him and ask if I can come."

This news was so heart-warming. Pieces were falling into place and suddenly what was a lonely unfinished landscape was becoming picturesque with purposed detail. Daddy called Chase his son, and Chase needed Daddy as a father. "Of course I'll speak with him."

I didn't wait to tell Bishop Prunell the good news. "Daddy, are you seated? I've got some big news."

"What is it, darling?"

"Swanson left me $1.67 million to do whatever I want, but requested I start a program to help women or girls like me."

"$1.67 million?"

"You heard it right."

"What are you going to do with it?"

"Tithe to you. And then be led by the Spirit of God. Whatever I do, I'm not spending a dime of it on me because God has already blessed me. I'll look at it as if it never came to me and do something that I'd probably never do on my own because I couldn't afford it. So some sort of program will definitely be in the works."

"That is beautiful. You deserve it, kiddo. If anyone can make that money grow and help the community, you can."

"This is for the girls. God will let me know exactly what I need to do. And, Chase wants to come sit with you for a little bit. He needs to talk with you."

"When is he coming?"

"Home with me. Is that good?"

"He's a son. He has my ear whenever he needs it. I know I've got to help him now."

These tears were tears of joy. To live to see the day that my father would be a father to my son is a day that speaks of God's mercy and grace.

Harlan was next on the list. We met at the Bistro on the main level of the hotel. I told him about the meeting and the gift. He encouraged me to pay down my debt and to increase investments.

"I can't do that with this money, Harlan."

"This is the same opportunity for you that the lady who gave the man money did for him."

"I'm not on the breadline, Harlan. I do have some debt, but most of it is student loans and debt for the practice. I could stand some money here and there, to make things tighter across the board, but God has given me the ability to accomplish that within the next four years or so. I'm not hurting. This is the opportunity for the girls who need a helping hand. I definitely feel more comfortable using the money as requested."

"Jewel, don't you now have two boys to take care of? Why not use this for you? You're technically a program yourself."

"There would be nothing wrong with that, but there is so much more that could be done and help people way beyond me. I want to use the money in the same spirit in which it was given. Moderation is enough for me. I'd rather give to those who need provisions. If I pay off my student loans in a chunk, that's going to deplete so much funding for the program. This is a great start for a charity. But it's only a start."

"How much are your loans?"

"Why?"

"Just tell me how much you owe. I'm a businessman, remember? I'll tell you what to do."

"I should be down to around $200,000.00 in student loans and around $500,000.00 total including a business loan I took out when I started the practice. I've already paid back a considerable amount of money over the years. I'm on easy street now compared to where I used to be."

"Okay, so based on your thinking, if you didn't have the loans then you'd do something with the money you would normally issue for loan payments, and act as if you still had the loans to pay, correct?"

"That's a reasonable assumption. Where are you going with this?"

"And based upon your commitment to stick with the donor's request, you should stick with my requests, if I became a donor as well, correct?"

"If your requests were honorable, hypothetically speaking."

"Good. Then I'm going to pay off your loans. Half-a mil means I have to work a bit harder this year, and you can work a bit easier over the next four. The only request I have is this: that you take what you would normally expend as the loan payments and apply them to your mortgage one month, and to additional investments every other month. So for example, in January, you send the money you would have spent on the loan payments to your home mortgage as payment toward principal, and in February, you pay the money you would have spent on loan payments into your investments. You will shave probably a decade off your mortgage, and have your money making more money for you and the boys. You get it?"

"I got it. But I can't let you do that."

"Can you stop me?"

"Why would you do this Harlan?"

"Because I know how to get blessed. That's why. We aren't just supposed to help the poor. We also help those who help the poor. As you give out, someone else is supposed to be pouring into you. I'm a farmer, remember? You are taking on two children and then starting a program at the church, and a charity. You need to be completely secure. God has given me the ability to see to that in one swipe of my signature."

"Thanks, but no thanks."

"Jewel, can you buy your own plane yet?"

"No."

"Then trust me. There are no strings attached. You are probably skeptical, but I'm not a manipulator. I'm not giving to you to control you, our relationship, or what you may even do in the future. You can never speak to me again after I zero out your loans. I'm not trying to buy you. If I could buy you, you'd be too cheap of a woman for me. I'm trying to bless you. Learn how to receive and make room for increase. Just because you're comfortable doesn't mean you can't afford some help. You can use a cushion and the God we serve doesn't want you to worry about a thing."

"Are you sure?"

"This is how the Kingdom works, Jewel. Those who have, give so that those who don't have can be sustained to see the move of God. That's what giving all goods in common was about, not just giving to the apostles so that they could plant some seeds for a harvest to come back to them. Or for the apostles to decree a blessing on those who gave because they gave. Or for the apostles to become wealthy and live lavish lives. They saw the harvest in the gospel going forth right before their very eyes. That's what we are supposed to do. Those girls are going to see the hand of God in their lives and I believe you'll set up something that will really influence their lives. Today is a day where you get blessed as you bless those girls who are waiting for what will come to them because God wants them to know there is a better way."

"Wow. All of this is overwhelming. And you know a lot about the Kingdom for someone who doesn't go to church regularly."

"Get used to it. Get used to the blessings. I may not go to church but a few times a year. But I'm connected. You better know that."

By the time we were waiting for the lunch check, Harlan had already reached his assistant and commandeered that the loans be paid in full immediately. "By the time you get back home, wait about twenty-four hours and see if the payment has been received."

I've heard of people preaching and testifying about seasons in their lives just about all of my life. I guess this must be my season. Finding Chase. Restoring the relationship with my family. Forgiveness. Facing the past. Walking in healing. Releasing the bitterness. Finally seeing Xavier, Jr. Serving in church again. Astronomical financial blessing. The only thing left was working out the kinks with Xavier.

UNTIL WE MEET AGAIN
Like A Champion

Sometimes the most magnificent things happen at the same time you may have to jump a hurdle. All of this exciting stuff simmered down when Chase and I arrived at Aliyah's bedside. Years of telephone conversations, movie nights where we didn't watch a darn thing, nights at our favorite restaurant, crashing at each other's pad, or some long weekends at a resort somewhere would culminate with this curve at Aliyah's bedside. Aliyah and I were supposed to be there for one another. Our plans stated that. We would be there for the long haul. She was supposed to be preaching and going to the nations. She was supposed to enjoy the Rashaun and Tysheem that we were all coming to know, as they began to "find" themselves while flourishing at swimming and all of the other constructive character-building activities.

Who would get on my nerves as royally as only Aliyah could, if this was the end of the road for us? Who else in this world, who occupies space and time, is known as mass and matter with a specific identity as Aliyah Lewis Jones, who would have me running around to buy shelled no-salt non-colored pistachio nuts to send to her husband in jail? Or, who would insist that I drive past fifteen critically acclaimed eateries to hit the chain store in the midst of the ghetto to get the over-the-counter roasted chicken for her to eat? These demands were custom-made high-class ghettrocities that only Aliyah could pull off. Aliyah is the justifier for Jewel to reach beyond her own stratosphere into a world she wouldn't have otherwise known. I would have to learn how to survive without the simplistic voice that always sees the best in me and the same voice that would break me all the way down in 2.2 seconds or less. We all get each other real good if necessary. Aliyah is definitely the least of us by everyone else's perception including her own. Yet, we all knew that in many respects she is truly the greatest of us. With the least in life, Aliyah gave the most of herself to God, be it with zeal without knowledge or excellence. She gave her all according to her own ability and understanding. My sister was suffering and I had stayed away. Although there were real legitimate considerations, we both knew that the distance was the only way I could cope, she could process and we could both let each other go.

I walked in and saw my sister who could no longer breathe on her own. I leaned over and kissed her.

"Hey girl," I uttered softly.

"It's about time you got here. I didn't think you'd make it in time."

I still spoke as if there was a viable alternative. "In time for what?"

"Jewel, I'm not scared. It's just uncomfortable with this breathing. It's getting worse." Aliyah wasn't scared, but seemed uncomfortable because of the unknown.

"I would have come sooner, but I was under the impression you really didn't want visitors."

"True that. But you do know how wishy washy I am. You should have been in the spirit and just come anyway. I don't like doing all this talking to the doctors myself."

"I'll find out everything. Do you understand exactly what's happening with your body right now?"

"Pretty much, Dr. Prunell. I'm dying. They want to send me to hospice. I told them the devil is a liar. I'm not dying. I'm living. Either way you cut this, I'm gonna live. And, I'm not going to no hospice." I know Aliyah told every hospital personnel what was on her mind with a righteous indignation encrusted with the stereotypical black women's swivel neck attitude.

"So what are you doing? What's next?" I asked. Aliyah was hardheaded and determined to die with dignity.

"I'm going to stay right here. One way or the other, I'm not letting them send me to no hospice. I don't want people dying in my atmosphere. If I'm going, I'm going in the Lord."

"You don't think anyone else with your same outlook would be in a hospice?"

"Are you trying to run me till the very end? Cause I'm not going to let you. Just fly me back to New York and let Bishop Deuce have the homegoing service for me. Let the people here have a memorial service or get to New York. Bishop Deuce took care of me most of my saved life, and he's the only real father I've ever had, not just a pastor, but a father. So it's only right that he bury me. And, I'll be close enough for the boys to see me. Make sure they come and visit me, Jewel."

"You've got all this worked out, huh?"

"No, you've got to work it out. That's why I'm telling you now. So you'll tell Bishop Deuce. He'll take care of the funeral and anything else. Please ask Kamoi to sing. And if Laurel can keep it together, let her sing too. She may cut the fool. But none of y'all better cry too long. And get that Stephen and Phyllis to do a duet. Praise Him like I will be in eternity. Keep doing the work of the Kingdom. Don't play with it. This life is nothing to play with. If you need anything else, ask Mother Johnson. She has plenty of loot and she loves me. And the boys. I probably won't be able to talk much longer. So they need to call me. I don't want them to see me this way. I want them to remember me when I could breathe on my own. They've already seen enough."

"Okay, do you have any type of insurance or anything I need to know about?"

"Yes, Bishop Deuce, Mother Johnson and you. Whatever you need for the boys, let them know. They'll get it to you. And make sure the boys keep in touch with both of them. They were the only people who ever acted like a father and mother should to me."

"I surely will. I just wanted to know if they had anything coming to them. I'm going to adopt them and raise them as my own."

"Don't change their last names. Leave it as mine. And, that's if BJ doesn't try to stop you. But don't worry about him. God will take care of him."

"I'm not thinking about BJ, Aliyah, I'm thinking about you and the boys."

"BJ doesn't care nothing about them. If he thinks there's money involved, that's the only way he's going to try anything. He never bought Tysheem a pamper or a can of milk when he could. God is going to deal with him."

"Have you spoken to him?"

"I wrote him a long letter and haven't heard back from him. He probably doesn't have nothing to say because I told him it's all God or nothing. We haven't spoken in a minute. He knows how to reach Mother Johnson. I told him to get with her, but she says he hasn't called. But I'm good. God already has him. Just don't let the boys forget me, Jewel."

"How could they? You gave them life, and you showed them the way. You've been the Harriet Tubman to your family. You got out of bondage and darkness and it almost cost you your life. Because of your faith, and their witness of your faith, prayerfully, they will never see the days your forefathers saw. I will never let them forget you. I give you my word. That would be impossible."

"Give them something special on birthdays, and when they get married and tell them I left it for them. I'm leaving them a rich inheritance. You. So don't make them feel as if I died and left them with nothing. And don't be naïve with them. They're from the streets. Tell them everything about girls. Don't let any of these hoochies trap them. I know the streets. Tell them what I would have said, not just what you think. You're naïve you know."

"Okay. They're going to do fine. The same God that kept both of us, is going to keep them. He is sovereign."

"They'll be the first to ever graduate high school. Thank you Jesus. Lawd, I give you the praise. Hallelujah! I give you the glory!" Aliyah usurped so much of her waning breath to declare the goodness of the Lord. I was an eyewitness to "with every breath I've got, I'll give God the praise." Many people say it, and complain all day long. But Aliyah, even while fighting in her last precious moments to live, commanded her spirit to laud the God that would care for His children, her children. They would, by faith, go farther and further than she did.

"Remember Rashaun acts hard, but he needs just as much love as Tysheem. The devil fights him so much because he is a prophet. And Tysheem, that's the evangelist. Don't push them with all that intellectual stuff and they neglect their callings that matter."

"Momma, remember, God has them. They can hold a revival after they leave the board room or on the basketball court. What matters is what they desire according to God's will. He is the one who has their steps ordered."

Tears engulfed Aliyah's eyes and broke free to flow down her face. "My boys will do more. I guess that's why God has me handing the baton of their lives over to you. Win the race. All you have to do is endure till the end with them. See them through. They are going to need you. I gave them all I know. They've been through so much already. But God can do anything."

"Yes He can. Now take it easy. Your breathing is stressed."

"I'm not always going to be able to talk, so let me say what I need to. Don't be pushy."

"Ok, Aliyah. You're right."

"Thank you, Jewel, for being a true sister. We moved way beyond friends. You're the only one I know I can always depend on, no matter what. I wore everyone else out. But you, you never not been there for me. That's why I know God wants you to take the boys. Cause if you love me like that, you'll love them like that. If God gave me a best friend kit, and told me to make one, I would have made you. You know, I went looking for a card to send you, and every card I read, I put it down, to buy. When I turned around, I didn't have enough money to buy the whole store. Words can't express."

"I love you too, Li." Li was my nickname for Aliyah, when I really just wanted to hug her and never let go. Since she got on my last nerve most of the time since she became gravely ill, I rarely called her "Li." Aliyah was terribly moody since she lived in unbearable pain, sickness after sickness because of full-blown AIDS. This was a "Li" moment. All of a sudden, I felt so small for not cherishing more "Li" moments and ignoring her banal lunacy and ridiculous demands in the last couple of years. "I don't know how I'm going to live without you."

"You will. You all will. My covenant sisters. Only God could have given me you, Danne, Laurel, Noey and even Chante. Even Phyllis and Delcosa. My God. When I think of Geniver. Y'all are my family. Y'all took me for who I was and never made me feel less because of where I've come from. I expected you to be a snob. Cause you a doctor and I used to be a crackhead. I used to see us as being so different. Always admired you. If I had time to do my life over, I would have wanted to be just like you. So much wisdom. Only thing is, when I thought about it, you had the same demon assigned to your life as mine to take us out. We were both raped as little girls and I hit the streets and started hoing and shooting up to cope and you mastered hiding and hardly living. But when I look at us now, you got the victory and I got the victory. No one in my family has done what I've done. I lived without drugs and saved. And my boys—our boys—are going to go to college. Don't ever forget how much I love you Jewel."

With everything that was within me, I tried not to break down in front of Aliyah. With all of my professional experience in dealing with people who suffer and die from AIDS, watching a human being who had been joined to me through an unbreakable friendship, had the doctor helpless. I needed God's strength in this weakness.

"You betta go now. And one more thing. Don't let it be said that I died from AIDS. Whatever you have to do, make sure it's not AIDS. The devil is a liar. AIDS don't have the power to kill me. And let the people know I was a fighter. I want some red boxing gloves on my casket. Yup. Red ones. That's it."

I leaned over and kissed her forehead. Suddenly I felt as if I was about to faint.

"And don't have me sitting on no machine for twenty-two years. We already discussed this, and I haven't changed my mind. When it's over, just turn the machines off. I'm ready to live forever with Jesus."

I managed to keep my composure enough to muster, "Fine. Things won't be the same without you. I love you, Li."

Talk about manifold temptations and back-to-back trials. Chase's family and his father's death seemed weighty in and of itself. Maybe the timing was strategic. Enough simultaneous "other things" wouldn't give room for me to succumb to figuring out how to cope without one of my dearest friends in life. Chase still needed me, and so did Tysheem and Rashaun.

Chase offered, "Do you want to sit a minute, Momma?"

"No. We've got to get home. She could slip into a coma any second. The boys need to speak with her."

Once we arrived home, Chase and I were exhausted. I couldn't ignore Xavier in good conscience. After all, he had re-arranged his life for me again to care for the boys. So much had changed between us. I used to do most of the accommodating to please him. At this point in our non-relationship relationship, he's the one who would do whatever is necessary to make things happen for me. Although I was near delusional, I sat and attempted to talk with Mr. Johnson until the wee hours of the morning. I told him about the bequest from Prophet Swanson.

"I'm happy for you, Jewel. I really am. So what kind of program are you going to start? Have you figured it out yet?"

"No, I can hardly think. I'm so drained right now, I can't focus on that just yet."

"Something that would provide temporary housing for young pregnant teens with an emphasis in family communication and reconciliation would be nice-a strong counseling component with practical parenting modules, or alternative child placement options. My mind is racing with so many options. You want to see the girls opt to make it, just like you did. Of course, the program would have to include proper prenatal care and I think you should put something toward completing education in there too. I remember you telling me that out of everything you went through, the worst time for you was when you were isolated from your family. You felt like you were out there all by yourself in the midst of a dark sea overboard in a storm."

That woke me up. With zillions of words I've shared trying to communicate with Xavier, he did pay attention.

"I know you don't think I hear you most of the time. But I do. When you told me that, it affected me. So, that's my suggestion. And take some of that money to get grant writers to get additional grants. Or hire a fundraiser, or at least make it part of someone's job description. And—"

"How about you take the ball and run with it. I like what I'm hearing and love the fact that you didn't suggest that I take any money and spend it on myself."

"Why would I do that? Didn't you say the man gave it to you so that you could help other girls like you? You're important, but you're already blessed. It's time for us to start making sure that we can at least match our giving with what we keep for ourselves. That's why God chose you. Cause He knows you'll give it and do something to change someone else's life. Speaking of which, we need to tell the boys about their mom."

"We?"

"Okay. Jewel, don't get it twisted. Who do you think they are going to want to be there for them? Just you? I don't think so. I have a rapport with them too."

"I realize that. Really I do. We'll call her first thing in the morning. Aliyah doesn't have much longer."

"I'm going to bed. Xavier will be up before you know it."

"Shouldn't you find a nickname to call him? It's got to be confusing for him to know if people are addressing you or him, when the two of you are together."

"Don't you worry your pretty little head about that. If you're so concerned, call me Chocolate Daddy, then."

"At two in the morning, you still got jokes. You never stop."

"Chocolate Daddy doesn't ever need to stop."

If persistence were the key, Xavier would unlock the door. He was a hot mess.

By the time we called Aliyah, she could hardly utter a word. The breathing was so much more strained and the respiratory function was failing. I urged the boys to tell her they loved her. That they would serve the Lord. That they were happy with the life they've had with her. That they would miss her. They would be all right. Rashaun was overwhelmed with emotion. He told his mother he didn't want to see her suffer another day. He watched her suffer, and knew how to "go through."

Two hours later, Aliyah slipped into a coma. She never regained consciousness. Although I had seen death up close and personal with my grandparents, a few childhood friends, and with so many of my patients, this one hit in a different way. I screamed and hollered and so did Danne, Noey, Laurel and even the emotion-blocker, Chante. The news spread faster than a wildfire in the forest. I couldn't even manage the boys who were a whole lot more calm, cool and collected than any of us were. This was a place I had never known before. I'd known looking at the lake and wanting to jump in, feet first with forty pounds of brick tied to each physical extremity. I wanted to live, but found it difficult to bear the heaviness of no more Aliyah, or her ghettrocities, in this life.

I looked at Chase and Xavier and wanted them to tell me something different. Tell me I was about to wake up from a nightmare. This was not happening. We all had our specific place in the help one another survive, thrive and enjoy life unwritten sisterhood network. Our lives were intertwined and worked like clockwork. Someone was supposed to tell me that the last pages of the book of Aliyah's life weren't written and about to be sealed with "The End." We had to retire her jersey and her numbers. No one else could ever fill in and do us justice.

Everyone tried to calm me down. Daddy called, Ma was on her way over and Ford was too. Chase had never seen this part of me. Neither had I to tell the truth. I gave birth to my son at twelve years old, and hadn't carried on like this. When Xavier got the guts to take a grip on what would be roasting material for the rest of my life, he walked over to me and said, "Jewel, quiet down now! You're about to give yourself a headache and Rashaun and Tysheem don't need to see all of this."

I looked at Xavier with duplicitous eyes, one to see if I could knock him out if I tried and the other, to see if he'd whip me for striking him. I opted to be quiet. Xavier then told me to lay down, held me, and I couldn't fight his comfort. After a few moments, he disclosed the fact that I had to make a call on whether to pull the plug. I did what Aliyah asked me to do. By the time the respirator was turned off, within six minutes, Aliyah was officially declared deceased. As a physician, I knew that she had long departed if all of her vital signs ceased that quickly.

While everyone took a chance at trying to console me, I just wanted to go to sleep for two weeks. Aliyah's death showed me the real bond I had with Xavier. All of a sudden, I needed him. My daddy, brothers, and even the girls couldn't cut it. A few words and directives from Xavier ministered to me. He also sat with the boys when there was nothing I could say to them.

Their mother was gone. None of us wanted to see her suffer. But we didn't like the alternative either. But the Aliyah we all knew wouldn't come back to us if she could. Once she got a glimpse of the eternal light of God, Aliyah would live in the perpetual worship of our Creator and act like she never knew us to be without sickness, pain, or suffering. She lived to see what she had to have embraced in entering eternal rest. Aliyah got hers.

Meanwhile, I knocked out and self-medicated.

Chase was dealing with so much grief I didn't want him to have to attend another homegoing. But, he insisted. I stood with him, so he would stand with me.

So Chase took the opportunity to sit and talk as much as he could with Daddy. I was literally in a daze, and couldn't function without someone else being there. Meanwhile, Chase and Daddy bonded like they were father and son. Daddy promised to cover him in ministry and I saw a brokenness in my father that I hadn't ever seen before. Almost thirty years later, everything was coming full circle. Bishop Prunell assured the elders and Chase that he would help them. Chase looked like a twenty-pound monkey that wouldn't let go had finally jumped off his back. Every day, something new unfolded that had never even entered into my thoughts, but was always part of the plan.

Trusty Danne and Noey planned every detail of Aliyah's homegoing. I was in a daze and for the absolute first time in my life, could not function. Danne did it all the way up. She hired a make-up artist who had a roster of A-listers in entertainment to do Aliyah's face. One of her stylists selected Aliyah's clothes and jewels. She was laced in a St. John's knit suit and even had her worst physical feature completely concealed. Danne had Aliyah's forty-five percent angle bunions that distorted every shoe and boot known to man concealed. Ha! Even the bunions were hidden. Had Aliyah known she was going to be so done up and that her homegoing would be the ministry event of the year, she wouldn't have died. Thousands of people packed out the mega-church to pay their respects for a woman who knew how to serve the Lord. We never had a full glimpse of how many lives Aliyah touched in such a short span of time.

We praised God for six hours at Aliyah's homegoing. There was praise for God in that edifice in a way I hadn't seen in a long time. Aliyah praised God ever since the day she came off the streets, until she took her last breaths in this life. The dignified people who only talk and quickly wipe tears in order to not be unseemly in church cause they have good sense, would have been offended. Folks ran around the church like they were in a marathon, fell out, lifted hands, and danced, danced, danced. The spirit of praise was so alive that I couldn't cry anymore. We celebrated a life well lived, one of triumph and of dignity, even in the face of scathing criticism because of a debilitative condition. The fighter fought and her prize was receiving the liberty wherein we have all been made free, two sons in good health, no drugs, no abuse and on their way to whatever they dared to pursue as their space in this world. We all looked at what used to be the fleshly body of an irreplaceable friend. She looked as if she was napping and graduated before the rest of us.

Rashaun, Tysheem, Danne, Noey, Laurel, Chante and I all had to keep on living knowing that we would never see her again in the flesh in this life. Even though our day-to-day activities had not changed one bit, just knowing she was gone was heavy. So the boys and I committed to talking about her as much as any of us needed to. We went to counseling and had to go to family court to begin adoption proceedings. The only hurdle was BJ.

THE PRICE OF A CHILD
Will The Real Father Please Stand Up

Elder Barron Jason Jones stood in the way of Tysheem's adoption. He did not want to relinquish his parental rights, nor did he want to see his son who never visited him once in jail, the son he never supported or took care of. He needed a visit from the crew. And he got one.

"Hi Elder. How is jail treating you?"

"Jail doesn't treat me. But I'm doing fine."

"How long are you going to be in here?"

"I don't know. I thought I would have been paroled by now."

"How's your health?"

"I'm fine."

"Good. Well, your wife died. She's fine now. Just in case you were wondering, she didn't die alone."

"I know my wife died. None of you all tried to get me out so I could see her. That's messed up. You didn't ask me what I wanted done with my wife."

"Are you kidding me, BJ? Why should we get you out to see a corpse when you didn't communicate with her when you had the chance? Oh, might that have something to do with her inability to get you what you wanted and send you your packages? And why should we ask you one dag on thing about what to do with Aliyah? Did you have anything in place to do anything with her body? Her children? We didn't ask you to pay her bills every month and take care of her for years, so, please forgive me for thinking that I needed to consult you to do what I've been doing for years-taking care of your household." BJ has always tested every ounce of my temperance and character.

"Well, I couldn't do anything from here. You know that."

"Good. So you don't get to run things from here either. You know that."

"What did you come here for?"

"To find out face to face why you are opposing Tysheem's adoption."

"He's my son. I'm not giving him up."

"And what are your plans for him? Cause you're not getting him when you get out either. No judge in her right mind is going to take him from his brother, or from the home he has stability in right now. He barely knows you."

"That's why I'm not giving him up. When I get out, we'll be together. He's all I've got left."

"You are incredibly, unbelievably selfish. You knew you had AIDS, yet got with Aliyah and now she's dead. Now, you know you're sick, and want your son to have to be with you, after having seen one parent die from AIDS. Did you think about what's best for Tysheem? Did you think about him when he needed pampers? Milk? School Supplies? A hug? A mother? Do you just think about him when he needs a father?"

"Look. You can say what you want, he's still my son."

"He is your son. He is first and foremost, Tysheem. He is a human being with worth irrespective of you. Irrespective of your never letters, never phone calls, and never been there. So cut it out. He is not a possession that makes you a father, or a man. When you love, BJ, you DTRT. Even when it's hard."

"So what do you want me to do?"

"Stop blocking the adoption. That would make it easier for them. I will be their legal mother. But regardless of what you do, their mother wanted them right where they are. And she sought the Lord for direction. So Elder, know that whether it's adoption or mere physical custody, Tysheem is staying right where he is. Period and point blank. He's going to have the life he is entitled to."

"You threatening me?"

"Not at all. This is the way it is, brother, Elder. It's not going down any other way. If you want to see Tysheem when you get out, then give me a call. We'll arrange visits. But I'm not bringing him to jail. Maybe someone else might. But jail is not part of my agenda. He doesn't ever need to spend too much time here."

"But I'm his father."

"Who is in jail. Who has had every opportunity before you were here to be a father. To take care of him. But you didn't. Maybe you can help me understand how it is so easy for some of you fellas to just make babies and think you can show up once in a while with a bag of chips and a smile and think everything is okay. Meanwhile, every dime you have is on your own backside, some woman or taking care of things you want. What about Tysheem?"

"I had to do me. No one else ever took care of me, so I had to look out for me."

"And you should have had no children then, so you could do you. Children can't do themselves. They are children. They are supposed to be taken care of by a whole lot of fellas who are doing themselves."

"You don't get it. You have always had a family."

"I'm so tired of hearing people think they know something they know nothing about. My life has nothing to do with your selfishness. You have no idea what I've dealt with in life. And that doesn't even matter. You had a family. You were born again into a family where you are supposed to get the lessons and apply them. Tysheem doesn't just need prayers and occasional letters. He needs supervision, love, clothes, food, guidance and all of the parenting that Aliyah and the rest of us have been giving him while you've been 'doing you.' He needs a father, and you know what, I'm going to believe Aliyah's take was on this situation. God got Tysheem and He has you. If you want to communicate with Tysheem, write him or call. And if you do good with that and don't cause any confusion, then he can come with someone else to visit. Prove yourself. I'm not Aliyah. I'm not going to fall under your swagger and let you corrupt Tysheem."

"You came all the way here to go at me like this?"

"I came here to tell you to get out of the way. If you want a relationship with Tysheem, then work at it. You have to do that. But you're not going to play with him like a yo-yo. Either you're in, or you're out. You decide."

"What about my food and stuff? Who is going to take care of me?"

"Father, did it ever occur to you that you should be grateful that people have taken care of your wife and family the entire time you've been here. And that you should be thankful. No. You want to know what about your palate while you're here? I'll let our prison ministry know you'd like visits and prayer and you can contact them. I do not have a prison ministry, or nothing for you."

"If you send me what I need while I'm here, I'll give up my rights."

"Are you serious? You'll give up Tysheem for some food and clothes?"

"I don't know when I'm getting out, and I need support. I don't have anyone else."

"What about the church?"

"No one keeps in touch, and no one responded to my letters."

"Okay. Fine. I'll expect you to cooperate with the adoption. Do you want any contact with Tysheem?"

"Just send me some pictures and let me know how he's doing. I don't want to mess things up for him. I know I probably won't be consistent, so I'd rather not get started. Just send me pictures all the time."

To think, I didn't even have to go hardball on him. All I had to do was offer to send him groceries every month, and he'd give up parental rights to his only son.

"Did Aliyah say anything about me?"

"She said God had you. So, I choose to believe that too."

"Just make sure you have me every month with some food. I'll write to let you know what else I need. I'm trusting that you'll keep your word, Jewel. I know Tysheem is going to be good with you. You act like he's yours already."

"Somebody has to fight for him, BJ."

And somebody did. The syndicate was prepared to do anything necessary for Rashaun and Tysheem. Aliyah's boys would always have a home. Their mother—in all of her craziness—worked hard enough to make sure she left them with an inheritance.

ONE YEAR LATER
A New Family

Rashaun, Tysheem and I went to visit Aliyah's grave today. This was a momentous day for us. It was our first visit to her gravesite. We had discussed going many times before, but never made it. We even pulled up to the curbside and stayed in the car. But today, we had to. Although we know she was asleep in the Lord and couldn't really hear us, we somehow needed to just let her know that we were moving on as a family.

Rashaun had matured so much since Aliyah's death that he surprised all of us. There were many things he wanted to communicate to his mother, if he could have spoken to her. So, he chose to speak as if she were listening. "Today, we are going to get our final adoption papers from the judge. And we know you wanted us to keep our last name. But, we talked about it in counseling, and we want to take Jewel's last name. It took a lot for us to get here. But, when she's at my swimming meets, or graduation, or any of that, I'm going to be a Prunell-Johnson. I don't think you realized that we would have a real father. And, he deserves for us to carry his name. We are a family now, and we have to move on. So, I'm sure you'd be good with this Ma. We're going to be Prunell-Johnsons. Xavier has been there for me and Ty so we owe him this. We came to let you know that everything is going good. We'll never forget you."

When I asked Tysheem if he had anything he wanted to say to his mother, he added, "And, we're getting ready for our little sister. Mommy is pregnant." Tysheem asked me two weeks after Aliyah died if he would ever be able to see her again. I told him no, she went to be with the Lord and she was never coming back. If we both lived for Jesus, we'd catch up to her later on. He had one question, "Who's going to be my mother? I can't live without a mother." So I told him his mother left him with me. I would be his mother just like Ms. Edie was my son's mother. I explained to him Chase had two mothers and many people do. From that moment on, Tysheem called me mommy and I never stopped him.

I just gave Aliyah the updates that she probably couldn't care less about since she was no longer involved in the cares of this life, and was resting in the Lord. Our non-existent dialogue was just a matter of release for me. "Girl, Chase still calls me Momma, and I love him more and more. I never told you all of the drama with his family, but his other mother, Ms. Edie and I are quite close now. We speak at least three times a week. Chase told us he put us both on the altar and we better work it out or else. So, we did. Although she never apologized, she told me she had to respect me. She never thought Chase would be with his birth mother, or that her husband and I would ever connect. It's funny how life is. We all have expectations that life doesn't always meet. Sometimes life supersedes what we expect. She schools me left and right about how to deal with Xavier Jr. and even Rashaun and Tysheem. As for Rashaun, he is still trying to be grown and calls me Jewel, and slips with an occasional 'Ma' and I love him. He's got some tutors to help him get through his schoolwork. Tysheem calls me Mommy, and I love him. He makes my heart melt. He and Xavier Jr. get along well even though they fight quite a bit. Most of that stuff, Xavier takes care of. They fear him and don't give him a second of trouble. Turns out Xavier's X-Box, PlayStation, Wii and online gaming skills have proven to be handy in fostering healthy competition between him and the boys. For all the loving Xavier gives me, I even love his dirt, girl. I almost missed God's choicest blessing with Xavier. You taught me how to appreciate the simple things in life and I'm doing it.

Rest in peace, girlfriend. We all miss you. There's no one else like you."

So we left a picture of our new family portrait on the headstone: Xavier, Xavier, Jr. Rashaun, Tysheem, Chase, and me holding a picture of Aliyah all with our jeans and white shirts on. We also left a portrait of Danne, Laurel, Noey, Chante and me on the headstone. Her memories would be with us forever.

We had a long day ahead of us. After all, we had a huge exquisite celebration to prepare for that evening with the girls, the entire Prunell family, Chase, Evey, Ruth, their new baby Charity, and even Ms. Edie. Yes, Ms. Edie.

What had once been a solitary existence in a great junior mansion was now a vibrant home getting ready for our new daughter. I can't wait for Sapphire Golden to get here to help me combat all the testosterone from our four sons and the biggest baby of them all, Xavier. The males have completely taken over the house and I chose to love every second of it. As much as all of my young men needed me, I needed them, especially Xavier. Jewel is no longer just existing. Jewel is now living. Life hasn't been crystal stairs, but after trying and trying, I began to live. At the right time, I decided to give love a chance, and stopped fighting Xavier. Daddy ended up being right. Love them that love you. Before I delved into Chase's world, I couldn't comprehend real love staring me right in my face because I harbored the voids that were filled with unforgiveness. Ms. Catherine, Ms. Edie and even Prophet Delayne Swanson prepared me for Xavier. We have forgiven one another and I realized I don't ever want to be in this world a day without my husband or our new family. We've overcome our past and expanded the borders of our hearts to face the world and our responsibilities together. We are both ready to love and with God, only heaven can offer something better than this!

CPSIA information can be obtained
at www.ICGtesting.com
Printed in the USA
FFOW05n0822220916